COCET

COCET

By
I.R.TYLER

QCBC

This story is based on actual events. Incidents, characters, and timelines have been changed to protect the innocent and legal obligations. Characters may be composites, or have one character mixed with an entirely fictitious one. Names and identifying details have been changed to protect the privacy of individuals. To maintain anonymity, identifying characteristics and details of some Police agencies, physical properties, occupations and places of residence have been changed. Any resemblance to actual persons has been done with their consent, or otherwise, is purely coincidental. No character in this book is to be inferred as an accurate or actual representation of any person, living or dead, as the traits, habits, and mannerisms of many were combined and meshed with the author's imagination to create the characters contained in these pages. This is a work of fiction.

The author shall not be liable for any physical, psychological, emotional, financial, or commercial damages, including, but not limited to, special, incidental, consequential or other damages as a result of the content of this book. You are responsible for your own choices, actions, and results.

All rights reserved. I.R.Tyler asserts the moral right to be identified as the author of this work. No part of this book may be reproduced or transferred in any form or by any means, graphic, electronic, or mechanical, including photocopying, recording, taping, or by any information storage retrieval system, without the written permission of the publisher.

Copyright © 2015-I.R.Tyler, ianrtyler.com, Hope without Borders, COCET, GOPOL, CB Network, GOPOL 360 child alert system, Tom Ross and all COCET characters. Published by QCBC, New Zealand. Paperback edition 1, Vol 2, of the 'Hope without Borders' trilogy.

ISBN 978-0-473-33612-7

A catalogue record for this book is available at the National and the Alexander Turnbull Libraries of New Zealand.

DEDICATION

This book is dedicated to my family who continue to lose out whilst others benefit; and to Karen and Anne-Marie, who together with thousands of other New Zealanders have been subject to child sex abuse, and still seek justice. It is an irony that the Government which should serve to protect you, and deliver that justice, in fact, leaves you to your fate.

ACKNOWLEDGEMENTS

Writing can be a lonely existence, yet there are many to thank by the time the manuscript gets into print. I must start with the four proof readers; Mark Grevan, Nine Scott, Tim Ford and the Welsh Quack. The latter, particularly, for the endless discussion on the correct use of English grammar, and that pesky comma! You have all given your time for free and willingly, and for that, I am not only grateful, but also amazed at what you can always find. Thanks also to Gallowglass Security Ltd, Anita Overgaauw, Wietske Van Der Pol and Associate Professor Evgeny Pavlov for your translation skills. Everybody needs some technical backup, so I must thank my guru, Dr. Sam Type. Even though you are a busy mother of four, selling a house, commencing a new house build, all whilst managing a busy company, you always find the time to support me and provide advice. How do you do it? Thanks also goes to Michael Bilton, for critical author advice, made more palatable of course with Mumm bubbles! Finally, and not least, I must thank Jim Gamble for writing the Foreword. You were the original founder of CEOP, without that, this story would never exist. Crucially, the many thousands of victims that have been given the hope of a better life as a result of the existence of CEOP, would have been left to their fate at the hands of their abusers. The original CEOP model, and the whole founding team, set the bar high. Child protection worldwide, mainly due to apathy, ignorance, arrogance, education or politics, even today, still fails to meet that bar.

Victim Advice

If you are a victim of child sex abuse or an adult that was subject to sex abuse as a child, and need assistance; you should go to the Police, your Doctor, the Samaritans or other similar victim advocacy group. Their details can be found on the internet or in the telephone directory. If you are a hidden victim, such as the mother, father, brother, sister, husband, wife or partner of an offender, and want to understand more about what happened to you, then the helpline that is available through www.ianrtyler.com is available to you for free wherever you are in the world. This helpline is also available free to victims who are considering reporting a crime, but wish to know more about the process before they do.

Advice for Child Sex Offenders

If you are a child sex offender; internet viewer, maker or supplier of child sex abuse images, or someone who sexually assaults a child of any age and you read this book, stop what you are doing, your actions are criminal. If you become distressed through guilt or fear, seek assistance or hand yourself into the nearest law enforcement station together with your hardware. If you are someone who is living with the disorder, who is managing it and have not offended, then your thoughts alone do not make you a criminal. But it does make you much more liable to offend. Help is available to you from confidential helplines that are designed to keep you from acting on those urges such as, Circles of Support.

Dramatis Personae-Consortium

ACPO	Association of Chief Officers of Police
ACC	Assistant Chief Constable
ADS	Acting Detective Sergeant
AFP	Australian Federal Police
Blown	Surveillance term for giving away position or person
Brass	Very senior police officer
CHIS	Covert Human Intelligence Source; also authority to use one
C.I.D.	Criminal Investigation Department
CII	Covert Internet Investigator
Civvy	Non Police
Cloggies	Dutch Police
Copine	1-5 scale used in UK for rating the seriousness of child abuse images, 5 being the highest
CPS	Crown Prosecution Service
CP	Child Protection
CPU	Child Protection Unit
Crops	Covert Rural Observation Post Surveillance
DC	Detective Constable
DCS	Detective Chief Superintendent
Det.	Detective
DHS	Department of Homeland and Security (US)
DI	Detective Inspector
DS	Detective Sergeant
Exposure	Surveillance term for the period prior to be being blown
Eyeball	Surveillance term for person having view of the suspect followed
Greasy Spoon	Cafe which specialises in fried English breakfast
Guv	Inspector or above
H/A	Home address
Hash	Images are broken down into mathematical Algorithm so they can be sent between law enforcement
Holmes	Police database system used in murder squads
HQ	Headquarters
HR	Human Resources

ICE	Immigration Customs Enforcement (USA)
IIMARCH	Later version of above to include ECHR
IP	Internet Protocol
Lift	Surveillance term for beginning surveillance
Morning Prayers	Meeting of department heads
MOU	Memorandum of Understanding
MPD	Metropolitan Police Department
NCIS	National Criminal Intelligence Service
NCS	National Crime Squad
Nick	Police Station
On the Square	Someone that is a Mason
OP	Observation Post
Ops Comm	Operational Commander
PC	Police Constable
Plot	Surveillance term for an area under observation by the team
Plotted	The area above is plotted when under control
P2P	Peer to peer
PM/PM'd	Private message
Proxy Server	An intermediary server behind which a person can remain anonymous
PSU	Professional Standards Unit
PTT	Press to talk
RIC	Remand in custody
Script	Police term for knowing what to do, also software term
SIO	Senior Investigating Officer
SO(10)	Met Police Covert Department
SPOC	Single point of contact
Stills	Photographs
Stupidoclock	Police term for getting up very early
Supt.	Superintendent
Trumpton	Fire Brigade
TVP	Thames Valley Police
UC	Undercover
Vanilla	American term for real good or 'sweet as'

FOREWORD

When I led the team that created CEOP we recognised that a different approach was needed to policing the online environment. The operational concepts described in this story, reflect the more holistic approach that we introduced, embracing law enforcement, harm reduction, intelligence, education, charities and industry, all cooperating under one roof with one goal — to protect children from abuse wherever they might be.

CEOP's success was the result of innovative approaches to a crime which many thought unpolicable. There were no procedures or policies in place that allowed us to operate effectively against criminals who acted in a world without borders. COCET, the second book in the 'Hope without Borders' trilogy, is based on true life covert operations that were led by the author. The success of these operations were as a result of Ian's ground breaking ingenuity, determination and leadership. Our successes allowed me to develop the concept of a Virtual Global Taskforce, depicted here as GOPOL, a multinational shield to defend against those seeking to perpetrate their evil brutality on our most vulnerable.

Developing a strong and innovative partnership approach, allowed CEOP to work proactively to prevent crime from happening; to deploy specialist investigating officers and bring to justice those who had committed such crimes; to create teams of educators helping communities to protect themselves and where to turn if they needed help; and, equally important, we developed a comprehensive network of support for victims. The number of victims rescued by the operations that form the basis of this book has never been repeated by any agency anywhere.

I hope that when people read this story they realise the potential that the original CEOP model demonstrated. The child-centred approach, which elevated the needs of victims above all other considerations, created a new pathway for law enforcement and the multi-agency partners that CEOP genuinely integrated into every aspect of its work. Learning was at the heart of our approach and sharing the lessons secured our vision to educate, empower and protect children and young people across the world.

Jim Gamble, QPM
Founder, and first Chief Executive Officer, of the Child Exploitation and Online Protection Centre (CEOP)

PROLOGUE

'If Jesus was a preacher, teacher and healer; are you really here in place of him? Are you looking to heal the whole person, not just the symptoms? Can you heal?'

"I am the resurrection and the life.
He that believes in me will live, even though they die.
For I am convinced that neither death nor life,
Neither angels nor demons, neither the present nor the future,
Nor any powers, neither height nor depth,
Nor anything else in all creation,
Will be able to separate us from the love of God
That is in Christ Jesus our Lord.
Blessed are those who mourn, for they will be comforted."

The minister looked around at the large gathering in confirmation of his last words before placing his right hand gently on the cross which hung around his neck. He turned to enter the church, then stopped momentarily, still facing the cortege and its mourners. It was as if he didn't want to walk in, but suddenly finding the strength he broke the padlock that grief held on the moment, and led the procession into the church, bringing the pall bearers to a resting place at the head of the nave. The minister waited by the coffin until all was quiet, then entered the chancel and stepped into the pulpit.

"Hushed are these walls that welcome you all here today," he said, pausing for what seemed like minutes, letting the reverence of the moment sink in. Lifting his voice he continued. "The stained glass windows that have been part of the sanctuary of this church for hundreds of years, weep their many colours. All of you have come to mourn a passing, a huge loss; one that has been so widely felt. Jesus Christ, our Lord, I beseech thee: let us find the strength to come to terms with death and bereavement that is to be found in your promises, in the hope of the Resurrection, and in the belief that our departed loved one is now safe in your hands."

The large stones smoothed by generations of hands, softened over time, interlocked each other with a uniform and recognisable bond, all solemnly and with reverence making their way up to the great heights of the wooden arches that held up the old roof. The ancient English oak beams, strong and roughly hewn, looked so small from way beneath. The pain and grief they would witness matched the strength needed to keep a protective watch over the congregation below.

"Our eyes, Lord, are wasted with grief;
You know we are weary with groaning.
As we remember our death
In the dark emptiness of the night,
Have mercy on us and heal us;
Forgive us and take away our fear
Through the dying and rising of Jesus your Son."
Amen.

Feet, side by side, rooted to the holy ground. Back, pushed into the oak pew, causing pain not felt. Now was the time, it had come. The epistle wanted its say. So did the room, the walls, the beams, the prayer books and mats, the sanctuary and its sculpture of Jesus upon the Cross. The cherished ones and the friends, they all wanted their say but couldn't speak. Grief had descended.

'Well! Can you? I have to know now!'

There was no thought, emotion or memory as the words floated out. *'Was it a miracle? Was it something supernatural? Or was it healing powers flowing around the room?'*

The minister who had been standing near the pulpit took back the service and moved to the centre of the nave.

"God of mercy, into whose hands your Son Jesus Christ
Commended his spirit at his last hour, into your same hands
We now commend this servant, that death may be for them,
The gate to life and eternal fellowship with you; this we ask
In the name of Christ, our Lord. Amen."

Soft hands on hand, calming. Strong hands on shoulders, giving strength. All flowing hot with the power of healing. Eyes fixed on the pulpit, waiting. Suddenly, and without warning.

"Though I walk through the valley of death, I will fear no evil; for you are with me; your rod and staff, they comfort me." Silence.

"Our Father, who art in heaven,
Hallowed be thy name; thy kingdom come;
Thy will be done; on earth as it is in heaven.
Give us this day our daily bread.
And forgive us our trespasses,
As we forgive those who trespass against us.
And lead us not into temptation;
But deliver us from evil.
For thine is the kingdom,
The power and the glory,
For ever and ever. Amen."

"We now commit this body to the ground.
Earth to earth, ashes to ashes, dust to dust: in the sure and certain
hope of the resurrection to eternal life."

CHAPTER ONE

Tom read the team list as he waited for Jane. It wasn't as big as he would have liked, but big enough. The real winner here was the mix of agencies, a dedicated budget and further monies he could bid for against operational need. A team title and separate identity went a long way to giving them 'esprit de corps'. The Combined Online Child Exploitation Taskforce (COCET) was the new team on the block. A new office, governance, management structure and declared political intention by Thames Valley Police (TVP) was a real wake-up call to the Home Office, and the larger forces around the country. TVP's 'Chief' had taken the lead and formed a new multi-agency taskforce. What had been unthinkable just months ago had been made possible by a few like minded law enforcement chiefs getting together and agreeing a plan, without the normal politics getting in the way. And why? Well, Operation Hope had given them a blueprint for success. What a difference a few weeks can make! He ran down the list again;

ADS Jane King
DC Archie Donaldson
DC Mitchell Hayes
DC Owen Marks
DC Anna Wilson
Patrick Smith
Anna Farley, National Criminal Intelligence Service, (NCIS)
Agent Adrian Smith, Australian Federal Police, (AFP)
Agent Jim Burgess, Immigration Customs Enforcement, United States of America. (ICE)

Niall Mullins, Interpol
Louisa Greenwood, National Society for the Prevention of Cruelty to Children, (NSPCC)
Sarah Dorsey, Corporate Communications, National Crime Squad, (NCS)
Dr. Nicholas Sharpe, Southern Digital Evidence (SDE)
Dr. Sue Tay, SDE

Then there were the fringe benefits, and not just for him. Mo had been granted an extension and was now the Acting Detective Inspector of Allensbury Child Protection Unit (CPU). In his place Katy Lansdale had been made Acting Detective Sergeant (ADS). This was particularly useful for her as she had already passed Osprey part one of the Sergeants Exam, so the supervision experience would give her some insight when it came to the role play required in part two. Paul Simmons had been successful in a request for an attachment to the Serious Sex Offenders Unit of the National Criminal Intelligence Service. This had, in turn, been good for NCIS, as Anna Farley had been nominated to be attached to COCET as a sign of their commitment, which meant they stayed even on paper.

The CPU had back filled Anna Wilson's position with Julie Merritt, the officer on shift who had challenged Tom one day for using their shower block, and who subsequently applied for the vacancy following a visit to Operation Hope. Jane, on a commitment to sitting the Sergeants exam and staying in the Police, had been made Acting Detective Sergeant; a source of real happiness for her, her family and Tom. He also had access to the Family Liaison Officer list, and agreement that he could select whom he wanted, which was a real step forward for child exploitation crime policing.

COCET had been allocated a dedicated corporate communications officer, Sarah Dorsey. Sarah was on loan from the National Crime Squad, which had, in turn, seconded her from one of the Yorkshire forces. As far as Tom was concerned, if the NCS wanted her, he wanted her more.

The Australian Federal Police, Immigration Customs Enforcement and Interpol had all signed up to the new team, allocating the same officers from Operation Hope to ensure continuity. They would work from their home countries, but had given a commitment to work together on whatever the current job was. He had a computer forensic budget that he could use to buy in the expertise of Southern Digital Evidence, on top of whatever TVP's Digital Evidence Recovery Team could do. Tom himself had been promoted after the Chief had set the group leader's position at Detective Chief Inspector. He had applied along with two other candidates, one of whom was DCI Carol Summers. Detective Chief Superintendent (DCS) John Troy had chaired the board, and had pushed Tom all the way during the examination. Afterwards, JT had said he'd given him a harder time to fend off any accusations that might come up as a result of him getting the position.

Finally, and not least, was TVP's Chief Constable's decision to embed a member from the National Society for the Prevention of Cruelty to Children in the team. Louisa Greenwood would work from the new office, with all her housing and expenses being met by the NSPCC. Tom had had a personal meeting with John Troy, when he complained that he should have been consulted over the appointment; citing good operational reasons why it wasn't a good fit with existing team skill profiles. It fell on deaf ears. Instead Tom got a lesson in corporate governance and political survival. The Chief had personally included the position as a 'checks and balances' safeguard to Tom's new position as head of a combined operational team involving three major countries and Interpol. He felt it more than prudent to ensure that there was an inbuilt child protection (CP) expert monitoring Tom, given his new position of power; and importantly, that the monitor wasn't Police. Tom sighed at the thought. But the fact was, had he been given this opportunity three months ago and had been told, 'All you've got to do is have one position open to the NSPCC', he'd have jumped at it. With that Jane walked in.

"Boss. We're all here and ready when you are."

Tom, who had his notes in hand, looked at them again, dropped them on the table, got up, and went to the conference room for his first address to the new taskforce and the many other invited guests.

As he entered the room and walked to the head of the assembled audience, he suddenly became acutely aware of all the hard work that had been involved in getting the new building refurbished to its current state so that he could be in this position right now. The new unit had been given first priority over all other departments within an already burgeoning Police Force. After many site visits all over the force area, a regional traffic department building close to Allensbury Police Station had been identified as suitable for internal conversion, its main plus being that it was already wired up for the TVP intranet. Its close proximity to the main road also meant that Jerry Stone was able to get the best internet speed possible for the area, still slower than central London, but the best possible in the circumstances. Tom knew how much it had cost, and from what he had heard it had been fully covered by TVP. He'd had a say in the refurbishment and the space available well exceeded the density employment regulations for full time staff, and he felt humbled as he started his opening speech.

Later that afternoon, with all the guests gone, and staff getting used to their new desks which had been arranged into distinct pods within an open office environment, Tom called a meeting in his office with Jane, the Intel Cell and the Ops team. The office was a little bigger than his last one at Allensbury CPU, big enough to include a large rectangular desk with eight chairs and still have room to move around. As Anna Farley, Patrick Smith, Mitchell Hayes; Jane King, Archie Donaldson, Owen Marks and Anna Wilson all took up positions around the desk with fresh open notepads and pens at the ready, Tom opened a new counsel book and dated the first page.

"OK. Let's get to work. From all the intelligence left over from Operation Hope there are a number of leads. It's my intention that we will work on two operations at a time. We don't have the luxury of working on one job. All of us in this room know that child abuse on the internet is way out of control, so we need to be doing as much as we can, all the time. Any questions on that approach?"

Tom wasn't expecting any, and he deliberately toned down his voice for Anna Farley and Mitchell Hayes, the newcomers. He could also see that Jane was wearing her new more serious Sergeant's face in approval.

"The way I would like this to work has been explained to ADS King. On a day to day basis, Anna, you are the Intel Cell team leader; but you will work to Jane and she works to me. I know Mitchell's and Patrick's skill sets and I know they will be a good fit for how we will be working. Business practices, policies and procedures are known to Jane, so have your own meeting to get to know them. They are not set in stone, so if you want to work it another way then just put a case forward and it will be adopted."

"Will we be using TVP's investigation system? And what about intelligence, what system are we using for that?" asked Anna Farley.

Tom knew Anna was a top notch intelligence officer, so he not only expected the questions, but was ready for them as well.

"We have been asked to use a system called Athena," replied Tom. "It's new to TVP. The company who developed and own it saw all the media surrounding Operation Hope. They have done some deal with TVP whereby we will use parts of their system for the first few operations. I have been given a brief on it, and it looks good."

"Is it just a crime investigation system then?"

"No. I think they have a number of modules, but we will be using only three of them. One will be investigatory, one intelligence and the other psychotherapeutic, which will only be used by Dr. Fiona Gordon."

"Will the Intel side be searchable?" Anna further enquired.

"Yes," said Tom. "Operations Benson and Hope will remain as standalone operations for the moment, so you will have to search across each of those. Jerry Stone, our IT guru, is working on a solution to merge those two together, but keeping their root source identifiable without manual inputting. He reckons a week. But, they won't be going on Athena."

"What about training, Boss?" asked Mitchell Hayes.

Tom had known but not worked with Mitchell, a quiet, deep thinking professional detective with a good track record in child protection. His other assets were his computer skills and an analytical mind which Tom assumed he had got from his maths degree. The additional big plus that came with Mitchell was that he was an accredited financial investigator.

"That starts after lunch. Their trainer will be here for the rest of today and all tomorrow. Look, the best way to learn this is on the job. Get yourselves skilled up. I've done some of it already, and will be joining you tomorrow for the rest. For now I just wanted to tell you what I have in mind to start with."

Tom took the silent pause as a Green for Go. "Owen, you are team leader for the Ops team. On top of that you will have to carry out other duties which you are skilled at, particularly comms."

Tom looked towards Anna Wilson. "Anna and Archie, you will form the rest of the Ops team. Again you will work to Jane. She has been fully briefed by me so have your own meeting outside of this one. If you want to change things now or in the future, just put the case forward and it will be looked at."

He could see the surprised yet pleased look on Owen's face. Tom waited for questions to come back at him but there were none, so he moved on. He opened his laptop and the large screen on the wall at the far end of the table immediately came to life, showing a PowerPoint presentation. The attending officers clearly didn't know what was coming as their seating had been arranged for verbal discussion, and they all, bar Jane and Tom, immediately set about rearranging their positions to get a clear view of the screen.

"You don't need to take notes. This forms part of a more detailed briefing Jane will give you," Tom said, as he opened the first slide entitled "Operation Ascent" then activated the next slide:

ORGANISED CRIME PAY-PER-VIEW
- Andrei Dmitriyevich Kuklin
- Sells child abuse images via the internet
- Uses offenders credit cards
- Engages in other fraud

Tom let the assembled team read the short trigger words.

"Andrei Kuklin. Russian father, Moldovan mother. He's from the breakaway region of Moldova called Transnistria. A country within a country, you might say. It's not recognised by the rest of the world other than Russia, which backs it. For us it's a 'no go' country. Luckily for us, though, he currently lives in London."

Owen Marks said, "How old is he, Boss?"

"Twenty three."

"Is he here legally?" asked Anna Farley.

"Yes. It's one of those grey areas. Moldova has its own language, but effectively it's a Romanian sub dialect which is spoken both in the breakaway region and in the rest of the country. Most Moldovans, irrespective of that, will probably speak Russian. When the EU opened its borders to Romania, many Moldovans applied for Romanian passports and got them. They put a stop to it, but not before hundreds of thousands got a passport, and using the gateway of the EU they left the country; many of them to the UK, including Kuklin. He has advanced computer skills and creates his own blank ready-to-go websites and sells them on the internet, taking the money through credit card transactions using another merchant. He captures the credit card details at that point, which he hands over to the fraud side of the organised crime gang, and they hit it till it gets blocked. He also has his own website with child abuse material. He loads this onto the internet using mainly legit servers all over the world, all through bogus emails and accounts. He operates for a short period and appears to have a ready-made paedophile list, to whom he sends emails, indicating he is operational. They or new ones log into the site, give over their credit card details and get child abuse material in return. He stays operational for short periods, hitting the customer as many times as he can. He then takes the website down remotely, cleans the server he has been operating on, then moves onto another company. Once he feels the customer is of no further use he passes the credit card details to the fraud side again and they hit it hard until it gets blocked. They have a built in time lag here. They know the customer won't want to make too much of a fuss, because they know what they've been doing with the card, and are therefore not likely to bring in the Police."

Archie Donaldson said, "Where's the money trail?"

Tom smiled back at the new team. He had made the right choices, their questioning was evidence of that.

"That leads me to this."

THE LAUNDER

- Three bank accounts in alias names
- Barclays, NatWest and Lloyds
- Kuklin back to Transnistria

"There are three known bank accounts linked to Kuklin," said Tom. "Intelligence indicates that money is drawn from the accounts in cash, and shortly afterwards Kuklin takes a trip back to Transnistria. This is where the Intel ends and you pick it up. Have your own meeting with Jane, the objective here is to dismantle this organised crime group. Trace all the users and undertake action with them. Get the website, or at least a copy for forensic and identification purposes. Trace and recover as much money as we can. Trace and recover as many children as we can. Finally, arrest and prosecute the offenders. Questions?"

Archie, Anna Farley and Owen all started to talk at the same time, then the two men stopped and let Anna go first. She acknowledged their decision with a smile and a nod.

"Will we be able to use surveillance?"

Tom replied, "Yes. That's for the meeting with Jane."

"Is there an Intel package on Kuklin and his associates?"

"Yes. Again that's for your meeting with Jane."

Anna this time picked up the hint that although this was their first day, it clearly wasn't Tom's and Jane's, so she stayed quiet.

"Are we dealing with the prosecution?" asked Archie.

"That's still in the mix. We are certainly getting it to arrest point. It all depends just how complicated it gets. I work to Superintendent Maggie Burrows on day to day stuff, but everything else to JT. He reports direct to the ACC or the Chief. All three say they don't want us bogged down in complicated, long drawn out prosecutions. Operation Hope taught them that our strengths lie in the architecture of the internet. It has no boundaries, therefore our approach has to be the same. Our job is to bridge the gap between borderless crime, where there are no police, and the real world where there are borders; and where there are hundreds of different nations, any number of which have separate law enforcement agencies within one nation. We are the trail blazers, and it's our job to show that a combined approach can work. That if you can remove the borders within police boundaries in the real world, we can be a cohesive fighting force where there are none. One reason why law enforcement worldwide is failing in the cyber environment is that the real world is wholly made up of borders, which you can't operate out of without some form of red tape. We can't operate seamlessly within the UK, let alone go from country to country. So, the chances are we will hand it over to serious crime or the fraud team, but at what point that's not clear. If it turns out to be much smaller then we will carry it. Anything more?"

With all of them remaining silent, Tom moved to the next slide and Operation Resolve.

WEB BASED PAEDOPHILE GROUPS

- Operation Hope identified web-based paedophile sites
- Identify sites for infiltration
- Identify targets for U/C replacement
- Identify locate and capture a copy of the server

"There are a number of web based sites linked to Operation Hope," said Tom. "We can't take them all on, so we need to come up with front and secondary runners. Your meeting with Jane will cover identifying likely targets so that we can replace them with undercover officers, then through them infiltrate the sites. SDE have already provided good intelligence products on two, and from that, I want to capture a copy of the server. Questions?"

The team had worked out that they were a number of days behind

Tom and Jane, and that this briefing was an overview, so again they stayed silent.

INTELLIGENCE AND EVIDENCE

- Deconstruct the server
- Understand & Develop
- U/C infiltration
- Key target acquisition
- Travelling sex offender

"Once we have a copy of the server, unskilled staff need to be able to investigate its contents. For that to happen, it will need to be converted into a readable format. From that, further intelligence will be captured that can be worked on and developed into actionable intelligence and evidence. The sites will be joined by undercover officers who will start to engage, infiltrate and identify key players. As the intelligence is developed they will 'target harden' using that intelligence, and look for a weakness that we can exploit by assuming their identity, and then further infiltrate. Intelligence indicates that there are a number of suspects who seem to travel to gain access to children. That needs to be fully investigated. Questions?"

A bank of serious faces stared back at Tom. They had all been excited when they walked in. None knew what was going to be said or done. Inside, Anna Wilson was virtually screaming with delight. She had been a straight A student at school, went on to University getting a BSc Honours with ease, and was tipped to carry on for a PhD. Instead she left and joined the Police. She had loved it until she met DCI Carol Summers. Everything in her life had come to a grinding halt as result of the bullying from her. She had been days away from resigning and going back to University when Tom had arrived. Within hours he had lifted that cloud. She was allowed to use her analytical mind and actually get thanked for it. She had been picked for COCET for her skills. Her dedication at school and University was paying off. Her degree per se didn't transfer across into a Police environment, but the skills in getting the degree did, this was her chance.

INTELLIGENCE DISSEMINATION

- Intelligence product preparation
- Dissemination Phase
- COCET coordinated action
- Exit strategy

"Intelligence packs will be put together ready for dissemination. There will be COCET coordinated action taken based on the intelligence captured. An exit strategy will protect our undercover officers and allow us to come back should we need to." Tom pushed straight on to the last slide.

MEDIA & CP

- COCET media strategy
- COCET CP

"Sarah Dorsey, whom we haven't met yet, has already started. She has been assigned to us from the National Crime Squad. You can take it from me, if she's from the NCS then she is going to be good. She will deal with all things media for COCET and that includes all the Chiefs. We have also been assigned an external CP specialist from the NSPCC. Louisa Greenwood will be here later today and will join you on Athena training. She is not a cop and hasn't worked in a situation like this before, so welcome her in. Jane, over to you," Tom said, signalling that he was finished.

"Everybody around my desk for eleven, we can take it from there," said Jane.

With that, the team got up and quickly left the room with smiles of expectation. Jane stopped at the door and closed it enough not to be overheard. "Any advice?"

Tom smiled at her, but was also smiling at himself, remembering the first time somebody gave him the reins and the new responsibility of command.

"Jane. The only advice I can give you is this: believe in your ability. Be yourself. Don't try to learn leadership from a book. The team needs to find their feet and will be looking for guidance. You are that guidance. You can only do it if you are at the helm. Have a plan, stick to it when the going gets tough, but don't be afraid to change a decision in the light of new information. Be inclusive, but there is only one team leader. Don't be too hard on yourself if you get things wrong. Sometimes that's how we learn best. And, if you do screw up, just tell me, because I will have almost certainly done it myself and know a way round it."

"Thanks. I know I can tell you anything. I guess it's just the weight of our profile and the new command. When I came out from the meeting with the ACC, Margaret Thrinton said, "Onward and upward, Jane." That was as far as Jane got on her own. She was joined by Tom as they said together "It's the only way!"

Jane immediately burst into laughter, which also served to break her inner tension. "How did you know I was going to say that?"

"Just a hunch. Now to your station, Detective Sergeant!" laughed Tom.

"Yes, Sir!" Jane snapped back whilst standing at attention, and with a smile left and headed for the small canteen off the central corridor at the rear of the building.

Tom picked up his desk phone and direct dialled an internal extension number.

Dr. Fiona Gordon, who was at her desk reading an article in the Journal of Contemporary Psychotherapy, glanced up at her phone, and seeing the extension number on her screen immediately picked it up. "How's my favourite Detective Chief Inspector today?" Fiona said, with more than a little bit of pleasure.

"This DCI is on top of the moon, but also a little apprehensive," replied Tom.

"Does the moon and the apprehension cover the same subject?" Fiona's tone was more than a bit suggestive as she said it.

"Well, I guess so. We have started, and you need to make your baseline assessments soon because I'm going to hit the ground running. Which brings me to the some of the apprehension. What about me? How's this going to work?" Tom said it in a tone that

30

immediately closed the gap between the two of them, even though they were each on the end of a telephone.

"Well, your timing is impeccable, Mr. R. I have just been researching peer reviews to get some names and details of other professionals I respect. I clearly can't continue to counsel you when I'm sharing your bed. So you will be counselled by someone else. The issue for me is who receives the assessment. Can I still have oversight and ownership of the outcome from the interviews? If I can't, then we have a dilemma."

"How bad a one?"

"Ethically? I would need to flag this up, and from now on you will be seen by another professional. That's not the problem. The problem is, who do they report to if they need to tell someone something?"

"The Force MO?"

"With the teams and your profile being what it is, I can't see the Chief wearing it. He will probably speak to Arthur. But once Arthur knows the full story he will decline, citing a number of well rehearsed reasons. He's been the Force Medical Officer now for over twenty years. He's seen it all, Tom."

"Is this going to be a problem for us?" Tom shot back, way too quickly, giving a glimpse of his private thoughts. "I don't want our relationship to damage you professionally."

Fiona took charge of the way the conversation was going with a gentle but firm professional voice.

"Tom. Our relationship started after Operation Hope concluded. I have been clear on everything I have done, so there is no need to worry. But the time has come for some decisions to be made, and there is more than one way to deal with this. I just haven't made my mind up which way yet. I can get started with the team in a couple of days once I've had my Athena training. It will take a couple of days to baseline the team, so we have a week; and I'm on the case, OK!"

"I love it when you dominate me," Tom replied in a sexual tone. The comment immediately broke the moment, causing them both to smile.

"I'll call you tonight," Fiona said in a caring, soft tone. Then ended the call.

'*It looks right, feels right; seems right.*' Tom thought to himself. But he still had the feeling from time to time, and he was getting it now, that it was dangerous. But how could it be? He went over it again in his head. '*Was it just that it was Fiona and who she was? That made sense. Was it because he was waiting to be found out lying about his nightmares? Yes, he knew he had to come clean soon over that. But that didn't account for some of those remote thoughts he suddenly got a glimpse of in his mind, the ones that made him think: Danger!*' His thoughts were interrupted by his desk phone.

"DCI Ross."

"Tom. It's Sarah Dorsey. How are you?"

"Hi, Sarah. I'm fine, thanks. I wasn't expecting to hear from you till you arrived, but welcome to COCET."

"I started two weeks ago, but I've been busy clearing a few things I was working on, and COCET Chiefs wanted their own strategy. I just needed to touch base with something that has come out of their strategy, the policy for which I have been asked to put together by tomorrow. Can you speak?"

Tom immediately picked up Sarah's Yorkshire accent. She also had a light but very assured telephone manner, from which he mentally got a picture of someone very good at her job. He didn't really expect anything else from someone attached to the NCS. But hearing her for the first time just gave him a boost, knowing he was getting the best.

"Yes. Of course I can. Great to have you on the team."

"Great to be on it," replied Sarah. "What do you know about the US Amber Alert system?"

"Not a great deal. It's a country wide child abduction media alert system."

"That's it in a nutshell. Right. COCET has an American partner called ICE, as you know, and they are part of the Amber Alert system. Now, although we aren't part of the USA, you will be working in a virtual environment where offenders capable of undertaking or planning this sort of crime operate, and you could be doing this using American agents. Agents that you ultimately, as head of COCET, will be leading. So we are being added to that list of outlets who will get the alert. I need three names to be on our list, you being one."

Tom knew his judgment was sound. This girl just gave him the 'feel good' factor. He quickly scribbled a note on his pad to bring up the NCS with JT when he next had an audience with TVP's head of C.I.D.

"Jane King and Anna Farley."

"OK. The next thing is that Sussex Police started a Child Alert system of their own. Your Chief and theirs have come to an agreement that we will be part of the UK alert system. Same three names?"

"Yep."

"Good. One of my jobs will be to expand the membership list and to include the virtual world. That's something we can talk about when we meet. I will be at the office the day after tomorrow, bright and breezy. See you then. Bye!"

As the phone hit the cradle, he was just about to reflect on Sarah Dorsey and Child Alerts, when there was a knock at his door. It opened, and Jane King walked in with another woman.

"Boss. This is Louisa Greenwood."

"Hello, Louisa. Come in, take a seat," Tom said, standing and shaking Louisa's hand.

Jane left, shutting the door behind her.

"Welcome to COCET, Louisa. Can you tell me a bit about yourself?" Louisa was in her early forties Tom reckoned. She was about 5'2" and had blonde hair cut short. She was smartly dressed, mainly in dark colours, and sat upright with a smile that immediately gave him the impression she had a bubbly character.

"I've been working for the NSPCC for the last 11 years, and before that for local Social Services. In all, I have about 16 years' experience working in child protection of one sort or another."

Tom picked up a northern accent which he thought was from the Northumberland region. He was also right about a bubbly personality. She wore a constant smile as she spoke.

"Louisa. Does your NSPCC line command have a view on what your job description should be here?"

"The only brief I've been given is an outline on the structure of COCET and how the top bosses want it to work. Other than that,

I was asked to be here as a non police CP specialist who can access the UK's Social Services network through contacts, and get things done quickly should you need it. Other than that, that's pretty much it really."

Tom thought she was telling the truth. She still wore the smile that clearly wasn't going to go away just because she had stopped talking. He was trying to gauge whether she knew about his reticence concerning her appointment, when she suddenly began again.

"I have worked with cops in the past you know, and I'm comfortable in this environment. I guess I have the same sort of outlook as police on most things, which makes it easy for me to get on with them."

Tom couldn't make out whether the last statement was solely said for his benefit, or it was Louisa just being Louisa.

"How about this. You get yourself settled in. In two weeks' time write me a job description for what you think you can deliver on for COCET, and send it to me. From there we can work out what's best for everyone. How does that sound?"

"Sounds great, Boss. Who will be my line manager?"

Tom didn't have a clue what rank Louisa held within the NSPCC, it was probably quite high once transferred to its Police equivalent. But as far as he was concerned, it didn't enter into the equation as he saw it.

"Jane King."

"Thanks Boss. I'm a hard worker and I won't let you down," Louisa said, as she got up and left.

'Bubbly!' He thought; as his mind immediately went back to Child Alerts. He knew a bit about the US Amber system. Its approach was: child gets abducted, let's get the message out using all forms of media, conventional and social, country wide. Tap into all the federal law enforcement agencies to maximise the spread, and cover all borders. Flick on one switch and the whole network lights up. But, that was point A in the real world to point B in the real world, using the internet to convey the message. What COCET was going to do was expand that search into the virtual world. Not only that, but Tom could see the possibility for reversing this to give 360° cover. Why couldn't they go virtual world to real world? And virtual to virtual? The hairs on his neck stood up and he got a cold shudder. Day one and they were breaking new ground. Here we go again!

CHAPTER TWO

We all have our time machines. Some take us back, they're called memories. Some take us forward, they're called dreams.

—Jeremy Irons

As Tom watched the closed door of his ensuite, he could hear the water from the shower move across Fiona. His stare made its way to the ceiling rose, whilst his mind wandered from the soft sounds of the water to the receding nightmare. Desperate to keep hold of the contents, he was drowning as his fear took hold and severed the link forever. He knew there was something there, some warning the dream held for him, something more sinister, but it was gone.

His senses turned to the present. He was wet with sweat, the bed covers were twisted, and he knew he must have been caught. There was no avoiding it now. He sat on the edge of the bed, waiting for the future to expose him. The sound of zips closing and suitcase handles extending gave warning the door was about to open, so Tom stood up. Fiona walked out fully dressed, pulling her overnight roller bag in her left hand and manually airing her almost dry hair with her right. She had a blank and serious look on her face, as she said, "How long have you been having those?"

It was more of a demand than a question.

"And don't try telling me that it was your first!"

"Well, I'm not sure what 'those' are, as I've never recorded myself sleeping. But for a while I guess."

"You know exactly what 'those' are! They are some of the worst nightmares I have ever heard about, let alone actually witnessed, Tom.

You've kept that back, you've not been truthful!"

Fiona stared into his eyes looking for a response; she wanted a reply but he was struggling with what to say.

"I can never remember any of it. It doesn't hamper me, so what is there to explain? I can't be asleep and awake at the same time." The moment he said it he wished he hadn't, as he saw a flash of anger speed its way across Fiona's face.

"I haven't got time for this now, we will speak about it later. But this isn't OK, Tom. I trusted you!"

As he sat through the rest of his Athena training that afternoon he struggled with maintaining his concentration. He had a 'slave' terminal which was being controlled and watched by the company's facilitator. The guy clearly loved his job and the software. He also knew, or had been briefed, as to who was in the pilot study group and what they had been set up to do, so he was trying extra hard. Tom was being caught out by not staying up to speed with the rest of the class, and it was getting to him. The training went right up to five o'clock with not a minute wasted. The Intel team seemed impressed with what Athena could do and Jane was enthusiastic, which was even better, as he could feel some of what he'd learnt draining away from him already. Back in his office, and alone, he wondered what Fiona meant by 'later'. He thought the best thing would be for him to let her make the move when she was ready.

Jane reconvened the COCET team in the new conference room and proceeded to deliver an Operation Ascent briefing, using the standard Police IIMARCH template through Microsoft PowerPoint. The operational plan or investigation strategy was a straight lift from the presentation given the day before, and she quickly finished and moved on.

"We will be using Athena for Intel and investigation. For everything else we will be using the TVP intranet. Non TVP staff have been given access, and Jerry Stone has created us our own space and restricted it to just us. For those not familiar, Owen and Mitchell will mentor you through it. It is police proof, so it's not a big one. You also all have access to Operation Benson and Hope through the two standalone systems opposite the viewing room. The Boss will be setting the strategic direction, and I will be directing the investigation through actions. I will be also using a decision log when I need to, but the intelligence and proactive face of what we do will be on Athena. Archie has volunteered to act as Case Officer for Ascent, which means he is also Disclosure Officer. Are there any questions?"

"How do we start, and what with?" asked Anna Farley.

"I will send you a single intelligence log from Operation Hope. It will contain everything we need to kick this off. As a team we meet daily, before 10am, to discuss investigation tactics. From that more actions flow. As time goes on, or as we get busy, our meetings by necessity may become less frequent; but at the beginning we stay close, so that we all know what we are all doing. From working on Hope, I know that the key to success in this particular field is teamwork. However, to give you a flavour, the first thrust will be to locate and house Kuklin. Mitchell is financially trained and will submit some production orders on the accounts we know of, and identify more. From analysis of those we'll identify the laundering outlets and other gang members. We will reverse investigate the purchasers and the purchases, get to the online merchant, and eventually to the latest server."

"Are we going to use covert internet investigators to make a controlled purchase?" Anna Wilson then asked.

"The Boss wants to use level one undercover officers who are also internet trained, so yes. I know he wants to try and use the same ones we used on Hope, but that is still being discussed at ACPO and SO10 level. Officers are controlled through SO10, and some regions, in this case the home force, are also weighing in."

Archie piped up. "What about surveillance? Who're we gonna use?"

"For static OP work, ourselves. Anything more, then we ask the Boss, and he gets a team in."

"Who will be responsible for surveillance authorities?" Archie further enquired.

"I will," replied Jane.

"How much victim identification work is there going to be?" Owen asked.

"Not a great deal, probably. Is there anybody here that has done it before?"

"I have done some," said Anna Farley.

Jane looked around at her team whilst she considered her reply. "I will do most, but if I need a hand are you OK to help out, Anna?" looking at her.

"Yeah, I am fine with that, but I wouldn't want it to be full time."

"OK. Well, in that case we move onto Operation Resolve. The outline for this will be to submit some data comms around a specific website identified by SDE as 'childscentcafe'. At the same time, our U/Cs will join the forum in a number of identities, and from there engage some of the members to infiltrate the site and capture intelligence and evidence on the members. We want to identify a senior member that is ideally resident in this country, with a view to assuming his identity; and from there locate the server, identify its membership, and then dismantle it."

"What about 'Michael' from Operation Hope?" asked Owen Marks.

Owen knew it was a thorny question, but felt it needed asking. He wanted to know what they were going to do about that particular lead.

Jane paused and stared at Owen, silently wishing he hadn't asked the question. She knew it would come up at some point, but was taken aback that it had come up so soon. Both she and Tom knew it was unfinished business as far as they were concerned, and she herself had had some sleepless nights and some agonising days with Dr. Gordon as a result. She had dealt with it and had moved on. The fact was, when you were dealing with the virtual world you never really knew what historical time zone you were working in, and they hadn't been as close as they had first thought.

"SDE have it as a single action allocated to them. You're the single point of contact, touch base with them and see if they have anything." She knew they wouldn't, as she had since formed a close friendship with Sue Tay and she would have rung her immediately if they had got anything; but it put Owen in charge and at ease. Jane brought the operational briefing quickly to a close and moved onto admin procedures, when the team took charge with a barrage of questions. Finally at 6.55pm, exhausted but satisfied, the new COCET team closed down on day two and went home. Jane, however, hadn't quite finished so knocked on Tom's door.

"How did it go?" Tom enquired.

"I gave them the outline, sorted out the initial plan, and covered a whole bunch of admin and working procedures, which is good. We will be ready to start first thing. I'm going to stay on for a while if that's OK. I want the Intel start up logs for Ascent and Resolve with Anna first thing, and I'm still catching up on some victim ID work. I shouldn't be more than two hours."

"Fine. I will be doing some admin here and a heads up report for the CPS, just to let them know what we are planning. They might want a briefing or a visit here. What ID work are you doing?"

"Some new material that has come in from forces, SDE and Holland."

"Come and get me when you start, and I'll join you."

1855hrs UTC, London, UK

At that same time in a small flat within the Purbrook Estate, South East London, Andrei Kuklin was working on his laptop adapting an off the shelf template, when he received an incoming text on his pay-as-you-go burn phone. He read the English content then immediately deleted it. He went back to his laptop and quickly accessed a web based mailbox, logging in with a long alpha-numeric password. Once in, he opened a new email and wrote the following;

'Перемещение сервера сегодня вечером. Очистить все счета завтра утром'.

He placed the mail in the drafts folder, logged out of the Hotmail account and then sent a text from his phone. A short while later he got a reply acknowledging the server shutdown and a cash collection. He deleted that, reopened the Hotmail account, removed and deleted the draft email, and logged out. He then connected to a proxy server in America and, knowing his IP address was now masked, entered the internet, navigating to a hosting company in Norway. He logged into the server rented by him at the company. Following authentication, he gained access to the server as Administrator. He then opened an overwrite software package, pointed it at the site and set it to run for seven passes. He left the program to run knowing it would take at least an hour. Andrei Kuklin knew some experts believed it was still possible to retrieve data even after a zero overwrite of the hard drive. A single pass maybe, which was why he was undertaking a number of them. If he had the opportunity he would physically destroy the drive by way of a shred, but he couldn't access it so that was out of the question. It meant nothing to him, as the best security he had was that the police didn't have the skill to recover it in any case. They were just a fucking joke, especially in the UK. He then made his way to another hosting company, this time in Venezuela, and logged into a server again as Administrator. Once in, he spent about 20 minutes completing the prep on the hard drive that he had started but not finished a few weeks earlier. He then logged out of that, disconnected from the proxy server, and went back to his script work.

1910hrs UTC, Stockton-On-Tees, North East England
As Kuklin was building his online empire, Philip Thompson was in a bedroom of a house that he lived in with his disabled mother. He was private messaging a new member of the forum called 'childscentcafe'. Thompson was using his senior position within the forum to impress the new member.

'librarian' wrote: "You know the rules, nothing illegal up or down."

'luvbabypanties' replied, "I was hoping that you might help me with meeting others that want what I want."

The forum librarian snickered to himself thinking, *'Yeah, we all want it. And I'm getting it!'*

'librarian' wrote: "Contact me outside of this, and give me an addie."

He immediately got a reply. He stored the address, sent him a cut & paste prepared set of demands on one of his email accounts, and sat back. He knew he had the upper hand and this guy seemed really new, and desperate. There was no telling what he might get out of it. Within minutes his inbox number increased and he opened the new mail up.

"I am so into 3/4yr olds. It's on my mind every day. I will send you a copy of my entire collection if you send me what I want, and intro to others."

Thompson immediately replied, "How big is your collection?"

'luvbabypanties' responded, "Two hundred or so."

Thompson nearly spat out the mouthful of tea he'd just been drinking, and typed back angrily. "That's pathetic! That's not a collection!"

Thompson, the forum librarian, was just about to log off when the mail box increased. He was pissed off and toyed with the idea of just ignoring it, but he was so annoyed at the newcomer he wanted to have another go at him. So he opened it.

"I know it is a small amount but they are my own kids."

'Oh, yes, luvbabypanties! You have made my day!' Thompson said to himself.

He typed an email which said, "Put them on a CD and send it to the address below. Make sure to password protect and email me the PW. I am the 'Librarian'. I will look after your collection offline. As you update it, update me with a new CD. Once I have it, you will get what you want."

He waited for a few minutes and got a positive reply. He was now really looking forward to it. In the meantime he had his own little kid to think about, and she would be sleeping over for a couple of days.

0215hrs ICT, Pattaya, Thailand

In a part of the world closer to the equator it was gone 2am as he got back to the bungalow he was staying in. He was glad to get into the sanctuary of the air conditioning after an evening in Boyztown. For him this was an early night. He stripped and dropped his clothes into the laundry basket then walked to the bathroom and turned on the shower, waiting for the warm water to make its way to the shower head. He looked at his tan in the mirror, admiring it and his well defined muscles. He turned to check his back and noticed that even the scar on his shoulder was tanning. He washed himself slowly, thinking about the young Thai boy he had just taken. It certainly wasn't the boy's first farang, but judging by the complaints of the gay mama san, it certainly was the first time he had been tied up and beaten whilst being buggered. He had paid the fine. Money made it all go away. Yes, he would probably be banned for a while. But who cared? There were plenty of other places to go for a drink. The boy was nowhere near young enough for him, but he had just needed a young fuck. Although he was fifteen he seemed younger, with his tiny frame. But he was here for much bigger and better things. Tomorrow he would check out the three other bungalows and set up the letting of them. For now he drifted off to sleep with the sounds of the aircon, and with the thoughts of the jerking body beneath him as the boy tried to escape the punches.

"Ready when you are, Boss!" Jane shouted from just outside Tom's door. She made her way to the viewing room and inserted the first of the discs. This one had been sent to them by Suffolk Constabulary. She quickly scrolled through the images, spending just seconds on some and more on others. Tom joined her and they spent most of the time in silence as they made their way through the discs and their content. Although Jane was operating the viewing software, the amount of time she spent on an image, matched the time that Tom also required for that image without having to say anything such was their working relationship. In a perverse way it was a welcome break for Tom, as he had been thinking about Fiona and that morning for the past hour or so. As they came to the last disc, Tom could see that it had come from Eindhoven and contained a larger amount of images. He checked his watch.

Jane, who hadn't turned her head said, "Let's see how far we get in the next 30 minutes." Tom agreed and they started.

The child abuse material had been divided into sections using the COPINE scale to dictate the level of seriousness of the image, for the benefit of the new COCET team; as it was a scale they used and were familiar with. There were not many level fives, the most serious level, and they quickly moved on to level four; and were still in that category when the thirty minutes came and went. It was 8.15pm by the time they got to the end of that section. There had been only two images out of hundreds that Jane had put to one side for further examination, otherwise there was nothing in the background or the images of the victims that warranted further inspection.

"How much more is there?" Tom asked.

"Loads. The biggest section is level three, and then downwards from there. Plenty of level ones as well. Then there is an offender profile chart, personal description details and other things surrounding the offender."

"OK. Cover the rest when you can, skip to the profile chart and description, then knock it on the head for the day."

Jane skipped forward to a chart which contained information on the number of images in each section and how many of those were videos. There was then a chart which grouped together the victims, which indicated series, and further grouped those across the levels of the COPINE scale. There was a further chart for overall date, time, location and camera, which when converted to a column and line chart indicated peak times of possible abuse in comparison to periods of no activity, if the raw data were to be believed.

"Jane, can you give this to Patrick and ask him what more can be done on this, and what more data he would need to do it?"

"Sure."

As Tom considered what the peaks or troughs might really represent. Jane skipped forward to the offender description. The intelligence was contained within one Dutch Police form which had been scanned in. There were a number of pages that pretty much contained everything that was contained in a UK Phoenix Form, the form that was completed on every person when they were charged in the UK. It covered everything from names and aliases to birth marks and tattoos. The form was in Dutch, but with some analysing you could make out what was being recorded. Tom noticed that the offender had a number of tattoos, and stopped Jane on that page so he could see the description of each one and its location on the body, this being ringed on a drawing of a human. One jumped out at him, and got his heart racing as he saw its location.

"Have we got images of the tattoos?"

"I don't know," Jane replied, and skipped forward until she found a standard Police mugshot. She forwarded again and got a side profile, and again until one image revealed homemade tattoos on his fingers, and then a professional one on the left forearm. That one immediately caused the hair on Tom's neck to stand straight up.

"We have seen that tattoo before!" Tom declared.

Jane was smiling as she left the screen she was on and brought up an excel spreadsheet. She quickly found what she was looking for, and then called up a set of images within a folder titled Michael.

She scrolled through until she found the one she was seeking.

"Yes!" She shrieked triumphantly. She then got nervous and called up the tattoo, but after a few quick comparisons it was definitely the same tattoo and the forearm was of the same size and shape.

"I will get an email off to Niall tonight to see what we can develop out of this, and create an Athena entry to kick off the tattoo image investigation. Start here in the UK to see how common a drawing it is, and then get onto forensics to see what they can do with the shape and size of the two forearms. I want to know if they can say it is the same arm."

"Will do, Boss!"

Tom left. He was about to email Niall, but deciding it was late, sent a text message requesting a call the following day. He got a reply within moments.

"Sure 10.30ish suit?"

Tom confirmed, then together with Jane locked and alarmed the COCET building and went home; not a simple procedure as extra security had been installed.

He was driving the familiar route home as his mind went into overdrive covering the possibilities of a lead into Michael. Alongside that he was thinking about Fiona. He was trying to decide whether to call her. In the end he took the soft option and did nothing, leaving him free to think up tactics around the Dutch offender. It was past midnight as he got into bed, tired from the emotion of the day, but excited at the same time for the new lead on Michael.

0015hrs UTC, London, UK

As Tom was drifting off, Kuklin was back on the web, his IP address hidden by a proxy server. He expertly and with real speed uploaded the 'pay-per-view' child abuse website, which now included new material from a recent visit back home. Some of his associates had no problem with creating new material, some even with their own kids if they were being paid for it in Euros or US Dollars. He completed the e-commerce side, enabling him to receive payments electronically, then the links to the child abuse images and videos. Finally, after he had gone over everything twice and was satisfied, he went live. He sent an email from the site to a few of the more avid and heavy users from the previous operation who had not been bounced to his fraud section. He logged off and opened a bottle of Vodka. He was looking forward to a trip to Tiraspol, and started to plan what he would do with his share, the largest of the latest collection run. He had no sexual interest in children himself and thought that the ones that did were weak, and therefore were there to be exploited, and money was to be made from them. The Western Europeans, with all their pathetic idealism, were just soft touches; and their law enforcement was a joke. He got great satisfaction knowing that he was doing it in their country, using some of their kids and making thousands from their weaknesses. He didn't go to bed until he'd finished the bottle and slept soundly. Not from the alcohol, for which he had a tolerance, but from the thought that, as he slept peacefully, money was pouring into his accounts from paedophiles around the world.

CHAPTER THREE

Both the criminal, and the reporter, albeit from different points of view, have sought the answer to the question, 'What is the perfect crime?' Experienced international law enforcement officers will tell you that there cannot be such a thing, as there is always a victim somewhere. Criminals live by different morals and codes from law abiding citizens. Each country and its culture affect those morals to a greater or lesser degree. The violent history of a few countries has led their criminal fraternities to move away from the terror of their ancestors. Others reflect their history in what they do now and how they do it; rooted to the past, a past where victims are of no concern.

Today, if one country's police force enters cyberspace to undertake an investigation, it must know where the criminal comes from, his past and his culture, and adapt to it. If they fail to recognise or acknowledge the difference in culture, they can lose; and in some cases, lose badly.

0900hrs UTC, Central London, UK

Vitaly Ivanovich Danshov, Pavel Mikhailovich Lachkov, Dobre Bakaly and Nicolae Vartik all met outside Victoria Underground Station at the Victoria mainline exit. From there they made their way through Victoria Station to the nearest Starbucks, on the corner of Eccleston Street. After a round of coffee, and during discussions over football, girls and vodka, Danshov put his hand in a breast jacket pocket and produced four brown envelopes. Keeping one for himself, he handed them out in a particular order known only to him. The others took their envelope and placed it inside a pocket, whilst continuing to talk as if nothing untoward was happening. It was a busy coffee shop with lots of noise and chatter, their Russian dialect and animated talk brought no attention. At the conclusion they all got up, shaking hands and bidding farewell. They left Starbucks and departed the area in different directions and in pairs. Danshov and Bakaly made their way back through the mainline station and straight to a HSBC Bank. Bakaly was the first to approach the ATM. He was wearing a hoody which was now up and pulled forward across his face to help obscure his features. He tapped in a memorised password, selected the current account option, and withdrew £200. He quickly placed in a second card and password, and repeated the transaction for the same amount, and then again with a third card. Bakaly moved away; and after letting another two customers make transactions, Danshov moved to the ATM, wearing a long billed baseball cap which was pulled down covering most of his face. He went through the same process but with different debit cards, then met up with Bakaly. They moved onto the nearby Nat West Bank, and then Lloyds Bank. From there they walked South down Vauxhall Bridge Road, went to a Barclays Bank and did the same again.

They then went back to Victoria Underground Station and caught a tube to Piccadilly Circus via Green Park, where they met up again with Lachkov and Vartik, who had hit the same banks in another area for the same amount, using different cards. Each gang member had twelve debit cards, and over another coffee and a McDonald's breakfast, the gang members slowly and covertly handed their cash withdrawals to Danshov. By 11.30am Vitaly Danshov was entering the Purbrook Estate via the Pope Street entrance and knocking on the door of 91c.

Over part of that same time period, COCET team members had been at their desks working on the new Athena management system, which had commenced Operations Ascent and Resolve. ADS King had called an informal meeting for 10.30am to discuss the actions that had now been allocated to officers.

"Starting with Ascent. Mitchell, do you have all the Intel you need, and is it in the right format to obtain the production orders for the accounts we know of so far?" said Jane.

"Yes," replied Mitchell.

"Great. How soon can you get the production orders?"

"All things being equal, I hope to get them this afternoon; and be in a position to serve them in the morning. I have already made contact with the bank's liaison staff and gave them the heads up on the nature of who we are, and what we are about. So I expect to get a quick turnaround."

"Good," replied Jane. "What about the ATMs?"

"They know about that, and are going to work on that in advance. But we won't get any product on it until they get their orders."

"Anna, what about an address for Kuklin?"

"Patrick is working on that," she replied, looking at Patrick Smith.

Patrick formed his mouth to say something, but just as the words were about to come out they became blocked, and the new team, who had only recently met Patrick, felt the awkwardness that Jane had felt when she had first met him. She had spoken with Patrick before the meeting and he had asked to be questioned. He needed to cross the bridge as much as the new team did over his stammer.

After a few seconds he said, "Immigration had an address in Whitechapel, which he is no longer at. The whole address w-w-was s-s-s-subject of a search by Police, n-n-n-nothing to do with him. They seized everything and there was a contract in h-h-his name for 91c, Purbrook Estate, SE1."

Patrick paused and took a soft sideways glance at Anna Farley that nobody but Jane picked up.

"We have done the usual utilities and he is shown as one of four occupants at that address, although it is believed to be a two bedroom flat," interjected Anna Farley.

Patrick, who had by now relaxed a bit, added, "We have a student ID photo of him."

"Good work, team," said Jane quickly. She knew that was a good piece of intelligence work.

"Owen."

"Yes, Sarge."

"Do an initial scope of the address, and plot it for an OP and further surveillance. Work with Patrick for the Intel, and then get it to me so I can get a directed surveillance authority for us to take it further."

"Will do."

"Archie, have you got anywhere with the flights?"

"Not yet. It could end up being a needle in a haystack. I am hoping that Mitchell may get something from the production orders which can help narrow this down."

"OK. In the meantime keep pushing ahead."

Turning her look towards Anna Wilson, Jane said, "Anna, anything to report on the website?"

"I have just got something back from the gateway team, who have traced it to Norway and what seems like on open resource, a hosting company. The Intel Cell are using Niall to get this confirmed, and if so, find out if they are friendly enough so we can make an approach."

"Time frame?"

Anna Wilson, who didn't know the answer to that, looked at Anna Farley for assistance.

"It will be today."

"That's a good start bearing in mind it's morning break. We will regroup later and Resolve won't come out to you until later today. Just so you are in the loop, I have a lead on a victim from Operation Hope. If it needs any input from the team it will come from me as an email and not on Athena. Also Supt. Maggie Burrows will be here to meet you all at some point. As soon as I have a time, I'll let you know."

The team broke up, pleased with what they had achieved and the way it had been received.

Just as Jane knocked on Tom's door, his phone went and it was Niall. Tom waved Jane in, and taking a seat, she listened in to the one sided telephone conversation.

"Morning, Niall. I will post an update to the international team later today, but in the meantime I have something from Operation Hope."

"I am all ears," Niall said.

"Jane and I were going through some images from the Eindhoven job. They had very intelligently graded the images, charted those, and provided an offender description. The offender Visser had a number of tattoos. One was on the left forearm, and is identical to the one on the offender from the images you and I have viewed before, when you were here on that trip early on in Operation Hope. Do you remember?"

"Of course I do! Do you want me to touch base with the investigation team?"

"Yes. See how far they have got. Has he been sentenced, where is he, are they prepared to re-arrest and produce him back to a Police Station for interview? Can we assist, and if so, what do they want? Do they need a letter of request or can it be done under the banner of Operation Hope? That sort of thing. The objective for us and for them is to hold Visser to account for all his criminal actions, and we want to identify and locate Michael. "

"No problem, this should be a no brainer. They may need another letter of request, though. What's the source of these images? I can't remember."

"They go back to Op Benson and Boyd." Tom looked at Jane to see if he was right, and whether she was following the conversation. She was, and confirmed it with a nod of the head.

"OK, leave it with me. Got to go, my other phone is going and it's probably the Kripos officer from Norway."

"Speak later," Tom said and hung up.

"Did you get enough of that?"

"Yes, who is he using there?"

"Sounds like he's talking directly to the National Criminal Intelligence Service, he mentioned Kripos, why?"

"I just wanted to know; keep tabs I guess after Operation Hope and all the secrecy."

"Good idea. Speak to Niall, he won't have a problem with it. It will be someone out of the Bryn office."

"OK. On that subject of secrecy. We haven't done a heavy lock down on these Operations. Do we need to?"

Tom sank back into his chair and rubbed his hands over the back of his head, looked up and thought about it. Jane was right. He hadn't done anything about it. Was that because it had all happened on a wave of success? Or was it because he just didn't feel he needed as much secrecy around these two operations as he had done over Benson and Hope? He searched his mind, knowledge and experience for an indication, but got nothing.

"We don't need to go overboard at this stage. I will just leave it to you to reinforce the need for a very high level of confidentiality. We are a new team, and the nation's ACPO ranks will all know and hear about us in the future. So we need to be careful. No discussions about operational activity with anyone other than the team, unless it is part of an action. Only use contacts we know or that we trust. That should do it."

"OK," Jane replied, and got up to leave. Then she turned and asked, "Is there a time for the Superintendent?"

"First thing after lunch. So no yawning, or there will be a tea fund fine of a packet of Rich Tea biscuits!" he said, with a bit of laughter in his voice.

Alone, he checked his watch, then his email and phone. Nothing from Fiona. He couldn't wait any longer and rang her office number. It rang four times, and he was about to hang up when it was answered.

"Hi, Tom."

"Hi. I just wanted to know if it was alright to chat. Are you OK?"

"Yes. I am. But I am not ready to talk about it yet. I am really fond of you, Tom, but this has got off to a bad start; which in turn has caused me to think again about whether this should be happening."

Tom felt his heart miss a beat. "Not at all?"

"No, not at all. Well, I don't know."

Fiona paused. Tom didn't know if that was deliberate or not.

"Look. What I mean is, not now, I think. And that is why I need time. I have to start on your team this week, I have a huge work load as well. Either way, you must be counselled by another professional. I will have to compile a written, and probably verbal, handover of all the team and that includes you. I can't be reading your results knowing what I know now, and still be sleeping with you at night. I care for you dearly, but this has got messy, and was always probably going to be. But for now, if we are going to continue, I must either get this cleared from above, or we stop now. Because your counsellor can't report to me."

"Well, I don't want it to stop now," he replied, trying to keep desperation out of his voice.

"I know, and neither do I. But I need time to think about this. If this went wrong, Tom, the Force could replace you on the basis that it would be better off for you and them in the long run." Fiona stopped talking to let it sink in.

Tom's mind was racing thinking about that possibility. He knew she was right. There would be others in the ACPO ranks who would take the work-life balance route for sure. He knew he had to trust her. She did care for him, possibly even love him. He suddenly got it. If she came out too soon it might go pear shaped. She probably wanted to know more about his true mental state first. Well, he was sound on that.

"I agree. Who have you got for me, and when can we start?"

Fiona paused before replying with a different tone. A tone which Tom took as her acknowledging him for knowing what needed to be done.

"Her name is Dr. Gloria Clayworth, and she will be in touch soon."

Tom thought about asking if Fiona was going to, or had already, admitted their relationship to Gloria, or if she was just going to leave it to him to spill the beans.

"I look forward to meeting her," he decided to say, thinking it might be some test to see if he was going to be honest or not.

"Tom. This will be worked through. You are busy, so am I. We can pick this up later. Is it alright if I start on Thursday? You have a small team, I can be done by Friday."

"Of course."

"In that case, know that I want what is best." With that she hung up. He sank back into his chair. *'If things seem too good to be true, it's probably because it bloody well is,'* he thought to himself.

"'I want what's best." What's that supposed to mean when it's at home?' He continued.

He let the emotion of it all go for a moment and immediately felt more relaxed. She was right, he was busy. He let his mind wander without really thinking about anything to see how he felt. He did feel something. What was it? It was gone in a flash. He had to drop it and trust her. However this panned out she would make the right call, even if he didn't agree with it.

The knock at his door brought him out of his thoughts and he looked up.

"Hi, I'm Sarah Dorsey," Sarah said in a bright chirpy voice which held the same accent he remembered from his phone conversation. Tom got straight up and walked over as she entered, and shook her hand. There was a time he kept well away from media staff, but he had learnt from Operation Hope just how valuable they were. Not only in their own right, but within a child protection context, a good one was pure gold. He immediately took to Sarah, and knew he was on to another NCS winner.

"Welcome again to COCET. And I want you to know I am really pleased you have taken this assignment."

"I am really pleased to have the opportunity and I'm looking forward to it." Sarah replied brightly and with enthusiasm.

"How are you managing this logistically? You are from Yorkshire, am I right?"

"Yes, that's my home. The NCS are paying for everything. I have a block booking at a hotel at the moment, until I can get some rented accommodation. The NCS are sorting that as well. I can go home at weekends if I want to."

Tom was making an appraisal of Sarah as she spoke. She had high heels on, but she must be 5'8" or more he thought. She was slim and very attractive, with straight blonde hair. She was professionally dressed and just looked the part. He recalled when he had first met Maxine. He had been taken with her bubbly, talkative and self assured

54

style as well. He made a mental note to speak to his male staff. The team was about 50/50 males to females. And he knew all too well how things could go when one was under pressure and vulnerable.

"Well, if there is anything more you need, just ask. And when it comes to work, I am not skilled enough in your area, so I'm in your hands. Ask, and you will get it. So, on that, how can I help you today?"

"I just want to meet the team, I guess, and fit in. Have I got a desk?"

"Yes. It is the slightly larger one set away from the team pods nearest the entrance door."

"Monitor, keyboard, and access to whatever system you are working on?"

"Of course," said Tom. "How do you want this to work on a daily basis?"

"Well, I thought it would be best, if you were open to it, for me to be involved at every stage of the operation. From the cradle to the grave. Full access will allow me to provide you with an initial media strategy, which I will maintain and update as we go along. From the strategy, I will advise you on a tactical basis of what options are open to you, where the risk lies to the operation from dealing with the media, and I'll provide you with personal advice on interviews upon arrest phase. It has been decided that since Operation Hope the Joint Chiefs want you to be the main front man, so I hope you are comfortable with that?"

She was nothing if not a straight to the point talker, which he admired and liked.

"You've got it."

"So, in the short term," Sarah continued, "I want to fit in, catch up with everything with regard to the operational activity, get the basics covered and let it roll from there."

"In that case, come with me and let me introduce you to the team."

Tom saw the outline of Supt. Maggie Burrows making her way to his office and took a last bite of his ham and salad sandwich.

"That Coke will rot your insides, Tom!" said Maggie as she entered his office, saying it with a fondness of a caring mother rather than his supervisory officer, and with a smile on her face.

Tom stood up, but only got halfway as Maggie quickly waved him down as she sat down in the chair in front of him.

"This is a just quick visit, Tom, and informal. I want to speak with you and then meet the rest of the team with Jane. Just around their desks with a cuppa, if that is OK with you?"

"Of course."

"You haven't been going long enough for a real update, but I am seeing JT tomorrow over another matter and he will surely bring COCET up. Can I get a very quick, headlines only, briefing?"

"Sure. Well, the first two days have been spent Athena training, but we have been busy nevertheless. I am starting two operations named Ascent and Resolve, intelligence cases to start with. These have come from Operation Hope.

"One, Ascent, targets a commercial online credit card, pay-per-view, crime syndicate which is Moldovan, or from the Russian backed area of Moldova, from what we know.

"The second, Resolve, will investigate a web based paedophile network who appear to be using a standard web based server and hosting company. Who, what, where, we don't know yet. The team has been working on the intelligence case around the main suspect on Ascent, one Andrei Kuklin, to start with. We want to identify Kuklin; and from there his syndicate, locate his server, trace the money and prove the criminal enterprise by making controlled purchases ourselves; by following the money and the laundering of it."

"Is he legally here?" Maggie asked quickly.

"We haven't got a definite on that yet, but we expect he will be."

"Just be careful around that. If he is not legally entitled to be here, or if he is an overstayer, then JT will want his arse covered."

"Understood," replied Tom.

He could see her concern. JT would say 'Get rid of him, get Immigration in, serve him a notice to leave, and put him on a plane.' Tom knew it wasn't that simple with alleged 'students', a case of which this probably was. And this was the internet, one can't pick and choose one's targets or where they come from. The banks were here.

Just removing him would cause Tom more trouble than he would gain from a minor deportation success. It was a real issue though. If they allowed him to remain when they could have got rid of him and then something really went pear shaped - like a loss of life - which was then tracked back to Operation Ascent, they would be heavily criticised. For a new team like COCET, it could be damaging enough to finish it. It would be a dilemma that he would have to face and make the right call.

"Resolve is about a web based network which operates off a website called 'childscentcafe'. We want to locate the server and get a copy. At the same time we will infiltrate it with undercover officers, and eventually do what we did with Operation Hope. Which is to totally dismantle it by arresting the suspects that administrate it, as well as all the members."

"Sounds amazing, Tom. Have you secured the U/Cs you want?"

"Not yet."

"OK, I will bring that up, and I notice you don't have an office administrator, do you want one?"

"I do, but JT said that if I had one I would have to lose an operational place to fund it."

"Did he! Leave that with me, if he persists with that tomorrow, I will get you somebody from division."

Maggie stood up quickly. "Let me meet the team Tom. But before I go, you should know that the Joint Chiefs want COCET to have its own identity. Sarah will be working on that with you and them, but they will have the final say."

Surprised, Tom said, "I think it's a great idea, and will be good for the team now and going forward."

"I have also heard talk," Maggie continued, "that the Chiefs want an identity themselves so they can have a bigger impact, not only within their respective countries, but also globally."

"Wow. That can only be good for child protection worldwide."

As Tom left Maggie Burrows in the safe hands of Jane King, he returned to his desk, mulling over the news about COCET having an identity and a platform to work from. It was essential that they get it, especially when they would be working internationally much of the time. A nation's law enforcement route to another nation is either through legal government channels or through Interpol; or in countries such as the UK, possibly NCS or NCIS, both of which would soon be subsumed into the new agency that the Government was creating: the Serious and Organised Crime Agency. So to get that footprint in now would be a real bonus. It would also clear many pathways in the future when they were dealing with police from all over the world, if they actually knew who COCET were in advance.

'Time to update the international side of the team,' Tom thought; and circulated an email to Agent Adrian Smith of the Australian Federal Police, Agent Jim Burgess of the Immigration Customs Enforcement, a department of the United States Homeland Security, also known as DHS, Drs Nick Sharpe and Sue Tay of Southern Digital Evidence and Niall Mullins of Interpol.

In it, Tom provided a bullet point update of what had been achieved thus far, and what leads his team were currently working on. Apart from Niall, there was no other action for international members, other than giving them heads up over the decision for branding by the Joint Chiefs, something which he expected would filter down to them in any case.

Tom checked the time and rang his ex-wife Sandra. It would be a slow start to the first two operations, he thought, so custody visits would be easier now. As the phone rang at the other end he felt happier and less in pain at making the call. Sandra's tactics and the marriage breakup no longer left him racked with grief. It was Sandra who answered the phone.

"It's Tom. Can I have Struan on Friday night?"

"What time?" Sandra spat out.

"Say, half six."

"That's too late. By the time you get him to your place and give him something to eat he will be eating near his bedtime. It isn't good for him."

"Give him his tea before I pick him up, then."

"That's not suitable for the rest of the house. Let's say you pick him up at 5pm."

Tom thought about it for a split second, then said, "How about Saturday morning then? Say 9.30am?"

"He's swimming with Philippa," Sandra responded, in a disinterested and huffy manner.

He knew she would have him doing something else, probably with her parents, on the Sunday; so he went back to the Friday option.

"OK. Five on Friday, but I may be a little late."

"If you are more than 20 minutes late, don't bother knocking, because you won't get him!"

With that Sandra ended the call.

Tom was about to say something out loud but his office phone went before he could speak. He picked it up thinking he may not be in grief any more, but he was just as frustrated and angry.

"DCI Tom Ross, COCET." He said in a deliberately calm and neutral voice.

"It's Niall. I have an update from Eindhoven and Norway."

"Go ahead with Eindhoven, and let Jane know about the Norway update, unless it is a major update."

"Gotcha. The magistrate is happy to look into it under the original letter of request. It will be part of an investigative briefing he is having later in the week. He expects to have him interviewed in relation to that, and wants an evidential package from us."

"I will get it to you a.s.a.p." Tom replied.

"I just read the update. I hadn't heard about the branding and identity. Sounds like a good idea, our Chief will be all over that sort of thing. I can see that being a big bun fight and who can shout the loudest," Niall said letting out a hearty laugh. "Right I'll ring Jane."

As the phone went dead, Tom made an Athena entry knowing that Jane would be with him shortly. He had hardly logged out when she entered.

"Got an update from Niall."

"I'm all ears," Tom said, privately thinking it was great to have good Intel.

"The hosting company is well respected, with nothing known on them. Anna is ringing them now."

"Great. Can you get an evidential package together for Niall surrounding the tattoo we found on those images? The Eindhoven team are going to interview him about it."

"Sure thing, Boss."

CHAPTER FOUR

The COCET team had moved their chairs and were positioned around Jane King's desk, waiting for her to come out from a meeting with DCI Ross. All of them were making last minute notes in their lecture books when she appeared. The meeting had been put back due to Mitchell Hayes being at the banks in the morning, collecting evidence.

"Ascent first. Mitchell, update us please."

"I got the orders yesterday and managed to get them served on the banks before close of play. I have been collecting the product this morning. I have a lot to get through, but on a first glance we have a large number of accounts, one of which has incoming e-commerce payments. It is then redistributed to the other accounts across four banks; HSBC, Barclays, Lloyds and Nat West. From there it is siphoned off through ATM withdrawals. It looks as though there may be a system to the withdrawals, but basically all the money is removed and then it starts building up again. I will know more once I have had time to analyse the data."

"Will you need to get some more production orders as a result?" Jane asked.

"Probably not on these banks, but there will be work to do on the e-commerce side so that we can trace the purchasers. Also if we want to do a controlled purchase in the future, we may want to evidence that as a standalone."

"Anything else?"

"Yes. I noticed a payment to a travel company. It may help with flights for Kuklin. I have given the details to Archie."

"Have you had a chance to do anything with that?" Jane said, looking at Archie.

"Yes. It's a travel company and they are checking at the moment. They have promised a reply today."

"How are the utilities paid? Are they coming from the accounts we know about?" Jane said looking at Mitchell.

"Again, we need more time, but Anna has asked me about those."

"The electricity is on a prepaid meter key, there is no gas, and I am working with Mitchell on the rest," said Anna Farley.

"On the address, Anna. Is there anything more known on the other occupants?"

"Nothing. They are all Nigerian names with nothing known on them. I don't want to investigate further with the council until we know more, as it may alert Kuklin."

'The Boss was right. This girl is a bright cookie', Jane thought to herself as Anna spoke.

"Owen. How did you get on? I hear you had an early start!"

"Yep. Five am start. It's a difficult area in many respects. I have plotted it, and the report is with Patrick. In short, the target's address is close to Tower Bridge, and runs between Pope Street and Purbrook Street. It is a first floor flat, in a block of flats. That block is one of a number that make up the Purbrook Estate. There will be some private flats in there, but it is mainly council housing. There are a number of ways out of the estate on foot and in a vehicle. There is renovation and building going on in the general area, but it is still bandit country and he has a good view from his front door onto Pope Street. If you want us to do static OP work we can, but we will need an obs van to do it quick time. And without doing a lot more work locally with home beat officers, I wouldn't want to try and locate an address to use."

"Who is a van driver here?"

Both Owen and Archie put their hands up.

"Anybody surveillance trained?"

All hands stayed down.

"Photography?"

With all hands still firmly down, Jane made a note, then said, "Anna, get me the Intel package and I will submit a directed surveillance authority. I will speak to the Boss about static observations, I wanted us to do that part, but we may have to get a team in." Jane paused before she continued. "What news from Norway?"

"It isn't good news," Anna Wilson began. "The company there was really helpful, they have located the server used. It is clean, it has been zero overwritten, and in the view of their top tech there it is forensically clean. They are happy for us to have it if we still want it, but they say it is pointless."

"Who is the contract made out to?"

"It is all done online, and was paid for in advance for a set period using a prepaid cash card. The name on the account is Ms. M Shultz. She was the subject of a handbag theft in the West End of London; in which, amongst other things, was the prepay card. They want to know if they can reuse the hard drive?"

"Let me speak to SDE first."

"Mitchell, your work is critical for us to move forward. In the meantime I want the Intel Cell to keep profile building on Kuklin and his associates. We will regroup before we knock off for a quick debrief."

With the team nodding in acknowledgement, Jane moved on.

"Operation Resolve. The Boss has directed that we put all our efforts into the web based group called 'childscentcafe'. Patrick, speak to Dr. Sue Tay, she knows someone is going to call her. Get all the information she has, and convert that into intelligence on Athena."

Patrick Smith nodded whilst still writing.

"How is the information b-b-b-being relayed?' Patrick asked.

"She will send it in an encrypted file. Any images will be sent as hash sets on a CD through the post," Jane replied.

"How much d-d-ata?" Patrick enquired with a facial expression that Jane knew all too well, and she knew what her reply would mean to him. But she also knew he was up to the task.

"It will be a week's work, with two hours per day overtime. Yes, you have football nights off!"

Patrick smiled back, gave a little movement in his seat that almost resembled a wiggle, and said, "Great stuff!"

The rest of the team didn't quite know how to take the last comment. It seemed a little insolent, but Jane knew it wasn't.

"Anna F. Once Patrick has it inputted, the Intel team will be best placed to analyse the intelligence. Can you prepare an intelligence briefing for the Boss? The aim is to identify a target who is worthy of us assuming his online identity, and whom we can get hold of. So UK based would be better."

"How much detail do you want in that briefing? Anna replied. "Do you want us to show how we narrowed it down for instance?"

"Not in the briefing. But we will need to cover how we selected some and not others," replied Jane.

"I can help there, Sarge." Louisa Greenwood interrupted. "I can write a child protection strategy for both Ascent and Resolve, and work with Anna so that the decision making process meets the needs of NSPCC policy; which in turn is fit for child protection policy in England and Wales, Northern Ireland and Scotland." Louisa finished with a smile.

Louisa had been sitting alongside Owen, and hadn't said a word in any of the meetings so far. So when she did speak it was a bit of a surprise to Jane and some of the team. The offer was genuine, however; and Anna Farley beat Jane King to the reply. "That would be fab, Louisa, and will put me at ease."

Jane smiled at both Anna and Louisa. "That would be great. Link in with whoever you need. Yes, two strategies, and can I get a peek at it before it goes to the Boss?"

"Sure thing!"

"Anna W, you will get an action to submit data comms to locate where the server is and who is hosting it." Again, Jane got a nod as Anna was writing in her note pad.

Meanwhile, Sarah Dorsey was sitting slightly at the back of the team, but not outside the vision of Owen and Archie, both of whom had been in avid discussion that morning on just what a, 'hot chick' this girl was. She was not going to be outdone when it came to her neck of the woods and strategies.

"Would you like the same from me for both operations? I can let you see it, but it is meant for the Boss. It will link in with one that I have done for the Joint Chiefs."

Jane was starting to realise that the vision that the Chief Constable and Tom had, although still a work in progress, was starting to bear fruit. "Yes please, Sarah."

As the team got back to work, Kuklin's collection team had already made another run on the banks. They had met up as before, paid the cash over to Vitaly Danshov, and two days' takings were now in the hands of Andrei Kuklin.

When Jane got to her desk, she rang Dr. Sue Tay to get in ahead of Patrick Smith.

"Hi, Sue. It's Jane King. How is it going today?"

"Good, but I'm not getting any of my work done. Nick keeps giving me deadline work of his!" Sue said, with exasperation in her voice.

Jane really liked Dr. Sue Tay. She thought Sue was incredibly talented, smart, and great at her job. SDE was one of COCET's best assets. She was really glad they were on their team.

"Sue, we have located the server Kuklin was using, it was in Norway. We have spoken to the company, and they say it has been zero overwritten a number of times and is forensically clean. They say we can have it, but there isn't any point. The locals say they are a genuine company and can be believed. What should I do?"

"Take them at their word, I guess. It will be a waste of time and money if it has been cleaned as they say. They might want reimbursement for the hard drive as well. It could be that the company may still have some comms data that we could capture, but I know from Operation Hope that it will probably just lead us to the proxy server. When you take out Kuklin, we should be able to prove that he was using the same proxy company, but then thousands of others are using that same company as well. I can do it, but it could end up being costly for not a great deal of evidential gain."

Jane dithered, wondering if she should make the decision or not.

Tom had told her when she took the ADS job that she should trust her instincts and make operational decisions at her level, and not feel the need to bother him. She thought this was probably one of those occasions.

"Thanks, Sue. It can go in the unwanted file. Patrick will be ringing shortly, sorry if the timing is bad."

"If it is about the Resolve intelligence, then it is ready to go, so no problems."

"Yes, it is," replied Jane.

2105hrs ICT, Pattaya, Thailand.

It was after 9pm when the boy, now man, known to Operation Hope as Michael, left the first viewing of an address just off Soi Chaiyaphruek, Jomtien. It was ideal in most respects, and had the extra benefit of a private pool, which was a bonus considering the budget price tag. It was gated and guarded, which was a downside, as more people meant more pockets would need to be lined. But it was not overlooked from any direction and it had an enclosed parking area. It was perfect for bringing boys through the gates inside blacked out cars or vans. It was a good distance from Walking Street, yet a 15 minute ride would still reach the centre of the action. This was a must, because if they had to start lining the local police pockets, and it was the centre areas that they patrolled, it would get expensive. You never knew when they might just change their minds, take the money and arrest you as well. The underbelly of this area had been well infiltrated by the Russians. They had heaps of cash, were violent, and wouldn't hesitate to inform on others. Or even worse, put a bullet in the head of someone they didn't like. Much of the extra Russian money had ended up in the hands of local Police, all of whom were 'on the take'. It was a just a way of life. If you wanted to live and work in this country, you needed to pay. The lowest ranks were sent out every day to collect the cash. When they got back to the Police Station it got divided up. The largest share went to the man at the top, and the lower the rank, the smaller the share became. The go-go bar areas were controlled or permitted to operate by the Police, they couldn't be in business without paying them. And there was also a Thai price as well as a 'Farang', or foreign devil price, for being able to open the doors and make money.

The foreign devil price had always been higher than the Thai price; but now the Russians had invaded the area, buying up anything and everything with their new found wealth. The Thais, who knew the smell of money at any distance, had adjusted the price accordingly, and expected it from everyone. Add to that the particular type of sex operation he was about to undertake, the bribe would be as big as it needed to be in the eyes of the collector. That, he thought, would be many bowls of rice for many officers and their families. However, he wasn't planning on operating anywhere near the main sex district, and had no intention of coming to the notice of the country's law enforcement, as he wouldn't be there most of the time.

He also had a good cover story for being in Thailand and needing the rental properties that he had. He hopped into the agent's vehicle, and made his way west along the same street, across a major highway and a railway track, until he came to a small lane leading to another compound of bungalows, which was also gated and manned. The compound was open to the front, with the bungalows being a mixture of shapes and sizes, all built around a large garden and water feature. He felt trapped just being driven through the small compound. The agent drove to the last building on the single access road, and parked on the short driveway in front of a garage door, which he opened with an electric fob. The garage was empty and big enough to get a saloon or small van in without a problem. Inside, it was new and well equipped. The price tag was bigger, but then there were three large bedrooms, all with double beds. The garden had a plunge pool and was completely private, being the last property at the end of the estate. It would do.

The final one turned out to be a few minutes away in Yaek Khao Makok Road, and as soon as he got out he knew it would be a good fit. It was up a little shared driveway and not in a compound. It was new with an enclosed gated drive; it had a pool, and was very private, not being overlooked in any way. It was off the tourist track, and once inside one felt secure and away from prying eyes. He immediately agreed to take all three and they left for the agent's office to complete the paperwork.

With a cuppa each, and the door shut, Tom said, "Go for it."

"We have an address for Kuklin and I have just sent you the Directed Surveillance Authority," said Jane.

"Great, I will get it off to the authorising officer. What's your plan?"

"I would like an obs van to do some static surveillance to get Kuklin identified and housed."

Tom, who had been leaning slightly forward and making notes of the conversation, let the request sink in. He paused and thought further about it as he moved away from the desk. There were issues here of training and authorisation. He knew he didn't have anybody on the team trained in surveillance. If he asked the Detective Inspector in charge of the surveillance team for his obs van, Tom knew he would win on a priority case, but not from a trained staff standpoint. The problem was that the evidence captured by his officers may end up being cross examined in court. The defence would have a field day if the officer performing the surveillance was not trained or authorised by the Force to carry out that specialist skill. He knew his team would be just itching to get into this type of policing, and they had the talent to do it, but it couldn't be on this job. He moved back to his counsel pad, and made a note to ask Maggie Burrows to get some officers trained.

"We can't do it, Jane. The officers performing the role aren't trained, I know they are willing as you are but it is a non starter, I would never prise the obs van away from the surveillance team with no one trained to use it. I will make the call today to see if TVP can do it. If not, it will go up to JT and from him to the NCS."

Jane, who was disappointed, moved on. "We have the product from the banking orders and we should be able to provide you with an analysis shortly. From there we can create an investigative plan. SDE say the hard drive in Norway is not worth getting. We have made a start on Resolve, but it will be at least a week before we can give you a briefing on what the analysis is, unless we use other staff on the inputting. Louisa will be providing you with a CP strategy for both operations, as will Sarah."

"That's a great start. Make sure the team knows that. Who do you have doing the inputting?"

"Patrick."

"Once he is settled into it, I want to know a best guess of how long it is going to take him, and whether another member of team would help or get in the way."

"Will do, but I think it will still take three to four days, even with another person helping out."

"OK. Just let me know as soon as you can."

As Jane left, Tom immediately rang the surveillance team DI.

"DI Andy Foster, Surveillance and Operational Support, how can I help?"

"Andy, it's Tom Ross, how're you doing?"

Andy Foster knew Tom, but not well. TVP was a large Constabulary with a big geographical area to cover, but it was small enough to either know, or at least hear of, every DI or DCI in the Force. He had also in the past few days received a verbal briefing from his Boss about the new COCET team, and been told that he could expect applications from them for surveillance assistance. His Boss had told the chain of command above him that they should do everything to support COCET. But with the doors shut, and just the two of them, he had been instructed that all COCET applications would just go into the queue along with everything else. This could end up being a difficult call for him. He had also heard rumours about how Tom had taken on the TVP Lodge and won, probably that was why his Boss had given him instructions to say one thing and yet do another. He had long suspected him of being 'On the Square.'

"Hi Tom. Busy as usual, one surveillance team, and many squads wanting their services. You can only do what you can do. How can I help?"

Tom picked up the neutral tone and the advance excuse. He didn't know much about Andy Foster, but he did know of his Boss. His name had been one of the many on that famous Masonic list left on the

69

photocopier. He was also a golfing buddy of Terry Miller. Tom had been working with this bullshit all through Operation Hope, and was not about to start again.

"Andy. I know that you will have been briefed about COCET. I want part of your surveillance team to start on some static obs on a target residing near Tower Bridge, E1."

Tom thought that if there had been some disruptive activity going on in the background his demand would flush it out.

"Tom. As I am sure you are aware, there is a procedure for applying for our services. If you would like to make that a written application, then it will go into the next tasking and coordinating meeting for consideration."

"And when would that be?"

"Not till Thursday next week."

"Just so I am clear, Andy. You want me to apply throughout the normal channels?"

Andy Foster shot back, "Yes, why should you be different to anybody else?"

That was all Tom needed. He was up for some disruptive behaviour himself. He might not have the actual evidence, but he did have the word of the Chief Constable that he could use all the specialist skills TVP had to offer, and that he expected him to use them.

"Andy, do you know your DCI's extension number?"

"Of course I do!" he replied sharply.

"Good. That saves me looking it up. Put me through, would you?"

Tom heard Andy's intake of breath, but no words followed. Instead the line went dead, and Tom started monitoring his watch. The time it remained dead either indicated that he couldn't find him, or more probably they were discussing him and what had been said. It was 55 seconds before DCI Peter Fewings came on the line.

"Tom, you just can't demand that we drop what we are doing, you have to apply like everyone else. There are other cases just as demanding as yours, and they have been waiting for weeks. I haven't time for this crap, do your paperwork and get it in." Fewings' voice had taken a tone of 'I am more senior than you are,' and was trying to treat him as someone junior in rank, Tom thought.

"Peter, we both know what this is really all about. I have the word of the Chief Constable that I can use all the available skills of TVP, and that includes the surveillance team. So I am giving you and Andy notice now that I will be calling JT to say that you take issue with the Chief. Have a nice day."

Tom put the phone down and immediately called Detective Chief Superintendent John Troy, the head of the C.I.D. for Thames Valley Police.

"Yes, Tom. Be quick, I am about to go into a meeting with the Chief over COCET."

"I am meeting some obstruction from Peter Fewings, he wants me to get into the queue and apply for surveillance through T&C."

At the other end, JT sighed and sat back into his chair.

"How much are you after?"

"I need a team for a day or two, not a full team but at least three to four, maybe more. Doing it his way will put us back three, maybe four weeks."

Tom was about to go on and talk about Terry Miller and his association with Fewings but held off.

"If you want them I will get them, or would you prefer that we use the fact that they are not available to go to the NCS?" replied JT.

"I will take the NCS, Boss, but the air needs to be cleared now; so that I am not in this situation again in the future with operational support. I also need a reply about the U/Cs."

"Alright, leave it with me. Go the NCS route, you have my authority." With that JT ended the call and made his way to the Chief's office and sat down, waiting for him to arrive. He used the time to think about his conversation with Tom. He knew that Peter was friendly with Terry Miller, it had come up when he himself had taken part in the match play at the golf club about two weeks ago. Peter had been one of the other pair. As the Chief walked in, JT knew it would be something he would have to nip in the bud quickly, before it got past him and to the ears of the ACPO team.

Tom knew the route to ask for the services of the NCS, but he wasn't going to take that path. If he did, it would get back to Fewings before JT had had time to speak to his uniform counterpart in operational support. It was a minor piece of one-upmanship, but it was one he wanted. Instead he rang Bob Sealy from the Surbiton Branch of the National Crime Squad.

"Hi Tom, it's good to speak to you. I hear TVP have created some new multi-national team, and you head it up," said Bob Sealy. Bob was whispering as he spoke to Tom.

"Have I got you at an inappropriate moment, Bob?" Tom said immediately, worried that his call may spoil something.

"Nah. I'm stooging on a current CROPS course. I'm just about to play a part so can't speak for long, what can I do for you?"

Mentally, Tom had a picture of 'Seals' creeping up on some student and catching him off guard, or worse, asleep.

"I am looking for some surveillance and wondered if I could persuade you guys to help out again?"

"Would love to, but you will have to get it past the DI again. I think he is up for it, what are you after?"

"Some static obs on an address near Tower Bridge, it's a difficult plot."

"What's your aim?"

"Identify who is living there, we suspect it is a Moldovan or Russian national we know, see who else comes and goes, smudge them up, modes of transport. That sort of thing."

"Static only?"

"Yes, but it's on an estate with a number of ways in and out."

"What's the job in a sentence, Boss?"

"Organised crime, commercial pay-per-view using child abuse images, Moldovan syndicate, money being laundered through UK banks into cash, and back into Moldova," replied Tom.

"You hit all the necessary triggers there for us to get involved, you still got my DI's email?" This time Seals whispering dropped significantly, and he quickly said, "Got to go," and the line went dead.

Tom put his phone down, opened up an email, and wrote a request for assistance, and, after having heard Seals comments about hitting all the right criteria, went large on the intelligence case. He concluded with the dangers to children and the fact that TVP couldn't provide the necessary assistance at that time; and that Surbiton officers had worked on a previous case thus having knowledge of his team, their working practices and child protection. He then rang Maggie Burrows to update her, during which he found out that he was getting Sam from Allensbury CPU as his admin, and the CPU were getting a replacement from division. No sooner was the phone back in its cradle, than it rang again.

"DCI Tom Ross, COCET."

"DCI Ross, I'm Dr. Gloria Clayworth. Is now a good time to call?"

"Yes, it is. I was informed you would be calling."

"Excellent! Now, we need to get together. I can come to you, that's not a problem, but when are you available? Dr. Gordon would like an assessment as soon as possible." Gloria said it with a tone of expectation, Tom thought.

"I can do tomorrow if that would suit."

"Yes, it would."

"What time is good for you, Tom?"

"Eleven, do you know where we are?"

"Yes. See you at eleven."

His mind went to Fiona. She would be here all day tomorrow, the team were clearly going to wonder why he was being seen by one shrink and the rest by another, especially when he had been seen by Dr. Gordon before. Whatever they thought didn't really concern him. Jane, however, was in a position to broach it.

1520hrs UTC, Stockton-On-Tees, North East England

As Tom thought about what he was going to say to Jane, Philip Thompson had just collected his niece from junior school. He got a real kick from collecting her from the school. The place was full of 7-8 year olds, and he just loved seeing them in their skirts, wondering what their knickers were like, and how they must smell after being at school all day. He knew how Carly's smelt. The ones from last week were getting weak and he was really going to enjoy having the new ones. He also loved the fact he could stand and chat with other mothers and fathers, with their kids playing all around him. They didn't know, but at the same time it seemed right. Carly didn't complain and he was a father figure for her. They did so much together, he was careful never to hurt her, and she loved him so much. It was right, and others like him should be allowed to have relationships with children. When the children wanted it of course, and most of them did. Carly saw Philip and came running over. He bent down and picked her up, swinging her to one side so her legs were either side of his body. It was a natural act that nobody in the school playground took any notice of. As he walked out of the gates he could feel her legs either side of him and he immediately started to go hard. She seemed tired.

"You tired, Baby?"

Carly didn't reply, but nodded her head and said, "I want to go home to Mummy."

"You can go home to Mummy tomorrow, Baby."

As he got further away from the school, he moved his left hand under her skirt and held her closer, and started to think about the CD he'd got that day. It was what he liked the most, and it was fresh. He'd had a great day so far.

"You are a sleepy head. When we get in, do you want a bath and a little sleep?"

Carly shook her head immediately, let go of her grip around his neck, started to fall backwards and scream. Thompson lost his erection as fear took over. He placed her on the ground, held her hand tight, and made her walk the rest of the way home at his pace.

CHAPTER FIVE

The COCET team, who were by now getting used to morning prayers, went straight into the briefing that day. They had all started early, knowing that some of their time would be taken up by a baseline interview with Dr. Fiona Gordon.

DC Mitchell Hayes was first up.

"The laundering operation is a simple but effective cascade system. The primary account is the sole account that is linked to the website, and from that account the money is transferred to 48 other accounts, spread across the four banks that we know of. I haven't found evidence of any others yet. On the primary account there have been 3025 incoming purchases, but that is increasing. Some will be the same buyer, but with multiple purchases. Exactly how many unique purchasers we have will take another day at least. Once I know that, I can make up a schedule of who is with which credit company; and then go back to court for more orders. That will give you your list of suspects who are buying from the site."

Mitchell stopped to see if Jane was going to ask questions about what he had said so far. As she didn't, he continued.

"There is a pattern to the withdrawals, but not what triggers them, other than it is every seven to ten days. The four banks are all targeted at the same time, in two distinct areas of London. One set is near Piccadilly Circus and the other is near Victoria Mainline Station. The cash is being removed at the same time, so there must be at least two suspects, but I suspect more; because the times of the withdrawals are in groups of three, one after another. Then there's a short gap of a minute or so, in some cases more. I have ordered the footage from the

ATMs, and the accounts are currently being run down. I got that on the QT and not from orders."

"Right. We are on countdown then," said Jane. "We have a directed surveillance authority, but we won't be doing the surveillance. The Boss is getting the same team we used on Hope." As she was speaking she could see the disappointment on Owen's face. "I wanted us to do it, but we aren't trained; and things could go all wrong at court if we were relying on some of the intelligence from our observations; plus we might screw it up. The NCS are the best the UK has, and they have worked with us before. I will try and get you with them for a day, Owen."

"You're on, Sarge!" Owen replied, now happy again.

"Archie, anything from the travel agent?" Jane continued.

"Yes. He paid for return flights to Chisinau. He has bought tickets from them once before. I am getting a statement today, and I will set up some sort of advance warning should he get another ticket from them. I have located him on two other flights and I'm working backwards on that. I have made arrangements to take statements from the airlines, and Mitchell can evidence that the money withdrawals fit the flights that he took to Moldova."

"Good. Patrick?"

"Nothing interesting on Ascent, but I have m-m-m-made a start on t-t-the intelligence on Resolve. There is some good Intel. If I c-c-c-could get another set of hands on this, and w-w-w-we both worked the weekend, we could get this d-d-done by Monday."

Jane looked around and started to weigh up who she could lose, and who had more pressing things to do.

Patrick had also been weighing things up, and added, "They n-n-need to be more than two finger typists." He had a smile on his face as he said it. It was a smile that Owen didn't care much for, as he thought Patrick was having a laugh at the expense of the cops in the room. He flicked a quick look at Archie, who he could see was wearing a frown of displeasure. In that split second none of it was lost on Jane. If there had been speech bubbles above Owen's and Archie's heads, the words within it would have been the same: 'Bloody Civvies!' The truth was, they were both thinking that, and more!

"I can do that, and I can type," Owen shot back. He needed the overtime as well. He had to put money away for his Man United season ticket, otherwise the missus would be harping on. It would mean he would have to miss the match against Arsenal this weekend; but then nobody liked the Gunners, other than Arsenal supporters!

"Great," said Jane. "Anna W?"

"I have submitted more data comms for Ascent, nothing back yet. Resolve, however, we have had a quick reply on. The server is hosted in Holland to a company called WebHostTwelve. Niall is on the case, he has already fed back that it is a middle sized legit company with nothing known to Dutch law enforcement or Interpol. Anna says there is nothing known about them in Elementary or other Police indices. Niall is getting a contact within the company through the regional intelligence service that covers that area."

Just as Anna Wilson finished her sentence, Jane saw Dr. Fiona Gordon and another, older, woman enter the main office, and added, "Is there anything pressing anybody needs to discuss now?"

With shakes of the head all round, Jane said, "In that case 4pm. Or later if these interviews are still going."

Jane got to Dr. Gordon just before Tom, and sensed an awkwardness around her DCI as Dr. Gordon did the introductions. She listened as Fiona explained that Dr. Gloria Clayworth would be meeting with Tom, and then leave, whilst she herself would remain and conduct the remaining sessions over the course of the day.

"Jane. Is there a particular order you would like team members to see me?"

She was still getting used to being in charge and people turning to her for decisions. But there was something not quite right about her being asked with Tom standing next to her. She didn't hesitate to reply, thinking she needed to urgently for a reason she couldn't identify.

"Anybody; but leave Mitchell till last," replied Jane.

"In that case I will start with you. Where can I set up camp?" she said, as she looked around the building.

Tom, who was feeling uneasy with the way things were going, just wanted the whole situation to go away before he was sussed by Jane.

"Jane. You take the conference room and I will use my office. Gloria, this way. Would you like some tea or coffee?"

As Tom moved away with Dr. Clayworth towards his office, Jane guided Dr. Gordon towards the conference room; not giving anything away, but silently thinking, *'Something is going on!'*

With two mugs of tea, and the introductions out of the way, Tom was still wondering which way to deliver the truth.

"Tom. You don't mind if I call you that, do you?"

"Not at all, that's my name."

"Good. I just want to set you at ease. I am here solely because Fiona has thought it wise she put some distance between you and her, in a counselling sense. You will appreciate her position. It is quite simply out of the question that she should continue to see you on behalf of Thames Valley Police."

As Dr. Clayworth continued, Tom inwardly sighed with relief thinking, *'Well that saves me a difficult decision. She knows.'*

"So I am not here to judge on your relationship. I am here to ensure that you get all the help that you need; and that your health and future is given the support by Thames Valley Police that it deserves. At the same time, Thames Valley Police, through me, understand what they need to deliver to achieve those objectives. Does that make sense?"

Tom knew exactly what this meant. It meant revealing all his worries, fears and nightmares so that the brass could then use it to guard themselves corporately further down the line; should he ever take out some civil action on how they allowed him to continue working, when he should have been removed from this kind of work. Work that had left him damaged mentally. That was what this was all about.

"Yes, it makes perfect sense. As it always has, Gloria," Tom said, knowing that he was already not being truthful.

"Good. Well, I have had a full briefing from Dr. Gordon. So how long have you been suffering from bad dreams?"

'*Straight to the point then!*' Tom thought.

"I guess they started after my marriage broke down. I wouldn't call them bad dreams, just not sleeping well."

"Did it stay like that or get worse?"

"I guess it got worse from time to time."

"Was there anything that may have triggered them?"

"No, nothing at all. Sometimes I just don't sleep well."

"It is not a crime to not sleep well, Tom. In fact with the work that you do, the responsibilities that you hold, and the pressures that naturally flow from that, it would be surprising if you slept like a baby, solidly, all night! Some people do, some don't. We are all different. However, if those natural sleeping patterns start to have a detrimental effect on you, then we need to assess your work life balance. Do you understand that?"

As Gloria was talking, Tom had been thinking that Gloria and Fiona must have had the same lecturer at University. There was a pattern to their approach. He sensed he was on dangerous ground; and would have to be a bit more truthful to keep her and Fiona happy.

"Of course I understand that, Gloria."

"Good. So what are the dreams about?"

"I don't know. I can't really remember them. The moment I wake up they are gone. I try to keep hold of them, just so I know what it is all about, but I can't."

"What about in a general context? They don't appear to be happy dreams?"

"Not sure. I wake up in a fright, I guess. The duvet is a bit twisted and I just know that I have had some sort of bad dream. That's it; there is nothing more in it than that."

Tom couldn't detect anything on Gloria's face, but his gut told him she was thinking, '*I'll be the judge of that.*'

"Do you dwell on them afterwards?"

"No."

"Do they prevent you from sleeping?"

"No."

Tom thought he needed to avoid one word replies.

"Do you get tired as result of them?"

"No. I get tired from other things though, such as long hours and constant battling at work just so that I can get my job done, which in turn make my day longer."

"What is your typical working day and week?"

With the discussion firmly in familiar territory, Tom expanded into Police politics, the team, work desires, personal desires and whom he confided in. All of which he spoke honestly about, until she brought the meeting to a conclusion.

"Tom. That's it for today. I don't expect to see you again for another three to four months, depending on my schedule. You can, however, contact me at any time," Gloria said, handing Tom her business card.

"In the meantime, I want you to think about three things that you can do to make your work life balance better, and take some form of action towards it. We can discuss that when we next see each other. How's that?"

Tom didn't think, 'No,' would be the right way to go.

"Sure. I will have a go at that."

"Great," Gloria replied, in what Tom thought was a decidedly flat, almost sad, tone of voice.

Back in his office he thought about the task he'd been set by Dr. Clayworth. His first action was to cut it down to two. He was about to get busy and the team hadn't found full steam yet, which would in turn create more opportunities, so he had an inbuilt excuse. He thought about who he did confide in. Prior to recent events it would have been Fiona, up to a point. But that wasn't open to him at the moment. The fact was he didn't have anyone; and he wondered when it last was that he'd had a good whinge, and to whom. The light bulb went on. He picked up the phone and rang his old office extension number.

"DI Mo James, Allensbury CPU," Mo said in a confident and authoritative manner.

"Mo, it's Tom. Fancy a greasy spoon?"

"Do I ever. Conference Room two?"

"Yep, 10-15?"

"See you there," Mo replied, putting the phone down. Tom quickly checked his email account, saw one had just come in from the NCS, and opened it. They had agreed to provide limited support on an informal basis, and his contact would be Detective Sgt. Bob Sealy. Great news. As he got to his office door his desk phone rang and he returned.

"DCI Ross."

"Use the correct TVP phone answering procedure!"

'Is there any wonder why I don't sleep well or have nightmares when I'm getting this sort of corporate bullshit,' Tom thought. "Sorry, Sir. Just a momentarily lapse of corporate memory."

"Don't get flippant with me, DCI," replied JT in a genuinely stern tone of voice.

Tom was about to offer a further, more meaningful, apology when JT continued.

"Right. The air is cleared with operational support. If you want anything from them, you come to me first; and it will be sorted out at my level. Understood?"

"Yes, Sir."

"They will continue to support your use of the NCS, so keep using them as long as you can. Have you managed to secure their services?"

"Yes."

"Good. I will bring it up with the Chief. It might be good if he had a conversation with their Director General, Bill Hughes. I hear the two of them have a passion for child protection. You can also contact SO10 for the two undercovers you used on Operation Hope. I have done a deal with them and the officers' home Force. The deal is this, you will not be able to work them as you did last time."

JT stopped talking. Deliberately, Tom thought, and he wasn't about to be a shrinking violet.

"Since when has there been a problem with the way they worked?"

"Look," JT replied. "You don't have a problem, I don't have a problem, and more importantly SO10 do not have a problem. The problem is with the home Force. SO10 say that the two U/Cs have gone back bragging about how much they got in overtime, and it hasn't gone down well with other undercover officers, their handlers, and some senior managers. There are also concerns about the merging of their undercover and real lives. The only way to get them released was to agree to closer monitoring of their activities, which SO10 have agreed to do. So you will have to work with them on this. It was either that, or you didn't get them."

Tom couldn't really argue with it. They had been a nightmare to manage. And they had worked too much overtime, there was no question of that. In fact, they had worked until they dropped. But what other option was there? The country didn't have the police response he needed. He could just imagine the two going back to their home Force and bragging. When offered an inch, they took a mile. They were constantly looking for an angle, they were as cocky as hell, and they were probably living their undercover lives more than their real ones. But then they would not have been alone in that respect, they could point to a list of others who acted the same way. They would have rubbed it in for sure, and now it should have been backfiring on them, but it wasn't; it was just causing headaches for others before they were even deployed. He could also see their senior officers getting pissed off with them. And here he was again, starting from the back of the grid. They were both really good at what they did, but they came with a load of baggage which was getting bigger. He would have to come up with a strategy with SO10 to manage them. The one good thing on Ascent and Resolve was that they were not peer-to-peer investigations, so the infiltration strategy would be different and much more contained.

"I will work with SO10 and come up with a deployment plan; the main thing this time around is that their working exposure will be more confined."

"That's good to hear. Get to work." With that JT put the phone down abruptly. Tom sighed, just thinking about the constraints that might have to be placed on the U/Cs. But then his mind went to bacon and eggs, beans, two toast and a cup of tea, and he went in search of them, making a mental note as he went that he could now scrub his first of the two tasks he had been given off the list. He was about to go and confide in someone.

When Tom got back, fortified and feeling better, he found Sam Terry in avid conversation with Jane King, as she was shown around the new COCET building. Sam turned as she heard the office door close shut behind Tom, and left Jane to greet him.

"Reporting for duty, DCI Ross!"

"Sam! You are a sight for sore eyes, grab us both a cuppa and let's catch up."

As Sam Terry sat down in Tom's office, she said, "Feeling better for all that yummy grease?"

Startled, Tom said, "Have I got some of it down my tie?" looking down to see if he had spilt some fried egg on himself.

"My old spy network is working well," she said with a mischievous smile and a small wink from her left eye.

Tom laughed, which also got Sam laughing.

"How did you feel about leaving the CPU, Sam?" Tom asked, with a more serious tone. Tom knew she had been there for years.

"I was happy there. I had been there a long time, and I was happy to stay. But working with you over those two operations, seeing what you and the team achieved, I just couldn't pass this up when I was offered the opportunity. I want to be part of this, and you need someone to look after the administrative things that can cause a problem on things like inspections. You need to be freed up, to do what you do best, Tom, and that is arresting the bad guys and looking after the little ones."

Tom knew she meant it; and as he reflected on her kind words, the light bulb went on again and number two on Gloria's task list had been achieved. He had off loaded some of his work by gaining an Office Manager.

He knew that he needed her and he would come to depend on her again. She was one of those people you knew you could rely on to always be there and do the right thing; and make sure he wasn't 'blindsided' by something that on first glance appeared relatively small. She also knew the politics of working in the Police.

"It is really great to have you as part of the team, Sam. Mo said he was sad to lose you, but understood the attraction. We have only been going a few days. There is no office management. Do whatever you need to do. I will send you the budget plan; get whatever you need. Just make yourself at home. Has Jane introduced you to the team?"

"Yes, she has. I can't wait to get into it, Boss, so if it is alright with you I will make a start. Door open or shut?" Sam Terry said, as she got up to leave.

"Open," he replied for the first time in a while.

Picking up his desk phone, Tom flicked through his mobile phone contact list. Finding the number he wanted, he punched the numbers in.

"SO10, Sue Moore."

"Hello, Sue. It's Tom Ross."

"Hi, Tom. Congratulations on your promotion, your new team and those two jobs. Truly great work."

"Thanks. News does travel fast. Actually, I am ringing about the two U/Cs I used on those two jobs."

"Thought you might be. I was told to expect a call from you. We discussed it this morning and we have a plan."

It wasn't any real surprise to Tom that they were ahead of the game. SO10 was quite simply the gate keeper for all undercover work the Police undertook. They were known around the world; and were, in Tom's opinion, the best in the world when it came to this highly specialised area of policing.

"I'm loving this already, Sue."

"Good. Well they have both been summoned here for tomorrow, and will be given a yellow card. We have tried our level best to prise Dale Walters away from Northants for you to use, but they, and he, have genuine reasons for not releasing him in the short term. But he will become available after that."

"How long?" Tom interrupted.

"They don't know. He is working on a U/C deployment now, and my guess is it will be at least three months."

"That won't fit with the two jobs I'm starting with."

"We didn't think it would, which is why Billy and Mark are on their way here. During the negotiations with Northants and Dale, Dale mentioned to us that he would like to become a permanent member of COCET. We agreed to pass that on to you for the future."

Tom's mind was racing. He hadn't thought about having a permanent U/C of his own, but it made perfect sense.

"Isn't Dale a forensic examiner as well?"

"Yes, and a skipper."

Tom made a note in his counsel pad. "Could you flick me his contact details?"

"Sure."

"How do you want me to play this? I am on strict instructions from my DCS to manage them, as if I didn't last time!" Tom said it with more than a bit of frustration in his voice. "And I have to work with you on it."

"We know. We are sensitive around the politics with their home force, and don't want you to suffer operationally. So we will give them a yellow card. You get your authority in, so we can see the investigative plan, and we will provide you with a simple operational suggestion package around their deployments. It will relate to admin only. We won't officially send it until you are happy with it; and in any case we will need your input on it.

"What this is, Tom, is us providing TVP's Chief Constable and COCET with some protection. The real reason for all this is that there aren't enough Billys and Marks around. Because of that, they are in a position to hold it over managers and teams. And some of that is down to training, which as you know, is our area. So we will be looking to get trained some Covert Internet Investigators who possess the right basic skill set. We are currently canvassing our level one list, so we will keep you updated; but this will all be too late for what you want now."

"That's brilliant, Sue. Thanks. I will get the authorities to you as soon as I have the intelligence case, but it is likely to be a week away at least."

"That's not a problem. Have to go, Tom, all the phones are ringing."

0840hrs ICT, Pattaya, Thailand

Looking out of the window he saw that it was a grey cloudy start to the day in Pattaya, the heavy clouds signalling that rain was on its way. That sort of outlook made him think of it as being cold outside, it certainly would have been in his native country. Or his adopted one, Holland, for that matter. It was an illusion by his senses, with the temperature being so hot outside. The room he stood in was chilled down as far as the air con would allow, making him feel cold now that he was out of bed. He walked past the sleeping occupant and made his way to the living area. He opened his laptop, connected to the internet, and entered 'boylover.net.' He spent time checking to see who was online, and what was being discussed in the general chat room. There was nothing that interested him, and he could see that none of the particular members he was looking for were logged in either; so he typed a message to a private sub group called PTC.

To: PTC
From: LB

Hello JC, Y51, Cyborg, Mr. B, H, and Jack G. Have found the three items we are looking for. Commencement date from the 16th. Jack G, you will need to be here by then so I can return. Local talent tastes delicious!

After logging out of 'boylover.net', he logged into his Hushmail account, and sent an email to Mr. B solely.

From: LB
To: Mr. B

This will be fun, but short lived. Get in early before the others spoil the merchandise or draw too much attention to themselves. The product is smooth, small framed and their little cocks taste so sweet. Even the ones with hair, only have a few thin soft wisps. We must get our footage early and get out, leaving the others to take the risk. What news have you on our other ventures? Can't wait to get my hands on em!

He closed his computer down and switched it off. Standing, he realised that he had become hard just thinking about one of the ventures he had going with Mr. B. He stared at his penis thinking about that venture, and what was lying in his bed. He made his way into the bedroom and ripped the single white sheet off the young boy, who woke suddenly, disorientated from sleep and the drugs he had been given. In that split second he saw the fear in his eyes, and leapt to smother him from calling out.

With all the interviews done, a complete COCET team sat around the conference room table with Niall on speaker phone.

"Niall, do you want to go first with your update?" Tom said.

"I can. The cloggies have been in top gear. They have produced and interviewed Visser, who is not doing well in prison. He gave them lots of information surrounding others involved in child abuse, and others he says that are involved in the branding and who are also members of 'boylover.net'. They will give us an intelligence package on that in a few days. When they got to the images of his tattoo he broke down, and they couldn't get anything out of him. The tattoo is identical, and he never made any denials. They are doing some forensic work on the images, and have taken some evidential stills of him to go with our evidence, which should provide enough for further charges. Their view was that he wouldn't admit it without some sort of deal, as he isn't doing well in prison; and the thought of making admissions and getting more time is preventing him telling the truth. If they charge him anyway, and once he sees that the only way to lessen a sentence is to spill the beans, he might then cooperate more. So their intention is to heap more on him and visit him again further down the line."

Everybody listening was watching the speaker pod intently, and although Tom had heard enough, he knew that Jane, who was now running day to day operations, had a different set of requirements. He looked at Jane who took the cue.

"Niall, it's Jane. Are they going to need statements from us?"

"Yes."

"When can I get the Intel from the interview?"

"I will chase it up. Hopefully you will get it in a few days."

"Anything else?"

"Yes, but Anna W has it. So she can cover it," replied Niall.

"OK, Anna. What have you got?" said Jane.

"Data comms is back on Ascent and it's down to a company in Venezuela. Niall has already done some checks with his Interpol contacts; and it's a well known proxy server that is used by US suspects and others around the world. It is a non starter for an approach."

Niall interrupted. "I have had a bit more back on that from another Interpol Station which just confirms that it is a 'NO GO' for a law enforcement approach."

Jane looked at Tom for direction, who just shrugged his shoulders, and said, "OK, well no surprise there. But we have bottomed it out, so move on, Anna."

"Operation Resolve and WebHostTwelve," Anna W continued. "I have made contact with the owner who was expecting a call. He has confirmed that he is hosting 'childscentcafe' and that the content of the server is not breaking any Dutch laws. He has viewed the content himself, and agrees that it contains children that are scantily dressed and in erotic poses, and that some younger ones are semi naked, but the content is legal in his country. He says he holds the contact details of the owner, who is Canadian; but that privacy laws mean he cannot divulge his full identity, or give us a copy of the server, because in their eyes he isn't doing anything wrong."

"Niall, have you spoken to the owner of the hosting company?" Tom said.

"Yep. He really wants to help but says he will get sued if he reveals more. He says that he has contacted the Canadian owner of the server, and challenged him over the contents, and has revealed that he threatened to sue him if he did take his server offline. I get the impression, Tom, he is on our side; but he needs something to cover himself with. He has even run this past the company lawyer and he has advised him that he cannot breach the laws of his country without something more."

Tom put his head back and thought about the obstacle that was before him. He didn't want the server taken down, not yet at least. He wanted it to remain, but he wanted a copy of the server as well.

"Anna, work with Niall. Tell the owner that operationally we need the website to stay up. We will get him the extra intelligence or evidence he needs to cover him legally."

Tom looked at Jane. "Who is working the weekend on the intelligence from SDE?"

"Patrick and Owen."

Tom looked across at both officers. "I am going to want some UK suspects that we can put together an intelligence pack on. Get it out to the CPU teams, and get the evidence we need to secure the owner's identity and a copy of the server."

Owen Marks replied, "Sure thing, Boss."

Patrick went to say something and immediately got halted by his stammer. "W-w-w-we can't give it to you if it's n-n-not there."

There was a distinct pause in the meeting as Patrick finished his sentence. Jane knew that it was just Patrick thinking out loud, but she could also see the awkwardness of the situation in how he delivered it. Owen and Archie flicked a knowing look to each other, with Owen privately thinking Arsenal were looking pretty good at that particular moment. Jane was about to speak, when Tom decided that some leadership was required.

"Patrick, you are on this team with everyone else because you are all outstanding in what you do. I am confident that you will find what SDE and I believe is held within the data. Find it." Tom ended the sentence with just a hint of abruptness.

"Jane. What's next?"

"Mitchell, and Operation Ascent."

Mitchell Hayes produced some still photographs that he handed around the table. "These are our suspects who are withdrawing the money. They are the same team as on all previous occasions, and I have ordered the statements to go with the transactions. The MO is that once they are on a withdrawing phase, they do daily runs at virtually the same time every day until they have all the cash. As you can see, most, if not all of them are unidentifiable from the photos due to the placement of caps and hoodies; clearly a tactic to prevent them from being identified."

Mitchell stopped talking, allowing time for the whole team to get a good look at the stills that were being passed around the table.

Tom quickly noticed the same caps and hoodies on the suspects in photographs that had been captured on different dates. "When Patrick has the time, Mitchell, can you get an i2 chart on all of this to include the clothing?"

"Sure, Boss."

"Jane, maybe there is an opportunity here for some surveillance type scoping…" Tom deliberately left the sentence unfinished.

She picked up the hint in a flash. "Owen. Get to the banks in question well ahead of their withdrawal window on Monday, and scope them out for surveillance. Plot it for photographic work and foot surveillance away from the ATMs, and walk the routes in whatever order they go to the banks."

"Yes, Sarge." Owen replied, with a surprised look on his face, glad at the thought he would be able to finally get his hands dirty.

"Mitchell, can you set up a system with the bank, so that they can alert a single point of contact at the exact time of the withdrawal?"

"I am pretty sure that there will be a time delay. But yes, I will set up what their systems can deliver."

Mitchell's comment triggered Tom's memory of an old Regional Crime Squad case in London, where the main suspect, himself being a cop, was withdrawing cash; and that there had been real issues with alerting the surveillance teams at the exact point of withdrawal. Time had moved on and he was sure things had got better.

"Archie, what's your update?" Jane said breaking Tom's thoughts.

"Got the statement and have set up an alert system, that either I or Owen will get should he purchase another flight."

It was clear to Tom, and probably everybody in the room, that Archie and Owen were working well together as a team. He also clocked that they were seated next to each other and that the whole Ops team were sat together in a line. Which was good; now, and for the future. He also thought it would be good for Anna W to get the exposure of working with two experienced investigators.

Tom and Jane had been working together long enough for him to realise that he was being handed back the chair without the need for spoken words. "To update you, the NCS will commence surveillance on Kuklin and they will need our surveillance authority." Tom wasn't looking at Jane, but she nodded nonetheless and made a note.

Sarah Dorsey, who was watching the body language of the meeting just as much as she was listening to what was being said, realised that Tom had picked up Jane's small nod without breaking sentence. She had been briefed in Force that Tom Ross and Jane King had led Operation Hope to a successful conclusion, and that both were highly respected. They worked together well, which had a calming influence on the rest of the team. Their leadership style was having a real impact upon the newly formed group of officers, in that it fuelled its energy and commitment.

She had worked with many squads within her own Police Force, and so she knew that leadership success at the beginning of an operation could soon break down and cause a once tight working group to split into dysfunctional factions, which ultimately failed its initial promise. She wondered how this new team would fare in the long run. Would Tom keep the energy alive? There was something special being created in front of her at that moment that she couldn't put a finger on. They were a new team: strong, and yet vulnerable; in that there was no business continuity. The positive leadership effect on the team was huge, and yet Tom was potentially a single point of failure at the same time. If he went down, then so could the team.

CHAPTER SIX

There is a time when every lead investigator feels that he or she is about to move from intelligence gathering into evidence capture. The intelligence 'purists' argue that information differs from intelligence, and also argue about the point at which that intelligence becomes evidence. The senior officer of a proactive investigation, the one who is responsible for its failure or success, sees it differently. The game changes, and the risks are great; as both the intelligence and the evidence gathering phases merge. With evidence, one has to get closer to capture what is needed for a prosecution. It is at that point that a previously hidden presence becomes visible. If one is found out, it can lead to failure. The trick, or art, is to be visible and yet hidden at the same time for the life of the operation. Which in most cases is for months; and, occasionally, years.

Bob Sealy (Seals) and his team had been refining this skill or 'tradecraft' for years. Today's 'stupidoclock' start was just another day at their metaphorical office. Seals had managed to get a bigger turnout than he had expected on the first day, enough to undertake mobile surveillance. The target address lent itself to an extended plot, mainly covering vehicle exit points onto Tower Bridge Road or Abbey Street.

But he was starting from scratch on Andrei Kuklin. He knew nothing on how he operated, what his lifestyle was, or even if he owned a motor vehicle. The operational team didn't even know what he looked like. So he was glad to have some extra staff on the first day to cover all eventualities.

He had Purbrook Estate plotted for close monitoring of the home address doorway, so they could 'smudge up' the suspect for full identification, and then a number of foot units were double-crewed in cars to be deployed should he leave the area on foot. One of the surveillance team even had a folding bicycle in the back of one of the larger cars.

He then had vehicles plotted in an inner and outer cordon to cover a vehicle that had been deliberately 'laid down' by Kuklin a distance away as an anti-surveillance tactic, looking for signs of being followed before going to a car. If Kuklin thought he was being watched he would ignore the car, otherwise he would use it; safe in the knowledge that he hadn't led the cops to it.

The team had prepared themselves mentally and physically for the day with 'props' like shopping bags, tourist clothing, hats, coats of differing styles, jackets, umbrellas, suits and travel cards that covered the bus and tube. The main challenge for central London surveillance was the skill required to go seamlessly from vehicle to foot, tube or bus surveillance, and back again numerous times within the course of the day.

The NCS team were all experienced surveillance officers; having passed a rigorous three week residential surveillance course, followed by up to three weeks' driver training with the NCS's own driving instructors. They had been using their skills, some for years; and as their home base was located within Greater London they were adept at the craft that was required for following a difficult suspect in the London area.

Meanwhile, Tom, who was in early, was busy reading the media and child protection strategies that he had received last thing on Friday. They had caused him to be late, and he'd only just managed to pick Struan up in time. His eyes stayed on the monitor, as his thoughts drifted off to the weekend with Struan. They had gone fly fishing and Struan had caught his first trout. Struan's heart had been beating so hard as he fought the fish, that he had felt it through his layers of clothing. It was a huge moment, which both of them struggled with. Struan because he had hooked and landed his first trout, and Tom because he was there to do it with him. Pleased that he could be there; and yet sad, knowing that this one small opportunity meant he was missing so many more.

He refocussed on the print and read the document twice before making some notes. Sarah had put together an excellent strategy. Although it was early in the operation, it had every eventuality covered. She really could see what was required operationally for him and his team without it being explained to her. He would have expected that on general policing subjects, but he didn't expect her to be so insightful around CP. The only thing in the report he needed to think about was a highlighted section which Sarah had asked to discuss first thing on Monday. It related to the child alert system which they had touched on before.

He closed down that document and opened up Louisa Greenwood's child protection strategy. The opening paragraph told him that it was based upon current NSPCC policies and created from a standard NSPCC child protection template. As he read further into the document he became more concerned about the content. His mind quickly went back to the warning from JT. The one when he had deliberately placed Louisa with him as a 'check and balance' structure, to stop him from going too far, whatever that actually meant.

"I bet you wouldn't feel the same way if your operational day was constrained like this!" Tom said to himself out loud. As he read on, there were parts which he felt were intelligent child protection 'best practice', but it was interspersed with policies that had been put together mainly for the benefit of the NSPCC and not a combined law enforcement taskforce.

His concern lay in two areas. One, operational activity, and two, the way they would count and measure their success. The latter nearly causing his eyes to pop out of his head. It was no wonder that the NSPCC were seen as a success in the stats. He closed the document, and sipped his first tea of the day, one of the many that he knew he would never actually finish. The presence of a member of the NSPCC on COCET he knew to be a political hot potato, but it was starting to shape up as a problem for him far larger than he had first thought.

The way the policy was written constrained him operationally in that whatever he did, or whatever stage of the investigation they were at, if there was information or a possibility that a child might be at risk then he would have to take immediate action to negate that risk, no matter what the cost to the investigation. The issue lay in the language used. In Police circles information was something that was a precursor to intelligence. Once you got to the stage of having intelligence it was then graded by the Police on a national intelligence system. The grading would deal with words like 'possibility', in that it would rank it at a lower level. Police took action, or did not take action, based on the level of grading. All action taken by the Police was measured against the risk to a child, but it had to be measured, and not just any possibility as the current document specified. He thought about bouncing the strategy straight to JT with a big question mark and a one liner of '*Still happy to have them on board?*'

He knew JT well enough to know that he would probably just get to the measuring success part; and then, seeing just how easy it would be to present himself and COCET as a success story, leave him with the operational dilemma. It sure as hell wouldn't stop him demanding more operational success. What would Louisa do if he asked her to change it? Would it be reported back up the NSPCC chain of command, then across to his top brass? And then, like all shit that rolls downhill, make its way to him? And all at the same time with Louisa just sitting at her desk outside his office.

The second problem lay in the term 'safeguarding' by which they would claim success even if those children were not victims and had no contact with an offender. The Police traditionally claimed success on children rescued from abuse, and offenders arrested. The rest was called crime prevention.

Tom felt a definite shift in how he was going to have to operate as head of COCET. He was moving into politics more than he would have liked, but he thought he had the skills to do it. After all, he had seen enough senior officers in the Police protecting their niches and collective arses to know that the only way to play the political game was to join it and play it. Tom opened up the email containing the document, saved it to his Ops folder, and then returned it to Louisa asking for the NSPCC definition of 'possibility and safeguarding'. He wasn't going to challenge the NSPCC on their current working practices; this was going to be all about language and interpretation within a law enforcement context. The thing that bothered him most, was that the strategy made it so easy to make themselves look like a huge success; and yet at the same time it could be just one arrest.

This was Government politics in action, style over substance, and not one Tom was going to accept unless it was forced upon him. He forwarded the email to Maggie Burrows seeking advice around claiming successful action, simply asking whether COCET should be adopting NSPCC practice.

As he poured away a good third of his cup of tea, and was about to make a fresh hot one, he was joined by Sarah.

"Is now a good time?"

"Yep, sure," Tom said. Thinking, *'At least I'm on safer ground with this subject.'*

In his office Sarah handed him a hard copy of the strategy. Her fresh, open, genuine approach of being prepared and friendly had the effect of softening his mood, causing him to move to his discussion desk; and making him feel more relaxed than he had been moments earlier.

"Look, Sarah. This is fantastic, it really is. I don't have anything to add other than 'thanks.'"

"Thank you, but it is pretty straightforward really. But we do need to cover this child alert section and how it is going to fit in with the Chief's own strategy?"

"I had time to think about this over the weekend, Sarah. In the real world, you have us signed up, and that is how it should be. As for the virtual world, there isn't anything out there, and we should plug that gap. Not just real to virtual, but also from virtual to real. But there is no way of knowing who is doing what online in the rest of the world."

"Well, that is where your Chief and some of the others have been busy. They are forming their own alliance and it is being called, 'GOPOL', short for Global Online Police. They have all agreed, as heads of their respective agencies, that their online teams will be a part of GOPOL. I am still putting together the agreement based on their directions. The final agreement is currently being bounced between them, and I expect it to be agreed today. I will send you a copy as soon as there are no more alterations.

"They will announce it at a meeting at Interpol HQ in Lyons next week. They see it as a global taskforce, where each agency will work independently; but will agree to work together jointly on online operations where the case requires it. Like you did with Operation Hope and are doing now with Operation Ascent. All without the need for MOU's or other long winded government letters of request. It will officially allow you, as a group leader, to request assistance from another country using the umbrella of GOPOL, and they will be able to do likewise from us. The alert system can piggyback that, whether you are working together or not, as you will all know each other and be connected."

"Wow!" replied Tom. "Whose idea was this?"

"Your Chief, and he will be the first head of GOPOL. I think they will take it in turns, but he will be the first, and has agreed to take the lead for the first two years."

Tom sat back in his chair and felt the hairs going up on this arm. This was brilliant.

"Do the other teams know?"

"No. You are the first one to know, and, it will be your Operation Hope that they will hold up as a catalyst for GOPOL, when they announce that the taskforce has already begun global operational activity. So no pressure on you, then!"

Sarah ended the sentence with a big smile and a flick of her long blonde hair back over her shoulders, and Tom noticed for the first time she had grey-blue eyes.

"Well, if it works, it will be a step in the right direction. In my view there should be a permanent global force; the problem will arise when we are all too busy operationally with our own stuff to drop it so as to undertake action at the request of another member. But that's not for now. What do you want from me?"

"Two things. First, an alert system structure between all the agencies at your level, so you all know who to contact 24/7, and a policy that covers it. You will need to write it, so it will be accepted by the others first time, otherwise it will be bounced back and forth, and I need it by end of play tomorrow.

"Second, I need a pre-record from you for Sky TV that will go out with the piece they are doing around the announcement of GOPOL."

The first request was easy, as was the policy. The second, though, caught Tom out.

"What sort of interview?"

Sarah gave nothing away in her expression or her body language to his question but, she did register Tom's immediate change of reaction.

"Have you done much camera work?" Sarah asked as casually and uninterestedly as she could.

"No."

"Well, in some ways that's good. All you need to do is be yourself. I will be there to guide you all the way and we will prep you before the interview." Sarah finished the statement and began to collect her things, signalling she was finished. She gave nothing away, and Tom never knew that she had already started to prep him.

Tom, however, still wanted to know more. "What sort of questions will I get?"

By this time Sarah was up and by the door. She knew the worst thing to do was lie, there needed to be trust between her and Tom. Yet, at the same time, it was her job to get the best out of him, so sometimes it was best to delay the truth. Her instinct told her he would be fine, but Police Officers in general were crap in front of cameras. Not just because they hadn't had the training, but mainly because of the way the Police Service as a whole was structured. They didn't know how far to go, what to say, how it would impact on another police action that they had no knowledge of, or how to handle difficult questions. The ones when only a 'Yes' or an admission would be a suitable response; but which they couldn't give, and which put the officer in a difficult no-win situation as a result. It was middle ground time.

"When they confirm I will know more, and we can chat again then.

It will only be a short piece; the bulk will be done in Lyons, but I need the policy soon as, please!"

"Standby, Standby, Standby! Movement at the door!" came the sudden command that broke the radio silence.

The officer speaking the words sat in the back of a specially converted and highly equipped observation van. Although the walls and doors had been soundproofed to a certain extent, the officer still wore a headphone set; the speaker of which, operating in whisper mode, allowed him to talk in a whisper.

The result at the receiving end was as if he were speaking with normal intensity and loudness. The words were spoken rapidly, increasing the sense of urgency. If there had been a camera in every surveillance vehicle it would have shown the entire team change from a relaxed state to one of sudden readiness.

Three 'footmen' switched their earpieces on and immediately exited their vehicles, and quickly, but covertly, made their way to a position where they could cover their assigned junction or footpath.

One of the positions was an early 'heads up' assistance for another vehicle unit which was covering an exit onto Abbey Street, whilst the other two were covering foot exits away from the Purbrook Estate towards Tower Bridge. All three surveillance officers had donned some form of clothing prop such as a coat, jacket or cap, which they would discard and change for a different item at the first opportunity.

They knew from experience, as well as training, that the most dangerous point in surveillance was the 'lift off', even when one had been surveilling the suspect before, and knew his habits and lifestyle. In this case, they knew nothing about the suspect other than he was Russian and involved in selling child abuse material over the internet.

The whole team that day were married or engaged, some had children, and one was about to become a father for the first time. They knew the next few minutes would be crucial for them and the COCET team.

The officer in the observation van was sitting in a comfortable computer seat which had been adapted to sit on a set of noiseless rails bolted to the van floor, the sort used by television cameramen. In front of him was a purpose built desk which had a TV screen, an operational camera selection panel, a bank of recording devices, the front part of a Cougar radio system and a number of red light emitting side lights. The officer couldn't see out of the van any more than anybody outside could see in. He was watching what was going on at the target doorway using remote control cameras, which were covertly fitted around the van. The cameras had been situated in such a way that from the inside, and using the camera selection panel, an officer could control a camera by zooming in or out, and by panning left or right. Upon reaching the arch of the next camera it was possible to select it to achieve 360° coverage. The operating officer was able to record what he was viewing and take stills at the same time. There were also microphones fitted in certain positions around the van that could record conversations going on close by outside.

In this case the officer had one camera zoomed right into the doorway of the target premises, and had seen the door open, but no one had left the premises. He watched the screen, waiting for someone to emerge. After about 30 seconds, with no one emerging, he updated the surveillance team.

"Door remains open, no change."

There was radio silence as the team knew the 'eyeball' needed the airway clear. Within seconds the silence was broken again.

"White male from the premises, locking the door, towards the stairs and out of view, temporary loss, wait!" The officer let go of the press to talk button (PTT), or pressel switch, which he knew would create a faint crackle. But he had given the command to the rest of the team to wait, so although he had relinquished radio command, it was still his.

He had taken some stills of the unknown white male, and the officer now quickly panned out and relocated the second camera and zoomed in again at the bottom of the stairwell. Within moments the same male that had exited the target premises came back into view.

"Eyeball regained. Subject One is around 5'10", medium build, short light brown hair, cut above the collar but not crew cut, wearing blue jeans and green parka jacket, on foot towards pedestrian exit one and

Tower Bridge Road and Charlie Two Foot, loss of eyeball."

As the officer put the information out he took a series of close up facial stills of Subject One, and relinquished the 'eyeball'.

"Charlie Two Foot ahead and waiting," came the reply in acknowledgement. In the gap between the loss of the eyeball from the observation van and the pick up by Charlie Two Foot, a number of other surveillance units announced their repositioning and their new or intended location. About a minute passed before the eyeball was regained.

"Contact, contact, contact! Charlie Two Foot has the eyeball, Subject One is crossing Tower Bridge Road and heading towards Tower Bridge and the bus request."

Normally a footman's radio signal would be relayed by a vehicle unit, the vehicle's radio having a stronger transmission; but in this case the whole team was so close by, it was assumed the whole team had heard the last transmission.

Without asking for permission to speak, another surveillance officer made a quick announcement, "Charlie Five Foot ahead at the bus request."

"Charlie Two Foot, yes, yes, letting him run, he is towards you now."

Instead of a verbal acknowledgement, there were three clicks of Charlie Five Foot's covert body set, which told the team he had accepted the eyeball and had responsibility for controlling the surveillance. Although Charlie Two Foot didn't have the eyeball, he quickly said, "He's at the bus request and waiting for a bus."

Seals, the operational commander for the surveillance team, said, "Ops Comm permission." Three radio clicks were immediately heard over the radio system from the surveillance officer, also at the bus request, who was now standing within a few feet of the target along with three other members of the public.

"One on the bus only, back to you eyeball."

Three more clicks were heard again in acknowledgement. Charlie Two Foot who was monitoring his colleague from a distance away, dispensed with normal radio procedure.

"Paul to Nick I will commentate for you if he gets on." Again three clicks came back in acknowledgement.

Within seconds Charlie Three, a double crewed vehicle unit, said, "Double decker on way, number 188 to Tower Gateway." Three clicks were again heard in acknowledgment.

Nick had deliberately placed himself at the back of the covered area of the bus request stand so that the target had his back to him. He deliberately didn't look at the target as he arrived, so that if he looked towards him he would only get his side profile. He'd put on a pair of glasses, which had plain lenses, and wore a beanie which was pulled down over his ears, and a grey jacket with a large collar which he turned up so that it covered up the side of his face. Getting in this close to the subject meant that for the rest of the day he would probably never get in close again, no matter how many props he wore.

Surveillance in London had its benefits in favour of the Police, in that a subject would have to remember hundreds of faces over the course of a day; but for now he just wanted to limit his exposure. He saw the bus making its way, and noticed from the information board that a No 188 would stop there. He saw the subject and three others from the group move towards the edge of the pavement, and noticed the subject put his hand in his pocket and come out with what looked like a bus pass.

He moved towards the group but kept himself at the back. As the bus stopped, he heard Charlie Two Foot in his ear piece begin surveillance commentary. The target got on second, and Nick closed in as tight as he could, in an attempt to catch any intelligence that would alert them to his intended destination. But Tower Bridge is a busy and noisy central London road and he failed to hear anything. Nick then hung back and waited as long as he could to allow time for the target to move well away from the entrance of the bus and its driver.

He was in luck. The target went upstairs and Nick boarded, remaining on the lower level. He made his way to the back of the bus and sat on the bench seat at the rear, in the middle of three other members of the public. This tactic had two benefits. Firstly, he could be seen through the rear window by the following surveillance team, but more importantly he could cover the exit point when the subject got off. The downside was he couldn't monitor what was going on upstairs, but then that call had been made the moment the Ops Comm had called for one on the bus.

As the bus moved off, he heard the surveillance begin on the No 188 bus. As it travelled along its designated route, stopping at request stands, Nick gave two clicks by depressing his covert PTT to indicate that the subject remained on the bus. The surveillance team commentated on the movement of the bus, as if it were the subject of the surveillance itself.

"From Charlie Six, the bus is off, off, off, and remains on Minories. Next stop is Tower Gateway, subject remains on, Charlie Six has the eyeball." As the surveillance team moved off, sudden and rapid multiple clicks were heard over the radio by the surveillance team.

"From Charlie Six, relaying rapid clicks heard, back up are you in a position?"

"Back up yes yes."

"Eyeball to you, we will go past and Charlie Six Foot will deploy."

"Back up yes yes. Confirming Charlie Four has the eyeball, nearside indication on Bus 188. Bus is pulling in and it is a stop, stop, stop, Charlie Four Foot deployed."

Immediately the airwave became free the team heard further rapid clicks, indicating that the subject of the surveillance was about to exit the bus. A few seconds passed with no commentary from a surveillance officer. Seals, whose vehicle was at the back of the convoy of surveillance cars, and who was imagining the scene up ahead in his head, knew this was a tricky moment.

Foot officers had to deploy and pick up the target naturally, as if he had just entered their space, and not the other way around. It was normal for there to be a short period when the target was not under control whilst the foot team located him in a busy London street.

As the seconds went by though, the chances of a loss rose; and everybody in the team felt it. Without warning Charlie Six Foot said, "Six Foot has him, he is making his way towards Tower Gateway Tube, I will go down with him if he enters."

"Ops Comm permission," said Seals.

"Go ahead," came the reply from Charlie Six Foot.

"Charlie Four Foot to go into tube and capture Intel, Charlie Three deploy your footie, this is the DLR with connection to District and Circle, back to you Six Foot."

"Yes, yes, Six Foot has him and he is still towards the tube, beware his eyes are all about."

"Charlie Four yes yes," came the acknowledgement from Charlie Four.

"Charlie Three Foot deployed," came the reply from the driver of the vehicle from which Charlie Three Foot had just deployed from.

Seals had taken note of the 'eyes all about' comment from Charlie Six Foot. The officer was letting him and the rest of the team know that he could see the subject looking all around him. There were only three possible reasons for this. He had sussed the surveillance at some point; he was deploying anti-surveillance tactics, or he wasn't doing either of those two and was just acting normally, and the officer had imagined he was looking all around him.

It was imperative that Seals understood what was really happening. There were degrees of being blown. There was the total blow, the absolutely no mistake 'we have lost our cover'. The sort that arises from poor surveillance, such as an officer going into a telephone box on a hot summer's day, keeping the door jammed open with his foot whilst speaking on his covert set, with the suspect right behind him listening to everything! Then there was the suspect just looking around as an anti-surveillance tactic without really knowing what he was looking at. Then there was the suspect who was looking, seeing, recognising and thinking that he was being followed. The latter was survivable if one pulled off the surveillance quickly enough, before he became sure that he was being followed.

Seals knew from experience that one could survive a number of those if they were handled correctly by the Operational Commander. His feeling on this occasion was to stick with it. The target was about to go down the tube, or on an overland rail journey; if there was a time to check behind his back it was now.

"Six Foot still has eyeball, and he is into the tube station. I am following."

"Charlie Four Foot also in."

"Charlie Three in, going deaf."

Seals and the rest of the surveillance team, including the motorcyclist, plotted up around the tube station waiting for intelligence on the destination, or at the very least the direction in which he was travelling. This was where the elastic got stretched. The tactic was that as soon as the team knew where the target was travelling to, they would make their way above ground in a race to get there first to pick up the surveillance with a new foot team, so the one currently following him underground, could peel off before their exposure clock ran out.

Getting there ahead was always a challenge, and would necessitate all cars using sirens and 'stick-on' magnetic blue lights in an effort to cut through the London traffic. This was one of the many areas where a motorcycle on the team became invaluable. One never wanted to use the same team to follow a suspect down onto the tube and then out and away again, even when the target was not surveillance aware. But in this case, when he had already put in some checks before he went down, they really needed a seamless pick up with a fresh set of footies. Seals knew he needed every edge he could get.

"OPs Comm, Charlie One and Charlie One Two."

"Charlie One Two go ahead."

"Charlie One go ahead," came the replies.

"Start making your way towards Central London, aim roughly for Lambeth Bridge, but don't commit yourself to out of comms range."

"Charlie One Two and Charlie One yes yes," replied Charlie One Two for both units, who had been plotted up close by, in sight of the double crewed car unit. Both immediately left the area and headed into Central London.

Back at the home address in Purbrook, Jason remained in the obs van with the camera trained back on the front door. He had been listening to the surveillance and was sipping a cup of tea. The pressure was off him to a certain extent, in that the team was following a suspect from the address, but nobody knew if he was the target or not. The subject of the current follow by his team mates could be an innocent visitor to the address, and so he didn't let his eyes off the screen once as he opened a Tupperware box and munched on a cold bacon sandwich.

Meanwhile, not far away across the River Thames in Victoria, DC Marks had found a busy bus stop right opposite Lloyds Bank, almost within sight of the nearby NatWest Bank. He had been pretending to wait for a bus that morning along with the many other commuters. A few people had used the ATM since he arrived, none of whom looked remotely like the one he was waiting for. After a while, another TFL bus arrived and passengers got on and off, during which, his vision of the ATM was temporarily obscured. As the bus departed and he regained sight of the ATM, he saw a hooded man at the cashpoint with another standing a short distance away. He couldn't see their faces, but he immediately knew it was the men he had been waiting for. He quickly scribbled a time down on the side of the newspaper he was holding, and moved position to the back of the newly formed queue for cover. As he watched, he saw the man at the ATM remove money and reinsert a different card, whilst the man standing nearby looked around, as if he were looking for someone or something.

As the man at the ATM moved away and took up a position nearby, the other man moved up to the ATM and repeated the process; then they both moved away.

DC Marks followed them for a short distance and took up a position near a hoarding barrier, which concealed most of his body whilst allowing him to maintain a view of both suspects. They had now travelled the short distance to the NatWest Bank and were already withdrawing funds. DC Marks had walked the route to the Barclays Bank earlier in the morning, and felt confident enough to leave the two targets of his observations alone whilst he made his way ahead of them to another covered bus request on Vauxhall Bridge Road, about a hundred yards from the Barclays ATM. He got there only a few minutes ahead of them, and watched as they repeated the process, withdrawing what he could clearly see as cash on this occasion. As the pair left the area in the direction of Victoria he rang the COCET office and got Archie Donaldson.

"Archie, me old mate, what's happening?"

"Ah, you know, combing the underworld. How did you get on this weekend with Patrick?" Archie replied suggestively.

"Good, we got all the data inputted and there are some good targets for what the Boss wants to do, one of them standing out from all the others. Pat just loves having a dig when he can, he doesn't see the problem with opening his mouth and saying what he's thinking."

"Should go far then," Archie interrupted.

"Yeah, right! Listen, can you let the Sarge know that I have seen the pair doing a run on the Victoria based banks. They have the cash and have gone. I'm on my way back and will evidence it on my return. Oh, and can you let Mitchell know for his alert system? I have the times."

"Will do mate!"

"From Charlie Four Foot, subject has travelled District and Circle line westbound, no destination."

Seals, who had prepared himself for a 'no destination' intelligence update said, "All units relaying Charlie Four Foot. Subject has travelled westbound on the District and Circle line, no destination known, make your way to Monument, blues and twos authorised."

The surveillance team, who had blended into their current surroundings perfectly, broke cover and made their way at high speed and with sirens wailing and blue lights flashing, cutting their way through the busy central London traffic. As they approached Monument they cut the sirens and blue lights and slowed, blending back into the environment.

Seals immediately called up on the radio. "Foot units Ops Com, receiving?'

Seals waited for about 30 seconds and repeated his transmission. With no reply forthcoming, he said, "All units make your way to Cannon Street, Charlie One Two and Charlie One hold at Mansion House."

With all units acknowledging, Seals activated his sirens and lights and the surveillance team once again sped its way through central London. The team repeated this process along the overland route of the underground's District and Circle line, whilst the target and the two surveillance officers monitoring him sped along a similar route, but way beneath the roads of London. As they approached Victoria Underground and Rail Station, Seals could hear broken transmissions of the foot team talking between each other.

"Ops Com foot team receiving?"

The fact was that the foot team could hear their approaching team mates, but the output capability of their body sets couldn't yet reach them. Experience told Seals that this would be the case and he waited until he got closer.

As Andrei Kuklin entered the travel agency on the corner of Grosvenor Gardens, he could just hear sirens in the far distance, a common occurrence in central London and to which he gave no thought. He sat down at the desk of an agent he recognised and purchased a flight ticket to Chisinau, Moldova. The sales agent knew who he was and undertook the transaction, receiving cash for the ticket; not an unusual method of payment at the office, where they also sold bus and coach tickets. As Kuklin waited for his printed e-ticket, the surveillance team had descended on his location and quickly had the building under control, with the foot team being replaced and another officer deployed ahead, close to the entrance of Victoria Tube Station.

As Kuklin left the travel agency, the concealed speaker in Seals' surveillance vehicle announced his departure and movement back towards Victoria Underground Station. The following foot team was well prepared, and as they entered and descended back into the underground system their communications disappeared. The mobile team readied themselves, planning routes, and getting themselves in a position to move quickly. Some of the previous foot team changed clothing, with one putting on a wig and another putting on a dark rimmed set of glasses. They didn't have to wait long.

"Charlie One Foot, target is travelling northbound on the Victoria Line."

"From Ops Comm all units make your way to Green Park, Charlie One

Two let me know as soon as you get there."

The team began the race towards Green Park, one that the motorcycle would win. Seals' mind was not on the race as his driver sped through the back streets of Victoria, as he trusted his driving ability. His mind was working on a plan for Green Park and the interchange problems it posed. He felt the elastic beginning to stretch again.

The biker got there well ahead announcing his arrival at Green Park, and Seals could hear him repeatedly calling the foot team with no response. The elastic gave a large tug and stretched to breaking point. The tactic he was using could be affected by many variables; time, speed, direction, traffic, roadworks, or a missed junction; all of them could cause the team to lose the target. To correct those variables, one needed experience, a calm head and a plan. This would all come down to split second decision making. Seals waited for a bit longer for the team to get closer to Green Park, then said, "Charlie One Two, position yourself to get Comms between Bond Street and Oxford Circus, rest of the team continue through To Piccadilly Circus."

As the team acknowledged the new instruction, Seals felt the elastic loosen again. His head had not risen from the tube map and the team list he was looking at, as the vehicle he was in jerked, twisted and turned, accelerating and decelerating as it made its way along Piccadilly, jumping red traffic lights and travelling in a bus lane. At least three cars activated traffic enforcement cameras. Anybody with a hint of car sickness would have been throwing up long ago, but Seals just got calmer as the pressure increased. The problem he now had was that there were further interchanges, and he had only half a team. He could split the team once more, but to cover for every eventuality, he would need to split it twice, and send two units alone to cover other tube exits. As he approached Piccadilly he made the decision that if no communications were heard at either this exit, Bond Street or Oxford Circus he would hold the mobile team centrally, and wait for the foot team to resurface to pick up the surveillance. As the elastic was about to break it suddenly retracted to normal size.

"He is out, out, out, via Regent Street East, exit one, and towards McDonalds, temporary loss wait."

Seals was about to speak, but the 'wait' command meant that he couldn't.

"From Charlie Five Foot, eyeball regained, he is into McDonalds, and I can't go with him."

Seals waited a split second to see if the team would naturally take charge, and he wasn't disappointed.

"Charlie Two deployed will go in alone."

"Charlie Five Foot deployed and will cover all movement to the nearside as he exits."

"Charlie Six Foot deployed and will cover all movement offside on exit."

Seals was making a note of the change of drivers in Charlie Two and kept a record of further plot assignments as the whole team took up responsibilities without the need for direction, a sign of an experienced team used to undertaking surveillance duty. He then heard three long clicks come over the radio, which meant the officer inside McDonalds required interrogation, presumably because he was not in a position to speak however covertly he tried, and that he needed to relay something important to the outside team.

"Ops Comm to Charlie Two Foot, do you require questioning?" Seals said.

Three clicks came back in the affirmative

"Do you have eyeball on the target?"

Three more clicks came back.

Seals wondered what was going on inside. What was happening would direct him to ask the right questions. He decided on a direct approach.

"Can you take a mobile call?"

Two clicks came back, meaning 'No'.

"Is he eating or drinking?"

Three more clicks.

"Has he met anyone?"

Three clicks.

"More than one?"

Three clicks.

"Has he met with two people?"

Two clicks.

"Has he met with three people?"

Two clicks.

Seals looked at his driver, Tommy, and said, "Fuck me, he's in there having a party!"

"Has he met with four people?"

Three clicks came the reply.

This got Seals intrigued. "Is this a meeting with friends and family?"

Two clicks came back fast and sharp which wasn't lost on anybody involved in the surveillance.

"Are they doing anything?"

Two clicks back

"Do you require further interrogation?"

Two clicks came back.

"You have the eyeball then, all permissions through Charlie Two."

Seals thought about what they had achieved so far and decided to ring DCI Ross.

At the COCET office DC Archie Donaldson was speaking to the travel agent, who was reporting that Andrei Kuklin had just been in and paid cash for a return ticket to Chisinau, Moldova. As the agent relayed all the details, Archie wrote furiously, attempting to keep up with the agent's excited delivery. As she neared the end of the information, Archie kept writing whilst his mind started to question itself; did he have it all, were there other questions he needed to ask? As the agent finished, almost out of breath, he thanked her enormously and promised to let her know the outcome of the investigation. As ADS King was not present he went straight to the Boss. At the door he saw DCI Ross talking on his mobile phone; he beckoned him in as the call was ending.

"Yes, Archie."

"Just took a call from the travel agents. Kuklin has just been in and purchased a ticket; and earlier Owen reported in that he observed our two Victoria based money launderers working the ATMs."

Tom, who had just been talking to Seals, felt privileged to have such good lines of intelligence; and he was excited because the game was afoot.

"Where is Jane?"

"Canteen."

"Tell her to come and see me when she gets back. Well done, this is bubbling nicely."

Tom went over the Intel in his head, and without really knowing it, graded it as he went along. He picked up his mobile and rang Seals back.

"Yes, Boss."

"The travel agent has just confirmed it was Kuklin who booked the tickets, have you got photos of him?"

"Yes."

"Also, DC Marks had the Victoria ATMs covered this morning; he thinks there was a run on the banks. There is a second group of banks close to your current location that we didn't cover, but I will get an enquiry made with them to confirm. If there has been a run, then the money has to be handed over at some stage."

"In that case we have identified and housed Kuklin," said Seals. "Do you want us to move onto the group of four with a view to trying to identify some of them?"

"If you see any exchange, then yes. Otherwise wait to hear back from me about the banks."

As Seals put his phone back into the cradle he heard three long clicks, followed by, "Charlie Two to Charlie Two Foot is there an update?"

Three clicks came the reply.

"Is the target still with the group of four?"

Three clicks.

"Has something happened?"

Three clicks.

Seals had rung Charlie Two the moment he heard there was an update.

"Yes, Sarge."

"There is Intel that indicates there may have been a run on the banks this morning, and we have Kuklin, the travel agents have confirmed it."

"OK," said the driver of Charlie Two, who ended the call and then over the radio said, "Has there been an exchange?"

Three clicks came the reply.

"Was it to our target?"

Three clicks.

"Could you see what it was?"

Two clicks this time.

"Do you need further questions?"

Two clicks.

"In that case, relaying from Charlie Two Foot, and for the log, there has been an exchange between the group and our target, with our target receiving the item, cannot see what it was. Intel update from Ops Comm is that our target has been identified as subject one, that having come from the travel agents via the operational team, back to you Charlie Two Foot."

"Ops Comm quick permission?"

Due to the closeness of the last transmission, Charlie Two replied, "Go ahead."

"We will be dropping our subject and taking the group of four, Charlie Two Foot move to the upper or lower level and get a description out of the men using your mobile, then cover the exit, foot teams prepare for further splits, we will always stick with the largest group, back to you Charlie Two."

"Charlie Two, Charlie Two Foot, did you get that?"

Three clicks came the reply.

At COCET, Jane was back and sat with DC Hayes in Tom's office.

"Mitchell. What have we got from the banks?"

"There has been a run on all the accounts, which amounts to a complete withdrawal. They have got the lot; there is more coming in every day but with the purchase of the flight ticket, and knowing the previous patterns, we can expect there to be a period where the accounts are left to fill up again."

"Footage?"

"I will collect it this afternoon, statements as you know need requesting; and I need to work out what we need first."

"OK. Jane, cascade it down that Kuklin has been identified and housed. Get all the Intel from Seals once they have written up the log. We will do it, just get a copy of the log. From that, draw up Intel packages on all the known subjects so we can identify the intelligence gaps. I want a meeting for a wash up before anybody goes home, that's all for now."

Tom was already ringing Seals before they left the room.

"Seals. There has been a run on the accounts this morning. You could be at a meet between the launder team and Kuklin."

"I think we are," came the reply. "There has been an exchange..." Right at that point Seals heard rapid clicks come over the air followed quickly by the words.

"Out out out!"

"Have to go call you back," said Seals, quickly regaining focus; imagining the scene that was only a few hundred yards away, but which he couldn't see.

"From Charlie Two Foot they're all together and hailing a black cab, one is pulling in, all four unknowns, so subjects two to five are getting in, subject One is staying out. Cab Reg is LD53XMR and it is off off off, towards Haymarket, wait for the split with Coventry Street."

Charlie Two Foot relinquished control of the airwave for a few seconds and his mobile unit quickly grabbed it.

"Two Foot will pick you up top of Haymarket."

"Yes yes, and it is a right right right, into Haymarket and out of my sight."

Tom felt Operation Ascent was ascending as he completed the child alert policy, which he then sent to the international partners of COCET, requesting they deal with it as a matter of urgency as it was required for the upcoming announcement of GOPOL in Lyons. All their respective Chiefs would presumably be there and so he expected it to fly back. The idea was brilliant and yet simple. COCET was making law enforcement history, and it was only the first month. He searched himself for a sense of the weight of responsibility, and, although he felt it a bit, he didn't feel the enormous pressure he would have expected. Yet there was something else that was there, something that made him nervous and worried, but he couldn't identify it.

He ignored it and opened an email from Supt. Maggie Burrows. It was in response to his referral of the NSPCC accounting rules. In short, she didn't like or agree with it either. But it came from the very top; he would have to adopt them.

He closed the email and pondered the directive, looking further down the path at the bigger national picture, and the impact on the country's Police Forces. And in some cases, their small and underfunded child protection units.

It would be all milk and honey for the first few years, and the politicians would accept all the praise and success. But it was just that, it was politics; and worse, it was playing politics with children and child abuse. It was like saying Arsenal had played Man United and lost One-Nil. But Man United had also had seven very near misses, so their supporters claimed it was a whitewash.

Further down the line this would bite them in the arse. The immediate problem for him would be to ensure he wasn't questioned on it in the press without explanation in advance. Safeguarding was a word that could, and did, mean a number of things. His international partners would not see it the way the NSPCC did. In fact they would just see it their way.

It was something he could deal with, in part, by taking a 'law enforcement offender classification' approach. By labelling an offender or case as a 'true paedophile' would help balance the claims of thousands of children having been rescued, when most were really 'safeguarded'; and he wanted that point made clear with the press. He had to deal with this now; or it could, in the end, take him down. He rang Sarah Dorsey's extension.

"Hi. Can you pop in if you have a sec?"

"Sure," replied Sarah.

As Tom waited he thought of his ex-wife and her uncle Dick, or Hugh Richard Xenophon D'Aeth, a distinguished educationalist and former Master of Hughes Hall, Cambridge, and former trustee of the NSPCC board. He was wondering what his view would have been on it, when Sarah entered the room.

"Policy?" She said looking at him with a look of expectation.

"Done and gone, but not back yet!" He replied in an efficient tone.

"Something else," he went on, "have you heard anything about how we are going to account for our figures? It's contained within the CP strategy that Louisa has submitted."

"Yes. I got that sent down to me from the Chief." Tom was taken aback by her quick response. He wasn't expecting that reply. "How did he get it?"

"Louisa sent it to her bosses in the NSPCC for checking before she sent it to you. They, I understand, made a few alterations and sent it back to her, as well as sending it direct to your Chief, and he sent it down to me."

Still absorbing the information, Tom said, "When did you get it?"

"Last week. Is there a problem with it?" Sarah enquired.

Tom didn't want to pursue the subject but assumed she had had it before him. Something he was pissed off about, but couldn't do anything about now.

"I am concerned about the way we are going to count our successes. The way the NSPCC count it is not the way we do it. But it has come from on high that we use the same rules. I am concerned about getting difficult questions from the press on it, and I was wondering if you could help allay those fears.

"Sure, that's an easy one. When I send a media release I will include an 'Information for the Press', or explanation of what we do and stand for. It is just so that we don't get misquoted on topics that broadcasters might use poetic licence with unless they've had the briefing note. What's your concern?"

"My concern is around the term 'safeguarding', and the way figures will be inflated unless there is a real understanding of it. Rescuing is one thing, safeguarding is another; but a headline will just read 'Kids

Saved from Sex Abuse.'"

"I know where you're coming from. I can cover you on that. Leave all the big claims to GOPOL media releases. With you, the media are not going to be interested in those, they're going to want to know what it is like to be in your shoes."

Sarah was so convincing that it put him at ease, and she must have picked that up somehow, because as she left the office, she said, "From what I hear the NSPCC are trying to get a foot in the door of GOPOL."

With Tom now staring at the empty doorway and the information making its way along his neural pathways, the ease disappeared; to be replaced by a feeling that he had a mole in his camp.

The desk phone rang. The sound of it on this occasion was angry, shrill and penetrating, leading him to pick it up with a tense forearm and an argumentative mind set.

"DCI Ross," he almost spat out.

"Hello, Sir, my name is Dale Walters." Dale sensed the awkward pause as Tom was trying to pick up the thread of new information, whilst releasing the one he had just been thinking about.

"I'm an undercover officer from Northants. SO10 have given me your number and suggested I call you. Is this a good time to talk?"

The penny dropped for Tom, helping him to focus.

"Hi there, Dale, I wasn't expecting a call from you. I was told you were tied up on a case at the moment."

"I was," replied Dale, "the job folded yesterday, a problem with the informant. I've just had a debrief at SO10, and they told me you might be interested to know that I am now available."

Tom's mind began racing with the prospects of having his own UC.

"Yes, I am interested. Are you in a position to come here for a chat?"

"Yes. Of course I can."

"Great," Tom replied, thinking he was already warming to Dale for not objecting to attending COCET, a building linked to law enforcement.

"When can you make it?"

"Today. I can be there say around 3.30."

As Tom thought about the endless possibilities in having a UC like Dale working for COCET, he was interrupted again, this time by his mobile. It was Seals, informing him that they had stood down for the day and were returning to base at Surbiton.

"We dropped subject one and went onto the team of four, they got a black cab from Piccadilly and went in with a key to 61A, Stanhope Street, Euston, NW1. There was an exchange between one of the four and Kuklin, don't know what it was, and we don't have imagery of it. But whatever it was, it was inside a Tesco's bag and was the size of a large book. We have got some product though on the four unknowns. I won't know how good it is till I review it, but it should be good enough. As we were standing down Kuklin arrived back at Purbrook, and we have product there of the Tesco's bag again in his hand. We will give you a copy of the log, the original stays with us. We will give you all the imagery as original exhibits, you will have to do your own copies and we will provide statements upon request." Seals finished the sentence with a satisfied tone that Tom felt was well deserved.

"That is just awesome again, Seals. What does it take to get a job on your firm?" Tom enquired.

"We are in transition to SOCA, now is not a good time. None of us know if we want to be part of SOCA. All the Cussies want in, no surprise there, as they have had their ability to prosecute taken off them because they screwed up too many times at court. NCIS has become a black hole, we don't even work with them any more, and we already have our 'Reflex Units' who have been operating now for a number of years. SOCA will still take the Immigration Service staff who are currently covering Human Trafficking, and failing in that area. It's a mess, and most of us sense that the cops will be fucked over. The NCS doesn't need the other partners, but they need us. But the way the new agency is shaping, it will be the others that benefit. So, in the long run, it will fail."

"Is that your view as well?" Tom asked. He really respected Seals, and valued his opinion. He wanted to know if it was his own.

"I am probably going to sign up. But that's only because my home force provides a window where I can go back within the first three years. I am one of the lucky ones in that respect. Hampshire, for example, have told their staff that if they sign up, that's it; there is no way back. My view on it is this. The NCS has been a total success, and it works; and has worked for years, in part because it was born out of the old regional crime squads, another success story. If you put three failing agencies with one good one, the chances are they will drag the good one down, no matter how good that other one is."

"Thanks for your honesty. I always wanted to be a branch NCS officer, but it now looks as if I have missed my chance. Expect a call from Jane to arrange collection of the exhibits. You have done us proud again, Seals. Please thank your team for me and I am sure we will be back in touch."

As Dale Walters arrived at the COCET building, DCI Ross was completing his decision log for the team meeting later. Dale, who didn't really know what to expect, was impressed with the building, its setup and the tight security that Sam had already put in place. As he was shown into Tom's office Dale wondered if his future was about to take yet another change of course.

"Dale, thanks for coming at short notice."

"No problems, I was interested to see and hear all about COCET," replied Detective Sgt. Dale Walters.

For the next 20 minutes or so, Tom basically conducted an interview with Dale. He got a full Police and qualification history, and in the process learnt that Dale was a level one undercover officer, which Tom hadn't known, as well as being an online expert. He was a computer Forensic Examiner, currently managing Northants Police Forensics Department. He had about 25 years of service, was calm, experienced and was clearly a safe pair of hands. Without asking, Dale also provided a number of examples of his work, along with referees who could verify what he was telling was the truth. Tom guessed, rightly as it turned out, that Dale had realised that he was being interviewed and so adapted what he was saying to match that intention. It was all going to be down to which officer broached the subject of joining COCET first. Dale decided that, as he had come all this way, and the time being right at Northants, he might as well declare his intentions and put his hat in the ring.

"Guv. I want to be straight up here. I would love to be a permanent member of COCET. I can do your online and offline undercover work. I can manage those operations for you if you use other U/Cs. I can be your 'in house' Forensic Examiner. I am ACPO authorised and fully qualified. I know personally most other examiners within the UK, including TVP, so networking with them would be easy. I could do your own Forensics where it is needed, but would need a lab and equipment. I have a Police history in investigating child protection cases and taking them to court successfully. I've had a briefing from SO10 on what you did with Operation Hope and I would love to be part of something like that."

Tom was impressed. It was what he wanted to hear. The only downside was that when someone was this successful, and this qualified, the home force would not want to lose their asset.

"How difficult will it be to get you away from Northants?

"Well, they will be disappointed, but before coming here I spoke with my Boss, who by the way had heard of COCET, and I told him of my wishes. He feels it would be something that Northants would want to support and be part of." Now Tom was even more impressed. The one thing that means more to a manager than anything else is someone who brings a problem and a workable solution to the table.

'But what rank was his Boss?'

"Who is your line manager?"

"Detective Chief Superintendent Hardy."

Tom didn't know him, and didn't need to. If the DCS had given his blessing, then it was game on.

"Where do you live?"

"Outside of Northampton. It has taken me just over an hour to get here, and I came from my home address, which is this side of the M1."

Tom knew each force would have their own regulations and policy around distance between home and work. This would probably be outside both the TVP and Northants areas. 'Just over the hour' meant more during rush hour, but he could add some travelling time to this, and the occasional overnight stay.

"What about family?"

"I am married. This is the third Mrs. Walters, and we don't have any kids with us."

"What does your wife do?"

"She is in the 'job', in Northants."

"OK. Well, I would love you to be a part of COCET as well. It will need to be seen as a secondment from your force to COCET, and I will do the approach to your Boss. When could you start?" Tom said tentatively, not really knowing if he could pull this off.

"Two weeks?" Dale replied as more of a suggestion. "But Northants may want more."

"Could you do some work for us before then?"

"Of course I can. What have you in mind?'

Tom discussed the online child alert system and what was being planned, and how he would need to contact all online undercover officers or their handlers within the UK in one easy communication. Dale thought that would be an easy thing to do, but it would need agreement from SO10, which he would seek to do on behalf of COCET. Tom then briefed Dale on Operation Ascent, and that he would require evidential access and purchases from the pay-per-view website. Again Dale said that would be easy, he just needed authorisation and instruction. He could do it with one of his current covert credit cards or purchase a preload.

"A preload will be fine. Don't waste your named covert ones, this is something likely to go to court." With Dale Walters gone, Tom, who could see that the main office was empty, went straight to the conference room and sat down; opening his decision making log. He knew that he was about to set the team on a course which would lead to their first success. But, not for the first time, he caught a sudden glimpse of some danger he couldn't identify, something sinister that would not unveil itself. It was just a thought, a flicker of danger across his senses, nothing more. He put it to one side knowing that Police procedure and correct risk assessment would keep them all safe. Looking up to see the whole COCET team present, he began.

CHAPTER SEVEN

The reactive policing mantra of 'We will go where the evidence takes us' is the antithesis of proactive doctrine, which intuitively seeks to go somewhere first, and there find the evidence.

—I.R.Tyler

It was decision time; it had come together over two days. Not unheard of in smaller investigations, but in something like this it was new territory again.

In child protection cases that could only be good, but it felt wrong. He had gone over the evidence three times and it was all there. The opportunity to interdict was right, in that it showed the complete cycle of the money laundering. No, it didn't help that he was getting pressure from above to take action on the very day that GOPOL was to be announced; but it wasn't just that, there was something else holding him back, something telling him not to take action.

He went through it all for a fourth time. The evidence was right, the time was right, and perhaps there wouldn't be another opportunity maybe for weeks. Or worse still, ever. There was no evidence that Kuklin would return to the UK after his trip to Moldova. Whatever it was that was getting under his skin he needed to deal with rationally, there was no reason not to go ahead. Mitchell Hayes had pulled off a real blinder by getting the data on the purchasers from PayPal in such a short time. In turn, the Intel Cell had pulled off an equally amazing feat by not only creating intelligence packs on those purchasers, but also disseminating them to CPUs around the country; all of whom were just waiting to be the given the word to act.

The surveillance product from Seals and his team was near perfect. To cap it all, he had managed to secure Detective Sgt. Dale Walters from Northamptonshire Police on a two year secondment to COCET; who was currently making undercover evidential purchases for the prosecution case. The timing was made all the better because Owen and Patrick had identified an admin nicknamed 'librarian' from 'childscentcafe' from the data supplied by SDE. The IP work had returned, and the target, Philip Anthony Thompson, had been identified.

With what he now knew on Thompson, and other users of the site, he had more than enough to approach Cleveland Police. To have Ascent in a prosecution phase in the next week was near perfect, so he called Jane King and Sarah Dorsey into his office.

"We're going into arrest phase on Ascent. The Bosses want it to coincide with the announcement of GOPOL in Lyons on Thursday. Jane, alert the forces who have actionable Intel and get a list together of how many they can do for Thursday this week."

"Yes, Boss!"

"Then get warrants for Purbrook and Stanhope Street. All hands on deck, only certified sick notes will do!"

"We won't have enough staff to cover both addresses," Jane replied quickly.

"I know that. But I want our staff making the arrests. As part of the bargaining chip for doing it now, HQ have agreed to provide search teams, and the Fraud Squad will undertake the prosecution post arrest. The Fraud Squad is providing two officers, one for each address, and then they'll team up with our staff to undertake the interviews. After charge they should be in a better position to take the case over. I will lead the warrant at Purbrook, and you at Stanhope. We arrest Kuklin at the airport, prior to going through passport control. Once he is in custody both warrants get done at the same time. I want everyone briefed the night before, so that's tomorrow night!"

Tom's slight change in tone gave the impression that he was laying down a challenge. It wasn't lost on Sarah, and she looked at Jane, expecting some form of reply.

"Challenge accepted!" replied Jane, without even hesitating and in a tone of voice that gave no hint of her inner thoughts. Thoughts that were already taking her to working until at least 10pm for the next two nights 'and then', followed by an early start to get into London by 6am.

Sarah, who was impressed by Jane's reply, looked back at Tom; enjoying the exchange and wondering what would come next. These two really did work well together under pressure, she thought. It was at that moment that Tom flicked her a glance, and she suddenly felt herself under the spotlight. She quickly found her body temperature starting to rise for no apparent reason.

'I hope I'm not flushing up, I think I could be!' she thought to herself.

"Sarah. Can you prepare a media release? And what else do you need?"

Feeling less in the hot seat, Sarah replied, "I can have the brief ready for you in about an hour. We should look to deal with Sky at the same time; in that they get to do an interview with you at some point after the arrest phase, but timed so they can run it with the piece they are doing on GOPOL. As I am covering both it will be easy to arrange, and it will fit nicely with what they want."

"OK, will you be here or in Lyons?" This time it was Tom's turn to feel some unease.

"They are all using Interpol's media team and they have their staff officers as well. I am working with the Interpol team and have overall lead on it, so you will be fully sighted and I will remain here."

"That sounds great to me," Tom replied, not hiding his relief.

"Have our international partners come back on the Child Alert Policy?" enquired Sarah.

"Yes, they have all signed up."

"Good. We now have dedicated press staff allocated to us from their respective agencies and I will be looking to include them in all our press releases."

"Thanks, Sarah. Great job."

"Jane, Dale will get everything to you once he has deployed and got the evidence. Get him to come in with it, and sort him out with a desk and introduce him to the team in advance. He starts in two weeks."

With the decision made and a new course set, he felt his ship lurch suddenly forward, picking up speed. The wind, now able to pass across the sails, filled them; placing strain on the mast, boom, forestay, kicking strap, shrouds and chain plates. He felt the increased pace transmit through his fingertips as he held the wheel. The ship - strong, capable and finely tuned - began to hum. The course was true, and the way was clear with an open passage of water ahead. Yet he felt he was heading straight onto rocks. Why?

"DCI Ross," Tom announced, picking up the phone.

"Hi, it's me."

"Hi, me," replied Tom.

There was a pause, as neither one of them knew where to start or what to say.

"You have a great team there, Tom. They are all mentally fit and raring to go. Jane is as strong as I have ever seen her. I won't need to see them again for another four months unless there's an operational need."

"That's good to hear, as we are going operational on our first case in a couple of days. What about me? I haven't heard back from Gloria, should I read anything into that?"

"That's the other reason I was ringing. On this first assessment she has agreed to report back to me. You have a clean bill of health, no worries there. This allows me to make a decision based on her assessment and recommendations. That decision is that I will only ever see your COCET staff, but not you; and I will report upwards accordingly, as required. I will also see other ACPO staff as required. Gloria will now be responsible for you and she will report directly to JT or above."

"Where does that leave us?" Tom interjected, only being interested in what was coming next.

"Well, that allows me the professional space to deal personally with where that leaves us."

"And have you?" Tom said, desperately trying to hide the frustration in his voice.

"No, I haven't. And that is down to the fact I have only just got to this point today, after concluding my write ups on the team and seeing Gloria's report. So I just wanted to let you know where I was on this."

"OK," replied Tom, feeling not much further forward than he was before, in that he was still waiting.

"What sort of timescale?"

"Couple of weeks. I am on some retail therapy this weekend, then in Nottingham for a week's conference. I am back in force, for a day, then in London for the rest of that week. Maybe we could meet up towards the end of that week, or at the weekend?"

Tom was searching for anything he could gather from her tone, but there were only the words, which appeared good on the face of it.

"I didn't set out to lie to you."

As soon as he said it, he wished he hadn't. It didn't matter that he was on the phone, he had closed the gap between them by his words, and she reacted to it immediately.

"Let's leave that until later, Tom. I have to go. I'll speak to you soon, and all the best for whatever action you are taking. Bye."

1410hrs UTC, London, UK

Andrei Kuklin peered out of the window and looked down at the car park below. He scanned the area, noticing regular cars and making a mental note of the make and colour of new ones whilst he waited to be connected. He had the flight details ready when the line opened, and as usual, he had to speak first.

"я приезжаю в Кишинев в 15:30."

"я забрать вас, она у вас?" came the reply.

Kuklin immediately recognised the voice of his 'Pakhan'. Although he had the utmost hierarchal respect for him, that respect came solely from a personal desire to survive. He was ruthless even in Russian terms, and it made him shudder to think he was collecting him in person. The question of whether he had the money was not normal. Of course he had the money. He wouldn't be coming back unless he had. Kuklin weighed up the merits of asking a question but dropped the idea and decided to play it safe.

"Да," replied Kuklin, confirming he had the money.

"Хорошо, помните — если у вас будут проблемы, вы сможете воспользоваться моей сетью. Они похоронят любую проблему," his 'Pakhan' said in a menacing voice.

"понимать," Kuklin replied, as the phone line immediately went dead.

He peered back out of the window and watched the scene below as he pondered the call. He knew he was on good terms with his 'Pakhan' but he was still uncomfortable in his presence. He recalled the last time he was with him. He had summoned him round for a coffee, only to find out that the man had just tortured a gang member because he believed he had fucked one of his favourite whores. He hadn't. But in the ensuing rage at failing to get that information out of him he had shot him, and slit the whore's throat as an example to the other girls. That sort of behaviour was all well and good in Russia, but this was the UK. If you did that to someone here, you could expect a reasonable response from the cops. And what problem did his leader think he had, or was going to get that would need such a violent response? He wandered away from the window and mulled over the content of the short call. He felt confident in his position, but knew in the longer term he would have to get away from the gang. And to do that he would need money, lots of it, and a complete new identity. There were only two ways to accomplish that in his position. One was to make money on the back of his current activities and not declare it, running the obvious risk of losing his head, and the other was to turn 'Stukach'.

Tom was still pondering his call from Fiona whilst writing up his decision log. He was frustrated by the need for more time and just wanted to know his fate. If he didn't put it out of his mind now, it would start to distract him at a time when he needed to be totally focussed.

In the end he had his work. Maybe that was all he ever really had. If he was honest with himself, did he care too much? Yes. Did he love, live and breathe his job? Yes. Could he put it down at 5 o'clock and go home? No. On that alone he was more of the problem than Fiona was, that was for sure.

He let it go as he knew he had to, and opened the email from Sarah Dorsey. As he read the media briefing he recalled her flush and wondered what that was all about. The briefing note was excellent and immediately put him at ease. Seeing the operation: what he was about to undertake, the presumed result and how it would be portrayed to the media and then the world, before he had even taken the first step, was a new but satisfying experience.

Of course, it all hinged on one thing: him getting it right, and getting the result. There was a huge amount riding on it. It was the first case for a newly formed team taking the fight to the child abusers, which included organised crime, no matter where they were from. The announcement of a new global law enforcement partnership of which COCET would be the UK's representative. UK formed, led and inspired. Yep, there was a great deal riding on it alright!

He made a handwritten list of the likely areas that would come up in interview with Sky News. It would be an exclusive with Martin Brunt, but prerecorded to run with his reporting live from Lyons in France on the announcement of GOPOL. There was nothing in the list to really worry him, and Sarah had suggested a short rehearsal before the event, once they knew more of the outcome from COCET action.

As he went to sleep that night, he felt he had it all covered; everything was planned, prepared and in place. Without further thought he dropped into a deep sleep, the first time for many months.

At 4.30pm the following day the COCET conference room fell to a hushed silence. Tom introduced his staff to the other Police Officers from the Fraud Squad and the Operational Support Unit, then provided the guests with an historical outline of Operation Ascent and delivered a TVP standard Police operational briefing using the IIMARCH model. Most, if not all, were just waiting for the 'M' section, the method, and Tom got straight into it.

"Archie and Owen, liaise with Heathrow Police and arrest Kuklin as he enters passport control. Take him to Heathrow Custody, they have been forewarned and have allocated us a custody officer and some cells. Once there, you will be responsible for all property found on him, and for conducting interviews along with DC Hallett from the Fraud Squad." DC Hallett, who was standing at the back of the room, put his hand up as identification for the two officers.

"We won't have surveillance on him so you will need to be there early; and just in case, put something in place to alert you should he have passed through passport control before you get there. Make sure you have a uniform officer nearby to assist. Once you have made the arrest, call me and I will inform Jane. That will be our signal to execute the warrants. It could be we will need his key from prisoners' property to get in. If so, I will make a decision at that time, depending on his demeanour, whether to have him at the search or not. If we can get in another way then we will execute the warrant without him. Officers for Purbrook will be me, DC Anna Wilson for exhibits, with PS Ford, PCs Henry, Budd, Morrison and Knight as the search team. Once complete, we will go to Heathrow for a debrief and breakfast. The Purbrook team will form up at Southwark at 7am and await the arrest of Kuklin. Officers for Stanhope Street will be ADS King, DC Hayes exhibits, APS Collins and his search team of PCs Egan, Travers, Baker and Floyd. Also at the address will be DCs Cartwright and Hallett from our Fraud Squad. DC Cartwright will team up with ADS King and DC Hayes to conduct the interviews on the prisoners who go to Camden 'Nick', they know four will be coming in and are providing a double crewed van to assist with transport. Form up point, though, will be Albany Street Station at 7am, where their van will meet up with you. DC Hallett when the search is complete you will need to relocate to Heathrow and team up with DC's Donaldson and Marks. Questions so far?"

After a short period of silence Tom continued. "Ops Comm for the day with be the Intel Cell run from COCET, staffed by Anna Farley, Patrick Smith, Louisa Greenwood and Sarah Dorsey. Louisa will deal with any CP issues that may arise out of the action we take, and Sarah will be dealing with the media, so any calls from the media put them through to her. From the moment the warrants begin, all intelligence and updates are to go through Ops Comm unless there is a clear need for brevity, and then you can go officer to officer, but in those cases back date Ops Comm. Anna will liaise with me as required and will update Jane and Owen regularly, so everybody will know what is going on. If you need a further update, ring COCET. They will only know what is going on if you tell them what is going on. So there will be three major update points. One, post arrest and custody issues. Two, initial interview. And three, subsequent interviews and charging. You are to report on those points as a minimum. Any questions on that?"

With no questions coming from the team, Tom pressed on and covered communications, personal protection and the human rights of the people they were going to arrest. At the end DC Marks was the first one to talk.

"Boss. If there is anybody with Kuklin what do you want us to do?"

"Arrest them as well on suspicion of being involved."

"What about keeping them apart, can Camden do that?" asked DC Hayes.

"Yes," replied Tom.

"What about phone calls?" DC Hayes asked.

"Kuklin has his delayed until we are in. After that he can have it."

"What about a solicitor acting for more than one?" asked DC Donaldson.

"We will play that by ear, but if Kuklin's brief tries to act for him and the other four then we will object. At the Camden end one to four would be too big in any case, so we will be on strong ground there. Representing two I can live with, four and we will object, especially if they all want interpreters and are going 'no comment' ".

"What about exhibits that we may need examining as an urgent case?" DC Wilson asked.

"SDE are on standby and can get to us within a couple of hours," replied Tom.

With no more questions coming from COCET staff, DC Hallett said, "Sir, at what point do you envisage us taking over?"

"When would you like to?"

"We would like it prior to charge or at the point of charge, so we can have some input around the first round of charging."

"Agreed. But what are your feelings for remand in custody?" Tom asked. This was something he didn't want to hand over without knowing more of their intentions.

"I see it as a suitable case. They are foreign nationals with no real ties to the community and are likely to abscond. It is down to the Custody Sergeant, as you know. But it's a central London station, and they will be seeing this sort of thing regularly; so I don't envisage a problem at the station, and our remand application will be strong. We do have quite a bit of experience when it comes to Nigerian fraud type investigations and normally get a remand in custody, due to the likelihood they will abscond. The money laundering side itself backs this up. The money isn't staying in the UK, it is going outside; and although it has initially gone to Moldova we know from there it disappears behind the Iron Curtain."

"Good. We are on the same wavelength then."

That night the ten COCET team members all found it difficult to get off to sleep, some more than others. Most had more than one alarm clock set, or had set one on 'repeat'. A few increased the volume of the alarm even if failing to hear it before had never been a problem. Most had their personal 'go bags' ready packed and by the front door. Some had their keys in the fridge on top of the box of food they were due to take with them, so there would be no last minute 'headless chicken syndrome', ending up with them forgetting something else in the process.

Most married or cohabiting officers had their clothes in another room so they could dress without disturbing their sleeping loved ones. For the ones that couldn't avoid it, male officers had shaved and showered the night before to save time, and left their electric shaver in the kitchen to deal with the small amount of growth that would still appear over the short night. Each got up at a different time, depending on time and distance factors, and how they dealt with early starts personally. Some got straight up, washed, dressed and went straight out of the door. Sleepy, but ready for work and not really hungry, just grabbing a coffee from one of the many outlets within London. Some needed a light breakfast, some needed something more substantial before they left.

DC Donaldson's wife set her alarm an hour before his and cooked him a full English breakfast before he left his house that day, something she had always done for him on early starts. Tom's routine had been the same for years. Although, when younger, he would have included himself in the 'last minute' brigade, he now identified the time by which he needed to leave his front door, then got up an hour before that. He always shaved, showered, dressed and then ate a light cereal breakfast, followed by a cup of tea. The whole process took just under an hour, and allowed him to wake up and think about the coming day's events. His brain, through this process, got into gear well before he was at work, and he was able to identify possible problems or obstacles that could present themselves as the day unfolded; and crucially, he would plan a necessary solution. This day was no exception; and as he entered inner London and became stationary at traffic lights, he quickly noted down in his counsel book solutions to problems that had been popping up in his head as he travelled towards Southwark Police Station. It was mainly logistical problem solving, but experience told him that poor logistics was the one thing that could cause, what was otherwise a flawless operation, to disintegrate into a counterproductive mess during a debrief.

DC Donaldson's wife had slept in another bedroom on this occasion so as not to disturb her husband when she got up at 4am to prepare his breakfast. So when both officers entered the Heathrow Airport terminal and DC Marks announced, "I'm 'Hank Marvin' Archie, I've got to get something to eat right now, do you want something?"

Archie's reply was, "Just a tea, Owen."

Both of them had decided to get to the airport early and had set up a meeting with one of the shift officers responsible for patrolling the terminal. They found him waiting near the agreed meeting point. DC Donaldson identified himself by revealing his Police warrant card and undertook the introductions, as DC Marks stood back and demolished a hot bacon roll within seconds.

The uniformed Metropolitan Police Officer made an enquiry over his radio, and then said, "He hasn't gone through security control, so we can go there now if you want. If you have a picture I can help you look for him."

Archie produced a surveillance 'still' that had been blown up, and although as a result the image was a bit grainy, it was good enough to pick out their target, even amongst the thousands of people that would pass them by. The officer held the photograph and stared at it for around twenty seconds, allowing his memory bank to fill with identifying parts of the person. He filtered in certain parts of the face and facial features so that he could quickly identify the person amongst the constantly moving mass of people from all over the world.

"Do you know if he will check in baggage?" the officer asked, handing back the photograph.

"No, we don't," replied Archie.

"In that case, as the shift can't spare anybody else, we will do best to monitor the security check-in entrance. Once we have him, I can get the airline to tell me if he checked in baggage; and if so, I can arrange for it to be pulled and seized. You can order footage and statements later if you need it."

Both COCET officers agreed it was a good plan, and the group of three made their way to the security entrance. The COCET officers positioned themselves on both sides of the hall so that the whole hallway leading to the check-in area was covered. The uniform officer stood close to the entrance way, far enough away from the plain clothes officers so they would not appear connected. As the hallway became busy, both Archie and Owen blended into the background and were able to remain covert, even when they had to adjust their position to gain a view of a single person hidden behind a large group of people. Although it required constant concentration, the people that passed through this mainly domestic and EU destination terminal were from a varied cultural background, and both officers naturally adapted to concentrating solely on white males. As the minutes went by, the uniform officer began to wonder if this was going to be just another 'no show' bit of police intelligence, when Archie spotted the target from a distance away. Enough distance for him to walk over naturally to Owen, inform him, and then back to the uniform officer to do the same.

Three sets of law enforcement hands landed on Kuklin at the same time, stopping him dead in his tracks. Although the ambient noise level of the terminal was fairly high at that moment, Kuklin couldn't hear anything as he struggled to take in what was being done and said. Archie and Owen had agreed that whoever spotted him first would get the arrest, so Kuklin's brain only began to register the position he was in as Archie stood in front of him, showed him his warrant card, and identified himself as a Police Detective attached to the Combined Online Child Exploitation Taskforce.

As the words 'Online' and 'Child' sank into his consciousness, his brain, which had already been in freeze mode, went quickly into flight mode, and he began to pull away from the grip of the two officers that held him. As he pulled away, their grip increased; and he in turn pulled harder until it became a full-on fight to get away. It quickly led to DC Marks and the uniform officer bringing Kuklin down to the ground as they struggled to contain him.

Archie stood above the group, smiling at his mate struggling on the ground, took out his set of 'quick cuffs' and attached one end to the wrist of Kuklin that was being held and wrestled with by the uniform officer. A passerby, who was witnessing the whole event, wondered how on earth the officer was going to get the other end of the handcuff on a person who was so strong and intent on escaping. His mouth began to fall open in horror, as both the uniform officer and the other plain clothes detective who had been struggling so hard, suddenly, and at the same time, let go of their prey as if they had been commanded to do so by some unseen fourth person.

The offender was surely going to get away, and indeed the moment he realised that he was not being held on either side Kuklin made a break for it. Archie, who had been trained in these situations, had other ideas. He held the other side of the handcuff and twisted it a full rotation to his right, just as Kuklin was about to get up and run for it. The action turned Kuklin onto his knees as the pain to his wrist increased in line with his attempt to get away. The pain was just bearable if he didn't move. So he didn't, and he became trapped like a tiger in a cage. He looked up at the source of his pain and for the first time Archie saw the sheer malevolence and hatred on the face of the person he had been seeking to arrest. Although he was in charge, he felt a chill travel through his body and it had emanated from the face of Kuklin. His face was full of pure evil and venom. The witness saw the other two officers get up and even take their eyes off their prey, as they brushed themselves down and adjusted their clothing. Only then did they both grab Kuklin's free arm and place behind it him to attach the other end of the handcuff. Archie broke eye contact, went behind Kuklin, checked the tension of the handcuffs and, once satisfied, locked them so they could not tighten up on his wrist and cause injury. Kuklin, who was considerably taller than Archie, peered down still full of hatred as Archie reappeared in front of him saying, "Andrei Demitriyevich Kuklin, I am arresting you for deliberately and knowingly distributing or causing to be distributed, indecent photographs of children, contrary to section one of the Protection of Children Act 1978. I am also arresting you for Concealing Criminal Property, in that you concealed, transferred and removed cash made from your criminal actions. You do not have to say anything. But it may harm your defence if you do not mention when questioned something that you later rely on in court. Anything that you do say may be given in evidence."

Archie waited for a few seconds to see if he was going to get a reply. Although he knew Kuklin was not a British National, he suspected he could speak and understand English but would play the game of 'I can't speak English', like the vast majority of others in his position. The Police had long taken the approach that if there was any hint that the prisoner couldn't understand they would get an interpreter, and they had developed a procedure that would cause Kuklin to be arrested and cautioned again as soon the interpreter was present. For now, though, it was all about safe transportation and custody procedures. Archie said, "I am going to search you and put my hands in your pockets to make sure you don't have anything that could harm us or you."

Kuklin, who hadn't even blinked during the arrest procedure, continued his venomous stare; which Archie met, only letting go to begin the preliminary search. The procedure didn't reveal much, other than some loose cash, two mobile phones, and a set of keys. Next was the carry-on luggage that was now at their feet. Archie picked it up, unzipped it, and looked inside. There were items of clothing neatly packed which he removed to find that the rest of the holdall was full of cash. He replaced the clothing and said to Kuklin, "The holdall has a large amount of cash in it which I believe are the proceeds of crime. I am seizing it as evidence, do you have anything to say?"

Kuklin continued his evil stare during the search of him and the luggage; something that was now starting to concern Archie who was going to be partly responsible for interviewing him. The interview procedure generally went better if there was some form of rapport between the interviewer and the interviewee, and he was beginning to suspect that might be something they would never achieve with this offender.

"Have it your way!" stated Archie, who moved Owen out of the way, took hold of Kuklin firmly, and marched him off.

CHAPTER EIGHT

Meanwhile, ADS King and her team were parked around Albany Street Police Station. The local Metropolitan Police van crew was present, the driver of which had brought with him an 'Enforcer', a Police battering ram which he was hoping to get the chance to use. Jane King's mobile rang just as she got to open the plastic lid of a hot cup of tea. She opened the car door, placing the polystyrene cup on the ground. Without the lid it was not so rigid, causing her to spill some of the hot contents on her hand. Shaking the tea off, she used her other hand to answer the call.

"Jane King."

"They have Kuklin and the cash, it's a go, let me know you are all safe by text, then it's over to the Ops Comm."

"Roger, Boss."

Jane poured her tea on the ground and informed her team to move to their prearranged positions around the address in Stanhope Street. The journey was short, as the crow flies, but it still took around fifteen minutes to get there, and a further ten until everybody was in position. With all units confirmed in place Jane, search warrant in hand, led the team to the door of 61A, Stanhope Street. Jane and DC Mitchell Hayes, both in plain clothes, stood directly in front of the door whilst members of the search team, all in uniform, lined up to the left of the door; out of sight from both the 'spy hole' and the two windows that faced outwards.

Mitchell pressed the doorbell but heard nothing, so he immediately knocked hard on the door three times. All radios had been placed in silent mode or turned down, and, although Stanhope Street was busy

Jane could hear herself breathing as she waited for a response. After about 30 seconds had passed, and with nothing heard, she looked at Mitchell, who took the cue and knocked again, but five times, and just as hard. Within moments sounds could be heard from inside the flat, as someone came to the door but stopped short of opening it.

On the other side Dobre Bakaly was still dressing as he peered through the small aperture in the door. His brain registered the man and a woman outside and he pulled away from the door to finish buttoning his trousers. He then took another look, this time his eyes more in focus as he studied their dress and demeanour. He looked left and right of the door as far as the wide angle lens allowed, but saw no one. He studied the woman and then the man. They were both official looking, with one carrying a briefcase and the other a leather folder. They could be Police, but they could also be other government or council officials, he thought. The rest were asleep, and he was unsure what to do. He was pretty sure they were not gang related, so they would just go away if he did nothing. Which is what he did. Both Jane and Mitchell knew there was someone there, but played dumb; and Mitchell knocked again. As he did this, Jane turned her back on the door and whispered to APS Collins, "Get the Enforcer!"

APS Collins called the van crew on a Met radio he had been given, and within moments the van driver arrived short of the door, having passed under the window so as not to be seen. Jane remained with her back to the door and whispered to the PC with the battering ram, "Are you ready?"

"Yes."

"After Three. One, Two, Three!" With that Jane took a step forward, and Mitchell a step back.

Bakaly had just put his face back up to the door when he saw a large uniformed Police Officer come into view, and then the biggest bang he had ever heard shattered the peace of the moment. Bakaly reeled backwards, as the door came crashing open and flew past him to hit the wall on his left. Such a loud and sudden bang caused his brain not to register sound, as both uniform and the plain clothed Police came rushing in, some past him and further into the flat. One grabbed him and placed him up against the wall in the hallway. It took a full ten minutes for Jane to restore order to the premises and get all four men in the flat dressed and in one room, so that the search officer responsible for videoing events could begin.

"I am Acting Detective Sergeant Jane King from the Combined Online Child Exploitation Taskforce and I have a warrant to search these premises issued under the Protection of Children Act 1978. Who is in charge of the flat?"

All the four young men she was speaking to understood her, but remained silent; giving no indication that they did understand her.

"I will ask you once again, who is in charge, who is the lead tenant amongst you?"

With nothing forthcoming, Jane moved straight to plan B.

"Mitchell, you're up," she said authoritatively, not taking her eyes off the group of four.

Mitchell went straight to the one that had hidden behind the door and beckoned him to stand, which he eventually did.

"I am arresting you for deliberately or knowingly being involved in the distribution of indecent images of children contrary to the Protection of Children Act 1978. You are also being arrested for Concealing Criminal Property, in that you have knowingly transferred the proceeds of crime to another, contrary to the Proceeds of Crime Act 2002. You do not have to say anything. But it may harm your defence if you do not mention when questioned something which you later rely on in court. Anything you do say may be given in evidence."

Mitchell waited to see if he was going to get a reply, and after a short period of nothing being said, a man he would later find out to be Dobre Bakaly was searched, handcuffed and removed from the room by two operational support officers. Mitchell repeated the same process with the other three men until all of them had been arrested and cautioned. With not a word from any of the suspects, the operational support team leader, whose officers were responsible for the search of the premises, guessed they wouldn't be getting any assistance from the occupants of the address.

Jane looked at APS Collins, and said, "Over to you, how do you want to play this?"

"The video stays on. The best course, I think, would be to take them one at a time into the bedrooms to see if we can identify which bedroom belongs to which prisoner."

"OK, good idea."

Jane texted Tom, "In, safe, all arrested, starting search." She then rang the Ops Comm and updated them. Whilst still in conversation with Anna Farley, APS Collins came back into the room and shook his head. Pulling the mobile phone into her shoulder, Jane said, "Keep one, the one that came to the door, and get the rest transported to Camden."

As operational support moved into a well rehearsed method of working, the Met officers arrived and began the procedure of transporting the prisoners to Camden Police Station, ensuring that they were kept apart.

Tom and his team made their way to 91c Purbrook Estate. The uniformed officers quickly worked out how to stay out of view whilst Tom and DC Wilson went to the door. Even though it was relatively early, their presence was immediately felt by other residents of the estate. There was no reply to repeated knocking, and after a short period Tom looked through the windows and letterbox and could neither see nor hear anything. He went to the neighbouring flat and knocked on the door, this time not so loudly. Within seconds the door opened just a crack to reveal two security chains and an Indian woman wearing a Sari. Tom immediately caught a strong scent of Indian spices and curry.

"I'm a Police Officer," Tom said, revealing his warrant card.

"Do you know anything about the man who lives next door? We would like to speak to him."

The Indian woman looked at the card and then wobbled her head from left to right but said nothing.

Tom knew a number of Indian police officers, so knew that her head sign could mean a number of things.

"Can you speak English?"

Again the woman wobbled her head without saying anything. He heard a man's voice, which caused the woman to smile and close the door. Within a few seconds it opened again; this time with a much older man at the door, probably the Grandfather. He immediately spoke a sentence in a language that Tom didn't understand, then shut the door. This also shut off the aroma, which by now had the two of them thinking about a 'greasy spoon'.

Tom returned to 91c and examined the door and its frame, weighing up the amount of damage it would cause to get in. On paper, the intelligence indicated there was more than one staying at the address; but physical surveillance hadn't confirmed that. In fact, it indicated that only Kuklin lived at the address; and from what he could see, that all confirmed what his gut feeling was telling him. Which was that there was nobody home.

He rang the Ops Comm, updated them, then rang DC Marks. As he waited for the call to be answered, he watched as a number of what only could only be described as 'spotters' emerge from a number of flat doors, taking up position and watching everything Tom and his team did.

"DC Marks here," Tom heard in his ear.

"How far have you got with Kuklin?"

"He has been booked in. Not saying anything. Waiting for the interpreter to arrive so we can go through this all again and get past the custody phase. He had the cash in walk on baggage."

"That's good news. What about house keys? Did he have any in his possession?"

"Yes, Boss."

"What's his demeanour like?"

"Not good. In fact, he hasn't said a thing. Both me and Archie reckon he is the most frightening prisoner we have ever had to deal with." "In what way?" Tom asked, surprised by the real concern in Owen's voice.

"We can't really put a finger on it, but it is just the way he looks at you. It's real hatred, real venom. He just exudes evil. Transporting him for the search isn't a good idea, Boss."

141

"OK, get the keys to me."

"On my way now, travelling time."

Tom checked his watch and knew it would be a while. "Two on the door please," Tom said to PS Ford the operational support team leader. "The rest follow me, we will plot up away so the locals don't get too panicked, and await the keys."

The rest of that day went the way of most multiple arrests of foreign nationals. A long slow slog, as Police procedure moved forward a bit at a time. Tom's team concluded its search by lunchtime, and had regrouped for a late 'MET 999' breakfast at Southwark Police Station. The search had confirmed that Kuklin was living there alone and had few belongings, apart from two laptops which had been seized for forensic examination. After the hearty, but possibly a little greasy breakfast, DC Wilson took possession of all exhibits and accompanying statements, and together with Tom left for the custody block at Heathrow, leaving the support officers to make their way home.

Jane and her team found significantly more belongings at their address in Stanhope Street, but the only thing of real evidential worth was an envelope containing a significant number of bank debit cards. Passports were found in each bedroom, matching the persons arrested. But, to cover all eventualities, scenes of crime officers were called to fingerprint the bedrooms, and specifically the one with the envelope in it. Her team were also back at Camden in time for a late '999' breakfast. In fact, it took so long for an interpreter to be found to match that of the duty solicitor, the Stanhope team had completed all their exhibits and statements long before it was necessary to begin the interview stage. The events at Heathrow and Camden virtually mirrored each other. As DC Donaldson, and DC Hallett began their first interview with Andre Demitriyevich Kuklin, DC Hayes and DC Cartwright were beginning their first interview with a person they now knew to be Nicolae Vartik. As the first taped interview got underway at Heathrow, Tom was in the station's car park being interviewed by Sky TV's crime correspondent, Martin Brunt. The interview took no longer than a few minutes, and with Sarah orchestrating the events Tom felt remarkably pleased with the course of the questioning and the outcome. COCET was set to be revealed nationally and then globally later in the day with the announcement of GOPOL. Their first arrests were already made, involving a Russian organised crime gang, who were distributing child abuse images on a commercial basis and laundering the proceeds through the London Banking system. It made good copy, and would sit nicely with the Chief's declaration of war on the internet abusers from Interpol's headquarters in Lyons.

Before returning to COCET with Sarah Dorsey, Tom went to the custody block to find that Kuklin was being returned to his cell. It was the first time he had set eyes on him. As he approached the group which included the solicitor and interpreter, Archie said, "Hi Boss, the interpreter has said she can't represent him, we are going to have to get another one."

Tom looked at the interpreter clearly with a 'Why?' look on his face, but she just looked away and walked past them to the main custody booking in area, where she spoke to the custody officer briefly. He in turn made a note on the computerised record of Kuklin, and then let her out through the heavy entrance door by way of a remote switch underneath his desk. Tom looked back to the group and caught Kuklin's stare. Owen and Archie were right, it was pure hatred and venom. Tom met the stare briefly but then broke it off.

"What's that all about?"

DC Hallett took hold of Kuklin's arm and returned him to his cell, with Kuklin keeping his stare fixed on the person he now knew was the head of the operation against him, memorising as many features as he could in the short space of time allowed. With the cell door locked DC Hallett then rejoined Archie, Tom and the solicitor to catch the end of the conversation.

"Whatever was being said between the two of them I have no idea, but about 20 minutes into the interview she broke it off. I can't wait around, call me when you get another one and either I or another duty lawyer will turn up." With that the duty solicitor signed herself out and left.

"Did she give any reason whatsoever?"

Archie replied, "Nope, but she was scared, really scared; and you could see that change in her after the consultation. She was shaking. Whatever was said in there has scared her off. She spoke only once afterwards, saying that we will find it difficult to get another interpreter to act on this case."

"Get another one, I'm off to COCET and will remain there. Let us know how the next one goes."

As Tom and Sarah got back to COCET, Jane and her team had completed one interview each on their prisoners. All of them requested solicitors, they all needed interpreters, and they had all gone 'No comment'. They were preparing for final interviews and would then wait to see the outcome of the interview of Kuklin. Tom and the rest of COCET meanwhile waited for Sky News to come on television. Sam had purchased three TVs; one each for his office, the main office and the conference room. It wasn't long before the breaking news tape at the bottom of the screen started to alert viewers of a breaking story involving a new Police Unit called GOPOL, and its operational arm, a UK elite squad called COCET. It was a surreal situation, watching their part in the UK law enforcement scene being put in front of their eyes; and Tom could see the pride on the faces of his staff. They were making history, it was their time, their moment. Eventually they would all move on, and others would follow to pick up the mantle, and they would in turn do it differently. But, those others would only get that chance as a result of this team. His team. He let it seep in, and left for his office moments before he came on TV.

Three hours went by before Archie, DC Hallett, the same duty solicitor and a new interpreter recommenced interviewing Kuklin. His attitude remained the same, and both officers wondered if the new interpreter would go the same way as the first. It was another female, a young Russian. She looked on edge as Archie explained the standard tape interview procedures, translating each sentence to Kuklin, only when the interpreter stopped talking did Archie continue. As Archie got to explaining the tapes, and how one would be sealed as a master

144

copy which could only be opened on an instruction of a court, it was clear to him, DC Hallett and probably the solicitor, that more was being said between Kuklin and the interpreter. Whatever was being said by Kuklin he couldn't understand, and, unless he got a grip of this, the new interpreter might go the same way as the first. Both he, and he was sure the solicitor didn't want to have to go through this all again, and he caught a warning look from her in confirmation of what he was thinking.

"OK. Stop. We clearly don't know what you are saying. But let's make this clear. The prisoner has had his consultation with the duty solicitor, the first interpreter in my opinion was scared off as a delay tactic. The tape is going on now, I will then continue and explain the rest of the procedure and why it is being done this way. You should understand we will get everything translated."

He looked at both the interpreter and then Kuklin. He didn't get any objections from the solicitor, so he switched on the tape, finished the explanation and caution and got into the interview. It was no surprise to anybody in the room what the result of the questions was going to be. In the interviews in Camden at least the prisoners said the words, 'No comment'. Kuklin just stayed silent all the way through; just staring at Archie or DC Hallett when it was his turn to ask some questions. Both officers had prepared for the interview and had a large amount of questions to ask, but it all went quickly with Kuklin saying nothing. Two tapes later it was all done, apart from the taking of non-intimate but evidential fingerprint and DNA samples. The solicitor, who had no wish to be present for the sample taking, left again but promised to return; her interest in the case now heightened, having been made aware of who the arresting officers were and the squad they were from. Her office clerk had recorded the Sky interview with DCI Ross, and the announcement of GOPOL, which she had watched. She had a major new case and saw many possibilities coming out of it, not just for her firm, but also for herself. The interpreter, who had explained the sample taking to Kuklin, also left as quickly as she could. But before she did she whispered to DC Hallett, "You may need more than two to get your samples."

The last interview at Camden was completed 20 minutes after Archie had finished at Heathrow. Tom and the team at COCET waited as Sam sorted out the conference call from Jane and the rest of her team, who were listening on speaker phone, and Archie who was doing likewise with Owen and DC Hallett. Once they had communications in place Tom commenced.

"OK Jane, go ahead."

"'No comment' all round. We have put names to faces through their passports. The cards relate to all the accounts and were found in the bedroom of Vitaly Danshov. They all have phones which we have seized. Two, Danshov and Lachkov, have got laptops. They were both working off sticks, no phone or broadband going into the address. Each of them had over £2000 and a quantity of US dollars. Danshov had the biggest 'stash', he had over five grand in his man bag. We got section 61 orders for fingerprints and DNA, which we have done, and it was negative on fingerprints using Live Scan. We have seized all their clothing to match up with the surveillance footage from the banks. We are just waiting to hear from Owen and Archie to see if there is anything more we can put to them."

"Owen and Archie, over to you," said Tom.

"He never saw us coming. He fought to get away upon arrest. He had a bag full of cash. We haven't counted it, it's been sealed and is in the shift Inspector's safe. He had keys to the address in Purbrook and a phone which we have seized. He had virtually no cash on him apart from what was in the bag. He is one of the most evil prisoners I have ever had to deal with. He went 'no comment' and the first interpreter refused to come back. So we got another one and he tried to scare her off as well, but we got the tapes running to record what he was saying and he then shut up. It wasn't a 'no comment' interview in that he refused to utter a single word, and still hasn't. We got section 61 samples, but only after a struggle. We couldn't get mouth swabs so went for hair, we got plenty of that with good root structure. We got nothing back on his fingerprints with Live Scan as well. He is a real risk, so on the remand file we should alert the prison authority."

"DCs Cartwright and Hallett, would this be a good point to come in on this?"

"Yes, Sir," replied DC Hallett. Both James and I have worked with the custody officer at each location and have the charges loaded. We would like to take it from here with your officers now supporting us. We can take possession of all the exhibits. So, if your officers can do their statements today, that would be good. We can charge later this evening, the custody sergeants have indicated they are of a mind not to give bail due to their flight risk. I have liaised with the CPS so they can all appear together at Horseferry Road Magistrates Court, we have a good case for remand, and we have most of the evidence we need from the banking system and will get the rest within a few weeks."

"In that case, Jane, you have charge of all COCET staff, continue with the Ops Comm until the point of charge and then they will close down. Support the Fraud Squad and stand down COCET as appropriate. Jane, both you and I will be at their first appearance along with the Fraud Squad. Mitchell, I want you there as well, and also either Archie or Owen. This is our first case, it has profiled in the news and I want us to make a statement of intent to the court. So, if you need to stay overnight ring Sam, otherwise I will see you at court in the morning.

Horseferry Road Magistrates Court was one of the most famous central London Magistrates Courts; second only to the famous Bow Street Court where Tom had given evidence at a few times. It being only his second time at this court, it took him a few minutes to find the Police office where Jane, Mitchell, Archie, Owen and DC Hallett were already in attendance. The room was full of uniformed and plain clothes officers. Some were in groups, clearly discussing their cases; others were alone, reading over evidence from either a statement or an incident report book, a one-off officer's notebook which was a system used by the Metropolitan Police. Others sat alone, staring straight ahead, probably preferring to go through their evidence in their own way. As he joined his staff, the internal court loudspeaker system called for all parties in the case of Kuklin, Danshov, Lachkov,

Bakaly and Vartik to go immediately to Courtroom Six. Tom and the others made their way there and entered.

Tom saw that it was a stipendiary magistrate sitting alone, which he was pleased about. Stipendiary magistrates had been renamed District Judges for magistrates courts and could sit alone. They were only a few of them, and most of them could be found in central London. The good thing was that, from a prosecution point of view, they were very, if not exceptionally, experienced over such a wide range of crimes. So it didn't matter who the defendant managed to field by way of a defending lawyer, as the magistrate had the knowledge to even up the scales of justice. Today was probably going to be an example of that. Tom saw on the left of the courtroom a lone CPS lawyer, almost certainly overworked and underpaid, who would have read this remand hearing about an hour ago, if not later. On the right of the room sat three lawyers and their assistants. DC Hallett went to join the CPS and remained behind her, whilst Tom and the COCET officers sat at the back of the room. Tom saw the Judge look and note the presence of Tom and his staff, and the press seating area that was full, with two standing.

A few moments later Kuklin and his gang filed into a large glass cubicle to the left of where COCET were sitting, and were joined by four security staff who stood at the back of them. The four prisoners from Stanhope Street looked at Jane and Mitchell, immediately recognising them, and had some form of discussion with Kuklin, who changed his position to get a look at them. Spotting Archie, Owen and Tom, Kuklin's face changed from curious to pure hate in a split second. Kuklin locked himself in a stare with Tom and wouldn't let go. It was a strange feeling, he felt uneasy about being challenged the way he was, he wanted to maintain the stare but knew he was being watched by the bench. Inciting anger within the defendants' box was not a way to make a good impression, even if he wasn't the cause of it. So he broke off and ignored him. Out of the corner of his peripheral vision, though, he was aware that Kuklin had maintained his stance to the extent that the security staff had become aware of it and had intervened to remove Kuklin to the far side. He became abusive to the officer, only calming down when proceedings began as a court interpreter made her way to the cubicle.

None of what happened was missed by the Judge, who maintained a watch on the activities at the back of the room whilst giving and taking instructions from the court clerk in front of him. After a few minutes the Judge said something to the CPS lawyer, and then looked at the defence lawyers, causing them all to stand up.

His voice then became clear as he said, "I understand, on behalf of the Crown, you have a remand application, Ms. Barrett?"

"Yes, Sir."

"How many?"

"Five, Sir."

The Judge then looked to his left, and said, "Who is appearing for the five?"

There was a short discussion between the three lawyers and the Judge, that indicated two of them were representing the four from Stanhope Street, two each, and the third lawyer indicated he was appearing for the fifth person; Andrei Demitriyevich Kuklin. The cut of the suit and the courtroom confidence of the last lawyer was not lost on the Judge. Maybe he felt he needed to express his own authority, or maybe he wanted to send a message to the defendants, the CPS, the last lawyer, COCET or even the Press. But whichever it was, his next words balanced the scales and let everybody in the courtroom know that he was in charge.

"And who are you, Sir?" said the Judge flatly, with just a hint of equal measures of respect and indifference.

"Thomas Latham, QC, Sir."

Nice one, thought Tom.

The Judge flicked his eyes to the back of the courtroom again, assessing the Police presence and then the defendants' cubicle. He took his time doing it, all the time the QC for Kuklin was on his feet waiting for the Judge to speak.

'If you think you are adept at court room theatricals, Mr. Latham, you are about to get a master class,' Tom thought.

"Are you indeed?" said the Judge, without looking at him.

"Ms. Barrett." The Judge said, addressing her, leaving Latham on his feet; the other two lawyers had quickly sat down by this point.

"I have read the indictments, they are very serious charges, very serious indeed. Do you intend to call the officer in charge of the case?"

The CPS lawyer, who was by now back on her feet, replied, "No, Sir. But DC Hallett from Thames Valley Police is here should you wish to hear from him."

The Judge said something to his court clerk which couldn't be heard, then he looked up again at the back of room to let his previous assessment of the charges sink in. All the time Mr. Latham, QC, was still on his feet. The Judge finally looked back to the defence, and ignoring Mr. Latham and the fact he was still standing, addressed the other two lawyers, who quickly got up.

"Is it your intention to contest this remand in custody application?" He said it with more than just a hint of surprise in his voice.

Both lawyers had clearly been given their instructions, they knew the futility of their situation and their body language suggested they wished they were in another courtroom, defending another case. They kept their submission simple, stopped abruptly, and sat back down again. In the meanwhile Mr. Latham, QC, had remained on his feet. The Judge appeared reluctant to address Kuklin's lawyer, and did so without looking at him. "Do you really wish to make an application for bail, Mr. Latham?"

"Of course, Sir," Thomas Latham QC replied, incredibly; not believing that he was being questioned on his presence at court, and yet suddenly very grateful for having a chance to speak. His reply and tone, however unintentional, was perceptively picked up by the Judge, who sat back in his chair with just a hint of exasperation. Leaving Latham on his feet again, he said to the CPS lawyer, "Miss Barrett, in that case can I have the facts please?"

Latham, realising he had to adapt his style for this courtroom, sat down quickly.

With the application for remand in custody on behalf of the Crown well delivered, the only people in the room that thought the defendants had any chance of getting bail were the defendants themselves and one of their three lawyers; and Mr. Latham was the first to speak. He spent a full twenty minutes of the court's time, after which the other two spent about three minutes each, bringing the proceedings to an end. Jane watched the dynamics of the five in the cubicle as they were updated by the court interpreter.

"This is going to kick off," she whispered to Tom. The press bench thought so too and had their eyes on them.

The Judge wasted no time in summing up, leaving his decision to the very last sentence.

"All the defendants are therefore remanded in custody."

Before he could go much further Kuklin started shouting from the cubicle, causing the others to start as well. More security staff appeared, and they began to take hold of the defendants with a view to removing them. As Tom and Jane looked towards the ensuing struggle they saw Kuklin, who was not held at this point but sandwiched between the other four, bring his hands and arms up to make the shape of a rifle. With his right hand he cocked the make believe rifle, and fired in the direction of Jane and Tom. Both officers' eyes made contact with Kuklin and he never let go until he was bundled down the steps to the cells.

Tom treated the team to a breakfast at a nearby well known London cafe which featured in the film Layer Cake, which he hadn't seen. But Jane had, and had since fallen in love with the main actor.

"We are at the same table, I think." Jane suddenly announced.

They all ate some form of fried English breakfast, stopping only to discuss the courtroom events between mouthfuls. The rest of team hadn't seen the gesture from Kuklin, but it was playing on her mind, and at the first opportunity she brought it up.

"Boss. That guy has got me worried. He's capable of it, don't you think?"

Tom had been concerned about it too, but had quickly consigned it to the past.

"Look at this logically. How're they going to know where we live? How're they going to find out? How're they going to get to us, they are locked up?"

"But what if he gets bail?"

"Do you really think he will?"

Jane looked away, and remained silent; but she was worried, and Tom could sense it.

"Would it help if I got SOCO to fit a panic alarm?"

"Yes." Jane replied immediately. It was something; better than nothing, she thought.

Pentonville Prison had broken the Russian team of five up, but they were all on remand in the same prison, so it wasn't long before they all met up; long enough to undertake a 'post mortem' of how they were caught. It was during this discussion that two large and heavily tattooed men arrived at the door of the cell. Dobre Bakaly, who wasn't doing as well as the others, started to tremble, thinking they were going to be attacked for being 'pederasts'.

"Which one of you is Andrei?"

Kuklin was weighing up the possibilities of the five of them taking the two men. But his gut feeling told him that if they wanted him they would have just come in and started.

"I am."

The one who had spoken, and in what they all thought was perfect English, suddenly spoke fluent Russian.

"Остальные вон!"

With that order, Bakaly was the first out of the cell without a second glance, leaving Kuklin alone in the cell with the two unknown, but clearly Russian, men. One of them reached inside his trousers to his groin area and produced a mobile phone. Kuklin, who had begun to think he was about to be killed, breathed a sigh of relief at the sight of the phone.

"есть один номер, кольцо это, у вас есть одна минута," said the man, offering him the mobile phone. Kuklin took it, quickly found the sole number and rang it, wondering how much this one minute would cost him in the long run. As the phone was answered he recognised the voice of his 'Pakhan', who immediately said, "Kak?"

Kuklin didn't really know how he had been caught, and told him that. "Не знаю."

"Насколько плохо?" his Boss immediately asked, wanting to know how bad the situation was. Kuklin knew that it wasn't that bad in real terms. His 'Pakhan' had many operations going on at the same time; and compared to his Drugs, Human Trafficking and Online Fraud operations this particular loss would not be great. It was the loss of himself, and the loss of the others, that would really hurt. It would take time to replace them all.

"просто мы и один платеж." Kuklin replied, letting him know what he had just been thinking.

The 'Pakhan' said, "Я вас вызволю. Кто полиция?"

The directness of the statement took Kuklin by surprise. Only the other day he had been thinking about getting out. Now he alone was being offered a way out. A way out that would inevitably draw him further in. Giving the officers' names, that was an easy one. He could have them. He couldn't care less about their lives and would be happy to put a bullet in their heads himself. A few days ago he had found it hard to comprehend that sort of action. Maybe this was his life. Maybe it was also his future. He had no other option but to tell him what he wanted to know.

"Росс является лидером, а Кинг — вторая, полиция Долины Темзы."

The phone went dead, which was picked up by the two men guarding the door. The man placed the mobile phone back inside his underpants then both of them left without a word being said. After a few seconds Danshov, Lackhov, Vartik and Bakaly returned to Kuklin's cell to find out they were all on their own. They had been cast adrift by Kuklin's 'Pakhan'.

CHAPTER NINE

"The press just can't get enough of GOPOL, Interpol's media chief has even allocated two permanent staff to it," Niall said.

"It's getting huge coverage here as well. Sarah has been busy every day on requests for interviews, fly on the wall type stuff. I guess it's new territory for them. Some of the papers are taking it too far with this 'wall' of names. It will end in grief somewhere down the line."

"You mean vigilante type stuff?"

"Yeah. You can pretty much guarantee somebody will take the law into their own hands thinking they have the public behind them to do it. So what's the news on Visser?" Tom asked.

"They have heaped on the extra charges and they expect him to go guilty. But if he doesn't, they may need a court appearance from Jane, or possibly even you."

"OK. No problems there."

"They think he is probably good for a further intelligence debrief now. But, as there's so much riding on it, they think it's better to wait a while and let him reach out to them. If he doesn't, then they will pay him a visit."

"Keep on top of it, Niall."

"Will do. Listen, I heard about Jane and Kuklin. How is she dealing with it?"

"Well, alright I guess. But it has spooked her, enough for her to have a panic alarm fitted. It was just Russian bravado, Niall."

"Tom, these guys don't think twice in their own country, so why should they in yours? They don't play by your rules. Bejesus, they even scare the crap out of some our own hardened criminals. Did you see him do it?"

"Yeah. He did it towards us."

"So where were you sitting?" Niall asked quickly, with concern in his voice.

"We were next to each other."

"Who was closest to him?"

Tom, who now felt this was turning into an interrogation, could also see where Niall was going with it.

"It was to the both of us. If others had been there it would have been to them," Tom replied, in a tone implying that he didn't really want to hear any more about it. Niall picked it up, but had other ideas.

"So you were closest. So it could have been, and probably was, meant for you, being the officer in charge of it all."

"He has no reason to know that I am in charge of COCET."

"Come on, Tom! Who are you kidding here?" Niall replied, incredulously.

Tom thought about his last comment, and how naive it probably was.

"Yes. It could have been to me alone, but I was there; and it was done to us both. The guy is evil; but he is operating here, not in Russia. I will promise to take some precautions!"

"Just watch your back, Tom. These guys are for real."

"Will do. Look, on Visser, this is our major lead into Michael and whoever is really behind all that. We are starting the build up phase on Operation Resolve. If it goes according to my plan I will need you personally to brief the CEO of WebHostTwelve, I'm guessing within the next few weeks."

"No problems. Just let me know. Bye for now, and watch your back!"

Tom immediately redialled Jane's extension, and within moments she arrived in his office along with Anna Farley and Patrick Smith.

"From the work done earlier by Patrick and Owen," said Jane, "we identified Philip Anthony Thompson. Building on that, we now know that he lives in Stockton-On-Tees with his mother on a council estate. I have set up an initial meeting for tomorrow with a Detective Sergeant

Becky Drysdale from the Force Intelligence Bureau, who is based at Police HQ in Middlesborough. She is keen to hear what we have to say; but has indicated that we will have to get an audience with the Detective Chief Superintendent for anything major to be authorised."

"How're we getting there?"

"Unless you want to drive, train. Sam is working on it."

"Train it is. Go on."

"Anna and Patrick have been working hard on the rest of the data from SDE, and have come up with four targets, all within the UK. They are all members of 'childscentcafe'. Anna, can you go through them?" Jane said, handing the briefing to her.

"Sure. The first is John Michael Black, aged 34, from Walsall, near Birmingham, West Midlands. Lives alone, welder by occupation and works at a company in Walsall. No previous convictions and no intelligence held on him on any databases we have access to. He appears to have been a member for over two years and he has more than one identity. He has 'buddy' status under one, and 'senior buddy' under the other. Our Intel package is ready to go, and we have spoken in advance to the CPU for the area and they are willing to undertake a search warrant."

Anna stopped deliberately for questioning.

"That's perfect, Anna. Please carry on," replied Tom, thinking just how good this girl was at anticipating what was required.

"Second, Arthur George Thomas, 44, from Blackwood in Gwent. He is manager of a shop in Blackwood. Divorced with two children, both of whom live with his former wife, who lives in Newport, Gwent. He is remarried, has no children by his current marriage, and this wife has none either. Again, nothing known by way of previous convictions or intelligence. He has been a member for 15 months and has 'Buddy' status under one identity. We can't find any more, but that doesn't mean he hasn't got more. The Force indicates that they will assist as long as they are given some notice. Intel pack ready to go."

Anna paused to look at Tom, who was making notes. Looking up, he just nodded.

"Third. Brian Leitch from Redhill in Surrey, aged 49, married with two children both of whom have left home. We have details of who and where they currently are if it is needed. He is an insurance agent for a local company. Again, clean for convictions and intelligence. He is a 'senior buddy' and has two identities, but appears to use only one. He has been a member for just over three years. Surrey are very keen to assist, and again the dissemination pack is ready to go."

Tom stopped Anna's flow, saying, "Get the packs disseminated today, please. I would like them all done on the same day, but that is a 'nice to have', rather than a need. So if they could do them within two weeks or as soon as they can, that would be fabulous. Carry on."

"The last is Simon Clark from Chelmsford in Essex. 27 years of age, software engineer, lives with his girlfriend we think, or she is just a flat mate renting a room there. Works in Brentwood. No convictions or intelligence. He has been a member for four years and is a 'member support admin'. Being a software engineer, he will probably have a high level of IT awareness. Essex say they will undertake action, but they want notice and say that their forensics department just can't take the work. Jane has spoken to Dr. Sue Tay and they can do it."

"Do we know how long the other departments will take?"

"No," replied Jane, thinking that was something that she should have thought about.

"In that case, get an assessment. We can wait a few weeks, but not a few months. If need be I will pay for Sue and Nick to do all the work."

"Is that it?"

"Yes," Jane and Anna replied together, with Patrick just nodding.

"OK. Get them off and let's get them done a.s.a.p. Patrick, well done for getting that work done in the time period."

As the taxi pulled up to the outer gates of Cleveland Police Headquarters in Ladgate Lane, Middlesborough, the driver, who must have done this trip before, quickly found his way through the sprawling complex and stopped at a large set of glass double doors, which Jane could see led through to an open foyer. Having signed in, and whilst waiting for Detective Sgt. Becky Drysdale to arrive, Tom began reading a TV screen that was playing Cleveland Police statistics on a loop. He was waiting to see if they included child protection figures when his attention was broken by a female voice behind him.

"DCI Ross?"

He turned. "Yes?"

"DS Drysdale, Sir. Nice to meet you," the officer said, offering a handshake. Tom took it then introduced Jane, after which DS Drysdale took them to her office which was at least a three minute walk away. Tom saw the interaction between what he expected were two female career Police Officers, both detectives. A rare commodity in any Police Force, and a bit like buses, there are none in sight then two come along at once. They engaged in eager and happy conversation, clearly nothing to do with why they were there. It carried on during the making of tea whilst he waited alone in DS Drysdale's office. As the two Detective Sergeants arrived back with the tea they were still in deep conversation, and he picked up the topic of Police Osprey exams.

Becky sitting behind her desk opposite Tom and Jane, said, "Right. First of all, I have heard all about COCET. Who hasn't? I am fascinated as to why you are here, tell me all!"

During the next 15 to 20 minutes he gave a short but succinct briefing on Operation Hope, the formation of COCET and GOPOL, Operation Ascent and finally Operation Resolve.

"We would like to undertake a similar operation to Hope on the users of 'childscentcafe', although this is a web based network, so the tactics will not be identical.

"In this investigation I want to seize the server in advance, whilst at the same time assuming the identities of a number of users, and specifically Thompson's. We won't know the extent of the membership until we get a copy, but we estimate that there will be thousands. Our experience shows that a major incident team will be required to handle the quantity of data that will be generated from our activities, and specifically the dissemination of the intelligence.

"Which is why we are here. Thompson is living within your Police district, the server is in Holland, and we are a small squad which does not have the capability of handling this amount of intelligence without support. Yes, we are located within Thames Valley Police, but we are made up of staff from various agencies, not just TVP. So I was hoping to secure your support on this current operation."

"Right. Well, I will be responsible for putting the business case across, and you have my support. But ultimately it will be a decision for the Detective Chief Super. Give me a couple of days to network this in Force, I will then put a business case together and get an audience with the Boss. He is an open guy, so I am confident he will support it. The major investigation teams are always busy, but I am sure they would love to get involved in something different like this."

Tom, who had been assessing Becky as she spoke, thought she was a forthright, no-nonsense person, probably as a result of living and working where she did. Cleveland was, in general, a working class area which had, over the years, seen a decline in industry with associated job losses and little reinvestment. The evidence of that was everywhere on.the drive from the station to Police Headquarters. As a young cop she would have had to adapt quickly to the changing times. Also, from the presence of the photographs of the two young children on her desk, she was a mother as well as a busy intelligence officer and manager. She would have to be committed to keeping all the bases covered at home and work. Tom thought she must be in her late thirties or early forties. What was evident was that she was open, and clearly not put off by something that was ultimately going to cause her a great deal of additional work.

"Have you got any time imperative issues that I need to be aware of?" Becky concluded.

"Once we have a copy of the server and have access to the contents in readable form, then yes; at that point we will have something tangible that we will need to be seen to act upon. Although that maybe two or three weeks away."

"I can have this sorted by early next week. Will you be able to travel here again on, say, Wednesday or Thursday to see the Boss?"

"Yes, of course," replied Tom, thinking this had all gone a lot quicker than he had expected. In fact, just over an hour later he and Jane were back at the station and boarding an earlier train back to London.

2005hrs ICT, Bangkok, Thailand

At the same time, a person who was never far from the thoughts of both Tom and Jane was in a cab on the way to Don Mueang Airport in Bangkok. It was a long drive from Pattaya to Don Mueang. Not the sort of distance he would call long in Holland, but long in Thailand. Add to that the wait at the airport, even if the flight was on time, the round trip would take most of the evening. The driver wanted a break in both directions, something that came as part of negotiating the price, and now they were stuck in traffic, probably about 10 kilometres away from the airport. At the rate they were moving the flight would have landed by the time they arrived. He had got somewhat acclimatised to the temperature since being in Thailand, but the air-con in the taxi was virtually non-existent. That, coupled with the cheap vinyl upholstery of the seats, meant he wanted to just get to the airport, get out of the taxi and into the airport terminal.

He was however, looking forward to meeting Mr. B, and to finding out more about the two new acquisitions and the recent arrest of someone who knew a little about their activities.

'Nothing to worry about,' Mr. B had said. But all the same, he still wanted to fully understand the nature of the arrest so he could protect himself.

As the taxi slowly made its way a few hundred metres at a time, he let his thoughts wander to what was in store over the next few days for himself and Mr. B. There was going to be some blood-letting that was for sure, so he needed to get in first before the merchandise was spoilt. He wanted his mind and body to be in balance, but that only occurred when he had taken action. The 'patients', as he now liked to call them, were simply there to serve him and his needs. One day they would be like him and need the same. They just didn't know it yet.

As they were travelling back to London Jane got a text from the Fraud Squad and DC Hallett, notifying her of another bail application by Kuklin listed for that Friday at Horseferry Magistrates Court. It abruptly brought her attention back to the panic alarm and her concerns around him. "Boss, Kuklin has another bail application on

Friday, time not fixed but in the afternoon, do you want me to go?"

Tom's immediate thoughts were, *'What the heck! How has he managed to get another bail application so quickly? What's changed in Kuklin's world to warrant this?'*

He looked at Jane and saw no level of concern. But that didn't mean it wasn't there. He didn't want her going on her own, but then he had done enough running around this week already, and DC Hallett would be there as well.

"Yeah, OK. Link up with DC Hallett though, and go with him. If he falls out for any reason let me know."

"Sure thing."

As he went to bed that night Tom felt strangely alone and in need of someone to be with. He'd been going to bed alone for ages, so what was different about tonight? He tried to work it through and nothing really explained it, other than the fact that he was still awaiting to hear his fate from Fiona. He recalled her movements, and with Friday not far away he risked a text. He got no reply, but with the message sent, his mind got some relief. He dropped off to sleep, only to wake at around 5am to find that he'd been fighting again with the unseen ghosts in his mind, all of whom had disappeared in the split second he awoke. Fighting to claw back some of the quickly receding memories in an attempt to understand why he was getting the nightmares, his grasp of the strands in his subconscious vanished in the moment his brain became aware of his surroundings. His failure, as usual, left him with just the mess of the bed as the only thing linking him to the truth he sought.

Tom travelled to London with Jane for the bail application. DC Hallett had pulled out, although he had a pretty valid reason. An anniversary, a hotel booking and leave submitted six months before. Tom couldn't argue with that. Maybe, if he had been more dedicated to his own work life balance, he would still be living with his family and doing things like that. His thoughts fell to Struan, his son, and wondered what he was doing. He would be at school by now. Was he thinking of his father as he was now thinking of his son?

He left those thoughts and transferred to others that had all the hallmarks of being just as painful, if not yet. Fiona had responded, and with him going to London they had agreed to meet. She had given no hint of what was to come, but it was decision time and he needed to know, and know now.

The traffic was heavy and he pulled away from his thoughts and concentrated on the fact that he had started to overtake about five minutes ago and was still in the outside lane. The traffic was so heavy that the lane had become full. They were all travelling at least 10 miles an hour over the speed limit, and it took careful signalling and patience to transfer to the centre lane. They arrived in central London just after 2pm; and whilst Jane paid the congestion charge Tom drove straight to the court. He then made his way out from there to find a parking space that wasn't controlled in some form. He found one in Maunsel Street, although it was on payment. They both went straight to court and found from the listing sheet that the bail application had not been assigned a court room. A quick enquiry with the CPS office and they knew it wouldn't be heard before 3.30pm.

"So, last thing of the day. Come on, let's get a bite to eat at the Regency Cafe."

Jane, who was really hungry, just loved the cafe and the standard of breakfast; and she fancied the pants off Daniel Craig, so for her it was a no brainer.

"I'm in," she replied with a grin.

As they made their way out of the court Tom took in the members of the public that were there. No matter which court you attended, it was always a mixture of the worst and best of society. The best stood out by their dress and nervousness. The worst had their eyes on him and Jane. Neither of them were dressed or looked like a legal representative, so they were the enemy, they were cops. He felt their eyes on them both right up to leaving the courthouse and turning out of view. As they made their way towards Regency Street, Tom noticed the pub near the Magistrates Court which he thought would be a good place for him to meet Fiona. The timing would be about right, so whilst walking he sent her a quick text.

'White Horse & Bower Pub, Horseferry Road, near the court, around 5pm.'

Within seconds he got a reply;

'See you there.'

'Giving nothing away, right till the end, eh Fiona?' Tom thought to himself.

Jane and Tom spent as long as they could at the Regency Cafe, with Jane managing to get the table that Daniel Craig had sat at again. At one point they had to share it with other patrons who also knew it was 'the' table. It was great food as always, and had a fabulous ambience of times gone by in London. The walls were adorned with photographs of that era, which made you feel as if you were there. It was like a time machine, the moment you stepped in you were transported back.

Even the food was cooked differently, and seemed appropriate to a time when everything tasted better and more wholesome. The staff were dressed like it was back then, and yet the clothes were modern. It was as though a spell took over the wearers, making them seem that they belonged to a different time. The smell of the food, the sounds, and the cries from the single woman orchestrating the ebb and flow of the hungry hordes held you in that time capsule, disappearing the moment you stepped outside.

Tom noticed two men who had been in the courthouse foyer earlier, one of whom had his back to him. He didn't pay any real attention to it, other than it was just a 'spot'. The cafe was famous before 'Layer Cake', but it had become even more famous with the great, the good and the bad of London, all sitting side by side in silent recognition. Jane checked her watch and announced, "Time to go, Boss."

Back at the Magistrates Court they found out Kuklin had been allocated a court, and having entered it, they found the court was in the process of trying two men for shoplifting. A witness to the event, a store security guard, was in the box giving evidence in cross examination. They both sat at the back and listened to the case. The defendants both looked, and from their names sounded, as if they were Vietnamese; and both elected not to give evidence. The summing up by the CPS and the defence was short and to the point. The Crown's case was that they were seen to take the items from the shelf, place them under their clothing and leave the store; they were then stopped. The items were found and seized, the Police called, and they were arrested. In interviews they refused to say anything. Their defence lawyer submitted that it was not them that took the items, but another two unknown suspects, who upon leaving the store, and realising that they were about to be arrested, accosted his two clients, forced the items upon them and made off. It was at that point the store security guard had come along. As the real thieves were also Vietnamese and unknown to the defendants, the security guard had made an honest mistake as they looked so similar, causing them to be here today. The defence submitted that it was as clear a case as any of mistaken identity. The bench took about 20 seconds of whispering which nobody could hear to announce that they thought otherwise, and having found the two guilty they were then told of a string of theft and kindred offences on their previous conviction list. A considerable list it was too, bearing in mind they had only been in the UK for two years. They were quickly sentenced to three months imprisonment, with the chair of the bench warning that they needed to heed this 'short, sharp' sentence, and learn from it. The room stood up as the bench left the court to their right, and once gone the CPS lawyer looked around, and having caught Jane's eye, waved her over.

She made her way over, and was sitting engaged in conversation whilst Kuklin was brought into the glass covered defendants' box. He glared at Tom and then broke away, looking ahead towards his lawyer who had entered the courtroom. Tom saw that it was not Thomas Latham QC, but again, from the confidence of the individual, he expected it was somebody just as good, and who would be better prepared this time. Jane rejoined Tom and he saw her glance over to Kuklin, who ignored her.

"Doesn't want either of us. He doesn't seem that good or confident, I had to emphasise the statement that DC Hallett had got from the language college. I think he is just going to rely solely on the flight risk, no ties etc."

"Well, something has changed. It must be the college and the course, he knows he has that statement to fall back on."

The room stood up again as a district judge entered the room. Unfortunately, Tom saw it was not the same judge as before. As the application got underway they learnt that Kuklin did indeed have another lawyer, not a QC, but someone who was from a well known and respected London Chambers, so a Barrister. He was good, and easily outshone the CPS official; announcing that his client did in fact have many ties with the area, not least the fact he had paid for and had been attending a North London college for nearly a year. In response the CPS lawyer relied on the fact that he was not a UK national, had no family ties and remained a flight risk. Both Tom and Jane couldn't believe he hadn't mentioned the information from the college; the fact he had not been attending the college for at least six months. The Judge took a moment to check over his file, and wanted to know more about the original offences, checking with his clerk, and then the CPS. The Judge questioned the lawyer for Kuklin and got more of the same, presented in a manner that was very reasonable and unbiased. The Judge went back to the CPS again, and just got the same response: flight risk, and ties. Tom shook his head in disbelief, an action the Judge picked up.

"Would you like to call the officer in the case?"

The CPS official replied, "No," then went on to repeat his application. The Judge quickly looked up and saw Tom nod, as did Jane, signalling that they wanted to be called. It must have been enough, because the Judge said, "Have you got anything to say about the fact the defendant has been attending college for the last year?"

Tom took a quick look at Kuklin, who was getting everything interpreted for him. He seemed pleased with the way things were going. Tom started to think the worst: *'Bloody Hell! He could get this!'* The CPS continued with the same theme, seemingly not hearing the request from the Judge, who then interrupted him.

"Mr. Webber. Have you, or have you not, got anything to say about the fact the defendant has been attending college for the last year?"

The counsel for the defence, who was now sitting down, took a long hard look at Webber, who looked down towards his file and finally found the statement that DC Hallett had taken. Tom didn't know what was holding CPS lawyer Webber back, he had his game plan and he clearly thought it was enough. *'He must pick up on the tone and manner of the Judge,'* Tom thought.

Finally, and right at the last second, Webber said, "The investigating team have obtained a statement from the college which says that he has not been in attendance for the last six months." With that he offered a copy to the defence counsel and one to the court clerk.

The Judge flicked a look up towards Tom, Jane and Kuklin then listened to another well constructed submission from the defence. It was a close run thing, but Kuklin was remanded in custody and bail was refused on the grounds listed by the Judge and put forward by the Crown.

Back outside the court Jane said, "That was unnecessarily fraught in there! Where are you meeting Dr. Gordon?"

"White Horse & Bower, there," Tom replied, pointing further down Horseferry Road. Tom checked his watch. "She should be there soon, I will go and nurse a light ale; so see you when you get back."

"OK. It shouldn't take longer than an hour. Why are you meeting her again?"

"Oh, she just wants to catch up on a few things, you know what the good Doctor is like!" Tom said, deflecting the question, knowing that he was sort of telling the truth but feeling uncomfortable with it all the same.

"Right, see you later."

Jane walked to the end of Horseferry Road where she turned left onto Millbank and made her way towards Big Ben. She had promised a young relative that the next time she was in London she would get a picture of The Houses of Parliament, Big Ben, and the gates of Downing Street, with herself in the picture. All three were not far away and close together. If she got a move on, there would just be enough light left to get some pictures.

As Tom waited he felt nervous. It was strange mixture of feelings fighting each other for dominance. At the moment the fear of not having a relationship with Fiona was winning hands down. He took a sip of his beer and felt the cold liquid hit his stomach far harder than normal. Nerves, he thought. He had taken a seat so he could see the door; now waiting to see who entered every time the door moved was just adding to his anxiety level. After about twenty minutes the door opened again, and this time it was Fiona. She looked around, not seeing him initially; then, having caught sight of him, smiled, and made her way straight over. Tom, who had been sitting slightly away from a corner, moved out to let her in. She was amazingly dressed, and looked great in a three-quarter length coat which had a pattern of horizontal stripes, the material being a herringbone black and grey. Her accessories were a matching scarf and a modern box handbag. She smelt wonderful as she passed close by him. Before sitting down she removed her coat, to reveal she was wearing a tightly fitted leather jacket which she then unzipped, tight fitting jeans and black leather boots that fitted over the jeans and which came up to her knees. He couldn't hold himself back.

"You look and smell fab!"

Fiona turned towards him and gave him a quick kiss on the lips as if it were the most natural thing to do in the world. "There are benefits to retail therapy, Tom. You should try it. One's wardrobe always needs updating!"

"What do you want?"

"Look. Can I ask a huge favour?"

With his nerves somewhat settled, the presence of her next to him, and the kiss he had just received, she could ask for anything. "Sure. What do you need?"

"I have some notes that I need to get to an occupational health specialist friend of mine tonight. Where she lives is too difficult to get to by train, and by the time I get home and then drive there it will be too late."

"Do you want me and Jane to drop them off?" Tom said, interrupting Fiona, thinking he knew what she wanted.

"No. I have to see her and have a quick meeting once she has had a chance to read the notes."

Tom interrupted her again, thinking he definitely now knew where this was going. "Do you want us to take you on our way back?" He thought he was probably sounding too enthusiastic and eager, but what the hell.

"Er, no, she is too far out of the way; and it will mean both of you getting back late. I was hoping to use your car. Now that you have a job car allocated to you, and I am authorised to drive it and I'm covered by insurance, I was hoping both of you would help me out on this and take a train back. I know it is a big ask, but it is very important that I get these documents to her. I have checked the trains, and from Marylebone you can get one an hour to Allensbury, up until about ten. You can bill it to my department and I will owe you both. And, I always pay my debts!" Fiona finished the sentence with what Tom thought was just a hint of sexuality, or maybe it was him just wishing it was so.

"Yeah, sure, why not? I am sure Jane won't mind, plus her car is at COCET."

"In that case, Mr. Ross, can I have a 'Henry'?"

"Half?"

"Yes."

It took Tom a while to get served, whilst all the time he was wondering what the best tactic was. Should he ask straight out, or leave her to talk? Thinking the latter was the best option, he returned to find out his fate.

"Tom. I know you have been waiting on me a while, but I needed to work through this. If I didn't get the space, I would have just called us off," Fiona immediately began after Tom was seated.

"I was thinking the best thing for us would be to start again. That would allow me to declare it properly. And, with everything now in place, we should be able to have the relationship we want without either of us being compromised."

It was what Tom wanted to hear, and was praying for. Fiona smiled, and kissed him again.

"Thanks for waiting, I have missed you, but you will have to wait a bit longer as I need to get going." She moved closer to him and snuggled in alongside his body and took a couple of mouthfuls of her drink. Tom's body eased with the words and the decision. It made him a little light headed, and with a sudden need for a drink he grabbed his pint and downed a third, feeling the effects immediately.

"Where's Jane? I thought she was going to be with you."

"She is, she is off getting some pictures of Big Ben and Downing Street, she'll be back soon."

"What you doing this weekend?" Fiona asked, getting her coat back on.

"Nothing, I guess. It isn't my turn for Struan."

"Right. Come and stay with me?" She enquired.

"Yeah, sure. I would love to."

"Great. I will pick you up and that way you get your car back."

Tom texted Jane with, "Fiona is taking the car, we have to take a train." He removed the car key off his key fob which contained a number of other keys, and handed it to Fiona. She, now dressed with coat and scarf, began to finish her drink. Tom began to do the same but had more to swallow. He felt his phone vibrate in his pocket, and checked it to find Jane's reply, which said, "No problem. I am on my way back now."

"I'll walk you to the car. It's not far and Jane is on her way." Tom said, as he finished his drink. They left, and as they walked along Horseferry Road away from the direction of Millbank, Jane was just entering Horseferry Road from that direction. Fiona linked her arm through Tom's, bringing them close together. It was a simple act, but one that seemed as natural as if they had been doing it all their lives. He suddenly felt a chill go down his spine, and questioning himself why, put it down to the moment; just being in a suit after night had fallen along with the temperature.

Also in Horseferry Road was a parked van, the driver's seat of which contained one of the two men Tom had seen both in the Magistrates Court foyer and later in the Regency Cafe. The other was behind him in the rear of the van. The driver commentated on what he was seeing, after which the one in the rear used a handheld radio to relay that the 'target' was in Horseferry Road. The driver then moved off to relocate his position. That message was received through the speaker of another radio which was in a Range Rover parked in Vincent Square, an area very close to Horseferry Road. The driver who had the radio said to the two men seated in the rear of the Range Rover, "подготовить для действий".

Both men opened a case that was between them and removed two virtually identical Russian firearms, known as AS Vals. The weapon, which had an integral silencer and folding stock, had been specifically designed as an assault rifle and was used as the weapon of choice on many covert operations by the Russian Special Forces and other secret government organisations in Russia and many of its former Soviet states. The weapon had many assets, one of them being the fact that it could take two types of the same 9mm subsonic round. One was armour piercing and the other a smooth ball shot. It also made very little sound and had next to no muzzle flash. The man who sat on the nearside did not extend his stock, he just loaded his weapon with a full magazine of armour piercing rounds, charged it to chamber a round, and switched to fully automatic. The other extended his stock, switched on a laser sight which was side mounted, loaded a full magazine of 9mm ball rounds and switched to semi auto. They took out full face balaclavas from their clothing and with one nodding at the other, the second one said, "готов".

Tom and Fiona quickly arrived at the car in Maunsel Street with Fiona getting straight in adjusting her seat and rear view mirror. "Have you paid the charge?"

"Yes," replied Tom, quickly getting into the passenger seat. Fiona knew why and lent over for a long kiss which both of them needed and loved.

"Gotta go," she said, breaking the embrace. Tom got out again and squatted down to blow her a kiss through the window. Getting up, he then left, walking back in the direction he had come. He quickly entered Regency Street, crossing over to the far side and then back into Horseferry Road, where he briefly stopped to text Jane, asking where she was.

As he moved off again, he began to look further down Horseferry Road to see if he could see her coming, wondering whether she had gone into the Pub looking for them. She had, and having not found them there, she guessed they had left for the car and was making her way towards Tom, who couldn't see that far along the road due to the oncoming headlights.

The radio in the Range Rover burst back into life, "Ataka, Ataka!" The two men in the rear put on their balaclavas and opened their doors slightly whilst the driver pulled out from his position without his headlights on. He travelled a short way along Vincent Square and pulled into the first junction on his nearside, blocking it with the front of the Range Rover facing directly into the street. Both men in the rear got out immediately the moment their vehicle came to a stop. Opening their doors to act as a shield and a makeshift tripod, they produced their weapons between the wall of the vehicle and the door, keeping their eyes mostly shut to ensure that their night vision was not impaired.

Fiona saw the vehicle enter her one-way street without its headlights on and assumed it was turning, so carried on towards it. As she neared the junction the vehicle in front put its headlights on full beam, causing her to stop abruptly and put her hands and arms up before her face to protect her eyesight.

The moment the Range Rover's headlights came on its driver spotted that the person behind the wheel of the other car was female and not male. But it was too late, the firing had started. The armour piercing bullets silently smashed into the vehicle's engine area at a rate of 900 rounds per minute, quickly destroying major parts of the engine, some passing through the engine compartment towards the driver. The volley then made its way up the bonnet to the driver's area, virtually slicing the vehicle apart. The 20 round magazine quickly discharged its lethal payload, leaving the other assassin to continue emptying all of his rounds into the upper body of the driver under the precision guidance of the laser sight and with minimal recoil. It was all over within 30 seconds with hardly a sound. The men stepped back into their vehicle, switched off its headlights again, then reversed it out onto Vincent Square and drove off.

Dr. Fiona Gordon died from the first laser guided round that hit her in the head. She never felt the other bullets that entered her. But in that split second, between the first and the rest, her neural pathways still operated, and she was crying out for Tom.

CHAPTER TEN

Grief and guilt do not always come together, but when they do, the black and deafening silence can last forever. Or you can use the grief as your anchor; and once ready, you can plot and navigate your course for the horizon, discarding guilt to the mercy of the wind and sea, leaving you free to see and hear again.

—I. R. Tyler

As Margaret Thrinton led Tom into the Chief Constable's office it had been over two weeks since the murder, and four days since the funeral of Dr. Fiona Gordon, the head of Occupational Health for Thames Valley Police. The Metropolitan Police had deployed a major investigation team from their Homicide and Serious Crime Command, who had made a number of early arrests.

GOPOL, after only being in existence for just two weeks, had no option but to refer COCET to the Independent Police Complaints Commission (IPCC). After assessing it they had referred it back to TVP's Professional Standards Unit for investigation.

For Tom, even through all the trauma, grief and guilt, it had in the end been a simple choice, and one that had to be made immediately. It was either break down, throw the towel in and walk away to a life of alcohol, misery and failed promise; or lower the anchor and set it on suitable ground that could weather the tempest. The motivation came from some known and some unlikely external sources, all of which quickly enveloped him; providing insight into the closeness of death, the real meaning of faith, and its effect on the present and the future.

The presence of something on that day in the church, something he could neither describe nor really see, but that was felt so strongly, made him see that he could be healed; that there was a way, and that he could find that way himself. He would never know how he got through his eulogy that day, but somehow he did; and now he had a duty to carry on.

He knew above all else, that before he could set off on a particular course, he had to be ready, his ship needed to be fully provisioned. The time for mourning and wishing he had taken another action or decision had to come to an end. If he wanted to stay afloat, he had to go on to the next stage, otherwise the maelstrom of emotions that encircled him was surely going to sink him. He had to slip anchor, and get under way even with a sail full of those mixed emotions.

There was however, one thing he needed to know. That was, was he still at the helm?

The Chief was sitting at his desk, with Assistant Chief Constable Peter Adams on one side and Detective Chief Superintendent John Troy on the other.

"Take a seat, Tom," said the Chief.

Tom thought his tone showed kindness, but with Margaret quickly disappearing, and blank expressions on the other two faces, he wasn't sure how this would end up.

The Chief began. "Tom, as you know, you and the team will get updates as necessary, and the latest is that the homicide team have made more arrests, one of whom is Andrei Kuklin. He is looking to turn Queen's, and wants a deal. You need to know that we only support witness protection once he has answered for his crimes, and he has provided the evidence that warrants it, whatever that turns out to be."

The Chief stopped to see if Tom wanted to say anything, and when he didn't, he continued. "The vehicle has been found in a container in Rotterdam, en route for Libya. It appears it was stolen for export, stolen again for the crime, then placed back in the disposal route without the original criminal gang who stole the car in the first place ever knowing. The two shooters have been identified and are back behind the Iron Curtain, their exact whereabouts unknown. The

Organised Crime Boss has also been identified and all three will shortly be placed on Interpol's most wanted list. I have personally spoken to the Met Commissioner and he feels it will take political pressure for these three plus the driver to be found. But these are early days, and it is about evidence gathering at the moment."

The Chief paused long enough for Tom to nod. "The Fraud Squad," he continued, "will work closely with the Met in relation to their prosecution, and our Professional Standards Unit will be undertaking an investigation into every aspect of Operation Ascent on behalf of the IPCC. I expect you to cooperate fully with our PSU, and I hope that you will not be found wanting. This is all about transparency and accountability, what it is not about is scapegoats, and you have that from me.

"I have told the PSU that I want the investigation fully completed this week, and the IPCC knows that I am looking for a quick decision. If there has been a case of negligence, and you are at fault, then you will be replaced, and the normal process of criminal and or police conduct regulations will be looked at accordingly. If there is a clean bill of health, which we hope will be the case, we need to know firstly, do you still want to head up COCET?"

The Chief stopped, waiting for the answer.

"Yes, Sir."

"And secondly, are you fit enough mentally to undertake the role, now or later? Before you give me your reply, it will not be just your view that I will be taking into account. I have read the reports from Dr. Clayworth, from before the murder and up to the present. So I know that Fiona was clearing the way properly before she embarked on a relationship with you. I also know the time line of events and why she was there that day. She was there to get access to a TVP vehicle, which she was entitled to do, so that she could fulfil her function with the utmost professionalism, something she always did.

"Her killers were there that day to get you. She was in the wrong place at the wrong time. The ACC and John have gone to great lengths to get access to the best specialists from the security service and industry to provide us with a current and ongoing risk assessment around this, and I am satisfied that you and your team are not at risk at the present time; and it is highly unlikely that this will change. Whatever they thought they could achieve with your death, they failed to take into account the level of response from the UK Police; and that has been a game changer for them. So for me, and for everybody here, it is all about your state of mind and whether can you come back from this."

Tom thought it was more of a statement than a question, but he wasn't sure; so decided to speak in any case.

"Am I over this, Sir? No, I am not, and, it will never be fully over. No matter how long I live, it will always be there, as part of my history. But I have received enormous help from Dr. Clayworth and Superintendent Burrows. Without them I am not sure I would have wanted to stay in this role, or possibly even in the Police. But they have helped me understand and respond to my feelings in a balanced way, and I am now in a position to use this to move on."

"Well, Dr. Clayworth and Maggie both think that as well. So it will be my decision that you will go back to work tomorrow with the following conditions that will be adapted as necessary.

"One. You will be assessed by Dr. Clayworth twice a week for the first three weeks. You will have access to her at any time should you need it.

"Two. Until further notice you will inform Maggie of all operational activity that takes you outside the office, and that of Jane King as well. Irrespective of what time of day or night, we want to know where you are, or intend to go, so that means reporting in advance. I am happy that there is a very low risk of another attempt on your life, but I still want, and there will be, an armed response team on the COCET building and both of you wherever you go. To do that effectively there will need to be good communication channels between you and Maggie. She has been given the responsibility for the ongoing safety of the both of you. Do I make myself clear?"

"Yes, Sir," replied Tom, thinking that the cost of this was going to be enormous, so it wouldn't last long.

"Three. There will be an armed response team at your home when you are asleep so you will need to make adjustments to enable that to happen without causing a problem with the neighbours. If it becomes a problem, you will be temporarily rehoused.

"Four. Whenever you are at work, whether at the office or not, you will both wear a separate panic alarm. So, are you ready to work with these conditions?"

"Yes, Sir."

"In that case I want you to go with the ACC and JT now to meet with Sarah Dorsey and come up with a workable media solution for the short term. Tomorrow you can expect a full PSU team at your office by 8am, so don't be late."

Tom got to the COCET building around 7.20am the next day, shadowed by an unmarked armed response car. Inside it were two Special Branch Royalty Protection Officers who were taking their job seriously. They had been given a full briefing on the possible threat, so knew their sidearms might not be enough. As a result, one, the passenger, was in possession of a Heckler and Koch MP5 carbine which he had in a rucksack at his feet. The driver had access to a second one in the rear of the car which he could reach without getting out of the vehicle. Once they were inside the outer perimeter of the COCET building, they undertook a reconnaissance of the building's exterior; and, when satisfied, they took up position in the car park at the front of the building. Their job was to stay there until relieved by a marked armed response vehicle; which would then remain on guard for the rest of the day in an overt capacity.

Tom knew he was first in, as he had to deactivate the alarm. It was a strange feeling. The last time he was here had been before the murder of Fiona. The building, being empty, added to his feelings of uncertainty and fear. If he couldn't manage today it would probably signal the end for him. He'd had days of being weepy and had cried himself dry; to the extent that he had no more tears left.

The guilt he was carrying, however, was a corrosive force that came in waves. On a receding wave all the common sense logic of *'It wasn't your fault, you could not have foreseen this.' 'They were after you, bad case of wrong time and place.' 'Fiona would want you to carry on.'* All made sense and allowed him to see a way through.

On an incoming wave, when the fear got under his defences, it was, '*You knew something was up, your sixth sense had told you more than once that something seemed wrong.*' '*You might have seen the killers at the court and the cafe.*' And the one that really got to him, and made him feel that he would never really get over it, was, '*If I hadn't lied about my nightmares, then maybe we wouldn't have had that break and she would never have been there.*'

He had discussed the last one many times with Dr. Clayworth, and he knew the answers to them all. When he told them to himself, the incoming wave would recede after a time and he would begin to feel better. It was all going to be about time and accepting that this was his life, his history. The good thing was that nobody knew about him and Fiona, not even Jane. However that would change; this was something he had to tell her. For the rest of the team, though, they knew nothing and that would help him. They had all been sent home on paid leave. Today they would be addressed by Maggie Burrows and himself, all whilst Professional Standards were pulling his Senior Investigating Officer role to bits. '*They can break a leg,*' he thought. '*They won't find anything there.*'

The kettle hadn't even boiled when Jane entered. "I'll have one whilst you're in the chair, Boss!" He saw her smiling face and found himself really pleased to see her. They had spoken on the phone many times over the last few days. But he had forgotten, being in her company so much, just how far they had come in a short space of time. Her presence gave him the lift he was seeking.

"You ready to get this show back on the road?" Tom said, hoping his confident tone sounded sincere.

"Damn right I am! Fiona's death has just given me more determination than ever. Those bastards will have won if we give in. Bollocks to that, Boss!"

Tom suddenly found himself laughing. It being a serious moment, Jane looked at him in alarm, which he saw and quickly moved to put it in perspective. "It's just that I haven't heard you use language like that much, and it's just so right! So, spot on! Well put, Sergeant King!"

Understanding a bit more, Jane replied, "Ah, OK. I get it now! Well, the way I look at it is this; we need to get back in the saddle before this all gets too stale."

"I couldn't agree more. Grab your tea, and come with me. I have something to tell you."

Once inside his office, Tom prepared to drop the bombshell.

"We are going to be busy today on a number of fronts. First off, the PSU will be here any minute to investigate my handling of Ascent. Once we have a clean bill of health, and we will, then we can get going. Second, Maggie Burrows will be here later this morning to address the team, I will be doing that with her. There will be one thing they won't be told, and that is something you don't know, but I am going to tell you."

"You were in a relationship with Fiona," Jane interrupted quickly.

Seeing Tom lost for words and with a startled look on his face made Jane seize the moment.

"I never knew for sure, but there were a few things that didn't quite add up along the way, and call it a woman's thing if you want, but Fiona just acted differently around you. It is a thing a woman would spot and not a man. Am I right?" she asked, knowing by his expression that she was.

"Yes. We started and then stopped. Professionally it was getting difficult, so she wanted a break to see if she could find a workable solution, and on that night she told me she had that solution and wanted to give it a go."

"Boss, I'm so sorry!" Jane said, and then dropping her head mumbled, "I'm so sorry."

"Jane, we are all sorry. We both know we could never have stopped this. There was not a shred of intelligence to say this was coming. They were after me because we were doing our jobs and targeting them effectively. It was because we dismantled their syndicate and stopped their source of money that made them do what they did."

Jane lifted her head and looked at Tom without saying anything. There was a long period of silence between them before Tom broke it.

"How are you taking it all?"

Jane thought about it. She had seen Dr. Clayworth a number of times, and Superintendent Burrows, and then her Mum and Dad had been all over her. The truth was that she was glad to just get back to work. She was never the target from what she had been told, but she could have been caught in the crossfire. If they had gone for Tom en route to the Court they would have got them both. But they hadn't, and now it was different.

"Actually, I am doing OK. Gloria and Maggie have been marvellous, and helped me a great deal to keep it all in perspective. To be honest, with my parents being all over me I just want to get back to work."

"Me too. I need this stage now, so I can move forward."

"I do have one concern though, Boss."

"What?"

"How will the PSU and the IPCC view me wanting an alarm because I was concerned about Kuklin's fake gun shooting sign, and you agreeing to it?"

It was something he had discussed with Maggie Burrows and it had gone right to the top. They had accepted his decision making on the matter. Enough, that was, to support him back to work. But with Jane saying it like she just had, it took on a whole new meaning. One that the IPCC might agree with as well.

"I have covered that with Superintendent Burrows. It's explainable," replied Tom, using his newly acquired confident tone, one that overrode the underlying fear.

Ten minutes later, six members of Thames Valley Professional Standards Unit, led by DCI Stuart Simmons, were at COCET. Stuart played it exactly by the book, and two hours after they had arrived they either had originals, copies or electronic access to every single item or decision related to Operation Ascent. The whole thing had been videoed with both Jane and him present, every question and reply being recorded. Tom and Jane had been told the internal investigation would take this form, and that they had the option to object. But both felt they had nothing to hide; and the easier they made it for the PSU, the quicker the result would come back. The truth was that at different times during the search, both he and Jane had recounted the actions of Kuklin at court, her request for a panic alarm, and the granting of it by DCI Ross. As the PSU left, an officer from the technical support unit arrived. He allocated them both a personal panic alarm and explained how to use it, how to switch it on and off, and what to do if they activated it accidentally. And no sooner had he left, Superintendent Burrows arrived, along with two large brown paper bags containing lunch.

"The COCET team will be here soon, so I thought it might be good if we all ate at the same time, food for thought sort of thing." She said it all with an upbeat tone and a smile.

"Great," said Jane, "I'll make a pot."

Around the conference room table Maggie produced three sets of sandwiches, all of which had been recently made and covered in white food paper wrapping. Tom saw that one of them had 'ham/salad/brown' written on the outside and he immediately wondered if it was his; and if so, how did she know? Then came a selection of small cakes, and finally one can of non-diet Coca Cola and a Kit-Kat. He guessed the ham and salad was for him and that Maggie had been doing her homework on him. He drew a small amount of comfort from the fact that somebody had cared enough to find out what his standard lunch was, when he had time for one that was. With Jane back, and a cup of tea all round, Maggie got straight to business.

"How did the internal investigation go?"

"It went well. They have everything, and there is nothing to hide.

"Good. How are you both?" She looked towards Jane, signalling that she wanted her to reply first.

"I am doing well, Ma'am. It is just a relief to be back."

"How are you with the armed monitoring and the panic alarms?" Maggie said, addressing Jane again.

"It's just a safety precaution. It doesn't hamper my personal life and I know it's for a short period."

"Tom?" said Maggie, looking towards him.

"Same as Jane on both."

Maggie, who had taken a bite of her sandwich, needed time to chew and then swallow before she continued.

"Well, I feel it is essential that the team are fully briefed today. Once they know the level of risk they were at before, and now after what's happened, they will be in an informed position. I know this is the team you picked, Tom, but they all get the chance to leave if they want to for personal reasons. Do we have accord on this?"

"Yes, absolutely. It's what I want as well," Tom replied.

"There will be a press release today in conjunction with the Met Media Department which will say that the murder of Dr. Fiona Gordon was a case of mistaken identity; and that the real target had been the head of COCET, DCI Ross. The Met will announce they have made further arrests, and that the killers' identities, along with the driver and the Organised Crime Boss who ordered the assassination, are known. They will say the murder was ordered as a result of the good work COCET had achieved in dismantling their commercial child abuse criminal network, and their money laundering system in the UK. After this release, Interpol will update their most wanted list to include all four Russian nationals who are wanted in connection with the murder of Dr. Fiona Gordon."

Hearing the words about Fiona and her death come so plainly from Maggie's mouth, placing her in the past tense, hit Tom hard in the stomach and he felt his appetite start to disappear.

"Tomorrow the Met, in conjunction with Her Majesty's Government, Interpol and the Crown Prosecution Service, will start to apply pressure through all available channels in an attempt to extradite the offenders to the UK for trial. Russian law currently prevents any Russian being sent to a foreign country for trial, and there is no bilateral agreement between Russia and the UK for extradition, so it would mean changing Russian Law, and we don't expect that to happen. But applying pressure and keeping it in the public domain will help. One thing Her Majesty's Government 'Russian Watchers' all agree on, though, is that the particular gang members we want do not hold favour in the high echelons of the Russian establishment, albeit some of them are former military special forces."

Tom and Jane, who had been listening intently, watched as Maggie paused, took another bite of her sandwich, swallowed the content and then took a sip of her tea.

"Nice cup, Jane." She looked up from the table and smiled at her.

"Questions?"

Both Jane and Tom shook their heads.

"Eat!" Maggie said, pointing at the sandwiches and cakes.

Tom grabbed his, wondering if it would go down. Maggie, having taken another mouthful of tea, sat back in her chair and said, "We expect there will be requests from the media, especially Sky TV, for interviews with you, Tom. To head this off, as we don't want a scrum outside here all through the day; they will get offered exclusives from the Met OIC leading the Murder Squad. If they persist with us they will get an interview with the ACC, which should do it. Any cold calls or being caught off guard, they get directed straight to Sarah. OK?"

"Yes," Tom replied with half a mouthful of sandwich, feeling relieved he could get it down.

"Sarah has dealt with our international COCET partners, and they will all put out a joint statement in line with the others, no interviews to get to Tom through the back door; and an attitude of 'It is business as usual.'

"As for the briefing today, I will conduct it with you and Jane to one side. After I am gone you can have your own. We will wait to see if we have enough of a team to move forward, or whether we have to place things on hold whilst we recruit again. Thoughts, Tom?"

"Good by me!"

Tom and Jane sat through Superintendent Burrows' briefing to the full COCET team. Most, if not all, knew something; and most of what she had to say to them was just confirmation of the gossip they had already heard. The rest filled in the gaps of what they didn't know.

At the end, they were all asked to take time to consider if they wanted to remain part of COCET, and Tom was humbled by the immediate unanimous decision to remain. However, they were all told to discuss it with loved ones before reconfirming their decisions.

With Superintendent Burrows gone, Tom called another briefing with his staff in the conference room.

"I can tell you all now, there is nothing I know about the case that you don't as well. If there is anyone here that feels they want to leave, then they will have my full support in doing that. You should not feel under any obligation or pressure to stay just because others do. Each and every one of you has a unique personal home situation, and I for one will not think any less of someone who wants to go. In fact I would think less of you if you stay when you actually want to go! The armed protection is short term and just belt and braces, nothing more and nothing less, and will go within a few days I am sure. As for us? The ones that want to stay, I expect you to be here first thing. We owe it to Dr. Gordon to move on, so it will be business as usual, and the next job is 'Operation Resolve' ".

On the way home that night Tom stopped to get a Chinese meal, of which he had alerted his minders. Once inside, with the curtains drawn, he realised he didn't have much appetite for the food. He was exhausted from the mental pressure of the last two days, and reached for a bottle of Wither Hills Sauvignon Blanc from the fridge. He slumped into his chair with the bottle in one hand and an empty glass in the other. He filled it and took a large mouthful, closed his eyes and swallowed; feeling the cold, dry acidity hit his stomach.

He saw the blackness inside the eyelids and heard the silence of the room. These senses would have left him in an empty void but for the slight smell of the Won Ton soup which still managed to penetrate his nasal pathways, even though it was sealed in a container. Opening his eyes, he took another mouthful of wine and removed the plastic lid from the polystyrene bowl, to find that the soup was clear, and contained real Bok Choy and not shredded cabbage, which was how he liked it. The smell that was released reclaimed his appetite.

He woke at 3am to find himself asleep in the chair, an empty bottle of the New Zealand wine by his feet, and the main Chinese dish cold on a plate beside it. He had the beginning of a headache, which instinct and the fact he had drunk a whole bottle of wine told him would be a humdinger. His throat was dry and sore, and his neck hurt from the position he had slept in. He took some Nurofen and drank a glass of water, before refilling it and switching off the lights, dropping into bed to be claimed by the darkness of the night. Outside, the two night duty armed Special Branch Officers noted the lights going off and recorded it in their log of events which would be transcribed the next day, the contents going to ACC Adams and Dr. Clayworth.

CHAPTER ELEVEN

Sarah Dorsey was sitting in Tom's office with her laptop plugged into the COCET intranet, monitoring her email account and her mobile phone, a Blackberry Pearl. Tom was at his desk doing much the same. The Metropolitan Police had made their media release, and from the second it hit the 'Sky Breaking News' feed it quickly made its way around the world. In 2005, if your news was worthwhile it could be beamed around the world in seconds and be read everywhere, however remote.

All the COCET partners had been warned overnight; and Tom received personal emails of support from key players like Adrian Smith, Jim Burgess, Niall Mullins and many others. He was currently reading one from Inspector Tony Maggs, who had been promoted since the last time they spoke. It seemed like ages since they had both strolled through Taunton Town centre eating 'pasties', planning the downfall of 'The Son of God'. It was only months, however.

It was Sarah's phone and email account that took the brunt, and it was as if a switch had suddenly been turned on, allowing the queuing journalists to break through without warning. Sarah had placed a sound alert on her email account to act as a signal when she was on the phone. She wasn't able to field the calls quickly enough, so while she was on one call, another incoming call hit the engaged barrier and diverted to the answerphone. Some left a message and then texted her, some just rang back.

The result was her phone was nearly playing a tune from the bleeps in her ear that announced she had missed a call, had a call waiting, had received a text, or messages had been left for her. Most of the callers had also backed it up with an email, and Sarah made notes to link which call featured with which email.

In fact she was giving them all the same press release that had been agreed by GOPOL, TVP and the Metropolitan Police. Nobody could have access to DCI Ross due to his current operational activity, which was unrelated to the murder of Dr. Gordon. It still left him numb, hearing the words coming from Sarah's mouth about Fiona's murder. It was almost as if he wasn't really there, or it was just a film or a play; where at the end, everybody went home just as they had arrived.

He had his phone on silent, so he made a mental note of who had tried to call from a name or number he recognised that appeared in the window of the phone. Most left a message, which the phone duly made him aware of later. His email account was an easier proposition, and he quickly cut and pasted an amount of text written by Sarah, which he personalised slightly at the end and sent back. It was nonstop for about 45 minutes, then another hour catching up on left messages or texts, and finally emails.

"Well, that's round one," Sarah said in an exhausted voice. "Most will accept what I have said and that will do for them, but it won't satisfy everybody. Some will go to the Met to see if they can get an interview with their SIO. After that, the few that persist may get an interview with the ACC. By that time though, we will know the result of the IPCC investigation and the Met murder team will have got to a point where they are in extradition mode. That for sure, will be more politics than anything else. So. Any direct calls to you, flip them straight to me. Have you got anything you need me to deal with?"

"Not that I know of, but I've had my phone on silent."

"Clear your calls and then back to work, I have you covered."

Tom met Sarah's stare after her comment and he knew she meant it.

Dr. Gloria Clayworth sat in ACC Tony Adams' office waiting for him to arrive. She quickly went through her handwritten notes, reading sections she had highlighted, then moved straight to her conclusion and recommendations. She finished just as the ACC arrived and threw himself into his comfortable executive chair.

"Nice to see you, Gloria. Want some tea?" He said reaching for his desk phone.

"No thanks."

He called Margaret Thrinton's extension. "Margaret, can I have my usual and two today please? I am famished!"

Removing his clip-on tie and undoing his top shirt button, the ACC said, "Gloria, thank you for coming at short notice. The reason is our Professional Standards Department has been undertaking an investigation on behalf of the Independent Police Complaints Committee, as you know. They gave word late last night that they have finished and will be writing their report conclusion today.

"In short, Tom Ross has had the microscope put on all his actions, going back before the inception of COCET and up to and after the murder of dear Fiona, and he has been given a clean bill of health. In fact he can't be faulted on his operational work. We want to move on that quickly, and that includes coming to a decision around armed response, which is costing us an arm and a leg. Regarding his continuing in post, where are we with his mental health?"

"He is doing well over all. However there are a number of significant areas of concern that will need close monitoring."

ACC Adams, who wasn't expecting to hear that, looked up at Margaret, who had arrived with a cup of tea and two well buttered toasted crumpets.

"Thank you, Margaret. Perfect!"

The ACC took a large bite out of one of the crumpets, which dripped melted butter onto the plate causing him to reach quickly for a paper napkin from one of his desk drawers, whilst keeping his face still precariously positioned over the small plate.

Gloria, who was watching the dripping butter, thought, *'There's enough butter on that to clog up a rhino's arteries. When was your last work up, young man?'*

She watched as he wiped away the butter to reveal a look of concern. "How many, and how significant?" He asked, with a facial expression as if the butter was off.

"First, he appears to be leaning on alcohol too much, and he isn't getting to bed on time. When he does eventually get there he won't be getting restful sleep, as he will have too much alcohol in his body to allow that to happen. That needs to be nipped in the bud."

The ACC, who was actually loving his intake of hot melted butter, thought briefly about the amount of very expensive but delicious port he had drunk the night before.

"You can't blame a man who reaches for the bottle at a time like this," he replied with a slight tone of annoyance, which Gloria immediately picked up.

"I am not judging Tom Ross. I am merely saying that he is leaning on it, and that needs to be checked before it becomes a problem."

"Agreed. What are the others?"

"His former wife, Sandra, has threatened to go back to court because of the events. She wants to prevent all access to Struan, his son, due to the risks to Tom. He is trying to negotiate, and has agreed a short break; but it will end up at court at some stage unless she changes her mind. It is something to be aware of; I am hoping to meet with her to help on this."

"Good luck with that!" The ACC said through a mouthful of crumpet.

Picking up that ACC Adams didn't see that as an issue, probably because it was seen as an ongoing one with Tom, she continued.

"And the last is his desire to throw himself into his work to an even greater degree than before, if that is possible, as a way of dealing with the issue. I think real consideration should be given to replacing him as soon as is viable. Not immediately, as that may have a negative effect, but maybe through promotion or another job where he wouldn't be so much a single point of failure."

ACC Adams was on his last piece of crumpet, and was annoyed that he couldn't savour it more. He had been waiting for some 'bean baggy', flimsy, psychosocial bullshit to come out and was prepared for it.

"Gloria. In a perfect world that might be, and I may even say would be, a good idea. However, the reality is that if we were to take that stance we would have to be rotating people in their positions every year, if not sooner. It's a non starter. Now, I will deal with your first concern personally and you can monitor it. Are there any mental reasons that prevent DCI Ross from undertaking his role?"

"None. But I will be submitting my current assessment, the highlights of which we have discussed."

"Fine. Now, on to another matter. We need to find a replacement for Dr. Fiona Gordon and will be advertising for it next week. I would like you to consider it!"

Tom had been humbled over the last few days by the response from his team in wanting to stay on; they weren't all cops, and some had probably never encountered real danger before. Without hesitation they had all confirmed their wish to remain as members of COCET. He had also been genuinely affected by the messages of support, not just from work colleagues and friends both new and old, but also from members of TVP and other Police Forces within the UK and abroad whom he just didn't know or have any connection to. It had given him a real boost, and was something that he needed. It gave him strength, knowing he had that many people behind him.

The issue of Sandra holding him to ransom at a time when he really needed to be with Struan was something that he hated her for, and yet at the same time he understood. He could live with it for now, but she would want assurances beyond what he could give, and beyond that of others too. So it would end up in court at some point in the not too distant future. He was contemplating what he could undertake next whilst the IPCC investigation still hung over him, when his desk phone rang and he wondered if it would be the first journalist who had managed to get his desk phone number.

"DCI Ross, COCET."

"Tom. It is Margaret Thrinton, I have the ACC for you."

"Put him through, Margaret," Tom said, whilst thinking her email to him had really touched him. There was a longer than expected pause, then suddenly the unmistakable voice of ACC Adams came on the line.

"Tom. The PSU have done a great job and turned their investigation around. They will be submitting their report to the IPCC tomorrow and you have a clean bill of health, not even any recommendations for the future, so well done there. This has been conveyed across to the IPCC in advance, and we have their agreement to act now on COCET although their official announcement will take another ten days. So it's under the radar until then, understood?"

"Yes, Sir."

"Good. Now that leaves your assessment from Dr. Clayworth, who also has given you the all clear, although she will continue to assess you, and I expect you to continue to work with her. OK?"

"Yes, Sir."

"The armed response is being withdrawn as I speak and you can send those alarms back through the internal post. Which leaves me with just one thing, and that is your level of alcohol consumption. She believes you are leaning on it too much and that it could become a problem if it isn't controlled. So, you need to get it back under control for you and COCET, and I expect more good results soon so we can put this terrible business behind us. Back to work, DCI." And the line went dead.

Tom put his phone back in its cradle and began to think about the content of the call. It was a relief to have the result, even though he knew what the outcome was going to be. 'Seek and ye shall find' was something he truly believed in, and yet you never really knew. It had been preying on his mind, especially his decision to support a panic button in Jane's house.

Seen in isolation one could read all sorts of things into it. The real truth was that she had been scared and he had sought to allay that fear, even though he truly believed she wasn't in any danger. Hindsight had proved him both right and then wrong, the latter for the wrong reasons, and that was how it panned out in the end.

That in turn left him with a lifetime of 'if only', which quickly made Tom focus on the comment on alcohol. Whichever way he played it, he was bound to get it wrong. The macho image of detectives and drink was a reality in the Police. 'Make it a double it will ease the pain'. The truth was it did. Then when you do become that person, or that image, some get on your back for being the person that they expected you to be in the first place.

"You can't bloody win!" he said out loud, hoping nobody would hear. And, as for being truthful with the 'shrink', *I got into this mess because I held back the truth; and now I do tell the truth you use it against me! Well Gloria, it will be back to the old days from now on! And if I can't use alcohol then I only have work left'.*

Tom called a snap team meeting in the conference room, with Sam to his right, Jane to his left, and the rest of COCET massed around the table.

"As you know, the PSU have put Operation Ascent under the microscope, in particular my actions as a SIO. I have just been informed by the ACC that the PSU have finished their internal investigation and have cleared us of any wrongdoing or other bad practice. In fact, there will be no recommendations; something which in itself is unusual. This has been relayed to the IPCC and they have agreed ahead of their announcement, which will take another two weeks, that we can get back to work. But we are to keep that to ourselves until the IPCC announce it. So Anna, where are we with the warrants?"

"The PSU's timing is perfect. They are all being done tomorrow. SDE are doing all the forensic work so that way the process will be in overdrive, and puts us on the front foot when you next speak to Cleveland."

"Great work. In that case, Jane can you speak with Becky Drysdale and see where she is with her networking? If possible I would like to meet with her Boss any time after the day after tomorrow."

"Sure thing."

"Sarah, any update on the media for Operation Ascent?"

"Most still want an interview with you, but they have accepted the invitation from the Met SIO; and Sky will soon get an exclusive with the ACC, so you have the freedom to move about."

"Good. Can you make contact with your GOPOL media counterparts and alert them to Operation Resolve? And tell them we will be commencing operational activity tomorrow."

"Yep, no problems."

"Dale."

"Yes, Sir."

"Can you put together an operational briefing document that outlines what you would need to assume the identity of Philip Thompson? That means everything; from location, staff, equipment and passwords, to authorisations. If you want access to the Operation Hope authorities let me know. It is a wish list, so don't hold back. As soon as you have that, let's meet and discuss."

"When would you like it by?"

"As soon as you can do it, and if that means you need overtime then it's authorised!"

"Understood."

"Mitchell, are you still carrying any work from Operation Ascent?"

"A small amount. It's all statements and exhibit continuity, but I can't do it until I get the information from the banks and the Fraud Squad, so I am free for other work."

"Good. I know 'childscentcafe' is not profit making, but I want you to get access to all the property that gets seized from the warrants tomorrow to see what property can be attributed to being used to undertake the crimes for which they have been arrested. I want you to look at asset confiscation under the Proceeds of Crimes Act."

"Will do."

"Also assess the forensics. So speak with Dr. Tay. Let her know you are looking at all financial aspects. So if the laptop has had extra memory fitted, then how much? It might be a small amount, but it all counts in a numbers game. And ask her to 'data mine' for anything that shows members are exchanging something of worth in exchange for images. We need to be creative around this if we want to hurt them financially as well. After you have everything, put together a simple financial strategy around it all and let me have it."

"Yes, Sir."

"Anybody here 'Holmes' trained?"

DC Donaldson was the only officer who put his hand up.

"Archie can you get onto training and see what it's going to take to get two staff trained on Holmes as soon as possible. By that I mean the next ten days."

"Sure, can I use your name to push the request?"

"Yes. If you need more rank, let me know."

"Anna W. Speak with Niall, and let him know that I want a meeting next week with the owner of WebHostTwelve, and ask him to pave the way for that to happen. We will work around their availability."

"Will do."

"Owen. You are getting another role. You already work closely between COCET and SDE, so it seems a natural fit that you assist Dale where you can. Dale, you will now be called 'Covert Ops', a department within Operations."

The officers looked at each other, and a smile quickly appeared on their faces.

"Sounds great, Boss," Owen replied; clearly for both of them.

Tom paused deliberately for effect, which also gave him time to think, then with a steely stare of determination and resolution he said, "Right then. Operation Resolve: let's do it!"

CHAPTER TWELVE

Jane entered Tom's office and taking a seat, sat down.

"We have the initial results from the warrants this morning and it's enough for a briefing. Do you want me to tell the whole team or just you?"

"Are we all here?"

"No. Mitchell and Archie are out and won't be back till tomorrow."

"Just me, you, Anna and Patrick then. You can do the rest of the team in the morning."

With the four of them present and the door shut, Jane gave the floor to Anna Farley, who began.

"John Michael Black was at home and about to leave for work when the Police arrived. They found a desktop PC and a laptop. The desktop area was littered with used tissues and there was some baby oil near the monitor. He was very nervous, and when questioned about some of the CD's they seized, he admitted that child abuse material was present on them.

"They did two interviews, one with and one without his solicitor being present. He admitted that child abuse material will be found on his computer systems, a number of CDs and two data sticks. He refused to comment on what material he had, but did state he was only interested in girls between about six and ten.

"He admits to being a member of 'childscentcafe', and is only a member in order to meet with others he relates to, and from whom he gets images and videos. He says that he may have sent images as well as receiving them, and that he uses a number of platforms to exchange. The main admission is that whatever they find is his, and that nobody else has access to or has used his PCs.

"He describes 'childscentcafe' as one massive meeting place for people who like to have sex with children. There is nothing on the site itself, as they all know the rules; but once a member they then contact each other outside the site and deal directly on a one-to-one basis, or in small groups. When pressed about the groups he clammed up, and he denied any offline offending. He has a short bail to return as requested by us, and the exhibits have already been collected by Mitchell."

"Brilliant! Exactly what we need," replied Tom. "Carry on."

"The next is Arthur George Thomas, from Blackwood. He was also at home. One desktop, three external hard drives, 26 CDs and four data sticks. He made admissions at the scene before the search had even begun.

"In interview he admitted to being a member of the site for the sole reason of meeting others like himself so he can trade with them. He provided a description of how the site works and operates, what the do's and don'ts are. He also mentioned that there are other groups within the site, but that he wasn't a part of any.

"The main thing emerging is that it was a meeting place, and that all trading was done outside the site to prevent it coming to the attention of law enforcement. He stated his preference was also prepubescent females, and that whatever they found on the exhibits would be his. He admitted to receiving and sending material. He was questioned about offline offending and his own children, which was when he suddenly got nervous and requested a solicitor.

"Once he'd had his consultation, and with the solicitor present, they restarted and he went 'no comment'. They have kept him in, and have made contact with the ex-wife with a view to start the disclosure process with the children. They are both now pubescent, but they were in his age range when they were together. The wife admitted to the child victim interview team leader that she had suspected her husband had taken nude photographs of them when they were younger, which was the main reason for leaving him; but that she was sure he hadn't physically interfered with them. Disclosure begins today and will take as long as it takes. He hasn't got access to the children or any others, so they may bail him; but for the moment it's their intention to keep him in overnight. Archie has the exhibits and has sent them to SDE."

Anna paused, indicating she had come to an end regarding Thomas. Tom had a hundred questions he wanted to ask immediately, and then work the answers through in his mind. But this was 'hot off the press' stuff and it wasn't the right time. However, their primary objective was being achieved.

"Next."

"Brian Leitch from Redhill. He wasn't home, and neither was the wife, but she returned thirty minutes later after walking the dog. She told them where he was, and they went and got him whilst keeping someone with the wife.

"There were two desk tops and two laptops together with a number of external's, CD's and data sticks. The wife had her own setup, which accounts for there being two of everything. Brian never said a word at the address, but the officers at the scene said that the hatred emanating from the wife in the direction of the husband was a clear indication that she suspected or knew something.

"They allocated an officer specifically to her after they left, and she disclosed that she had suspected he was up to something but never thought it would be kids. He wanted a solicitor and went 'no comment' throughout. His PC and laptop are protected, the wife has got one password for the PC but doesn't know the one for the laptop, and has never known it. Victim interviewers are seeing their two older children tonight when they get home from work. They are keeping him in too. The exhibits were collected by SDE and they have begun work on it already.

"And finally, Simon Clark from Essex," Anna continued, "the officers knew as soon as they stepped inside it was going to be positive. There was a single PC and a laptop, with plenty of externals and CDs and other data-holding media. He admits to being in possession of child abuse material and exchanging some for others. He has encryption but has provided the passwords.

"He has provided an identical description of the site as the others that have spoken, and states that all his contacts have come from the site. His preference is prepubescent boys and he is a member of an internal 'childscentcafe' group that exchanges certain images of boys just between themselves.

"He stated that he hasn't offended offline, but that he wanted to; and had been working to get into another group which had access to children. He says that his collection has over 350,000 images and videos. Mitchell has collected their exhibits and is travelling to SDE, but is not expected there for another hour or so. Clark has been given a short bail again as per our request."

Anna finished with a flourish, then fell silent. All four of them in the room were rendered speechless. Anna because she had been doing all the talking, the rest because it was exactly what they had hoped to get.

"If this isn't going to be enough to change the mind of the CEO of WebHostTwelve, then nothing will," Tom said, feeling elated by the news. This could be the key to moving this operation on, and it was far from over yet. Once the victim interviews were done and examination completed, it would only get better.

'*But, where to first?*' He thought to himself.

"Jane. Where are we with Cleveland?"

"The DCS there is making all the right noises, and can meet us mid afternoon at their HQ again."

"OK, get Sam to get us some tickets. I will take Anna, she has all the information in her head or at her fingertips, and I want one of us at the helm here for the next few weeks if possible."

As Tom paused to check his counsel notepad and decide what to consider next, he failed to see the metaphorical bubbles poking out of the heads of some of his staff. All of them contained a similar sentence: '*He doesn't want to be with Jane in public so soon.*'

The truth was that Tom's unconscious competence was working along those lines, but his immediate thoughts concentrated on whether he should get the server first before seeing Cleveland. Because without it, it would all collapse, but that thought lasted for all of a nanosecond.

"Right, Anna. Prepare to deliver that and whatever we get in overnight and tomorrow whilst we travel up there. We will get the server. Failure to do so is not an option!"

As COCET specialist intelligence officer Anna Farley and DCI Tom Ross sped their way north towards the market town of Darlington, Tom was working his way through the updates that had come in overnight, some within the last few minutes. He knew from Operation Hope that the world was just touching the tip of the mother of all icebergs when it came to child sex abuse on the internet, and that, even with the beginnings of GOPOL, the environment did not lend itself to coordinated policing. So the future was not going to get any better any time soon.

But even knowing all of that, he still felt he could make a difference as long as he went the extra mile. If nothing else, it was a way of hiding from the immense guilt that enveloped him the moment he tried to examine the sequence of events leading to Fiona's death. He shook it from his thoughts and read the notes that Anna had provided for him.

John Black, who had been bailed to return, had a catalogue of over 300,000 images and videos, and the examination was still not complete. It would be another two to three days at least, and it was a case that Dr. Nick Sharpe was undertaking personally due to the high numbers involved. The images covered 1-5 of the Copine scale, and there were many incidences of supplying child abuse material across that Copine scale as well. Nick had specifically noted that he had not found evidence of John Black being involved in a 'group' within the site, but there was much work yet to be done.

Tom sat back into his seat and looked out of the window, watching the rolling farmland that passed by as the train made its way through the countryside. He knew a catalogue that big would take as long as it took to look at every single image, and make an assessment of its level of criminality, including every frame of the videos. During that examination he would make notes as to whether it was worth further victim identification work being undertaken on it.

If it did, Jane and another member of COCET would then go over the images or videos looking for clues that might identify a victim. Not thousands, but hundreds of thousands would take days; and then there were email and chat logs across however many platforms he was using. The temporary folders and archives might hold other clues and SDE, he knew, would leave nothing behind.

Nick would be busy at his desk, the thousands of victims reaching out to him. How many would they be able to identify and then rescue from their abuse he had no idea, but the heartache lay in the true answer to that question, and that was on the basis of previous investigations, it would be less than ten per cent.

He let Nick and the farmland go and turned to Arthur Thomas from Gwent. His collection was around 70,000 images and videos. Like Black, he had material that had been categorised from the minor to the very worst in child sex abuse, and Tom knew what that was. It was something that would, to some degree, leave that child scarred and mentally ill for the rest of their life. The most unforgivable of deeds in this area of criminality was the sexual abuse of one's own children, and Thomas had gone there. Both children had made disclosures, and he was to be charged with a number of rapes of both children plus other sexual acts, together with his internet offending. Dr. Sue Tay estimated that there were many duplicates in his collection, together with many images that were either known, older, or Baltic in nature. However, there were two videos which were new looking and which contained background material that might be of use for victim identification.

Tom immediately inserted a hatch sign next to the entry, then moved on to Brian Leitch, who clearly had something to hide. This case had not gone the same way as the others. The wife's PC and laptop had been clean. His PC was also clean. However, Dr. Tay had found 'The Onion Router' artefacts, which probably meant that, he had at some point, either downloaded or used that programme to access, surf or communicate over the internet anonymously. Called The Onion Router (TOR for short) after the many layers of an onion, it acted in the same way in that it went through a network of relays to hide the real source. An unknown person communicating whilst using encryption to another unknown person meant a bad day at the office for a forensic examiner. The fact that remnants were left behind provided a hint of what was to come. His laptop was whole drive protected using TrueCrypt, and Dr. Sue Tay had made a request for the password, something which the Surrey Police search team had not found. Tom made another hatch sign note then continued.

Nothing illegal had been found on any of the external hard drives, CDs or data sticks. Which left just the interviews with the two older children, Jamie and Karen Leitch, who both wanted to be interviewed together. The Surrey victim interview team had prepared themselves for the meeting, but within minutes of meeting with Jamie and Karen it was apparent that Karen was doing the answering, and for a specific reason. Once she had all the answers, and was satisfied with them, she had told her brother to speak.

No matter how long you had been working in child protection, or how 'hard' you thought you were, seeing the years of pain, torture, and fear unfold before your eyes still found its mark. He'd made a huge mental and emotional down payment only weeks earlier, and hadn't expected to pay any more. As he read on, he simply relinquished; handed over more of his memory bank, which quickly absorbed the newly acquired information and which he knew would remain with him forever.

Brian Leitch, as an alleged caring father, had started to abuse his own son from the age of five and continued until he was eleven. He had groomed him, then abused him; and then continued that abuse together with threats and blackmail which had continued for his whole life until now. His sister had been and still was the only thing he trusted in life. He had only confessed to her in recent years, and only on the promise she would not tell anyone, a promise which she had kept until now. He still truly believed that his father would kill him and his mother if the truth came out.

With his father now arrested, and with the support of his sister, he finally had the courage to speak out. Surrey Police had obtained a Superintendent's detention extension for the father whilst they conducted a further evidential interview with Jamie. They were also breaking the news to the wife. On being told, she had collapsed and been rushed to hospital, where she was being monitored for a suspected heart attack.

The Police had gone back to court and obtained a Section 8 PACE warrant to search for the password, something that Dr. Sue Tay said she would need. He didn't have to read much further as he knew what was coming next, but he needed to know it anyway. In interview Brian Leitch had gone 'no comment' throughout, and his solicitor had let the interviewing officers know that his client would protest his innocence in court, meaning Jamie would have to re-live it all again within the dramatic and combative atmosphere of a courtroom. SDE were amongst the best, if not 'the best' in the UK at what they did. If anyone could get into that laptop they could, so with that thought he let it go and moved onto Simon Clark.

He had admitted to possessing and distributing child abuse material. His personal collection was around 350,000 images, mostly of prepubescent boys, and it was going to take Nick a number of days to check them all for categorisation and victim identification evidence, then more time for chat logs and emails. There was an early indication that he was either a member of a group, or was in the process of joining a group that appeared to use anonymising software. Tom went back to his hatch notes and called Jane King.

"Yes, Boss."

"Jane, can you speak with Dr. Tay and get the two videos she has highlighted in the Thomas case for victim ID? And whilst you are speaking with her find out what the chances are of getting into the hard drive of Leitch's laptop, assuming Surrey don't find the password."

"Will do. Can they get into that?"

"No, I don't think they can; but I do want to know what the bottom line is. The Leitch case is bothering me, my gut tells me that he isn't just hiding the evidence around his son. That stopped years ago as he got older, it's what he's hiding now I want to know."

"OK. I will ring Sue now and arrange to get those videos. I will get back to you on the encryption. The Surrey search team leader has rung saying they have started. The wife is doing well and has told the Police that her husband always spent time in the loft and the garden shed, and that she never knew why."

"Fingers crossed," replied Tom.

DCI Ross and Anna Farley were shown into the office of Detective Chief Superintendent (DCS) Mark Braithwaite. After a quick round of introductions DCS Braithwaite took charge.

"Becky has told me that you are seeking support from Cleveland Police for the arrest of Philip Thompson, who is on our patch, she has confirmed that. From there, I understand, COCET would like to undertake covert operations using his online identity to infiltrate a web based paedophile ring. I'm not an expert in this area, but I do have staff who are, and they tell me this is pretty ground breaking stuff and necessary. So I will be supporting it."

Tom had been in situations like this before, where he had gone into a meeting cold with a very senior officer, not knowing them or their background, wondering how he would fare. His sixth sense was making itself felt and it was telling him he was dealing with one of the good guys. In the Police, for the officers who wanted to get to the top it was very competitive. Tom had a view that the ones who wanted to get past the rank of DCS went into a whole new area of competition, probably due to the few vacancies around and the fact they had to be politicians as well as cops. For the ones that stuck just short of that 'kingdom', they had reached their final level. Some became tyrannical, some were just plain strict, and some ended up like Miller. Then there were the 'few', the ones who were gentlemen, the ones who could reach down and touch the 'beat', and feel and remember it as if it was only yesterday. They never lost sight of their core values and they never lost sight of the Constable or the Detective on shift or night duty; and probably more importantly, they didn't have an axe to grind or scores to settle. They were therefore more naturally gifted in how they operated and processed a simple request for help. Tom had hit the jackpot. He had one of those in front of him now.

Skilfully, and with real sincerity, DCS Braithwaite drew out all the salient points of what Tom wanted to do, what he needed to achieve it, and what the impacts were for Cleveland Police. He also made notes of the intelligence briefing from Anna Farley. All of which led to one question for Tom and COCET.

"I have one major incident team that has the capacity to take on another job, especially one that isn't a protracted case, so what I need to know from you, DCI Ross, is how long will you need them for?"

"Three to six weeks," replied Tom immediately, knowing that the question was bound to come up.

Whether DCS Braithwaite expected more or less Tom never found out, but his reply was, "In that case you can have them. Detective Superintendent Evans will contact you within a few days for a meeting. If things run over a little bit I am sure we will be able to accommodate you. Operational activity like this is something we should, and will, commit time effort and money to. I wish you both well."

Tom and Anna made their way back, both very pleased with the way things had gone. Tom now had the issue of Holland, the server, and the Dutch internal laws to overcome: something they had to do before they could get to the operational phase. He pushed the negative thoughts straight out of his mind, which was helped by his phone ringing.

"Boss, it's Jane. Anna W has left to get the videos, we will have a quick look tonight, and may work late if there is a need. Dr. Tay says she can't get into the hard drive without the password. Even if we get it, his files could be protected as well."

"It's down to Surrey then," he replied sadly.

"Hang on the line a sec, my desk phone is going, it might be them."

As he waited he found himself wishing for good news. He looked at Anna opposite; she had heard most of what had been said and correctly guessed the rest. It was a few minutes before Jane came back to her phone, and just as the train sped into a tunnel. "They have found a long alpha numeric password on a rolled up piece of paper and Dr. Sue Tay has it and…" The mobile phone signal had clung on as long as it could, but then failed, leaving both COCET officers desperately waiting for the train to emerge back into daylight.

CHAPTER THIRTEEN

Tom sat hunched over, listening intently to the conference call pod on the table, as Dr. Sue Tay explained how she'd accessed Leitch's laptop with the password found by Surrey Police in their second search. Elation had been short lived for all concerned, as it quickly became apparent that some files were protected by further encryption. The ones that weren't had yielded just over six thousand images and videos of young boys, mostly between the ages of five and ten, all of which had yet to be assessed. There was clear evidence of Leitch belonging to 'childscentcafe', which was the evidence he needed for Holland.

"Well, that's as far as we have got. We will continue working on this case and the others, and you can collect all the images and videos for victim ID work from tomorrow. When we get something we will let you know. Do you want our statements first, or shall we deal direct with the Force concerned?"

"Deal direct. We just want the intelligence and the leads. All the Home Forces know that, and it is what we agreed."

"Right. I'd better crack on then."

With the call disconnected and the room silent, Tom sat back up.

"Jane, get hold of Niall and set up a meeting with WebHostTwelve, tomorrow if possible. I will go with Anna W, she was allocated this action and will have most of it in her head. Collect the images and videos and make a start, once we get going with Cleveland we won't get the time."

Tom spent the rest of the morning catching up on his SIO policy log, and had just one more to go when Maggie Burrows entered his office. Tom was pleased to see her, but at the same time she hadn't announced she would be coming, causing his internal survival gauge to go up a few degrees.

"Hi, Tom. Sit, sit. I just wanted to update you on Kuklin and the others." Tom sat back down behind his desk whilst Maggie sat in a chair in front.

"As you know, Kuklin wanted a deal, and it's something the Met are taking seriously. But it relies on them getting the suspects out of Russia, which, although they will continue to try to do, it is anticipated Russia will never allow it to happen. Therefore, at some point there will be no deal."

This information didn't surprise Tom. He had read up on the extradition treaty, and Russian law itself stated that they would never send a national for trial to the UK or elsewhere.

"Well, I guessed as much, Ma'am."

Tom didn't deliberately use the rank word and had no idea why he did. He had a good relationship with Maggie. Maybe it was because she had come unannounced, or it was his survival gauge; but Maggie picked up on it and moved on to why she was really there.

"Tom. How are you managing?"

"Fine, considering. Why?"

"The ACC has asked that I follow up on a matter that he spoke to you about."

'So that's why you are here', Tom thought.

"I have cut back my intake and I'm now at the level I was before Fiona's murder," Tom replied quickly, probably a little too quickly as it came across as being defensive.

"Good. I am glad to hear that," Maggie replied slowly and with a hint of authority in her voice, immediately making Tom feel he was in a 'Me Superintendent, you DCI' situation.

"I've also had a conversation with Dr. Clayworth. She feels that you need to be monitored to ensure that you don't take on too much work. Are you?"

Inside Tom could feel the red mist rising. He knew from experience that he had to control it and quickly. "I'm doing the same level of work

I always have. I am not taking on any extra and I am not making the staff do so either. Dr. Clayworth has never suggested to me that I was."

From the expression on Maggie's face, Tom felt she hadn't been expecting that reply.

"Well, maybe she should have done. I can bring that matter up with her. I know we have stopped the security cover on you but I would still like to monitor your work load. So I will need your duty times sent to me, please arrange that through Sam."

"Sure, no problem," replied Tom keeping a pleasant tone and a facial expression to match. Once Maggie had left though he couldn't keep it together any longer. Putting his face in his hands he rubbed his face hard and thought, *'For fuck's sake! What more do they want to take away from me?'* He was about to call Gloria Clayworth and give her a piece of his mind, when Sarah walked in wanting to talk about Operation Ascent.

The discussion was one about back door extradition. The 'What if the Russians just want to hand them over?' debate that GOPOL and COCET had been asked to comment on. Tom wasn't really in any mood to talk politics, but it did serve as a distraction.

"Look. My view is that they would have to return voluntarily to the UK, and by that I mean they would have to hand themselves in over there. Our evidence would need to go before their court, our evidence would need to meet the threshold for extradition as if we had it between the two countries, and even then if we got them here it might not be enough. But we don't give up just because of what might happen. We still pursue the best possible course as long as it has been thoroughly thought through."

"Well that's good, as it is in line with what the GOPOL Chiefs are saying. The Media just want to know if it's COCET's view as well. It is just their way of developing a story." Sarah paused and then said, "Are you OK?"

The words caught Tom completely off guard. It wasn't just that he didn't expect them, but it was also the level of sincerity and care in the tone that made him lost for words. Sarah was a professional and used to working around very senior Police Officers, much higher in rank than himself, and knew how to handle the void that was fast developing in front of her. She shuffled together her pad and some other documents and got up heading for the door.

"The press will continue to badger GOPOL around Operation Ascent until they get something more to think about. The best course of action is to give them that," she said, smiling at Tom with a caring expression.

Tom felt alone and numb from the two short interactions. One had got him wound up and the other had calmed him down. The result left him feeling rudderless, floating in the moment, until the red mist started to get the upper hand again. He picked up his phone and rang Sam. The sting from the first meeting may have been removed by Sarah, but he still needed to know that he was in control of his life.

"Sam. Maggie Burrows wants to see my duty states from today and until further notice, what do you actually show for me?"

"Exactly what I have always shown you as, straight eights."

"OK. Well, until she doesn't want them any longer show me as an extra three and then four hours a week, sometimes rotating, some consecutively. Just mix it up a bit."

"Sure. It might be a good idea to show you as starting late to cover some afternoons and evenings, they always like to see that. It shows you are managing your workload and prioritising a better home, work and life balance."

In a few seconds Sam had grasped what had gone on in the room only moments before as if she had been in there listening to it all. It took her the same amount of time to put Tom back on an even keel.

"You do what needs to be done, Tom. I will cover the admin, just let me know where you are so if I am asked I can say something that fits the situation, and we both don't get caught out!"

Tom felt humbled by the unique understanding they had.

"Thanks, Sam. Have I ever told you that you don't get paid enough?" Tom said with genuine affection.

"Many times, Tom. Many times."

The following day Tom and DC Anna Wilson flew to Amsterdam,

where they met Interpol Agent Niall Mullins and a local Police Officer who took them all to the offices of WebHostTwelve. On entry they signed in, and were shown to a seating area of large comfortable leather seats to the left of the reception area. Within minutes they were collected by a young female staff member who took them into the office complex. They went up four floors to a room which was a medium to large conference facility, made up of a large oval table with numerous chairs on two sides, with a projection screen with a web conferencing facility at one end and a hospitality station at the other.

The outside wall of the office was made up wholly of solid glass panels, which lit up the room naturally and provided an impressive aerial view of Amsterdam. They were met by three men, two of whom were wearing jeans and corporate branded polo shirts, whilst the third was in a two piece suit and a tie.

They introduced themselves in almost perfect English, causing Tom, not for the first time, to wish he could speak foreign languages. The CEO of WebHostTwelve, Lars Bakker, went first. He was followed by his Operations Manager, Pim Janssen, and finally by the company lawyer, Gerrit Van Dijk. Once Tom had introduced his team and everyone was seated, Lars Bakker spoke before Niall Mullins got a chance to open the proceedings.

"All three of us would like to state straight away that child abuse in any form is abhorrent and we want to help you in any way that we can. To help me in making decisions that are legal, I have with me Gerrit, who is our corporate lawyer, and Pim who will tell me exactly what we can and cannot do technically. So the floor is yours."

Niall, who was thinking, *'Great, that's my job done,'* turned to Tom and said, "Over to you!"

Tom provided them with a history of Operation Hope, how COCET had come to be formed, and how the intelligence case for Operation Resolve had led them to Amsterdam and WebHostTwelve. Tom broadly explained his operational objectives, and how, to be successful in dismantling 'childscentcafe', infiltration police tactics alone would not be sufficient. But, with a copy of the server and the cooperation of the company in keeping the server operational until all Police activity had been completed, it would lead the investigation to a successful conclusion. He then discussed the latest intelligence.

"We understand the legal situation you are in," Tom began, as he opened up the latest briefing document Anna Wilson had put together. "So we have undertaken four search warrants on suspects all of who are, or were, members of 'childscentcafe'. They were all positive searches and have led to four arrests, and over 700,000 images or videos have been recovered. It has also led to the discovery of three children who have suffered years of sexual abuse by their fathers, and one suspect who was looking to offend offline in the near future.

"From what we know, none of the four know each other; and yet they admit, and we can prove, that they are all members of 'childscentcafe'. A number of them have admitted in interview that the only reason they are members of this web based group is to enable them to meet other offenders such as themselves, and to exchange child abuse content, outside of the site forum.

"In fact, they state that the forum rules are that they cannot post or talk about child abuse images within the forum, and that those rules are there to protect them from coming to the attention of global law enforcement.

"So, a key objective in the investigation is the identification of the owner, the supervisors, and the forum users. To do that we need a copy of the server. That way we will be able to dismantle for good the criminal enterprise that has an end goal of the sexual abuse of children."

Tom, Niall and Anna had all been assessing the body language of the three men opposite whilst Tom was speaking. They seemed genuinely concerned, yet at the same time they weren't giving anything away. That was until Lars spoke again.

"To know that you have that much success is heartening, but at the same time it means there has been much pain, sadness and fear in so many children. Two of the three of us here have children, Chief Inspector. Some young and some not so young. So it has a real impact on us personally and indeed corporately. I want you all to know that we want to help as much as we can. As for this new information, we weren't expecting that. So, Gerrit, does this change things?" With that he looked towards the man in the suit and tie.

The last part of Lars' sentence registered with all three of the COCET officers immediately. Tom was thinking, *'That has to be enough, surely?',* whilst Niall and Anna were thinking the same thing, *'They are going to say no.'*

Gerrit, who clearly didn't like making immediate legal decisions without considerable reflection, shuffled silently in his seat before answering.

"As you say, Lars, we weren't expecting this. I will need time to consider this new information. It may well be that it changes things, but there are significant ramifications for the company should I advise you wrongly. So for the time being my advice must remain, but I will promise to work on this immediately and get back to you within a few days." Gerrit looked back to Lars, signalling he had nothing further to say.

Lars looked back across the table at the COCET officers, sensing they had come to Amsterdam hoping for a result based on their new information. He really wanted to help them, but he had his hands tied.

Tom could sense that bad news was coming and wanted to give it another shot.

"This case is no different from that of money laundering where a legitimate shop sells products in a commercial market, but the money to buy those products or the rent for the premises has been funded from criminal activities. You can also liken this to a criminal conspiracy, when a group of men go to a house belonging to one of them and they conspire to rob a bank. The discussions in the house are secretly recorded by one of the men who is an undercover officer. The action of meeting, planning and discussion all go towards proving the offence, even though the Police intercept them as they enter the bank. It is all in the presentation and understanding of what is going on in 'childscentcafe'. We think these arrests show the end criminal result, and that the server is the meeting place for the start of the conspiracy."

"Chief Inspector, whilst I would dearly love to help you, and indeed want to, the advice from my lawyer is that I cannot hand over a copy of the server to you. It is not permitted by law, and you will need the authority of a magistrate for me to give it to you. I have been informed that you will not get that authority due to the way the users of the website are using the server within Holland. I can understand your frustration, but Dutch law is quite clear and I cannot breach it. Now, we will get back to you once we have had time to assess the new information. In the meantime I have asked Pim to be on hand to show you our operational setup, so that if we get to a position where we can lawfully assist you, then you will understand how we operate."

Niall was making decisions in his head as Lars was speaking. He didn't really know how Tom was going to respond. A month ago, before Fiona's murder, he would have been confident to let Tom reply, knowing that he would have spoken diplomatically and politically and would have delivered a response suitable for the situation they were in. After finding out Tom had been the real target of an assassination attempt which had ultimately killed a close friend, Niall was now not so sure.

"We understand your position, Lars, and would never seek or ask you to break any laws," Niall began. "We came today knowing that was the case. We wanted to put to you the new information personally to show you the level of seriousness that we give it; putting a face to a name is always good in situations like this, and we really do appreciate you taking the time to assess the new intelligence. I, for one, would love to see the operational side of things." Niall looked away from Lars and towards Tom and Anna. Tom was grateful for the thinking time and the path offered him by Niall.

"Niall speaks for us all. Yes, we would love to see the operational side."

The trip to Amsterdam was a sharp learning curve for DC Anna Wilson. She had expected to go there and come back triumphant with a copy of the server in her pocket. At home that night, alone in her bed, she couldn't get to sleep as she went from feeling mad at the Dutch and their laws, to admiration for how both Tom and Niall had handled defeat.

She was ambitious and wanted promotion. Working within all the politics of UK policing was bad enough; but adding in all the European law, and the different cultures in each country, when working globally on the internet, was another thing entirely. The countries of the EU couldn't work together offline in the real worlds of trade, industry and agriculture, when they had all signed agreements to do so. The 'One size fits all' approach to Europe would never work when the French could just ignore a ruling because they felt like it. Without a copy of the server she just couldn't see how they would be successful, and that thought stayed with her until sleep eventually came.

CHAPTER FOURTEEN

There are many skills and traits a modern day manager must possess to be successful in the role. Some of them one can get by without, some are nice to have, some are a must have. A rare few will earn the respect of staff and others alike. One of those is the ability to change a decision in the light of new information.

0905hrs UTC, Amsterdam, Holland
Lars Bakker opened a letter from the pile in front of him and started to read it. He was half way through when he threw it down and rang his secretary to request a meeting as soon as possible with the company lawyer, Gerrit Van Dijk. He made his way through the remaining correspondence whilst he waited for Gerrit to arrive, becoming angrier as time passed.

As soon as Gerrit walked in Lars thrust the letter into his hands and, without saying a word, left to make coffee for them both. Gerrit's first action was to check the sender, and seeing it was from the client who was the subject of the UK Police investigation, read on with interest. As he neared the end of the vitriolic content he had already formulated his advice.

It was 'No change.' They weren't going to hand over the server, so the threat of being sued by their client meant nothing. On his return, and once Lars was seated, the lawyer delivered that advice.

"Het is alleen maar een dreigement. Wij overhandigen sowieso de server niet, dus vergeet het maar."

However, for Lars, this threatening letter from a client was the last straw; he was using Dutch law and Lars' company to hide his abuse of children. He wasn't going to ignore it. He was going to take the client on, even if it was illegal. He was going to hand a copy of the server to COCET, the UK Police authority, and that was that. Gerrit was just going to have to protect him and the company as best he could. So he firmly told Gerrit of his plan.

"Nou Gerrit, ik ga hem niet negeren, ik wil met hem afrekenen. Ik wil natuurlijk wel dat je alles in je vermogen doet om ons bedrijf en mij te beschermen, maar ik heb besloten om een kopie van deze server aan de wettelijke autoriteiten van Engeland te overhandigen.

Dit is mijn definitieve besluit dus probeer me niet meer om te praten!"

Lars' request would leave Gerrit personally exposed to civil action at least, as well as the company, so he would need to take immediate action to cover them as best he could. There was a silver lining in it though: the more they assisted, the more likely their client would go to prison for a very long time and this current threat would, in all probability, just go away. That was his advice now, and it wouldn't change no matter how long he pondered over it. So he told his Boss that.

"Prima, zoals je van me weet zal ik alles doen wat in mijn vermogen ligt, En nu, het beste wat jij kan doen, is COCET zoveel mogelijk te assisteren. Als jouw opdrachtgever gearresteerd wordt en voor jaren de gevangenis in gaat, dan beschadigt dat ons niet. Waarschijnlijk zal het er zelfs voor zorgen dat dit allemaal in het niets oplost."

1605hrs ICT, Pattaya, Thailand

It was late afternoon in Pattaya, Thailand, and LB and Mr. B had got back to their accommodation, excited by the filming session they had just completed. It was the third in as many days and had cost more than they had expected in bribes and family compensation, but the end product was worth it. Mr. B went to the fridge and removed two bottles of Singha beer, handing one to LB before sitting down. Both men drank silently from the bottle, each of them reliving some of their recent pleasures. The young man known to COCET as Michael could see the other man was getting hard again from the bulge that was fast showing through his shorts.

"You need to go last! You ruined him for me, why can't you just play the fucking game!"

Mr. B didn't reply. Instead he let his head drop back, and with a smile on his face, unzipped his shorts and started to masturbate. LB, incensed, got up, walked over to him and poured his still cold beer over the man's erect penis. Mr. B, who hadn't seen it coming, jumped up in anger; spilling the contents of most of his bottle on the floor. Both men stood opposite each other, anger coursing through their veins, each one waiting for the other to start the fight. However, one of them backed down quickly. He knew what the other was capable of, he had committed at least one murder, and if pushed he would do the same again.

"Not hard now, are you!"

Mr. B zipped himself up and left the room to change. On his return he took another bottle from the fridge, this time just for himself.

"I want to go over the Visser thing one more time." "Why? We've done it to death," replied Mr. B.

"Because I fucking want to!"

Mr. B sighed, but not loudly as he could see he had pissed the other man off. He had one more day to put up with him before he left, so he went along with it.

"He's been arrested by the local police on a tip off from the UK. He's been jailed, and as I've told you before he will get a lengthy sentence. Even if he does talk, he doesn't know who we are because of the precautions. So stop worrying, he can't identify you or the rest of us." With that Mr. B left and went to his bedroom to relive the evening's events in peace.

Alone with his thoughts LB knew it wasn't OK, but he couldn't let the others know that. They would be arriving over the next few days and there was far too much to lose. The only thing Mr. B was right about were the precautions. Yes, that would stop the authorities coming to his door for now, but he would prefer it if they never knew about him in the first place.

If he could get access to Visser he would kill him himself in a heartbeat, but he couldn't get that access. Also, he didn't have the ability to put a hit on him in prison either. Even if he tried, there was too much risk attached to that idea. If the Police got to the killer, he would surely give him up if the authorities offered a deal. His real problem was that Visser knew one more secret about him. And that secret, despite all the precautions, could lead them to him if they joined the dots. It was time for action, and one that he had prepared and saved for.

Around the same time Tom entered his office, having just returned from a 'greasy spoon' visit to the local cafe, which he and Mo referred to as 'Conference Room Two'. He was feeling satisfied with his bacon, eggs, beans, two toasts and a cup of tea, and sat down to write up a report to the CPS. Not getting a copy of the server from Holland wasn't just a setback, it could end their current Operation if he let it. He stretched his neck from left to right quickly, hearing the cracks through his ear drums. Resigned to a long session of report writing aimed at getting legal action within Holland to secure a copy of the server, he set to work. However, within moments he was interrupted by a phone call.

"DCI Ross, COCET. Can I help you?"

"DCI Ross, this is Lars Bakker. I have some news for you."

Twenty minutes later Tom was in the conference room with the COCET team present and Niall on the speaker phone. He recounted the telephone call he had received from Lars Bakker, bringing everybody up to date.

"They made the right decision, but for the wrong reasons!" Niall cried out. Something that Anna Wilson was also thinking.

Tom was looking at the speaker phone but his mind was not only on Niall's words.

"Dale. Go to WebHostTwelve and get a copy of the server. Sam, I want Dale there tomorrow."

Tom looked at Sam, who quickly nodded.

"Dale, Anna W has the details for their tech guy. Speak to him today to make sure you take whatever it is that you need. If you haven't got it, buy it!"

"Yes, Boss."

"Jane. We haven't heard from Cleveland. Call Becky and find out what the delay is, we needed that delay, but not any more. Let's get some traction on it."

"Will do, Boss."

"Oh, Dale, whilst you are travelling, give some thought to how many UCs you will need to assume the identity of Philip Thompson over a rolling 24 hour period."

"Will do."

"Questions?"

"Are you happy for me to now include Cleveland in the media strategy?" Sarah asked.

"Yes."

"Do you want it put through GOPOL?" Sarah continued, knowing that she would have to let them have sight of it in any case.

"Do they have to see it?" Tom replied, not really thinking. If he had, he would have known that the answer was yes.

"Err, mm, yes."

He felt he was being defensive, and so took it for granted he sounded like it. He softened his tone deliberately, "Yes. Of course, Sarah."

Louisa, seeing her opportunity, got in quickly. "Guv, it would be good to make some early contact with the local NSPCC and Social Services. They don't need to know any details, but making the single points of contact early should get us a better response from them when we need it."

"OK, but no operational intelligence is to be released. And Jane, let Becky know we are doing this. I don't want the local contacts there coming in from the side as a result of Louisa making her calls in advance. Reinforce it with Becky that this is on a need to know basis."

DC Marks was waiting to see if anybody brought up what they were going to do with the server once they got a copy, and as it seemed the meeting was about to end, he thought he'd better say something. "Boss?"

"Yes, Owen."

"Once we have a copy of the server how are we going to read the contents? It's not going to be in a readable form."

"That's one of his jobs," Tom said, looking at Dale and then back to Owen.

Dale, who saw where this was going, and that the Boss was wrong, quickly interjected.

"I don't have the skills for that, and I don't know who has."

Tom, who wasn't expecting that, replied, "I guess that's one action for me then."

Back in his office Tom rang SDE immediately and got Dr. Sue Tay.

"Sue. We have had a breakthrough on Operational Resolve. The Dutch have agreed to hand over a copy of the server. One of my bright spark DCs has asked how are we going to read the contents. I was sort of assuming that Dale would be able to sort that, but he says he's can't. So can you guys do it? I would pay for it?"

"That's Nick's area, not mine, I'll just get him."

"Hi Tom, lovely to speak to you, what's the problem?" Nick said, coming on the line.

Tom recounted the intelligence update on Operation Resolve and the issue of the server contents.

"Well, hmm. Now, that is my area, but do you know what script and database language the company uses?"

"No. Would it help if I send you their Head of Operations phone number and you can speak direct to him? I will ring ahead and let him know you will be calling."

"That would be great. Once I know what they are using I will be able to advise you more."

Tom rang Lars Bakker immediately.

"Lars. One of my officers will be with you tomorrow and will contact Pim directly to make arrangements. Also, would you let Pim know that one of the directors of a digital evidence company we use, a Dr. Nick Sharpe, will also contact him about what software you use on your servers?"

"I can inform Pim for you," said Lars, "but you can take it from me that the database will be MySQL."

"Right," Tom replied, not having a clue what Lars was referring to.

Thirty five minutes later Dr. Nick Sharpe rang Tom back. "OK. Yes I can do this, but it isn't that straightforward."

"Go on," replied Tom, with the hint of suspicion in his tone.

"Well, the copy that you'll get won't be readable. And we won't know what the server really contains until it is converted into a readable form. There could be very little, or there could be a lot. The conversion needs to stand up in court, and the best way for this to happen is if I involve another expert in this area. Now Jeremy, who you used on Operation Hope, has the skills. But, if you remember, I did suggest at the time another person who works for GCHQ, but we went with Jeremy."

"Yes, go on."

"Well, on this occasion I would prefer to work with Dominic Newland. Jeremy is good but Dominic is great, and he might be able to help me on the Leitch case as well."

"That sounds awesome, but does that mean you haven't got into those files yet?"

"We are still working on it. But no, we haven't. Dominic would be a good person to collaborate with on it."

"Alright, I'm sold on it. But I need a meeting with him before I can authorise him to do the job."

"Leave that with me," replied Dr. Sharpe as he put the phone down.

The following day Tom was in his office playing mind games with himself, following virtual leads on Operation Resolve in his head. His experience and knowledge highlighted the countless possibilities that could accelerate one lead or end another. But in most cases the original lead took another pathway, only to be changed again by yet another set of hypothetical events. It took about twenty minutes but slowly a clear picture emerged from all his intensive thinking, and he quickly grabbed his counsel pad and scribbled down a four bullet point list.

This was his plan. A simple list of four words that showed how they would infiltrate a global group of child sex abusers, take control of the environment they operated in and identify their leaders, administrators and users, finally leading to their arrest and the end of their terrible crimes against children.

This was a global war, and the internet made it possible. What he needed to do was use their own environment, the one they felt safe and secure in, against them. He had a plan and he could see the end that was in sight.

Just as he let go of those thoughts, they were immediately replaced by an incoming tide of guilt and pain for Fiona. It caught him off guard, large waves of emotion pulling him down into a rip. Suddenly, and without warning, a hand reached down and pulled him out to safety.

"Sir. I have a Dominic Newland to see you," Sam said brightly at his door.

He had no idea what the skill set was of this officer from GCHQ, the Government Communication Headquarters being shrouded in secrecy and intrigue. The mere fact that he was working for them meant that he had to be skilled around computer forensics and the communication structures that used the internet. Whatever the man from GCHQ was really all about, Tom guessed he would never find out, but all the same, it felt good to know that someone with that level of expertise was willing to show up at COCET.

Dominic Newland was simply dressed, if not underdressed, and from a quick glance the labels would have been at the cheaper end of the scale. The upper clothing was also oversized, just enough to give the appearance of someone that you wouldn't necessarily take a second look at, although Tom sensed he was muscular under all the clothing. He wasn't expecting a pinstripe suit and bowler hat, but he also wasn't expecting this. The main thing that was missing was any form of briefcase or bag, maybe that was all tucked away in his brain!

"Hi. Tom Ross. Pleased to meet you, and thanks for coming here. I find it difficult to get out of the office."

Dominic offered his hand in greeting and Tom felt the strength in his grip.

"Thank you for the opportunity," Dominic replied with a hint of humour that made Tom think that he really was glad of the opportunity.

"I've had a conversation with Nick Sharpe," Dominic said moving on quickly, "and he says that you may need some help in decoding a server you will be getting a copy of; and that you want to be able to access the contents for intelligence that will ultimately be used for gaining evidence. Have I got the right end of the stick?"

Tom was taken aback with the mixture of forthrightness and simplicity in the line of questioning, particularly as it was coming from Dominic, and not himself. He thought it sensible though to give the GCHQ specialist the floor. After all, he had come all this way.

"Yes," replied Tom, simply.

"I can do that for you. It is extremely important that the process is fully documented, thought through and checked over. I would anticipate that you will get more than you think, and that the action you take reactively will be traced back to this one item of work in the end. If there is one single thing wrong then it could cause you a problem in court, not just in one case, but in many."

Tom felt there had been a subtle shift in who was doing what, and this would need to be crystal clear in his mind and his policy log.

"I agree with that. Are you helping Nick do this, or are you going to do it on your own?"

"I will be doing it. I have discussed the issues with Nick, and he feels that it would be better that I do the work and he assists me. I am authorised by GCHQ to give evidence at court on what I do, although my evidence will need to go through their lawyers first. I have worked for the Met before, and I will send you the details of two senior officers who will be able to vouch for my work and my ability to deploy in mainstream policing. I will also send you the name of a CPS official who will be able to tell you that I have their authority as a subject matter expert in this field of work, and I can either have my Boss ring you to agree my terms and conditions, or I will ask him to ring your Chief Constable, whichever you would prefer."

Tom had already slid back into his chair, making his own assessment as he was listening to Dominic. If it had been anybody else he would have taken him up on the call to his Chief, but something told him he could make it happen without a ripple. There was one thing though that Tom wanted to know, and that was something Dominic hadn't mentioned yet. He expected that was out of politeness, but nevertheless he still needed to know.

"If you could send me the details you have offered I will make the checks, and a call from your line manager will be fine. As for terms and conditions, it would good if you could give me a steer on that, and just for my own understanding what is your transferable rank to Police?"

Dominic, with the slightest hint of a giggle, said, "I will send you the Police contacts now," as he got out a mobile phone. After a few moments Tom's mobile went off, alerting him to text messages that had been received.

"The first two are the Met officers," Dominic said, without lifting his head, "and the third is the CPS. You can expect a call from my Boss in a few minutes." Dominic looked up and caught Tom's eye. His facial expression had changed completely to an uneasy frown and he shifted a bit in his chair.

"I think it might be better if I wasn't here when Stephen rings, so if it is OK with you I will go outside for a fag. If you could make your calls to the Met and the CPS after he rings, we could come up with the terms: a simple email will be sufficient I expect. And you don't need to worry about rank, we don't work like that." With that Dominic stood up and removed a packet of Virginia Tobacco, a packet of roll ups and a throwaway lighter from his jacket pocket, indicating that he was about to leave.

Tom didn't like being steered the way he was, but he didn't detect any arrogance in it either; and he did need the GCHQ officer's help.

"Out of the front, turn to the left and go all the way to the back. That's the smoking area."

As soon as Dominic was out of earshot he checked the names of the two Met officers. He knew one and had heard of the other. He wasn't going to wait for Stephen, he wanted more intelligence before that call came in, so he rang the officer he knew.

"Hi Bill. It's Tom Ross. How are you?"

"Hi, Tom. Can't complain. Well, I can, but it wouldn't get me anywhere!"

Tom laughed loudly at the response.

"So, Tom. What can I do for you?"

"Do you know Dominic Newland, and what can you tell me about him? In short, he says he can solve a problem for me, but that means letting him into my operation and I don't know him. I have only a few minutes, Bill, his Boss is about to ring me."

"Take him. He's cleared to the very highest level. He's a genius. The way I describe him is this: down in the bowels of GCHQ there are some windowless rooms. In one of those rooms is a man trying to fit a nuclear bomb into a matchbox and nearly succeeding. That's Dominic. Don't hesitate, Tom, but I do have one word of warning. With brains like his there are always downsides; his is that he sees and feels all the hurt. He wears his heart on his sleeve and will work all the hours of the day to the detriment of his own health. You think he's OK, but underneath you don't know what's going on."

"Thanks, Bill. One more thing, any idea what rank he converts to?"

"Chief Superintendent or ACC from what I hear."

As Tom finished one call he took another, this one from Dominic Newland's line manager. After a short, polite and very accurate conversation that lasted no more than five minutes he decided there was no point in making any of the other calls. His brain was screaming at him, 'Is this OK?', and he was desperately trying to make sense of it. He reflected on the call he'd just had, what it really meant, or didn't mean, to him and the world he worked in.

All he knew was that the caller called himself 'Stephen', he didn't even have a surname. He could be anybody. He had some genius outside smoking rollups, whom he didn't know, and who could fit

224

nuclear warheads into a matchbox. He had never met him before and he had just rocked up offering help. What was OK about all of this? *'The murky world of spies,'* he thought to himself as he got up and entered the main office where he saw Owen Marks about to leave the building.

"Owen. Where are you going?"

"Out for a quick ciggie, Boss."

"You will see a random guy down there smoking roll ups. His name is Dominic. Tell him to come back, will you."

"Yes, Boss."

With Dominic back, Tom said, "I have spoken with Stephen and the Met, you pass muster! So, terms and conditions: I think it might be best if you write something and send it to me to look at."

"I thought the same. I have done it whilst I was out, it's in your email account," Dominic replied quickly with a hint of satisfaction.

Tom, who was loving the dedication and commitment of the other man, didn't want to waste time either. *'This guy is really on the ball,'* he said to himself as he opened his emails and found the one from Dominic. *'How the hell did he write all this on a mobile phone in that time?'* Tom asked himself. As he read through the content, taking it all in, Tom had the feeling he was surrounded by spies. He had one in front of him now, that was for sure. As he got to the end there was only one thing he needed to do and so he rang Sam. With the phone still ringing he looked at Dominic and asked, "How did you get here?"

"Train. I have a return ticket." Before Tom could say anything else Sam answered.

"Sam. Dominic Newland will be attached to COCET from today. Can you get him an ID card, pin codes, the whole works, as if he was one of us? No need for intranet email at the moment. Can you arrange a rental car and a 'Shell' card? He also needs reimbursement for a train ticket. Once that is done, ask Helen in transport for the loan of a pool car."

"Send him to me, and I will take care of him," Sam replied eagerly with a mothering tone in her voice.

With the room back in silence Tom looked across at the man in front of him. He didn't have a clue who he really was, or what his motivations were. But Tom needed his help.

"Welcome to COCET, Dominic. Let me introduce you to the team."

CHAPTER FIFTEEN

It was 1.20pm in The Netherlands as Detective Sergeant Dale Walters arrived back at Schiphol Airport for his return flight to London. He found his gate then sat down to call DCI Ross. He had everything they needed; it was just a matter of what to do with it now.

"Boss, it's Dale. I have the goodies, my flight leaves in 40 minutes, do you want me to come straight to COCET?"

"No. Take it straight to SDE. If you can't make it home in time get Sam to book you a hotel."

"OK, Boss. I will update you when I get there."

Tom rang Dr. Sharpe and told him of the imminent arrival of Dale and the precious exhibit he was carrying. "That's great, Tom. I hear Dominic is on the team now, that's good. He is making his way here now as well. Dominic and I have discussed the time element on this and my available capacity. I don't have a clean system for us to use on this case. Now, I can build one and bill you for it, but we both think the quickest way to deal with this is an off the shelf purchase. Can I have authorisation?"

"Yes. What is it you are after?"

"Dominic says the best purchase would be the top of the range Mac Pro for its processing power."

"OK. Can it be reused?"

"Yes."

"OK, go for it and send the bill straight in."

"Will do."

No sooner was the phone in its cradle than it rang again, this time with Sam on the line.

"I have Detective Superintendent David Evans from Cleveland Police for you."

"Put him through, Sam."

"Tom. I am Detective Superintendent Evans from Cleveland, I understand you are expecting my call?"

"Yes, I am."

"Good. I work in major crime and I manage one of the four major crime teams. We have some spare capacity, so Mr. Brathwaite has allocated me your Operation Resolve. I need a meeting to work out what you want to do and how it can be worked by us. Now, I can do tomorrow at your place at 2pm, how does that suit?"

"Good by me, do you know where we are?"

"Becky does, apparently. She will be working on the job as well. Also, I will be bringing one of my Holmes indexers with me."

"Great. See you here at 2pm."

Tom rang Sam immediately. "Sam. We have a meeting here at 2pm with Cleveland Police, they are bringing three. Can you arrange for tea, coffee and snacks? I would like you at the meeting for notes, and alert Jane, Anna Farley, Patrick Smith, Mitchell Hayes, Archie, Sarah and Louisa that I would like them all there as well."

"Will do. This is getting exciting!" Sam replied proudly.

Tom arrived for work early the next day. However, on this occasion, unlike others, he parked his car around the back of the COCET building. He had checked the records for Maggie Burrows' home address and worked out that her route to work would probably take her past the COCET building. The current operation was at a crucial stage, and although he knew Maggie would have his best interests at heart, what he didn't need now was a 'confined to barracks' bleeding heart order at exactly the time when he had to go into overdrive. He needed the preoccupation of work right now, the kids needed it now, and in a perverse way, some offenders needed it now. He just couldn't take any chances for this meeting, although his four words were all he needed, he could not turn up for such a foundation block conference with just four words scribbled on a piece of paper. So, within two hours as the rest of the staff were beginning to arrive, he had produced the meeting agenda and his investigative plan was prepared too. He was enjoying his third cuppa of the morning and was feeling satisfied with himself when Supt. Maggie Burrows arrived in his office, unannounced for the second time.

"I thought you would want to hear this from me personally, Tom," Maggie said as she sat down. Tom was already preparing his excuse for being in early, a half day off to go fishing, when his concerns as to why she was there were allayed.

"The Met got word from the Embassy in Moscow this morning. Their Russian watchers are saying that the extra pressure and attention on this particular gang from what went on in London has caused an internal power struggle within the gang hierarchy. It was well known amongst the Russian Mafia and the Police that this gang leader was particularly vicious and had many enemies, but this unwarranted attention on them appears to have caused a takeover bid. Maksim Mikhailovich Sorokin's body was found floating in the Moskva River this morning, their time. He'd been shot in the head. Diplomatic pressure will continue, but the intelligence from our Embassy is that there has been a change in posture and language from their counterparts. The way they are reading it is that the two killers, who would never have been handed over in any case, will continue to be looked for in word only. Sorokin's dead, and they see that as a fitting end to the matter. The Met feel the best thing now is to request a tasking meeting with MI6. That is also the advice of the Embassy."

As Maggie let the information sink in, Tom, who was still taking in the new intelligence, was also feeling relieved at not being caught at work early. The fact that Fiona's real killer, the man who had ordered the assassination attempt on himself, was dead at the hands of his own men: that was in Tom's mind justice, and something that he could identify with. He couldn't say that to Maggie, however.

"Looks like my wish for him to spend at least 20 years in an English jail won't be granted then."

Maggie stared at Tom for a considerable time before she replied, during which time both officers were searching for the true feelings of the other.

"Well, I think it is an outcome. Maybe not the one we would have wished for, but one nevertheless. It may also help you to move on, don't you think?"

Tom didn't reply immediately. Both officers were still locked in eye contact and he thought he caught a glimpse that Maggie might be thinking the same way that he was. Her question at the end was seeking a reply, for sure. He needed to trust his gut instinct here. It looked right, it seemed right, and therefore it probably was right.

"As you say, it is still a result of sorts. All positive stuff, and good for me."

Upon hearing his reply, Maggie dropped eye contact and became more relaxed.

"Excellent. I see you are managing your time as well, which is also good. What's the news on Operation Resolve?" Maggie asked in an upbeat tone as she got up to leave.

"We have a copy of the server and Cleveland are due here today for a meeting."

"That is good news, Tom. I will let JT know of this advancement. How do you see this playing out?"

"Reactive investigation on the server, arrest and prosecution of Philip Thompson, a main admin, undercover infiltration, dissemination and dismantling," Tom rattled off without pause or real thought.

"You never even thought about that, Tom! That's unconscious competence, which tells me you are back in the saddle," Maggie exclaimed.

As Maggie disappeared, Tom thought about her comments. Sorokin may not have had his personal finger on the trigger, but it was him that really fired the shots, so to get a bullet in his own head from his own men was very satisfying. The moment he thought that, he pondered what Fiona would have said if he had admitted to those thoughts in counselling sessions. As he did so, it in turn triggered an incoming wave threatening to spoil the moment, so he dropped it, knowing he probably would have lied to her just has he had been doing to Maggie.

Instead he rang Dr. Nick Sharpe to take his mind off the situation.

"Nick. How's it going with the server?"

"Hi, Tom. Dominic has just set it to run. We don't have any idea how long it will take, it could be over 24 hours or even more, but the Mac is awesome, so we are both interested to see how its processing power copes with it."

"Any update on Leitch?"

"Not yet. Dominic will be looking at that next though."

"OK. I will be in a meeting with Cleveland for most of the afternoon. I will call you when I come out."

"OK. Speak later then."

Tom was about to pay attention to his policy log when he received a call from Niall Mullins.

"Tom, how the devil are ya?"

"Good. You heard about Sorokin?"

"Nope. What about the filthy scum bag?"

"He's dead. Shot in the head by his own men, he was found floating in the river in Moscow."

"Nothing more than the bastard deserved," Niall said. Then, softening his tone, he continued, "You OK with that outcome?"

"Yeah, I guess I am."

"Me too, he lived by the gun and he got to die by it. Look, I have some intelligence on Visser, is now a good time?"

"Of course it is, fire away. Pardon the pun."

Both officers chuckled and were thinking roughly the same thing. Tom thought, *'Well, at least I can make a joke out of it, even if it is black humour,'* and Niall, *'If he can crack a comment like that, then he's going to make it.'*

"OK. Visser Intel update. The 'cloggies' went back to him and he was all over them like a cheap suit." The way he said it made Tom smile again. It didn't matter what the subject was, whenever he spoke to Niall there was always a smile to be had, and the feeling gave him a lift.

"He's admitted to being a member of a group that call themselves PTC, short for 'Protect That Child', which is why he had a key ring with the pagan sign on it, which means the same thing, and that's why Michael was branded with the same sign.

"The deal was this: you could only get entry if you first proved yourself and supplied home grown child abuse material. He satisfied the criteria and was made a member. Now that's the good news; the bad news is that he only met Michael once, and he paid for the father and him to travel to Holland, cash on landing.

"He skirted around the assault on Michael and never told the full story, but he did admit to being the man in the pictures. He said he met Michael one more time when he was older and living in Holland. There was no sexual contact between them as Michael was much older by then. It was then that Michael confessed to killing his father and disposing of the body on farm land to revenge the murder of his mother."

"Did he say where?" Tom replied, with a real sense of urgency.

"No, but he assumed it was in Holland. Visser also said that the father and Michael were Canadian."

"What's Michael's real name?"

"He doesn't know. He says that he was always referred to as 'LB' but that he doesn't know what the letters stand for."

"Where does he live? What age is he now? What car did he arrive in? Does he have an address?" Tom blurted out quickly.

Niall interrupted Tom firmly but with compassion. "Tom. They have asked all those questions and much more, they are all negative. An Intel log will come through within a couple of days. Sally is going to work on it personally, and you know she is our best analyst."

"What about a digital trail?" Tom asked in a more patient tone this time.

"All PTC members must communicate through proxy, and messages must also be encrypted, and that's at both ends. So if one end doesn't have it they are not accepted, or they're kicked out if they had it and then stopped. He thinks some of the group may communicate through other methods, but he didn't know what they are. Also, he hasn't been in contact with all of them, and had only ever communicated with three. One being LB, his father when LB was younger, and another called JC. It was JC that recruited him."

"How many are there in the group?"

"He doesn't know."

Tom pondered on what to do. He really needed the final Intel log before he could get to work. Also, once Sally got her teeth into it, more would surely fall out. But one of the biggest leads lay in Canada, and that was something he could get going on.

"Niall, this means as much to you and Interpol as it does to me and Jane, but I want the lead on this."

"I knew you would. The allegation of murder on Dutch soil is down to the Dutch. They don't have much to go on, and accept that. So they need to liaise with COCET. I have agreed to be the SPOC between them and us, that way you will know what is going on. If they ramp up their response then I can request that a Dutch Interpol officer gets embedded into their team to help with communication."

"Good thinking, Niall, I agree."

"As for anything outside Holland, they will go through Interpol and COCET in any case."

"Good. Do they have an estimate age for LB?"

"Yes. 20 to 25yrs, but that is a guess. It could be as low as 19."

"Great. Look, the main thing I'd like done, and this is something Interpol could achieve for us, is to obtain a list of outstanding missing persons within Canada and Holland going back to not just cover LB, but also his father within Canada and Holland, and his mother in Canada over the relevant periods"

"Hang on whilst I get this down," Niall replied, as he grabbed a pen and a notepad.

Niall quickly recorded the details of what Tom had said before speaking again.

"OK, ready. What about the murder being on Canadian soil?"

"We can go there as COCET make the enquiries, for now I need that list as a starting point."

"Agreed, later then."

"One more thing before you go, Niall," Tom said quickly. "The unknown subject Michael needs a subject name change from today. I will get the Intel Cell to send a memo on it, but from today he becomes subject LB."

"Yep, agreed."

"Oh. And another thing, Niall," Tom said, trying to keep up with his mind, "could you find out if Canadian immigration keep a list of Canadian Nationals who have left the country and who haven't re-entered?"

"On the list, Tom."

Tom called Jane into his office, and with the door shut he updated her on what he had just heard from Niall. Jane sat impassively as she took in the intelligence update. Over time she had become reconciled to being wrong in thinking she had been close to saving Michael during Operation Hope; she'd probably been years too late.

A boy, whose whole life had been taken away from him by the very person who should have been protecting him, had in the end himself become a child abuser and now a murderer. Or at least that's what the intelligence indicated. Was it distorted fate that led him to commit the most serious of crimes? The point when Michael became 'lost' as a boy had haunted her, and probably always would. She had wanted to find him, to stop the carnage in his life and take him back in time through professional intervention and save him. But now her job was to find him and stop him doing more harm, creating more damage, more victims, and ultimately more death. If he had murdered once he could do it again. He was lost, and that was that. It was time to move on.

"What can I do?"

"Send an email to all COCET partners and update our team that, as of today, the subject known as Michael will now be known as LB, an intelligence update surrounding this will follow in a few days. We will both be working on this in the future, Jane, and I may give it operational status, but after we have completed Resolve."

"Will do," Jane replied, thinking that the name change was good for her personally. "Cleveland will be here any minute, shall I get the team together?"

Ten minutes later both Tom and Jane were sitting in the COCET conference room with the news from Holland still at the front of their minds, as personal introductions were being undertaken clockwise around the table. Cleveland Police were represented by Detective Superintendent David Evans, the SIO for one of Cleveland's major investigation teams, Detective Sergeant Becky Drysdale, from the Force Intelligence Bureau, who was being seconded to the major investigation team for the duration of the Operation Resolve, and Linda Holdsworth, a Holmes supervisor who would also be on the investigation.

The COCET officers introduced themselves, explaining their roles within COCET and the reason why they were present. As this concluded, Tom handed out the meeting agenda which everybody started to read. The agenda had been constructed to follow the investigation plan together with its time line. Each person around the room could see a part or parts that they were involved in, so they immediately started making notes in their notepads.

Tom kicked the meeting off with a historical overview of Operation Resolve leading to the present time. First, he outlined the investigation plan, then he moved onto the investigative time line, breaking down the plan into sections, during which he passed the discussion to other COCET members so they could elaborate further on their part in it. As the plan reached its conclusion Jane handed the meeting back to Tom who summed up the phased approach to Operation Resolve.

"So, phase one will be to get the contents of the server to you in readable form. What those contents are we don't know yet, but we expect there will at least be some IP addresses that will need resolving to members. Phase one also contains the surveillance workup on Philip Thompson prior to arrest. This needs to include either a rapid entry or subterfuge capable of securing the PC in an open state, or a trespass authority to gain access to the house to install a key logger to capture his passwords.

"Phase two will be the arrest, interview and prosecution of Thompson. A remand in custody is paramount for the ongoing success of the operation. As this is happening the undercover infiltration of 'childscentcafe' will commence using Thompson's online identity and that of others, that the undercover officers have already created. As other senior members are arrested early, and it is inevitable that some will need to be because of child protections risks, we will assume their identities as well, and infiltrate further.

"Phase three will be dissemination of Intel both within the UK and globally.

Phase four will be a coordinated arrest phase and media release. Which leads us to Cleveland activity," Tom said, looking down at his agenda sheet then up at Superintendent Evans.

David Evans quickly looked around the table before beginning. "First thing is, the plan sounds great by me. Now, Becky got a directed surveillance authority and deployed an obs van in the street. I had the product reviewed before we came down, and a covert entry to fit a logger on the keyboard is a long term thing. There are no natural opportunities. That is mainly because the offender lives with his disabled mother and she rarely leaves the address. So it is going to have to be a rapid or subterfuge entry, and I favour a rapid one. Our support group has been tasked to come up with a plan and I will inform them of your needs surrounding the PC. Will you be on the ground on the day?"

"Yes," Tom quickly replied, impressed that they had taken the initiative to begin the surveillance phase.

"And you will be able to tell us when the PC is in an open state?"

"Yes," replied Tom confidently, knowing however, it wasn't as simple as that.

"I have tasked two officers to prepare for the interview of Thompson, after this meeting they will want a briefing from your intelligence cell so they can prepare properly. The interview team will work with a file officer, who in turn will be responsible for taking the case to court. I'm putting my best team on it, and we will need a statement from COCET about ongoing undercover activity to help secure a remand in custody." David Evans stopped and looked at Tom for direction and a reply.

"Yep, you will get one."

"Well then. That leaves me with the processing of the intelligence that we gain from the server and the Police undercover activity," Superintendent Evans said, picking up from where he had left off. "All I have to go on at the moment is what Hertfordshire Police told me from when they worked with you on Operation Hope, and that is to expect an avalanche of data communication submissions and a pile of dissemination packs the size of Ben Nevis. All mixed in with a number of life threatening cases that will give me a few more grey hairs! Have I got that about right?"

David Evans was smiling at the conclusion of his statement, but all the same Tom needed more convincing before he decided whether the smiles were just a smoke screen from someone who had been given a job he didn't want. The fact that he had gone to Herts Police was a good thing, and that he'd started the surveillance gathering, or at least Becky had. Tom flicked her a quick look and got a smile back confirming that all was OK.

"Yes! I can't, and I wouldn't, dress this up any other way," Tom began. "You can expect a mountain of data comms work and an even larger amount of intelligence products that will need to be assembled and then disseminated. How big the data comms commitment will be is anybody's guess at the moment. To a certain extent the number of intelligence packs will reflect the amount of data comm submissions."

"When will you know how much the server contains?" David Evans asked.

"Next couple of days," Tom replied, thinking he didn't really know, but that should cover it.

"Right then, after speaking with Herts, who worked a hybrid incident room procedure, we are going to run our activity fully on Holmes. My reason for that is so it can be cross searched in the future when more operations like this are conducted. At the moment, if we want to do a cross search, it means undertaking a separate system check with requests through Herts or COCET. So on that issue, I will need a COCET officer with the ability to check everything you have previously captured in my incident room. Can you do that?"

Both Tom and Jane had been prepared for the request and Tom nodded for Jane to reply.

"Yes. We have officers that are Holmes trained and some that are familiar with working in a Holmes environment. Officers have already been identified and they will have a copy of Operation Benson and Hope with them. How many do you need?"

"Just the one," replied David Evans. "With that one sorted," he continued, "Becky has told me that you have your own CP strategy. Are you expecting me to work to that within the incident room?"

Jane looked back towards Tom, who picked up the hint that this was something she didn't want to deal with. He could also see Louisa Greenwood out of the corner of his eye moving in her seat, wanting to speak on it. However the issue was something that would need to be thrashed out between David Evans and himself.

"Have you seen it?"

"No. I suggest we break for coffee, and if I could have a copy now we could sign this off."

Louisa, who had a copy, in fact several, interrupted, "I have one for you," quickly producing one from her folder.

"Good idea, let's break. Louisa, provide Superintendent Evans with a copy, would you?" Tom said, thinking the contents were going to raise the Superintendent's eyebrows.

As the COCET officers led the way to the tea, coffee and biscuits, Tom noticed that both David Evans and Becky Drysdale declined the break. Instead they spent all their time reading the CP strategy. Before too many officers had reassembled around the table, Tom approached both David Evans and Becky Drysdale, who were in deep conversation with each other.

"It's not your normal CP strategy," Tom said in a tone and delivery that didn't give away any of his personal thoughts.

David Evans looked up from the document he was reading and locked eye contact with Tom, as he placed his copy of the CP strategy on the table before speaking.

"Have you signed off on this?" David Evans said in an enquiring voice, with a hint of surprise in it.

"I did challenge it, but my line management didn't support my views and so it's there."

Tom didn't like producing 'dirty laundry' in public, but this was a case where he had no option but to tell it just as it was.

"How far up has this gone?" David Evans further enquired, with a dead pan face and tone. Tom didn't need to look at Becky, but he sensed she was looking at him intently and waiting for a reply, and that his reply was going to be crucial to David Evans. Luckily for him he could tell it how it was.

"All the way to the top of GOPOL, the Chief. It's what they want. I made my views known, but it was non-negotiable for me. If you guys can't sign up to it, then you should work to your own, and, when it comes to the number crunching at the end, the media departments will have to thrash out what they will and won't go with."

David Evans frowned and rubbed his chin with his right hand before answering. "This isn't how you count success," he said.

"It's not, I agree. But it is how the NSPCC count it, and GOPOL have signed up to that."

"OK. We will work to it," David Evans replied quickly, "when the stats are challenged we will direct all questions to you and I will instruct our media regarding that decision. Let's get this meeting finished."

Tom felt relieved, yet at the same time he was annoyed as the meeting got underway again. As the room became silent David Evans recommenced.

"OK. I have read the CP strategy and there are parts of it that I, and therefore Cleveland, do not agree with."

At this point he specifically looked towards Louisa before he continued. "However, we will work to it. If down the line we are questioned on the stats, we will direct them to you," and with that he turned his attention directly to Sarah Dorsey, who nodded in acknowledgement.

Louisa Greenwood, who had been listening intently, could sense that the meeting was moving away from her strategy; and she had a question of her own that she wanted an answer to, now that Cleveland had undertaken surveillance at the home address of Thompson. So she quickly interrupted.

"Excuse me, hi. Can I ask if there are any signs that Thompson has access to children at the address?" she asked, with a smile on her face.

Tom knew where Louisa was coming from. But, crucially, Becky Drysdale and her Boss Superintendent Evans did as well and it was Becky who wanted to point that out.

"There have been no signs of any children at the address and we have no intelligence to suggest he has access to any. If there had been you would have been informed." Becky delivered her words with a smile and a neutral tone which satisfied Louisa, but it left Tom under no illusion that he was going to have to juggle Police imperatives alongside NSPCC policy for the foreseeable future, and it was something that was not going to go away.

"As for the media strategy," Superintendent Evans said, picking up from the interruption, "that will be something that will be signed off on when we get back. It isn't something I concern myself with. The media department will tell me what they have agreed and I will go along with it, so that's about it from us. Linda here will set the room up on Monday next week, we will be working out of a Cleveland satellite Police Station. We can't use your Operational name within Cleveland and we need one: we have been allocated Operation Elm. Finally, I expect operational support to be in a position to arrest Thompson from next Wednesday onwards.

CHAPTER SIXTEEN

Unlike Pandora's Box; a box or 'Pithos' which contained the evils of the world, the internet has a tank full of victims. Some law enforcement agencies turn on the tap to that tank and arrange their response around it remaining open. Some turn the tap only when it suits them; then turn it off again, leaving victims to their fate inside the tank. Others view that dilemma differently, and never turn the tap on in the first place. Both Pandora's Box, an artefact of Greek mythology, and the Internet Tank have one common component, they both contain 'Elpis,' the 'Hope' of many souls.

At 5pm that same day, and about an hour after Cleveland Police had left, Tom's 'tap' which had been open for months began to flood his response capability at a faster rate than even he could have imagined.

"Tom, it's Nick. The work on the server, it's done!"

"What?"

"I know right! We had no idea how long it would take. We thought maybe like overnight. We had a coffee break and went to check it and it's complete!"

"Does that mean there isn't much on it?" Tom asked with a sense of foreboding.

"No way! It's the Holy Grail! And not only that, listen to this, there are over twenty two thousand members!"

"How many?" Tom asked, needing to hear that again.

"Twenty two thousand! Honestly, twenty two thousand! We haven't had time to look at the growth rate, but by the time you take this site down it will be way over that."

Tom's mind was racing, but suddenly the words 'Holy Grail' grabbed back his attention.

"What do you mean by 'Holy Grail'?"

"Dominic is making a tactical assessment now, but on first glance the way it has been setup is to capture the IP when they first become a member together with their email address. It seems to grab most ISP provider names as well. It also stores chat logs and messages, right, and captures what IPs relate to those logs. And it does the same with images posted and, crucially, downloaded. We don't know how far back it goes yet, but there's a host of other good intelligence gathering captures in there as well. And we should have that assessment by mid-morning tomorrow!"

"That's just awesome, Nick, and tell that to Dominic as well. The timing couldn't be better, Cleveland are ready to roll from next week!" Tom said ecstatically.

As he put the phone down he felt the hairs on the back of his neck stand up. His mind whirled with thoughts of the opportunities his experience told him would be presenting themselves over the next hours, days and weeks. But for now there was one major obstacle he would have to get over and that related to the numbers involved. They couldn't all be overseas IP addresses, there had to be a sizeable figure that would be UK based, and it would certainly be bigger than Operation Hope. He picked up the phone and rang Maggie Burrows. COCET was going to have to help fund the cost of the communications bill, Cleveland couldn't be expected to foot this alone. Ten minutes later he was ringing Supt. Evans.

"David. I wasn't expecting to call you again today but I have an update on the server."

"I'm listening," replied the Detective Superintendent from Cleveland Police.

"The team at SDE wasn't expecting to get a result so quickly, but they do have a new Apple Pro and its processor has done the work faster than expected. In short, we have a membership of over twenty two thousand and that is going to impact on your communications bill to ISP providers."

"How much is this going to cost Cleveland?"

"We can't tell. There will be more overseas subjects than home ones, and some of those will be behind proxy, but you will still have to do them. I can't really say, but my guess is that it will be higher than the bill Herts Police had."

"I'm going to need to flag this up and get back to you."

"I thought you might. What I have done here is get authority to pay half of the bill."

"That will help. But what if the bill comes to 50K? Even half of that could be too much."

"I don't think it will. From the few I have done my experience is it might go as high as 25 but not much higher."

"OK. In the end it won't be my decision, but I will make the call now. How soon will you be able to get the content to us?"

"Not sure. But I would like to work towards that Wednesday date of yours if that suits you?"

"Yep. Let's go for it," the officer replied, just as the signal from his mobile phone was lost.

It was well before mid-morning the following day when Tom received the call from Dr. Nick Sharpe. "Tom. We're done here on the server, and we're going to bring it to you. We will be there by lunchtime. Will you and Jane be there?"

"Yes."

"In that case we are on our way."

Tom alerted Jane for the meeting and then called in Detective Sgt. Dale Walters.

"Dale."

"Yes, Guv."

"Can you put together a CHIS authority to assume the online identity of Philip Thompson?"

"What's the end goal?"

"I want you to assume his identity and infiltrate the site whilst it remains open. The plan should include identifying all his contacts and other members of the site with a view to establishing the extent of their past or ongoing crimes, and to identify their victims."

"Yep, sure. Before deploying as him though I will need to do some intelligence gathering around his MO."

"I agree. There is a meeting here around lunchtime with Dr. Sharpe and a specialist from GCHQ. I want you there."

"Will do. With regards to deployment times. Will this be like Operation Hope? If so, I will need more staff."

"No. I don't see it being the same. The circumstances are different, but I would prefer you to work as a pair with someone," Tom replied, knowing that Dale was probably the one who should make the choice.

"I was involved in the training of CIIs," Dale began. "If you want, I could see if they would allow me to train Owen and Archie here at COCET. If it was agreed, I could start tonight, and if we were authorised to work over the weekend they would be ready for Thursday next week."

It was 'pure vanilla' as ICE Agent Jim Burgess would say. And indeed it was.

"Yes, make it happen. Anything you need, let me know!"

"Will do, Guv," replied Dale, grinning as he got up to tell Owen and Archie the good news.

Alone, Tom was thinking about the possibilities that three trained undercover officers within COCET would give him when the light bulb in his head switched on. He grabbed his counsel pad and turned to the page of notes from the intelligence briefing he'd read whilst travelling to Cleveland. He found the entry made against Simon Clark, read it once, and then read it again whilst recalling his last conversation with Niall Mullins. He dialled Dale's desk number and felt a gathering tingling sensation move through his body as he waited for Dale to answer.

"Yes, Guv."

"Dale. When you put together that CHIS, add Simon Clark and Brian Leitch. All the intelligence you need will be with Jane and Anna Farley."

"Will do, Guv."

Back with his just his thoughts, Tom felt his brain move up a gear as he assessed the numerous leads and their possible outcomes. At each outcome, his knowledge and experience suggested further leads and possibilities, which in turn led to further potential outcomes. Some leads came to a halt after a few outcomes, some went on for several. All of them were affected by a number of static and dynamic factors contained within his knowledge and experience. A way of working, knowing from experience what would work and what wouldn't. In the back of his mind, within the grey or 'soft' intelligence areas, two ideas were working in tandem: containing the 'It hasn't been done before' and the 'It might just possibly work'.

The factors like child protection protocols, lawful surveillance, encryption, staff capability, intelligence gaps and risk assessments all contributed to his decision making processes as he passed along the spider web of pathways. He stopped abruptly, making a mental note of where he'd got to. His experience told him that he had already made crucial decisions that could affect the outcome of Operation Resolve, and the fate of another paedophile and possible murderer. He needed to get these down in his policy log now before it all got away from him.

Just after 1.30pm, and fortified by a ham and salad sandwich, Tom began the meeting with Dr. Nick Sharpe and Dominic Newland. Also present was ADS Jane King, who brought Anna Farley, Patrick Smith and DS Dale Walters.

Tom introduced Dominic, then provided an intelligence update, after which he handed over to Nick.

"Right. OK, well. You really have a gold mine here. The site, as of the time we grabbed a copy, contained 22,361 members in total. Some will be duplicates, but that will be a very small number. At the point of joining, the site grabs and then retains the name they use, the email address that was used to join, and the IP address.

"It then stores the level of activity for each member. So if one member uploads, say 100 images, it will log that by the day, date and time and from where in terms of IP and email address. It's possible then to see if one member has joined using a throwaway email but later or straight after starts using another or several addresses.

"It is also possible to see that one member may actually be five members, but yet the same person. It also logs and stores all downloaded activity in the same way, and it's mostly the same for chat logs. We do know, however, that most use this as a meeting place and don't discuss real criminality, but we won't know if that's always the case until somebody actually reads every post.

"Now. This data has been held since the site started and hasn't stopped, so in historical terms the intelligence goes right back to creation point. On top of that, we are able to see who set it up, and who the admins are, so effectively who the organisers are. With that you will be able to target critical points to bring this site down for good. What do you think of that then!"

Nick stopped talking with a flourish, and with a very satisfied look on his face as he looked around the conference room table. Tom and the rest of COCET remained silent, trying to take in all that Nick had said, whilst at the same time placing it within an investigative context. It was Jane who broke the silence.

"Nick. Have I ever told you that I love you!"

Her comment was perfect in its timing. The room broke into spontaneous laughter, causing Nick to feel even more satisfied, and giving the whole team a feeling of success against the odds.

It was Tom who broke the laughter and brought them all back to business.

"Who is the owner?"

Upon hearing the question Nick put his serious face back on. "It is someone who calls himself 'The Lord', his ISP places him in Canada."

Tom, who was about to speak, was beaten to it by Jane. "What is it with these paedos and religion? Do they really think they are some God like being?"

Jane's comments weren't lost on anybody in the room, and her tone pushed the recent hilarity to a distant past in a nanosecond. The room remained silent for a few more seconds, and by the time Tom spoke again everyone wore facial expressions depicting various levels of grimness and determination.

"Have we got a clear picture of the hierarchy, and is Thompson part of it?"

"Yes and yes," replied Nick.

"Look. I want to deal with this in three stages," Tom began. "We need to get the data into a form that can be inputted into Holmes by the incident room. Jane, any ideas?"

"Yes. We have been working on a solution today, and Patrick thinks he should create a spreadsheet from the data Nick has, and which Cleveland can then use. I spoke to Nick earlier, he thinks it will be too difficult to lift it from the form it's in now. That leaves us with an inputting problem, but one that solves the question about who goes to Cleveland."

"OK, tell me more," Tom replied, liking solutions to problems.

"Patrick thinks it would be better on Access, which he is familiar with. He is also fast on the keyboard. So if he starts today, by the time he gets to Cleveland, and he is willing to go, then he will also have a head start. If they catch up with him, then we can send additional staff or they can go at his pace. My guess is that, just like Herts, it will take time for them to get going, probably a full week, by which time Patrick will be far enough ahead."

Tom looked at Patrick, who nodded in agreement to what was being put forward.

"Right, Patrick it is then. I want a reserve. Who will it be?"

"Mitchell or Anna," Jane replied.

"Who is going to oversee the makeup of the intelligence packs and the intelligence flow?" Tom asked.

"I am, and Niall will be dealing with the overseas dissemination as before, and we will get a full copy of everything."

Tom looked at Nick and Dominic before speaking. "Is it in a form that Patrick can read easily? Or are there hidden problems?"

"It's easy, and there are no problems. We can work with Patrick on it before we leave to make sure," Nick said, replying for them both.

"In that case, that will get us going on stage one. Jane, you have command on how COCET works with Cleveland on the Intel side.

We need to have daily debriefs. There will be teething problems, just as there were with Herts."

"Yes, Boss."

"Stage two is arrest and undercover tactics. Dale, I don't see you going live with Thompson's identity until a few days after his arrest. So, in the meantime learn all there is to know about him from his posts. Work with Nick and Dominic to get that intelligence. Make contact with the interview team for Thompson, you can get the details through Jane. Request they set up a downstream monitoring capability that you can have access to for their interviews with him. That way you will be able to learn more about his online style and profile."

"Will do, Guv."

"Anna. I understand NCIS has access to a Forensic Psychologist called Dr. Joe Sullivan. Do you know about that?"

"Yes. Not sure he has his PhD yet, but everybody calls him by the title. But yes, I know him."

"Great. Could you see if he has the time next week to work in Cleveland for a few days? Working for us, advising Dale and the interview team."

"Yes, sure. He is quite expensive. And he also lives in Ireland, so there will be flight costs as well. Can I see if NCIS would be willing to pay for him as part of their contribution to this operation?"

"That would be awesome, thank you," Tom replied, before continuing. "The undercover plan is to infiltrate the hierarchy as far as possible whilst the incident room undertakes the intelligence gathering phase. The infiltration will continue after the arrest phase for a period to capture intelligence that might assist prosecutions.

"Dale will also be our advance warning system should particular members become suspicious. If that happens, and they are a threat to the ongoing operation, then they will be arrested to preserve it. Dale will be training some of our own staff as covert internet investigators which will give us greater capability.

"As part of this phase I want to undertake some further forensic work on the hardware exhibits of Visser, Leitch and Clark. Nick, I will send you an email later stating what I would like done. Are you in a position to do it?"

"Yes."

"Dominic, are you available to assist in that?"

"I should be able to, it depends on what you are asking for. I haven't been able to get into TrueCrypt files so far."

"It's more data mining in nature, it will be the subject of a further briefing."

"Sure," said Dominic.

"Jane, can someone speak with Essex? I might want Clark re-interviewed, just put it out there with them. The reason comes later." "Will do, Boss," Jane replied, wondering what this was all about and making a mental note to find out.

"Dale, can you request a further copy of the server in say a week, so we can see what the difference is in size? And whilst you are speaking to them ask for all the details they hold for the owner, and that includes payment. If you need assistance on that side speak to Mitchell."

However, Jane got in first before Dale could speak. "I can do that for you, Dale. I have been speaking lately with Pim, the operations manager. He is visiting England the week after next and staying with me whilst he does some sightseeing in Oxford, so I will ask him to bring another copy with him. I can get the other intelligence when I speak with him tonight."

Jane finished her statement feeling pleased she could help. The rest of the room, apart from Nick and Dominic who didn't know the office politics and personalities, and Anna Farley, who had suspected a relationship was blossoming, were all thinking the same question. 'Wow! What's going on between Jane and Pim?'

The silence, and the expression on their faces wasn't even picked up by Jane for at least five seconds. When she did, her body language just confirmed the others' silent suspicions. Tom felt a strange mixture of sadness and pleasure, but quickly ignored his feelings and got on with stage three.

"Stage three will be the arrest phase. That, from experience, is months away, so it will be subject of a further briefing. Jane, the team will be on a fully operational footing from Monday, probably two hours a day until Wednesday when it will go up as needed. Anybody working late can have overnight accommodation when it's warranted, and staff should make arrangements at home to cater for long hours. It will be all hands on deck!"

As the team started to leave the room, buoyed up by the content and the tone of the meeting, Tom asked Jane, Nick, Dominic and Dale to remain behind.

"Nick and Dale, you will both know to some degree that Jane and I have been trying to locate a victim who is now also a suspect, who we named Michael. Dominic, you are playing catch up, Nick can fill you in later. Jane will shortly be receiving Intel from Interpol in Lyons that indicates Michael was known as LB by the now convicted paedophile, Visser. We had him arrested as part of Operation Hope. We don't know what LB stands for. Further to that, LB has been implicated in the killing of his own father in revenge for killing his wife, LB's mother.

"The Dutch are dealing with that information, and I have tasked Interpol to secure intelligence on our behalf relating to missing persons in both Canada and Holland over a certain period. Visser said that LB and his father were Canadian but that they were now living in Holland. That Intel will go to Jane as and when it arrives. Visser also provided intelligence that he and LB were part of a secret group who called themselves PTC. That's short for 'Protect That Child', and from which came the sign that Michael and others were branded with.

"He was recruited into PTC by someone known only as JC. I would like a fresh search made on the hardware I mentioned before to look for anything linked to LB, Canada, PTC or JC. That falls to you, Nick and Dominic."

As Dominic nodded, Nick said, "Sure. As you know, I did find some chat logs relating to Clark trying to gain access to a group. I would need to do further work on that, now that I know this."

"Well, you need to know as well that the group insisted that all members used anonymising software, and that they were not allowed in unless they had it, and if they were caught without it they were kicked out," Tom added

"If you get me the Dutch hardware I can look at that," Dominic offered, "I'm not sure I can do much more on Leitch that Sue and Nick haven't already done. As for Clark, I haven't seen his exhibits."

Nick spoke before Tom could. "There was nothing like that on Clark's exhibits. But that's not to say he didn't have it, then removed it, or was simply using another PC somewhere else."

"That's why I want another look at the exhibits. Dale, speak with Niall and get a copy from Holland, send Mitchell to get it if you are busy. Also keep in contact with Nick and Dominic around Clark, anything you can learn from his chat logs will help if you get a chance to assume his identity. One final thing. A common forum that most of the homosexual paedophiles belonged to on Operation Benson and Hope was called 'boylover.net', so keep that in mind. And Dale, the moment the other two are authorised, I want you and them to join that site!"

"Yes, Guv."

Tom returned to his office and rang Niall Mullins.

"Niall, the owner of the server in Holland is a Canadian who calls himself "The Lord", I will be getting his details soon. Who do you deal with in Canada?"

"Well, I could go through Interpol channels in Canada. They have two options based on where the scumbag lives. One, go federal and go through The Royal Canadian Mounted Police who then deal with it. Or two, go to the local Police that cover the location where he lives. If he lives in Toronto, we should deal straight with Kim. We know her and we know she will do a good job."

"I agree. It would be good to work with them again. If it's not in her area, then as a national team ourselves I think we should make contact with the 'Mounties'. But do you know if they have the expertise?"

"They do have some teams that work in this area. But they are new on the block, and from what we hear, and have indeed seen, they are playing catch up with the likes of Toronto."

"Mm. Let's hope it's Toronto then."

2335hrs ICT, Don Mueang Airport, Bangkok, Thailand

As Tom got back to his policy log, LB was waiting in the Arrivals hall of Don Mueang Airport. The late flight from London was on time and people were already pouring through. He spotted Jack G amongst the many passengers long before Jack had seen him. He wasn't hard to miss, being such a big person. LB thought that his age must be affecting his eyesight as Jack almost walked straight past him.

"You blind as well as stupid!" LB said, grabbing him by the arm.

Jack G, who was excited to be there, wasn't that excited at being called stupid.

"You fucker! You're so small I can't see you!"

LB had met Jack G twice before. He hadn't changed a bit. He was over twice LB's age, and although he had a belly that had come from drinking too much beer, he was still a powerful man. It didn't bother LB one bit that the other man was so much bigger than him. The man who had access to the young boys was King, and that was himself.

"Let's find a place we can talk with more privacy," LB said, taking charge.

"Why couldn't you stay a few more days and show me around properly?" Jack G enquired with a moan and a facial expression to suit.

"The flight was booked, you know the times. It was you who should have got here earlier."

"Yeah, well. I hate that fucking Mr. B. He gets right on my tits."

Both men made their way away from the meeting area that had become packed with people, some pushing trolleys stacked with suitcases. It was the same scene that was played out at most times of every day at the airport, but seen and felt for just a few minutes by people from all over the world arriving in Thailand full of excitement and expectation. There were backpackers, young couples, single travellers, businessmen and women, and families of all sizes, some with very young infants. The many Thai nationals who were meeting the incoming tourists wore infectious golden smiles and greeted their future companions, most of whom they had never met before, like long lost brothers or sisters. It was in stark contrast to the scene around them that the two men sat down to discuss plans that would bring so much fear, pain and torture to some of the youngest and most vulnerable children of that golden country.

LB handed over one medium sized envelope with the number '1' clearly printed on the outside. "That's base. The address is inside, as are the keys and a detailed explanation of everything you need to know. Just go there and settle in. There is enough food for a few days."

"What about the rest?" Jack G asked in an abrupt manner, taking hold of the envelope and putting it inside a plastic bag which contained two bottles of duty free American bourbon.

"They are sitting in other envelopes in the kitchen at base."

"Contacts?"

"All there."

"Can they be trusted?"

"Yes."

"Bet you and that fucking Mr. B have had the best!" Jack G said, hardly able to keep his anger from showing.

"I didn't share any of mine with him. You know as well as I do that would be counterproductive. I suggest that when you speak with Lim, you make it known you don't want any Mr. B has had. At least not for a few weeks."

"Mm. Too fucking right."

Neither man spoke for a few minutes whilst Jack G looked around him, taking in the environment. It was good to be back he thought to himself. He didn't care much for the little shit next to him, but he held all the cards, so he had to be nice to him.

"One last thing. Money. Have you made it plain to Lim not to put the price up just because you have gone and I have arrived?"

"Yes."

"Good," Jack G began. "Because if he does, it will be the last thing he ever does. And the party will be over then, for us all!"

With that he got up, grabbed hold of his trolley and walked away, quickly disappearing into the thick moving mass of people.

LB remained seated for a few seconds, pondering the threat and wondering whether the whole venture had been worth it. He had a great position in 'childscent' and an even better one in 'boylover'. If it wasn't for Visser, he could return to just that, but now he couldn't. It was time for a new beginning. And he had a plan.

CHAPTER SEVENTEEN

Although he'd had Sunday off, Tom hadn't switched off for a second, spending most of his time writing up a huge list of things he wanted to do, then another one containing items that had to be done. There was a large difference between the two lists, and he knew he would have to compromise somewhere along the line. Not because of his own effort or input, but because many of the items in one list required some action to occur in the world before he could progress or undertake them.

He was checking his email account when Jane arrived at COCET for the day. She made two teas and headed straight for Tom's office.

"His name is Michael Stephens and he lives in Brantford, Ontario. Niall says it's not that far from Toronto, but it isn't covered by them, so we lucked out there. Niall also pulled some strings through his Interpol network and got his previous convictions. He has a long history of criminal offences and been to prison for some of them, but none for child sex offences. Here is his conviction sheet," Jane said, handing a printout to Tom who then went through it.

He could see from the date of birth that the offender was in his forties and had convictions listed from a juvenile age. As he read on, it quickly became apparent he was a career criminal, and there was a repeating pattern to his offences which became more serious as he got older. In English terms he would be called a 'blagger'. He had convictions for theft, breaking and entering, robbery, armed robbery and assault. He really didn't fit the bill.

"Are we sure he's 'The Lord'?"

"Yes. No question about it."

"Is he married?"

"Not according to the checks Interpol made, but then they didn't go very far. Niall wants to know which way you want to go, local or Federal?"

Tom looked at the conviction sheet again. He was a career robber prepared to carry and use lethal weapons during his crimes. He'd been caught quite often as well, and yet there was no hint of anything sexual in his history.

"Well, Jane, we both know that child abuse occurs across all levels of society, even hardened career criminals. Tell Niall, Federal; and to get on with it. I want to have him arrested and taken out of the equation sooner rather than later. If we can replace him with, say, Paul from Toronto, it would be just awesome."

"I agree. On Cleveland, their interview team is here today for a meeting, so they can prepare further for the interview of Thompson. And the NCIS shrink is coming to meet them as well. On Wednesday, where do you want me?"

"With me, up there. Once they have him and it starts to settle down, I will return here and I would like you to remain up there until you are happy the room is working well. The way I see this going is arrest and interview in the background as the number crunching starts from the server data. I want to start at the top and move down. Dale won't get going for a day or two, perhaps even a week or more, depending how quick the data gets copied across, and then there is the wait for the communications data to come back.

"I have written a mini briefing note and have added it to the policy log. It's mainly for my benefit, so I can then make a large number of entries relating to intelligence dissemination and link it to that without having to explain my rationale all the time. I will send you a copy which you can let Becky have. I will speak to Superintendent Evans personally."

"OK. In that case we should go up by train tomorrow. Becky wants to start the arrest phase from 8am."

"What? Through the doors?"

"No. But to be in a position from that time."

"What time is Dale starting?"

"Just before eight."

"Alright then. Are you ready? Is the team ready?"

"Yes, everybody is primed and ready to go," Jane replied, with energy in her voice.

As Jane got to the door to leave she stopped. "Do you think we will ever find Michael?"

Tom looked at her, and for the first time in a while really thought about one solitary thing. "Yes. Yes, I do. But it won't be the Michael we knew."

Marshalling his thoughts, Tom rang the Cleveland Superintendent.

"Good timing, Tom. I was about to ring you about the Comms Data costs," said Superintendent Evans.

Tom's stomach lurched. So far, it had been one-way traffic on the success front. At some point it had to end, and maybe this was it. "What's the decision?"

"It's good. As long as you pay half of whatever the bill comes to!"

Tom quickly thought about ringing Maggie Burrows. But his experience told him she would see it as an issue, and then escalate it because of the costs being open ended. He was the person there and was in the right position to make a best guess. So he went with that, even if his reputation went on the line with it. "I can authorise that."

"In that case it's a done deal. How can I help you?"

"I use written policy logs, and to help with my wrists, I have made an entry referring to a mini briefing document stored elsewhere. Thought you might be interested in hearing it."

"Fire away. But if you can get it to me on email as well, that would be good."

"Sure. The bigger picture is the content of the server, then transferring and analysing that data to decide on the best way to process and act on it. We will have the ability to identify the site's hierarchy. If we had the ability to resolve their communications data to actual addresses then we could arrest them all, but in doing so, we would have to replace them with undercover officers, or the site would fail to function and in the end, the word would get out. The reality is, though, we won't be able to resolve all their communications to an address. So the tactic around the main players will be a fluid situation, governed by knowing who they are, where they are, what risk they pose to children and whether they can be taken out effectively while keeping the operation going."

"Are there any shortcuts we can take to ID these people quicker?"

"Countrywise, yes. Jane will be with you for a few days and can explain that to you. Also, we have a list of known proxy IP addresses which you can have as well. Otherwise, I suggest it is a top down approach: go after the organisers first and then the members."

"That sounds like a plan, Tom. Send it to me please. Are you ready for Wednesday?"

"Yes. Jane, Patrick and I will be up late on Tuesday and we'll be with you Wednesday morning by 8am."

"Excellent. See you then."

The next thing on his list was the media strategy, and he went in search of Sarah Dorsey and found her at her desk. Tom grabbed a nearby chair and pulled it up so he was facing her. "Sarah. Are you up to speed with everything?"

"Yes," she replied, smiling.

"Even the updates on Michael?"

"Yep, Jane has regular team meetings."

Sarah was looking at Tom as she spoke, but feeling herself starting to blush she looked away quickly and opened an email on her PC, something Tom missed as he was looking for some notes he had made earlier. When he looked up, Sarah had her eyes fixed on her computer screen and was typing. Tom thought she seemed transfixed by the screen and perhaps he was disturbing her. It was at that point he realised that she was blushing; it was something he had noticed with her before, but this time he was closer to her. His first thought was to look away, which he did. His second was that his sudden approach and relaxed handling of the situation was probably not appropriate.

"If you could let me have the latest copy of the media strategy when you get a chance, that would be great," Tom said, getting up quickly, and leaving in search of a cuppa.

At 1am on Wednesday, all ten COCET staff were in bed asleep, their alarm clocks set for different times depending on what task they had the next day and the travelling time to their place of work. All except two that was, DCI Ross and Sarah Dorsey. Tom was in a hotel bed drinking tea made with UHT milk, which he hated, but he was drinking it anyway. Policy logs for Operation Resolve were spread across the duvet, as were a number of blue counsel notepads. He was reading an email that had just arrived on his new Blackberry phone, a recent and enforced addition from Sarah. The email was from her and he checked his watch, saw the time, then read the mail and the attachment. It was an updated version of the media strategy and a work of art for sure, and he replied saying as much. He added two suggestions and then sent the file back.

Sarah was at home in Yorkshire, having been authorised to work from there for the next few days due to its proximity to Cleveland, should she be needed in person. She was dressed in pink and blue Fat Face pyjama bottoms with a colour coordinated cami top, and was about to go to bed when she heard the Blackberry mobile phone notify her of a new email. She was going to ignore it, but checked to see who it was from first, expecting it to be from Maria and the AFP, and was surprised to see it was from Tom Ross. He was up, which meant he knew she was too. She saw his comments, checked the suggestions and was about to reply 'OK' but stopped herself. Instead, she switched off her phone, closed down her laptop and got in to bed, quickly falling asleep.

As Tom finally drifted off to sleep, he was the last of a thirty seven strong law enforcement team, all of whom had one focus that day. And the object of that focus was still awake, and not far geographically from most of them. He was actively re-victimising one very young and particularly vulnerable child. The video wasn't his, it belonged to someone else, that person having sent it to him through the post on a

CD for safe keeping. His role as 'librarian' had risks as well as perks. In this case the idiot hadn't placed a password on it, something he checked for every time. If they hadn't, he would make a copy and place one on it for them, mainly for his own protection, not theirs. This particular video had a girl in it who was the perfect age for him. The sound was amazing, and he had to wear earphones so he could play the video loud, not wanting to miss a single moan or cry. Without the earphones his mother would hear for sure. He had watched the video many times, probably too many. So this night he had his eyes shut, just listening to her noises as he masturbated. Having finished and cleaned himself up, Philip Thompson logged out of 'childscentcafe' at around 3am and fell asleep, thinking there was a good day ahead, and one that would see him have access to the real thing within hours.

It was a little before 8am when Tom, Jane and Patrick arrived at the incident room, which was situated above a divisional Police Station on the outskirts of Cleveland. Morning coffee break came and went, as did lunch. And it was 1.55pm before Dale rang Tom, informing him that Thompson had logged into 'childscentcafe'.

"Do you want to see if I can engage him now?"

"No, wait. Stay on the line for a moment."

Both DS Drysdale and Superintendent Evans could only hear one side of the call but it was enough for both of them to know they were about to go live.

"Shall I get Operational Support to go to advanced positions?" asked Superintendent Evans.

"Yes," replied Tom.

The Cleveland Operational Support Unit was made up of a different number of departments, one of which was the Firearms Department. Apart from their firearms role, they also trained and provided staff for rapid entry into dangerous or stronghold environments. Unusually for them, this operation called for extra planning and preparation in a form they had never encountered before. The address, a single floor semi-detached house, from the intelligence they had been given, contained the target, Philip Thompson. This raid was different from others they had undertaken in that the target was secondary. The main target wasn't drugs, guns or money that an offender might try to disassociate himself from, but a PC, and one that had to be protected at all costs and not switched off.

The team leader, who had gone to the extent of obtaining floor plans for the address, still wasn't satisfied with his team's reaction times. Believing this was due to not having a realistic training environment, he secured an identical house away from the area that was empty and available to be used for practice. This had proved invaluable when simulating the arrest of a resisting offender. The narrow corridor and entrance would have placed the officers at a disadvantage when using a team of three at the door, which was the initial plan. Only using two, however, presented other problems. One being there were not enough men at the door to undertake a forced entry, meaning they had to resort to a combination of subterfuge followed by force and speed if necessary.

The team selected for the initial approach at the door included two of the strongest and fittest men in the department. They had obtained a full set of council clothing which they would wear over their personal protection gear so that they could not be seen or identified as Police. A council van big enough to carry a back-up team of four would be used by the two officers to drive right up to the address. Having secured a confidential contact within the local council, a letter had been sent to the address in advance, informing the householder that two workman would arrive sometime on the Wednesday to undertake an inspection of the guttering, an item of work that was overdue. The correct headed paper and contact details had been used, in case enquiries led the householder back to the confidential contact, who had also been trained in what to say should that occur. The team was sitting ready about ten minutes from the location when they received the call.

The two officers who were going to the front door put on their council two-piece reflective overalls and checked their communications using a concealed body set. With both officers having close cropped hair, it was necessary for one of them to wear a beanie hat to disguise an earpiece in case they be required to abort at the last minute.

The four officers who climbed into the rear of the council van took two types of entry equipment with them. One was a hydraulic system, the second a simple but heavy battering ram, which could be used on its own or in conjunction with the hydraulic door opener. All four officers wore one piece tactical fire-resistant clothing, Kevlar protective vests together with leather gloves, riot helmets, and knee, shin and elbow protectors. Each officer had a radio and a 'press to talk' or 'PTT' switch situated in a place of their preference so they could speak over their radios whilst maintaining focus on a given situation.

The group leader assembled the entry team in the satellite Police Station car park. His team had already been briefed, but he wanted to say one more thing before they set off, as experience told him nothing more would be said between now and securing the scene, other than aborting the operation.

"You are all married and most of you have kids. You all know the intelligence and what is riding on the further success of this operation. We are a small cog in this. But if we get it wrong, the whole undercover infiltration side will not just fail, it won't even get off the ground. Whatever your thoughts are on these offenders, you put them to one side. Our aim is to secure that PC and to stop all attempts at switching it off from the wall or from the consumer unit. That will give others the chance to save many children from sexual abuse. The key to this is Fast! Furious! And Focussed! Are you ready?"

The team replied in unison with a loud resounding "Yes!", then got into the van and set off.

The officer in the passenger seat called the incident room on his radio. "We're setting off now, received?"

Tom, who was in the incident room, heard the transmission being received. Becky picked up the radio, which had been left by the window to improve radio reception.

"Yes, received at India One. Sierra Two, Echo team are en route now."

There was a short pause then, "Yes, all received we are in position and standing by."

"Who is Sierra Two?" asked Tom.

"We have two full public order support units on standby because of the area the target address is in," Becky began, "we expect significant interest from the locals, and although we are taking as much precaution as we can, if the locals find out Thompson has been arrested for child abuse offences there is a strong likelihood of public disorder."

"OK. Sounds like a good idea then."

"It is for that area. We have an ambulance standing by at the nearest Police Station, and we've alerted 'Trumpton,' just to be safe," Becky said, placing the radio back down on the window sill.

"Time for a cuppa then. Jane, do you want a tea? The boys can get their own."

Jane, who was standing next to Tom and who had been listening to everything thought Becky's timing was perfect, and just what was needed to break the growing tension. As she moved past Tom, she said with a hint of smile, "Don't worry, Boss. You trained me well, I'll get you a tea!"

Tom was grateful to both career detectives for their humour. All the same, for him this was a time when he needed to stay fully focussed and he put his phone back to his ear.

"Is he still there?"

"Yes, Boss. You want me to PM him now?"

"Yes, but something nice and open."

"Sure. Just putting the phone down."

Tom heard the soft tap tap tap of the keyboard as Dale sent Thompson a private message, then a pause before hearing a louder single tap before Dale came back on the line.

"I've asked him if he is available to chat over a membership problem. He hasn't replied but he is still shown as online."

The minutes that went by seemed like hours. Jane and Becky came back, and Jane handed him a cup of tea which he took a sip of and then put down. Patrick Smith had got straight to work, knowing that his role was crucial for the rest of the staff to be able to do their job. However, he was listening intently to what was going on, and he noticed that his heart rate had increased significantly. Superintendent Evans, meanwhile, was reading emails whilst the rest of the Holmes team were either standing and looking out of the window, or sitting and looking at blank computer screens. Becky seemed to sense that it was about to get serious, and she herself started to stare out of the window whilst drinking her tea.

The rapid entry crew must have had a quick run, because well within the allocated ten minute drive time to the address the radio burst into life.

"India One. This is Echo One, we are at RV Two, what are your instructions?"

Becky turned and looked towards Superintendent Evans, who in turn looked at Tom. "This is the point of no return for the entry team. It's your call, is it a 'Go'?"

Tom, who still had his mobile next to his ear, didn't have to ask Dale because he had heard the question and replied straight away.

"He hasn't answered me, but he is still shown as being online and I have just refreshed."

"Stay on the line, Dale," Tom said, looking first at Becky Drysdale and then at Superintendent Evans. "He isn't in chat with the undercover officer, but then we have no way of knowing when or if that will happen. He's online now, that's as good as it will get. It's a 'Go'!"

Superintendent Evans had been a career detective and just about had his thirty years in. He knew a 'hot' decision when he saw one, and he also knew how it could be manipulated later so that others were at fault. Tom Ross from COCET didn't have the best intelligence and was going to have to do better than that. "This is your call. We can wait if you want?"

Tom knew the politics of the situation just as well as the Superintendent, but he knew his job better. "It's a 'Go'. Get them in there now."

Superintendent Evans picked up the radio and said, "Echo One, this is India One. Strike, strike, strike!"

"Echo One received, en route now," came the immediate reply.

The Superintendent gave Tom a small smile as if to say 'Down to you then', then went back to his PC and emails.

Jane sensed the Police politics that were in play around her and moved closer to Tom in support. Because nobody was speaking, the incident room went so silent you could hear a pin drop, and the tension increased. There was nothing more to be done, Tom thought. It was all now in the hands of the entry team.

At that moment the entry team had pulled up outside the target address. The officers in the rear let go of the ropes they'd been holding, and three of them moved close to the rear doors with one of them taking hold of the internal handle, whilst the fourth officer looked through a peephole in the side of the van facing the address. All the officers felt their two colleagues exit the van and shut the doors. The officer looking through the peephole whispered, "They are walking down the path now."

The four officers still in the van knew they were moments away from action and tensed up their muscles in readiness. The two officers in council work wear reached the door, and the officer with the search warrant in his pocket rang the doorbell. Neither of them heard a bell chiming, so the second officer knocked as well. As they had expected the door was made of wood with an oval central glass insert that was frosted so that someone on the outside couldn't see in, but nor could anyone inside see out.

However, there was enough clarity to see the outline of someone coming to the door, and as a shape appeared before them, the officer who had possession of the warrant reached inside his jacket pocket and took hold of it, whilst the other officer took hold of his Police identity badge. As the door opened their target, Philip Thompson, came into view. The officers had trained for this moment and knew exactly the course of action they would take, and they were sure the element of surprise combined with their speed and strength would not be matched.

Philip Thompson had woken late and had just viewed some child abuse material, but he hadn't masturbated, knowing he would have access to the real thing later in the day. He hadn't eaten anything and was still half dressed and not fully awake when he saw the two council men standing before him. His mother had told him they would be calling at some point, so to see them on his doorstep was not a surprise.

However, one of them suddenly produced a piece of paper, and said, "Police! We have a warrant to search the premises," whilst the other one shouted, "Police! Police!" and produced a Police identity card.

At the same time one of them leaned in and grabbed one arm while the other officer moved into the house, taking hold of his remaining wrist and upper arm whilst moving around him so that he began to get closer to Thompson's bedroom door. It had all been a blur until that point. The words 'Warrant' and 'Police' had little effect on him, even the officers taking hold of him hadn't really registered that much. That was until one of them started to get between him and his bedroom.

At that point, somewhere deep within him, a danger loomed. So big and real was the fear of being found out that it produced a volatile response, and he started to fight back with all his strength. He ripped his right and stronger arm free, and immediately struck the officer to his left a blow to the side of the neck. He used the fact that the officer had hold of him as leverage, and stepping back he began to force himself between the door to the bedroom and the officer, and then pushed with all his might.

He felt the officer give way at first, but then the other one put his hands around the back of his head and neck and pulled down hard. So hard that he bent over double, and the officer lost his grip as his hands fell away across the top of his head. Able to stand again he punched the officer who still had hold of him.

He had to stop them getting into his bedroom, they couldn't be allowed in there at any cost, not until he switched his computer off. He grabbed the officer around the neck with his free arm and ripped and pulled back as hard as he could. The result was that the officer pivoted back towards him, and they both fell to the floor with their upper bodies wedged between the sides of the bedroom door, with their lower bodies still in the corridor. The standing officer had bent down and taken hold of Thompson's leg and begun to straighten with the intention of pulling him back into the corridor, when he was hit over the top of his back and neck twice in quick succession. He looked up to see a third strike coming his way from Thompson's disabled mother, as she used her walking stick to hit him. He let go of Thompson's leg to fend off the blow just as reinforcements arrived.

The team leader was the first to see that their objective had not been achieved. He took a step to the left, not entering the house himself, and propelled the first backup team member in, shouting, "Computer!"

That officer had no option but to trample over the two fighting on the floor, whilst squeezing past his other colleague, who was still busy fending off blows from Mrs. Thompson, who was by now screaming at the top of her voice. As the second support officer crossed the threshold of the front door he saw the walking stick rise up and quickly moved into the corridor. Together with his colleague he grabbed hold of Mrs. Thompson's arms and pushed her backwards all the way back into the kitchen.

The team leader instructed the final officer to secure the consumer unit, and taking two steps into the house, as that was all he was able to do, he fell on top of Thompson using his knees and legs to protect himself from being kicked. The officer who was still struggling with him, considered himself one of the strongest in the team. He couldn't understand how a person much smaller than himself was not just matching his strength, but even with the weight of the Sergeant on top of him was still managing to pull away into the bedroom. He saw the Sergeant get one handcuff on Thompson's wrist, and whether it was that, or he had just finally run out of steam in the end, he suddenly let go and gave in.

Meanwhile, the incident room was in stark contrast to the scene at Philip Thompson's address. Each person was wondering what was going on, and whether they would be successful. They had all been told that if they failed at this stage the undercover side was probably doomed. The silence was suddenly shattered.

"Echo One, India One. Scene is secure, objective is secured. Send in your arrest and search team, over."

The change in the incident room upon hearing the transmission was fascinating to see and be part of. Within seconds Tom's doubt and fears dissipated, to be replaced by a sense of achievement, whilst others smiled or laughed. A few even clapped and cheered the success of the entry team.

"Stage one complete. It's game on then!" Superintendent Evans announced loudly to the whole room.

The rest of that day, or what was left of it, was taken up by the house search and the custody procedures for Philip Thompson. The entry team had managed to secure the PC whilst it was in an open state, and the resulting forensic work required at the scene took over five hours. Thompson, who had fought so hard at the beginning, started making admissions even whilst at the scene and throughout his journey to the Police Station.

There had been no plans for any interviews that day. But with Thompson talking so freely, and not wanting a solicitor, a decision was made to get two interviews in before he was given his rest period for the night. When Tom arrived at the Holmes incident room the next day, he was expecting the team to be still on a high, and they were. But there was also an air of concern which he quickly picked up on. Jane, who had arrived an hour before, approached him; his concerns were confirmed by the look on her face.

"What's up?" Tom said enquiringly

"They had problems at the address throughout the night. The support group had to stand down in the end, and they were replaced by the night shift. It went quiet, and due to another urgent call the car got pulled away, which was when somebody tried to fire bomb the house with the mother still in it. She's OK, but the fire brigade was called."

"What about the house and contents?"

"It's OK, some of the outside and door is burnt and there is damage to the house elsewhere. The Boss here is at a meeting on it. The plan is to move her and all her contents today to another location. They have a heavy presence down there now, and the local CID are investigating."

"They did say it was a bad area. Where's Becky?"

"Coming in late. She's got kids, so she starts later on some days.

"Is anybody in trouble for this?"

"Nope, not from what I've heard."

"I'm going to the custody suite first to see Dale and then get on the rattler. I want to chase up the 'The Lord' lead and see where we are with LB. This will take days to settle and get going."

As Tom waited to be collected and taken to the custody suite, he rang Sarah Dorsey.

"Hi, Tom. I hear it went well?"

"Yes, it did. They have had some collateral damage to the address though, are you aware of that?"

"Yes, I am. I have a good contact in their media department and I have seen their release. It covers everything, and the local press have all been covered. So you are good to go for now. The next stage will be when he appears in court, and we are ready for that."

"Are you able to stay up here until that occurs?" Tom asked, thinking he would prefer if she did.

"Yes. I've made arrangements to do so."

"Thanks, Gotta go, Dale's just arrived."

"Morning Guv, this way," Dale said, before leading him through a number of doors and corridors, until eventually they came up to a large heavy door. It didn't have any handles and could only be opened remotely from the other side. Dale pressed a switch to the right of the door, and a few seconds later a loud click was heard followed by a constant buzzing, which only stopped after they had passed through the door and it had shut again. Once in, Tom could see that Thompson had been given a whole custody suite with a dedicated custody sergeant and a civilian detention officer. Dale made the introductions, then took Tom down another corridor to an interview room that had a number of large wires running to it from another interview room some further distance down the corridor. The door to the interview room was open, and he saw that it contained two plain clothes officers and another person that he thought must be Joe Sullivan.

"Guv. This is DC Roper, and this is DC Webb. They are the interviewing officers for Thompson, and this is Joe Sullivan the Forensic Psychologist,"

The interviewing officers acknowledged Tom and then went straight back to the tape they were listening to.

"Hi, I'm Joe Sullivan, thank you for thinking of me for this interview. It's been really useful, I think, for the guys here who are interviewing Thompson. And Dale is learning a great deal as well for the undercover role you have planned."

Joe was a tall man with close cropped, almost grey, hair who was dressed smartly in a two piece suit and tie. He was wearing a trendy pair of glasses which looked expensive, and he spoke with a soft Irish accent.

"Well, I'm pleased to hear it, and I'm even more pleased to know NCIS are paying for you," Tom said with a smile and a laugh. "So what's the plan for today?" he continued.

"They are going over the two interviews from last night again, now that Joe has given them his input on it. Then they will prepare for the next two. We can listen and make notes here," Dale said, pointing at two sets of headphones, "and we can see his reaction and body language on the screen there."

Tom saw a large TV screen that had been placed on top of a metal cabinet, and although it was not currently switched on he got the feeling Cleveland had done yet another good job.

"Great. I hear he has been talking. Has he given all his passwords up?"

"Yes," Dale replied.

"Has he said anything that I need to know about that would require urgent action?"

"There is something that Joe picked up on. He has mentioned someone called Carly, and Joe says that his method of dealing with questions changed when he discussed her. The guys are going to press him on it in the next interview."

Tom's inner alarm bell started to sound in his head. "I'm off back to COCET for a few days. This will run into extensions of detention for sure. Just keep me updated on this Carly. The moment you know, Dale, let me know."

Tom had been on the train for an hour when he received a call from Detective Sgt. Dale Walters. "Guv, Can you talk?"

"Yes," replied Tom.

"Carly is a seven year old relative who sleeps with him in his bed at least once a week. He is refusing to admit to sexual abuse of her, so the interview has stopped whilst they make arrangements to locate her and get her interviewed. Once they have that underway they will start again with him. But they think he won't cough that unless she makes a disclosure."

"OK. Let Jane know."

"Will do."

Tom wondered how Cleveland's surveillance had missed the child going there once a week. His mind fell to Louisa Greenwood and what she would make of it. Her strategy called for her to be in the decision making process in cases like this. This was a matter for Cleveland to deal with. They might not have wanted to sign the CP strategy, but they had, so they would now have to honour it and work with it. As Tom returned to his seat, it was not the first time that he had pondered the wisdom of bringing the Police and the NSPCC together under one roof.

CHAPTER EIGHTEEN

Tom was in his office reading a briefing note from Jane. He could see it had arrived in the early hours of the morning. Philip Thompson was into his third day in custody, and although he now had a solicitor, he was still freely admitting to most things that were being put to him.

Cleveland's computer Forensic Department had worked full time on the job. With the aid of overtime they had got the images categorised and to the interview officers in time, together with evidence of possession or supply, and even some chat logs. No small feat, considering the size of his personal collection and others he held on CD.

Carly had been located and was still being interviewed, and it was likely to be a slow process. Louisa Greenwood had visited her school, and found that teachers there had raised concerns that Carly was displaying sexual behaviour in the playground, and which they had raised with her mother. The mother was due to be interviewed today. The prosecution team was expected to formulate the charges this morning with a remand appearance afterwards. The incident room was not yet fully operational, but they had made a start on the intelligence from the interviews, forensics, and the intelligence coming from Patrick. A number of communication applications to trace real addresses through IP addresses had been submitted, but none had yet been returned. Thompson's description of the site 'hierarchy' matched that of the actual server. More important, was that he had admitted it had been set up to run in the way it had been, specifically to avoid the attention of law enforcement, something that had been passed to the Crown Prosecution Service in the remand file. Dale was returning today, and had more than enough background to assume the identity of Thompson and begin the infiltration phase.

Tom closed the email. He was pleased with the information, but what he needed now was a result on 'The Lord'. He was about to ring Niall when he decided to keep the 'brass' happy first, so he compiled a comprehensive update report and sent it to Superintendent Maggie Burrows. He then readdressed the update report to all COCET members and made a cuppa, hopefully giving the email chance to reach Niall before he rang him. It had, and Niall rang him first.

"Blinding result, Tom. Can I send this up the chain?"

"Yes, of course."

"Well. I don't want to burst your bubble, but I have some not so good news, and some bad news. Which do you want first?"

Tom thought about it for a second, wondering which one to choose, then plumbed for the worst. "One step forward, two steps back! Give me the bad news!"

"The Canadians say they can't get a warrant without an actual offence, and as he isn't doing anything illegal in Holland they can't take action."

Tom simply couldn't believe what he was hearing. "Tell them to get a warrant and go find the evidence!" Tom replied quickly, with more than just a hint of frustration in his voice.

"It doesn't work like that there, it appears they need an actual offence before they can apply. Well, technically that's not correct. They could apply, but they wouldn't get it. So it's one and the same thing."

"How the hell do they ever conduct proactive investigations, where you go looking for offences based on good intelligence? Don't they have informants there?"

"They probably do, but it's their legal system. It's not the cops, they have to work to the way their system works, and they want to help. But say they can't do anything until we give them an offence."

"That's just bullshit, Niall. Are you sure they aren't just stalling you?"

"Nope. That is the way it works there. And what makes it worse is that they are still very raw in this area of work. If it had been covered by Toronto then we would still have the same problem, but Kim and the team would have found a way in. But as I said, it isn't covered by Toronto."

"OK, look. In that case, I want a formal request made for them to open an investigation into him. Intelligence build-up work. Data comms work-up on his landline. From there get his mobile and then do the same on that. Ask them to request a snapshot of what he is looking at online through his ISP. They don't need an interception, just historical intelligence, from that we should be able to push them harder."

"I can try, but I don't think it will work, they just don't seem interested."

"What level are you going in at?"

"The officer in charge of online CP work for the RCMP."

Tom paused to gather his thoughts. He had two issues here. One, the fact the RCMP were saying they couldn't help. The other concerned how he would look when it got to media release time. Not being able to arrest 'The Lord', the 'kingpin' of the entire site, when he had mounted a global online child abuse investigation involving the UK, Interpol, Australia and America, all part of GOPOL. He was not looking forward to that! And it would certainly not look good for the Canadians, when the rest of GOPOL were saving children from sexual abuse, to say they couldn't arrest the man responsible.

"Niall. I can go to my Chief now, but let's see if we can broker a deal. If I go straight to the head of GOPOL then there's nowhere else to go. Can you start with a formal request from COCET, copy me in as well as the AFP and ICE. Ask for the intelligence work, and let's see how they shape up to that. I want their reply in writing. Explain the media embarrassment that will descend on them when this all comes out. We arrest everybody and they leave the 'kingpin' in place. How's it going to look for them? If that isn't enough for them to do something, then my last play will be the Chief."

"Sounds like a plan. Do you want the not so good news?"

"Is it involving Canada?"

"Yes."

"What can't they do now?" Tom replied sarcastically.

"They have been able to help on the missing persons, but it's huge. There are over two thousand two hundred for just 2005, but I think some of them are outstanding from previous years. We won't know for sure till we get the intelligence. It could be a very big undertaking."

"Well, let's wait and see what we get. What about immigration?"

"That's in the 'not so good' bracket. They are very guarded about the software they use, where it's all stored and what can be searched for, certainly in a historical sense with the parameters we have given them. In short, they are saying that they can't supply us with what we want, because they cannot guarantee its accuracy. I have already said that we will take what they can give us, but they wouldn't accept that. I have made enquiries within Interpol with some immigration specialists, and they reckon the software and the architecture was probably purchased from America. Even if it wasn't, what they are using now may not be working as it should be. By assisting us, it will lead to their systems being known within law enforcement circles, and they don't want that. You can go as high as you want on this one. They won't be playing ball."

"I thought we had it hard here," Tom said reflectively. "Time line on the missing persons data?"

"Soon, was all I got," replied Niall.

"What about the Dutch side?"

"That side is looking good at the moment because it is something they want as part of their investigation."

"OK, Niall. Can you get that email off today?"

"Yep. Will do it now."

With the call ended, Tom realised he hadn't been this frustrated since his run in with Miller. This would have been a brilliant opportunity for GOPOL to ask the RCMP to join the club, but apart from their Federal name, what did they have to give? If their laws prevented them working on intelligence led policing to obtain evidence, then they could end up being a hindrance. His thoughts were broken by his desk phone ringing.

"Tom, Maggie. Great result! JT and the Chief know, and they both send their congratulations. So you can pass that along to the whole team."

"Thank you. It's early days though," Tom replied, pondering whether to tell her about the Canadian problem.

"It is. And I know there is a long way to go, but I am very confident you will succeed. There is something I need to discuss with you though…"

Superintendent Burrows paused, as her tone changed to concern from the congratulatory one she had been using moments before.

"The Chief has received a call from the NSPCC about the child who wasn't picked up prior to the arrest of Thompson, and he wants a report on the facts around it. I'd like to see it as well."

"Is there a problem?" Tom enquired as neutrally as he could, whilst underneath there was a bank of red mist rising.

"Well, that's what we want to see, so a report of what we did would be a good start in making that assessment." Maggie matched Tom's neutrality perfectly.

"OK," was as much as Tom could muster before the call ended.

He wasn't sure what bothered him more. The fact that Louisa had pushed it straight up and hadn't come to him first, or that they had gone on some witch hunt without assessing if there were a need for a hunt in the first place. If this had been a cop he would have recalled the officer immediately and demanded an explanation, but she wasn't. They had the right to question him, and all the way to the top, but he wasn't able to do the same with the NSPCC.

This was embarrassing, to say the least. Louisa knew what Cleveland had done, and they hadn't uncovered anything, but she clearly suspected that either he or Becky were holding something back. He wanted to control this, but the truth was that he couldn't. A few weeks ago he would have told them to stuff it, but now it was a mixture of anger and disappointment. At the end of the day he was a cop, and he was going to do the right thing by them first, so he rang Superintendent Evans.

"Are you in a position to talk?"

"No. Wait a second whilst I go outside," came the reply. Tom waited and heard a number of doors open and shut before David Evans came back on the line.

"Go ahead, is this about the NSPCC?"

Tom's first thought was that he must have fallen asleep and missed a day somewhere, because everybody seemed to be ahead of him today.

"Yes, it is. I don't know what you know, but I have been asked by the head of GOPOL for a report on the circumstances around the identification of the victim 'Carly.'"

"I thought as much. Louisa has been sounding off here. You do what you have to do. I will ask Becky to put something in writing with my name on it, and I will bring the matter up with my Boss. He in turn will mention it to the Chief Constable. We have nothing to hide, and can I suggest that as soon as Louisa finishes her CP work around Carly, she returns to COCET where she will be of more use? I'm quite happy for her to return if we have any more direct victims on our patch, but she isn't a cop, she doesn't know how to work in a Holmes environment, and so isn't any use to me!"

"As long as you know, and you clearly do," Tom said, wondering if the credibility of COCET would be enhanced or hindered within policing circles in the future.

"Thompson has been to court and has been remanded," Superintendent Evans said, changing the subject. "So we move on. It's a good job, Tom. You work with the NSPCC so you have to adjust to that way of working. We don't. Speak to you soon."

Tom was left with a dead dial tone in his ear, and the realisation that he did need to adjust, or he was going to be forever reacting to events. So he wrote an email to Louisa and copied in Supt. Burrows, ADS King, DS Drysdale and Detective Supt. Evans.

In it, he requested that she provide a full report on her concerns around the victim 'Carly' as soon as possible. The report was to include any evidence that she had found where COCET or Cleveland Police should, or could, have taken any other action that would have led to the victim being identified and located earlier than she was. The report was to include best practice suggestions, any other relevant information and to be sent directly to him for minuting before passing further up the chain. Tom pressed the send button, and then texted Jane to inform her she had a new email that she needed to read. Wanting some good news that wasn't affected by politics he rang Dr. Nick Sharpe.

"Nick, Hi. It's Tom Ross. How's it going?"

"Hi, Tom. Good and not so good. There isn't anything we can do with Leitch; Sue has got as far as possible on that. There was a great deal of imagery on Visser's hardware together with chat logs and other Intel, but nothing that we are looking for. We have kept a copy for Jane and the incident room once they start to get going. Clark, however, is a bit more promising."

Tom, just glad to hear some positive news, blurted out, "Great! Is this the good news?"

Nick laughed, and replied, "Yes. It is. The initial work I did picked up some interesting signs that he had been trying to join a group. With the Intel you gave us we were able to identify some whole chat logs which, although deliberately clipped in nature, indicate that he may have joined that group PTC, or was at least trying to join it. We can't find any trace of him using anonymising software, but that is not to say he didn't. The most interesting thing is that we have identified a Hotmail email that is linked to PTC. And there are five incoming mails as well, so you will want to get them resolved; and when they are, you should cross check that with 'childscentcafe'."

"Great work, Nick. Can you give me the Hotmail account now, then get the rest to me on an email as soon as possible?"

"Sure!"

Tom rang Jane King, who upon answering wanted to talk about nothing else but the email he had copied her into, but fell silent when she knew the call was something to do with LB.

"That has to wait for the moment, Jane, did you speak to Essex about Clark?"

"Yes. As long as you have new offences they will contact him and get him to come in. They can only provide the OIC though."

"Great. In that case, who do we have spare?"

"Mitchell or Anna W."

"Any preference?"

"Probably Mitchell. Anna has the most on at the moment," Jane replied.

"That email," Tom began, now prepared to deal with Jane's initial line of questioning. "Louisa must have brought up the 'Carly' issue, and the fact we didn't identify her with her line manager within the NSPCC, whoever that is. I think his first name is Colin. He must be pretty senior because it's made its way to the Chief."

"What!"

"Look. They are part of the team even if it is just one. This is the way they work and we have no option but to work along their lines. So, if Louisa has evidence we or Cleveland did something wrong, then she has to tell me what that is and I will forward it on up the chain."

"Alright, Boss. But we need to sort out how matters of concern are handled within the team. If she feels the need to go running to NSPCC senior officers, then she hasn't integrated with us in my view. And that is reflective of an 'Us and Them' situation, which isn't good in the long term."

"Agreed," replied Tom, "but going back to the first matter, I'm going to task Mitchell now and will be giving an email to Anna Farley to resolve from Clark's PC."

"Righto. What is the email? I will get it checked against our copy of the site."

Tom told Jane the email address, and went in search of DC Mitchell Hayes and Intelligence Officer Anna Farley.

At just after 4pm the following day Anna Farley walked into Tom's office with news.

"That email is back. It looks fake, same name as the Dutch prime minister. The mobile number given on registration, which is Dutch, is a throwaway and non-traceable according to Niall. He has had it dialled from within Holland and there was no tone. The IP that created the email account came from a TOR exit node, so it cannot be traced. Out of the other five incoming emails that we have for that account, two of the IPs come back to Thailand. We will need to make enquires there to see if they can be resolved, the other three are Dutch and Niall has asked them to resolve it for us. If we get to an address, then we may have identified LB."

Tom, first thanking Anna, felt an adrenalin hit and rang Jane immediately.

"Jane. Have you checked that email yet?"

"Yes. You want the details?"

"Yes. Anna got a quick result on the email. Can you send me what you have and copy in Anna as well?"

"Sure."

Tom went to make a cup of tea that he didn't really want, and would probably never finish in any case. He watched his screen, sipping on hot tea, when he spotted the incoming mail from Jane and opened it straight away.

Tom was still reading the contents when Anna Farley arrived back in his office with a smile on her face.

"Have you seen it?"

"Yes. And it's very interesting!" Anna said excitedly.

"Tell me more!" Tom replied eagerly, wanting to know what Anna knew.

"The email is registered to a member and admin called D512. First registered 16th May 2003. The IP at that time was a Dutch one, so I have added that to the three Niall is asking the Dutch to do for us. Since then he has posted a total of seven times, comments only. They are comments on images, or comments on other comments on images, or direct chat to other members. The members are all admins and that includes Thompson. Notably, he hasn't uploaded anything. The IP addresses allocated to these posts, and we don't have all of them - for some reason on a few it wasn't recorded - are all on our list of known or suspected proxy servers that Dominic and Nick provided us with. So, if you analyse that, it could mean that he registered from a real address in 2003 and then started to use a proxy, which means we could have him! The IP address, though, is not the same as the other

280

three. But then, if they were dynamically assigned, they wouldn't be."

"What a result, Anna, we could have him at last!" Tom exclaimed, thinking Anna had finished.

"That's not all," Anna replied quickly.

Tom's eyes widened and his mind screamed, 'Tell me!' as Anna continued.

"There is another member called D528 who joined on the same date and has the same joining IP. There are only two items attributable to that member and those are two posts, both IPs again are on our list of suspected proxy servers, but we will still submit them. So, it gives more weight to the fact that we may have a provable IP address. The two posts are comments on two other members' comments, and those two members are Thompson and Clark."

Anna signalled she had finished this time by closing the notepad she had been reading from and then placing it under her arm.

Tom's mind was racing with possibilities again, and he needed the time to assemble them.

"Thanks, Anna. Great work."

Alone, Tom put his tea down and began thinking. He took out his counsel pad and drew first a circle and then many arrows emanating from the centre of the circle. At the top of each arrow he wrote one word. By the time he'd gone right round the circle he had seventeen arrows and words. Then he wrote a number next to each word, in reverse order from 17 to 1. He put a cross through number 17 and got up and went in search of his undercover team.

Dale Walters, Owen Marks, and Archie Donaldson had obtained more desks through Sam and set them up behind temporary office screens in an attempt to provide themselves with some privacy. Their 'Covert Operations Room' was situated at the end of the building between Tom's office and the tea room. Tom walked in and took up a seat next to Dale. Both DC Marks and DC Donaldson were busy typing at their keyboards, and he could see from their screens, from where he was sitting, that they were logged into 'childscentcafe'.

"How's it going so far, Dale?" Tom asked.

"It's going very well, Guv. The incident room has identified twenty six top level and fourteen medium level administrators. They, and we, are only working on the top level at the moment, as they haven't processed all the data yet.

"Six of the top level are behind a proxy. Out of the remaining twenty, eight are in the UK, and the others are either in America, Canada, Australia, Europe or Brazil. The incident room is going through these targets and their profiles to see if there's any intelligence that would suggest they need to be arrested immediately, or whether they can be left to be targeted by us. We are waiting on that, but in the meantime we are logged into the site as both Thompson and Clark as well as six of our own identities. We have been really busy, even though we haven't actually engaged anybody ourselves.

"We are currently infiltrating eleven members after they engaged with us. Three of those are top level admins. Two are from the US and one is from the UK. Four are medium level admins; two from the US, one from Canada and the last from the UK. Most have just sent us child abuse material without us even talking about it."

"How is the Intel being exchanged with the incident room?" Tom asked, concerned about continuity and the CP strategy.

"We are cutting and pasting everything we do along with screen grabs into target folders, just like you did on Operation Hope, and getting it straight to them by way of email. Images and videos are going through a triage with us first. We view them, and decide what action we need to take from a victim identification perspective, or for further infiltration. Then they go onto a CD to be looked at here again by Louisa when she gets back. They get a serial number which is cross referenced to the target, and the material will then be stored here for further victim ID work. The serial number is also assigned to the subject in the incident room."

Tom was happy with what had been set up. They had been told to look at and use Operation Hope's set operating procedures, and they had. The only issue for him was the monitoring of the undercover investigation plan and the provision of sufficient written and logged instructions as the infiltration developed.

The potential areas for dangerous situations that could quickly get out of control were twofold. First, giving the undercover officer too wide a brief that allowed them to go too far, leading to a catastrophe such as a child being abused as a direct result of police action. Second, being too restrictive, to the point where a child is put at risk. The only way to get the balance right was to monitor it closely, and be part of the decision making processes that the undercovers performed at all stages of the infiltration. He was about to lose a lot of sleep and gain a few more grey hairs.

"What's your shift pattern?"

"UK time zone, long hours. One officer is doing eight to eight, and the other two doing three to three am. Anything else by demand."

"Is there anything urgent for today?"

"There are three cases that have the potential to develop into urgent. Two in the US and one in the UK. The incident room is aware of them, and you are going to be alerted if it escalates."

"OK. Until we get into a groove, I want a debrief every evening, sooner if operational circumstances dictate. All officers need to have pocket books up to date, and to be ready for them to be signed daily with fresh or continuation instructions from me."

"Yes, Guv. One more thing, Guv. It was a good call to be there for the interviews with Thompson. Turns out one of the members who had sent him material to be stored offline is one of our early customers. It came up, but because we knew about it, we were able to infiltrate him further. Without that knowledge we could have failed and been caught out within the first few hours."

"We create our own luck, Dale," Tom replied, thinking about the decision to have downstream monitoring of the interview, and to have Dale there.

"I want you to go steady on the Clark identity. Be consistent online with his profile, but don't engage. Anybody that engages you I want to know before you reply."

"Sure, no problem. What's up?"

"We have a lead on LB. Clark and Thompson appear to have been in contact with him. Whether they know who he is, is another matter.

Our intelligence indicates that Clark seems to have known who he was, or that he was a link to PTC. I want to use Clark's identity to get to him, but we may be able to get to him via some IP addresses. But they won't be resolved for a few days."

"OK, Guv."

Tom returned to his office, opened a large metal cupboard at the back and took out a folding stretcher bed, a sleeping bag and a pillow. He assembled his portable bedroom in the corner, then picked up the half drunk and cold cup of tea and left to make a fresh one.

At that moment, if it had been possible to see the combined efforts of COCET's Operation Resolve and Cleveland's Operation Elm, from a fly on the wall perspective, you would have seen a UK major investigation team in full flow supported by specialist staff from COCET, the first of its kind: a National Child Protection Agency. At COCET headquarters officers were working covertly on the internet, with its new online investigators supported by its own specialist Intelligence Unit.

Further afield, officers from the international arm of COCET representing GOPOL, Interpol, the Australian Federal Police and the Immigration Customs and Enforcement Department, (a section of 'Homeland Security' for America) were collaborating with other Law Enforcement Agencies around the world, taking action where it was required to preserve the lives of children, and to prevent them being sexually abused.

Their efforts were focussed on over twenty two thousand members of a single web based group, mainly made up of men, whose sole purpose of being a member of that group was the sexual abuse of children.

Whoever and wherever they were in the world at that very moment, they were living their lives as husbands, fathers, sons, brothers, boyfriends or colleagues. Some were in employment that involved working with, or caring for, children. Others held every conceivable job or position across the employment sector. They were all completely unaware that the safe haven they had made or found for themselves was now compromised. As every minute went by, the 'good' guys were peeling back their veil of secrecy, and closing in, to hold them to account for their actions. All apart from one, it would seem.

CHAPTER NINETEEN

Tom let his head drop to the table and banged his forehead on the wooden surface, before raising it again.

"They cannot be serious! They want to take no action on 'The Lord', and then they ask to become members of GOPOL! What are they going to bring to the table? If they can't get a warrant and go and search for evidence, then they can't work with us! What's the point?" Tom by this time was now out of his seat and pacing up and down the office.

Maggie Burrows, who was listening to Tom's rant, was beginning to think they may have been subject of a smart piece of political manoeuvering, a thought that was very much in the front of Tom's brain as well.

"Maggie, I know what's behind this. I've explained to them that it will be hugely embarrassing when it comes to arrest day. That when GOPOL, COCET, Cleveland and countries all over the world take down the largest web based group of child sex offenders, and we arrest thousands of them, and rescue hundreds of kids from sexual abuse, and They don't arrest the owner because They say he hasn't committed an offence: the press will crucify them. If not in their own country, they will elsewhere.

"That's why they want to become a member of GOPOL now. They want in now, so that when the shit hits the fan - in fact even before then - they know the situation will put us under pressure to give them a way out. If they are part of our team how can we point the finger? We can't do anything because we will be just shitting on ourselves! That's why they want in now!"

Tom ran out of steam. He knew exactly what was going on, and was powerless to do anything about it. He had made the threats to the RCMP, and they had just turned it back on him by joining his team; knowing that he would never let a team member down.

"Tom," Maggie began in a soothing voice, "I think you may be right. But it doesn't matter if you are. The Chief sees this as an opportunity to recruit another Federal Agency. So they are now part of GOPOL and you aren't going to want to hear this. They have assigned an officer to Operation Resolve and they have given it operational status there, they are calling it Operation Montreal. They will take our intelligence on their nationals and will deal with it according to their laws. When we send them evidence of an offence in their country they will arrest and prosecute. Make friends, Tom. And by the way, the Chief has had another conversation with the NSPCC. Apparently your inclusive email approach to dealing with Louisa hasn't gone down well. It's not the way they work. I have agreed to speak to you about your management style of non-police staff. Consider yourself spoken to. Now, I have somewhere I have to be. Concentrate on the bad guys and don't let it get to you."

Before he could begin some form of protest he had a dead dial tone in his ear. Tom threw his mobile phone down on the table, pushed himself back into his chair, looked up towards the ceiling, closed his eyes and started to count to ten.

Upon opening them again, he found Anna Farley in his office looking at him with a facial expression that was a mixture of surprise and wonder. In that split second he thought about Anna. She was the best intelligence officer he had ever worked with. She was immensely bright and clever. She was hard working, honest, trustworthy and worth her weight in gold. *'I wonder what she would think about this?'* Tom thought to himself.

He dismissed the idea immediately, knowing it was wrong to even contemplate it, let alone ask her.

"Yes, Anna?"

"Bad day at the office?" she enquired in a caring tone.

Tom thought *'Well, she cares. That's enough for me!'*

"Yes, you could say that. How can I help you?"

"The three from yesterday have escalated, and Dale and I would like to brief you in Covert Ops, if that's OK?"

"Of course," replied Tom, getting up and hearing for the second time Maggie's words, 'Concentrate on the bad guys'.

"Fire away!" Tom said to both Dale and Anna, as he took a seat in his new undercover officers' department.

Dale began. "The three admins I was talking to you about yesterday have all supplied the same images to us over the last hour. We think they are new; and the chat that comes with it sort of indicates the victim might be a daughter of one of them."

"Let's see the images," Tom said.

Dale was prepared for that and quickly pulled the images up on his screen. "There are fifteen in all. Not all of the targets have sent fifteen, but you can clearly see they are from the same collection," Dale said, as he toggled through the images.

The victim was a girl aged around ten. She didn't have any pubic hair yet, or breasts, and was alone in three of the images. In the others there was a male who had his erect penis inside her vagina. In the images where she was alone, her face could be seen. But when she was with the male, her face couldn't. The image resolution was high and there was no doubt it was the same girl, and none of the officers watching was in any doubt that the girl was being raped. Tom started to view the background of the image just as Anna spoke.

"The wallpaper seemed similar to some that I have seen before at B&Q, so I made an inquiry with them. They can't say for sure that it is the wallpaper they stock, but they agree it looks the same, and it is something that only they stock in the UK, and from what they know, only a limited amount went for sale in the US."

"Well done! Has the data comms been done?" Tom asked looking at Anna.

"Yes. It went in yesterday and came back this morning. Target is in Bristol, no previous convictions, lives at an address with his wife and two daughters, aged three and six."

"Anything on open resource to identify the kids?" Tom asked next.

"Nothing that we have been able to find," replied Dale.

Tom looked back at the image in front of him. There was no way the child was six, and there wasn't anything obviously English, or non-English, in the background to give the location away.

"What about the chat?" Tom enquired.

Dale went back to his keyboard, opened a folder and produced a screen grab. There was only one sentence and it said, "Homely girl, getting home attention."

"That came with the images from one of the US suspects. The best course would be if you can arrange all three to be done at the same time. The reason is they may well be connected as they have the same collection, and we can't say for sure who has access to the child. And indeed, maybe none of them do!" Anna said emphatically.

"How quickly can Avon and Somerset do it?"

"Today if we ask now," Anna replied, quickly and confidently.

Tom checked his watch. Agent Jim Burgess would certainly be at work by now, that was for sure, even allowing for the time difference. But Anna had already done the data comms work so they were ahead of them by half a day at least. Tom's experience of working with ICE was that they would make enquiries once the data comms work was back, and if they had no record of children being at the address they probably wouldn't work to the UK deadline. The UK suspect had access to kids, so action was needed on UK soil. But the Americans didn't appreciate the urgency like the British did. All he could do was to try and get it coordinated and worry about 'What ifs?' later.

"How long will it take you to do the dissemination packs?"

"Ten minutes to add the latest Intel and they will be ready to go," Anna replied, getting up ready to go to her desk.

"In that case, you get the UK underway, and send me the US ones and I will get them off to ICE," Tom said, getting up and leaving for his office. Once there, he texted Agent Jim Burgess alerting him to two intelligence packs coming his way within the next 20 minutes. He got an immediate reply of, "I'm on a course. Send them anyway, and I will get them actioned. Are they urgent?"

Tom texted "Yes," but never got a reply back. A short time later the dissemination packs arrived in his inbox. He had to sign off on the intelligence logs, although he didn't need to read them as the author was Anna. It was a requirement, so he skim read it, signed it, and got it off to Jim. All they could do now was wait.

Next on his circle of arrows was 'The Lord'. Striking number 14 off the list, he opened a new email and wrote a message to his GOPOL partners, introducing John Bressman from the Royal Canadian Mounted Police as the new team member of GOPOL. He kept the introduction brief, requesting other lead agency officers to make their own contact with John in due course. He informed the team that John's department, The National Child Exploitation Coordination Centre, had begun its own operation called 'Montreal' to assist COCET. Tom added a list of contact numbers for John's benefit and then sent the email. Then he called Sarah Dorsey into his office.

"Hi. Have you heard about our new partner in GOPOL?" Tom asked Sarah as she sat down.

"Yes. I've had a briefing this morning. They are joining Operation Resolve I understand. I am due to have a phone call with their press relations officer in about an hour."

"Did your briefing elaborate on their capability to arrest 'The Lord'?"

"What do you mean?" Sarah asked, looking perplexed, not really understanding the question.

"As it stands today they can't arrest Michael Stephens. That's because the site he owns and pays for isn't committing any offences in Holland. Now, that is not the issue as I see it. The issue is that they can't get a warrant to go looking for the evidence as we can here, based on graded intelligence or other information. So they won't be arresting him when we have our arrest phase on Operation Resolve. So factor that in when you speak with their press department."

"If that's their law then that's what they will fall back on, I guess. There isn't much we can do about it. If some of the Press pick up on it then we can cover it by referring to Canadian Laws. It won't be a problem, Tom."

Sarah delivered her view with such kindness that he didn't really know how to tackle her on it. In fact, it left him not wanting to fight her.

"Well. As long as you have it covered, then I'm in your capable hands!"

"That sounds like a corny chat up line, Mr. Ross!" Sarah said, getting up and heading for the door. "Don't worry. I will bring up your concerns," she said just before disappearing.

Just after 7.30pm that evening Anna and Dale approached Tom in the kitchen; he was pouring away yet another cup of tea he hadn't finished.

"Positive news from Bristol," Anna Farley said with a satisfied look.

"Tell me!" Tom demanded.

"They are still at the house, so we won't know the full result until tomorrow, but he made admissions at the scene to possessing and supplying child abuse images. His children will be victim interviewed tonight, but the officers don't think he's abused them. And they don't think he's got access to any other children. So the victim may be an American."

'The Americans would still be waiting for data comms to be done,' Tom thought to himself.

"What are they going to do with him tonight?"

"It's going to be interviews and bail, as long as he has another address to go to. The wife doesn't want him back."

"That gives ICE some breathing space. I haven't heard from them, but we had a head start and they know it's urgent. This was good work, both of you. Having an undercover team working alongside tactical intelligence is a model everybody should follow. Well done. Let's regroup first thing tomorrow."

As Anna Farley, Patrick Smith and Archie Donaldson finished for the day, for Tom, Dale and the team of newly trained undercover officers the evening was far from over. As the late shift, comprised of Dale and Owen, settled into their assumed identities, it was not long before Owen, who was pretending to be the 'librarian', aka Philip Thompson, began to infiltrate more of the twenty six top level admins.

He was busy communicating with four of them at the same time, and was at different stages of infiltration with each of them, when one of them sent him a small video clip. As Owen watched the clip he saw that it showed the rape of a little girl aged around six years. The video lasted for one minute and 25 seconds, was of good quality and showed nothing of the offender other than his erect penis. It appeared to have been cut from a larger section of footage.

There was nothing in the background that gave away the crime scene, so he sent a quick reply thanking the sender, 'amourdegarcon'. He then began a large number of set operating procedures that he had been taught in his recent training, knowing that his teacher, who was also his supervisor, would be watching. Owen knew that this target was one of the admins working behind a proxy, and therefore wasn't expecting this particular case to go much further, but he still wanted to know if there was anything he could possibly do to identify him.

"Sarge. That Froggie who is one of the admins behind proxy has just sent me a small clip. I want to try and identify him, am I authorised to work outside the site?"

"Yep. What have you got in mind?"

"I was thinking of asking him what he does for a living, that I like France, have taken holidays there, that sort of thing, all with a view to getting an occupation. If I can get an occupation, maybe there would be an opportunity for me to communicate with him further across different platforms. If there was, then it might well be outside the proxy."

"I taught you well, Owen! Go for it."

Owen turned around, grinning, to find Dale hadn't even been looking at him while he spoke. He was too busy typing to another one of five targets he was in the process of infiltrating, all at the same time. Some were in the assumed identity of Simon Clark, and some in two of his own identities, both of which had recently, and unexpectedly, been promoted by an administrator called 'librarian'!

Owen got back to his target and sent him the following message. "I guess you are from France. I love it there, and have been on holiday to France, love the wine. What do you do for work?"

With the message gone, he put up his volume, grabbed his cigarettes and left the office.

"Going for a quick ciggie, Sarge. Back in a jiffy."

"Roger," replied Dale, who still had his head down typing.

Within a few minutes, and with Owen still gone, Dale heard the 'bing' of Owen's speakers alerting him that there had been a new communication. Dale finished the chat he was in, quickly checked another, then got up and walked over to Owen's screen. Dale moved the mouse to disable the Manchester United screen saver to reveal a new message from 'amourdegarcon'. He then went back to his screen and continued where he had left off with his particular targets and their different levels of infiltration. A short time later Owen returned. Dale, without looking up again, and still concentrating on his own work, said, "Your 'Froggie' is a nurse, and on night duty tonight."

Owen raced to his screen to confirm that indeed his target had replied to that effect.

"What do you think about risking a chat tonight, whilst he is at work?"

This time Dale stopped and looked at Owen. "Owen. You are the 'librarian', use that advantage and go for it."

Hearing the advice was exactly the confirmation he wanted to hear, so he sent the following message to 'amourdegarcon'.

"Hi. I will be up most of the night, do you have an email so we can chat about places in France to visit?"

Within moments Owen got a reply and an email address!

During the rest of that shift both Dale and Owen managed to infiltrate eight of the top level admins and four of the medium level ones, most of whom incriminated themselves by sending the undercover officers images or videos of very young children being sexually abused. One of those was the target known to Operation Resolve as, 'amourdegarcon'.

Early the next day, bleary eyed and tired, Tom left the office and took the short walk to Allensbury Police Station. He made his way to the men's uniform changing rooms where he took a shower. The night duty uniform officers didn't question his presence, instead silently acknowledging that the senior Detective must be in the middle of another operation. On the way back, Tom stopped at a bakery and purchased a large bag of hot bacon rolls and got back to his office as COCET staff began to arrive for that day. Fifteen minutes later he was in the conference room, along with a full team apart from Mitchell Hayes, who was interviewing Simon Clark in Essex that day, and Patrick Smith who was still working in the Cleveland incident room.

Tom placed the food on the table, and although the officers had just arrived at work, they were all hungry and quickly demolished the freshly cooked bacon rolls gratefully.

"Jane. Update us all on the incident room, would you, please."

Tom knew the update, so as Jane began he checked his emails through the Blackberry mobile. Something that Sarah Dorsey noticed, and was pleased about. He quickly scrolled through looking for one from Jim Burgess and saw it towards the end. He opened the email to find out that ICE had completed data comms and background checks on the intelligence packs that had been passed to them. One had access to children, and would be the subject of a warrant the next day, their time. The other would be placed on the 'to do' list. It was a good result. As Tom started to hone back in on the briefing Jane was about to finish.

"So. In short, Patrick has finished converting the site, and 90% of that has been inputted onto their Holmes2. They are around 75% complete in the number of data comm submissions that they will need to do, and of those, 45% are back. This has led to sixteen UK urgent arrests so far. The team has got up a head of steam now, and have even started to assemble intelligence packs, which is why I have left Patrick up there. He will assist on that, and as more of their staff become available he will return. They are estimating three more weeks, which will tie in nicely with plea and directions on Thompson, which is the week after."

Jane looked at Tom to signal she had finished.

"Thanks, Jane. Anna, where are we with the Bristol case?"

"He was interviewed last night and admitted that all the material the Police found on his computer belongs to him. He admits to possessing and supplying. He says he has been a member of 'childscentcafe' for about 18 months, and all his activity and offending has been online. He thinks he has around twenty thousand images and videos. He admitted sending the images to us and has been bailed to return at a later date. The children haven't made any disclosures, and they don't believe he has gone 'hands on'."

As Anna finished, Tom began. "The Bristol target was part of three disseminations, the other two being to the US. They will be acting on one later today. The other they don't think is urgent, so we will have to wait and see how that develops. Archie, do you want to tell the team where you guys are?"

"Yep. Between us we have successfully infiltrated twelve targets so far, all of them admins. The three you have just been talking about were our first urgent ones. The latest is a French member who operates behind proxy when visiting 'childscentcafe'. Owen managed to lure him out and got an email. Because he uses technology to prevent being caught, we deem him to pose a higher threat to children. Niall has alerted the French, and they say that if we get the intelligence to them this morning, and the data comms resolves to a physical address, then they will get him under a warrant."

"Get it to me, and I will have it ready within the hour!" said Anna.

"That's it for now," Tom said. "We are already making a real difference, and it will only get better. Well done all of you, you should be proud of what you have achieved so far. Jane, my office, please."

As the team dispersed to their varying tasks, Jane followed Tom to his office where he shut the door.

"I haven't had that report I requested from Louisa. Any idea why?"

"Yes. She isn't going to submit one, her NSPCC Boss has told her not to."

Tom, who couldn't believe what he was hearing, rubbed his right eyebrow between his thumb and forefinger in an attempt to rid himself of tiredness and no small amount of frustration.

"Does Cleveland know?"

"Yes."

"That accounts for why I haven't had a report from them either. What's your take on it?" Tom asked, knowing that Jane had been with Louisa for the period.

"She feels that had Cleveland made more of an effort with local social services, then they may have been able to make a connection, but we will never know. It's best left. We have all learnt something from it," Jane replied.

Tom thought about what Jane was proposing. It wasn't beyond the realms of possibility that Cleveland had not made the enquiry, knowing that the COCET CP strategy could cause more harm than good. But he still had to deal with his report to the Chief.

"OK. Put it behind us. We have more important things to think about, and one of them is Clark. Let me know the moment Mitchell has anything."

"Will do. Now that I am back, can I have Saturday off? Pim is coming to stay."

"Sure. If it's quiet take the Sunday as well."

With Jane gone, Tom had to make a decision on what to say to the Chief. He put together a short report on the events surrounding the identification of the victim known as 'Carly'. He highlighted lessons to be learnt for the future, specifically a wider and more dynamic use of resources open to him by attached NSPCC staff. He attached it to an email and sent it to his line manager, Supt. Maggie Burrows. He never got a reply.

Later that morning, Tom's mind was taken off GOPOL politics.

"Guv, can I have a moment?" Archie said, standing at the door without coming in.

"Of course. Here?"

"Covert Ops, if you could?"

Tom followed Archie into the Ops room and to his computer screen. The screen had a number of pages minimised and the uppermost one contained an image of a horse in a field.

"I've been infiltrating this target for two days now. He is quite a new member, wants to impress, and has clearly had communication with the 'librarian' before. From his chat here," Archie then clicked on another page, which was a list of chats, "you can see he has sent me a folder. He states the folder is encrypted and then says it's the normal password. Well, from the interviews with Thompson we know that once he's got what he wants he deletes passwords. So I told him that, and he sent this saying 'Here you go again'". Archie then clicked back on the picture of the horse in the field. "So now I'm wondering what this horse means. I tried a few passwords like 'gelding,' 'chestnut' and 'stallion' but haven't got anywhere."

Tom himself wondered what the password might be, and suggested a few equestrian possibilities of his own which also failed to open the folder. Tom pulled out his mobile and rang SDE.

"Sue. It's Tom Ross. How are you?"

"Great, Tom. Lovely to hear from you. How can I help?"

Tom retold the story that he'd just heard.

"Mm. First of all, I wouldn't suggest asking him more on it. It sounds like the password might be hidden within it, using Steganography software. Can you trace him?"

"Hang on a minute," Tom replied, not knowing the answer to that question.

"Archie. Is this target traceable?"

"Yes, Guv. I am just looking to expose his criminality."

"Sue?" Tom said putting the phone back to his ear.

"Yes, I heard that," Dr. Tay began. "My advice would be to execute the warrant on him sooner rather than later and send the forensic work to me. With his PC and the file that you have I would be able to show the chain of events involving the 'steg' technology and that would be a really good aggravating factor when it came to summing up."

Tom, who had been taking everything in, started to think ahead. "Great, we will do that. On this subject, do you mean it's possible to hide an image within another image?"

"Well, only if the original image or carrier file was huge, and you would, or should, be able to see that. What I'm talking about here is an amount of text, something that doesn't take up a lot of space."

"How about all the images that are on 'childscentcafe', could they all be hiding another image within them?

"I don't think so. Dominic is here, would you like to speak to him?"

"Yes please. Before you go, Sue. What about Leitch? Did he have some images that weren't illegal and that might contain a password?"

"Yes. He did have legal images. He didn't have any known steganography software on his PC though, or any footprint of it, and even then he could further encrypt the password. If you want, we could undertake another examination to be sure."

"Yes, please. And bill me for it, Sue!"

"Will do. Here's Dominic."

"I heard most of that. I am sure that none of the images actually on the site contain other images, but if you want I can check again."

"Yes please, Dominic. That would be great."

"I guess you heard most of that as well, Archie. Tell Jane that I want this out today, and if it needs me to make a call I will. He's a risk to the ongoing operation. Log off for a while in that identity. Use one of your other ones and log back in again after a few hours. If he messages you for any reason, don't reply. Come and see me or speak to Dale."

"Yes, Guv."

"Have you had access to Thompson's historical chats?" Tom enquired, thinking the answer to this problem might lie there.

"I have and I did check it. It didn't reveal any contact, but we know that the site didn't capture it all."

"That just raises the risk around him even more. He needs to be arrested to preserve the ongoing infiltration. Make sure it happens, Archie!"

Meanwhile, DC Mitchell Hayes was in the process of concluding the interview with Simon Clark at Colchester Police Station in Essex. Having got Clark to sign the master tape label, he peeled the back off it to expose the sticky side and then wrapped it around one of the interview tapes. He then took Clark back to the Custody Sergeant who bailed him to return to Colchester Police Station. Once back at his car DC Hayes called Jane King.

"Hi Sarge, Mitchell. Done the interview."

"How did it go?" Jane eagerly enquired.

"Well. He knew it was coming and what it was all about. He didn't request a solicitor, and so it was all wrapped up in one interview."

"Did he talk?"

"On what he knew, yes. I don't think he held anything back. He says he found out about PTC through 'childscentcafe'. He lied about having his own kids and was in contact with someone who called himself PTC. He says he had a number of email exchanges with him and got accepted into the group, but he had to provide evidence of his own children before he could go further. He couldn't, and in any case he was arrested before he could do much more."

"Can Dale and the others become him?"

"I don't see why not. It took a while to talk around the content of the emails, so as not give away our intentions. But in short, the emails were very brief. The stumbling block is he has to provide access, or evidence at least, that he has his own kids. And so will we!"

"That's where the skill of Dale comes in, Mitchell. Well done, get yourself back here."

"Roger."

As Jane was finishing her call, Anna Farley was receiving one from Niall Mullins, who was calling her from Interpol Headquarters in Lyons, France.

"Anna. Got a result from Holland."

"Fire away," Anna replied, grabbing her notepad and pen, expecting to have to write a number of addresses down.

"They all come back to the same internet cafe in the centre of Amsterdam. Sorry, but it's a dead end."

Anna's mounting expectation was abruptly destroyed by Niall's information.

"Is there anything that can be done?"

"Live time, I am sure there is. But now? Nothing."

"What about the Thai ones?"

"I need to speak to Tom about that. His line is engaged and his mobile is going straight to answerphone. I will call him later and let you know the result."

"OK," replied Anna, who then went to see Jane to let her know the bad news.

Tom, who had been talking with Agent Jim Burgess, concluded his call and went in search of Anna Farley, to find her updating Jane King. He caught the end of the conversation relating to Holland.

"Dead end, then?" he said, privately thinking that his best lead to finding LB had evaporated.

"Looks that way," Jane replied. "But the good news is that Clark did make contact with PTC through that email. The reason he didn't take it any further was because he had to produce his own kids to get further, and he couldn't do that because one, he didn't have any, and two, we arrested him in the meantime."

"Dale will be in shortly," Tom began. "Let's see if we can at least make contact. If PTC is LB, and we have some form of contact with him, then we can get to him. And some very good news, Jim Burgess just rang. They made the arrest this morning. The child in the images is his daughter. They weren't going to do the other suspect quick time, but they are now. Well done, all of you!"

Anna Farley went back to her desk full of mixed emotions, she'd had a great lead snatched away only to be replaced by a success. Tom went back to his office, thinking that whilst he had lost his best chance to identify LB he was even more determined to make this one work. Jane King saw past the mixed emotions, having been there before, and was thinking about the weekend she had off.

Niall Mullins had been just as deflated about the news, and tried calling DCI Ross again.

"Tom. It's Niall. That's a bummer about the IP addresses."

"Tell me."

"Look. I have been chasing up the Thai end and it's going to need a visit. The Royal Thai Police do have the contacts with some of the service providers. And they have an Interpol liaison officer. But they won't do 'jack shit' unless you are there and standing over them."

"You are pushing at an open door, Niall. Authorised. Do you have the international arm of Operation Resolve covered though?"

"Not yet. So I wouldn't propose going away until the incident room gets close to completing its work."

"Agreed."

Alone, Tom looked at his circle of arrows and crossed off numbers 12, 11 and then 10. Thinking more about the offender Clark, and the fact nothing more was likely to come from that source, he crossed off number 9 and rang Dale, who had by that time arrived for work.

"Dale, the email we have for PTC is good. Come the last week of the operation I want you to make contact with PTC. Clark couldn't get any further with them because he didn't have his own kids. You are going to have to come up with a work around!"

Dale chuckled. "I love a challenge, Boss. Leave it with me. We'll be ready."

For the rest of that day Cleveland Police continued to work its way through a mountain of intelligence, and COCET's Covert Operations team infiltrated a further number of admins and began their attack on the wider membership of 'childscentcafe'.

Tom went home that night, the first in a while, and spent the night in a proper bed. Milk and food in the fridge came out to meet him when he opened the fridge door to see what he might still have to eat. Sarah Dorsey had already eaten, and was preparing for bed in the hotel she was staying in. She wasn't going to send the new media strategy to Tom until the next day, having been caught out sending something to him late once before.

'*What are the odds of getting caught twice*?' She thought to herself. She read it once more, and, deciding the odds were low, sent it to him, and then went to bed with it and Tom on her mind.

It was just after midnight when Tom got into bed, and as he still had staff working, he checked his Blackberry one more time to see if there was anything new. There was. ICE had made more arrests, and more children had been rescued as a result. Just as he was about to place the phone into standby mode, he saw there was mail from Sarah Dorsey. He could see from the subject line that the mail contained the updated media strategy to cover for the new Canadian team member. Tom was about to reply when he stopped, recalling the previous time this had happened. Instead he put the phone into standby, and went to sleep wondering about the strategy and Sarah.

0850hrs ICT, Bangkok, Thailand

About an hour after Tom was asleep. LB arrived back in Thailand and went straight to a meeting with his trusted contact Lim. Lim was a Chinese Malaysian working and living in Thailand. He was very well connected to a number of Chinese and Thai criminal groups, in both Bangkok and Pattaya, and was the head of his own gang known as 'Red Moon'. He made a very good living out of his activities, and the thought of ever being caught never crossed his mind: simply because all the authorities were also making a good living out of him and his activities. He saw his latest pay day in the distance and waved at him, flashing him a smile of white and gold teeth. With customary hugs and many shakings of hands, Lim eventually calmed down and became serious as he leaned across the cafe table.

"What is it you need, my brother?"

LB produced two red and gold European passports, one of which had its corners cut off, and a folded slip of paper.

"The one with the corners cut off is my old one, in my old name. You can keep that as the master copy. I want a new one, but with these details on."

LB then handed him the slip of paper. Lim placed the folded piece of paper into the passport and placed that into his shirt chest pocket.

"We make the very best passports in the world here in Bangkok. The price, though, depends on how good you want it to be."

"What does the very best cost?"

"Twenty thousand dollars US," Lim immediately replied, matter of factly.

LB knew Lim was lying, and that he had probably just increased the price by a hundred per cent because there was a pay day to be had.

"If the product is that good then I will pay it. But not until I have seen it."

"Done!" shouted Lim, smiling again and flashing more gold teeth. "Now. Photo?" Lim continued.

"That comes later."

"No problem. No problem for you, my brother. You just let me have the photo when you are ready."

CHAPTER TWENTY

Over the course of the next two weeks, the Major Investigation Team from Cleveland Police kept their word and completed their Operation Elm, a full week before the final court appearance of Philip Thompson. By the end they had worked on a child abuse website that contained an overall membership of 22,893.

Out of that number, just under 20%, or 4,532 members, were operating behind some kind of proxy. Eighty nine, fewer than 1%, had either joined more than once or had multiply identities. Members from the site were traced to thirty one countries around the globe, but nearly half of them came from America, Canada, The United Kingdom or Germany. The team had produced thousands of intelligence dissemination packs, many of which contained evidence that would lead to offenders being held to account for their sexual abuse of children.

All the organisers and administrators of 'childscentcafe', the offenders who had designed and engineered that web of evil, had either been arrested as urgent cases or were marked for first phase Police action. All bar one, of course. Interpol had contacted each country, and, working with local law enforcement officials, had organised a week of action to coincide with the final court appearance of Thompson, which would see the major offenders arrested and their houses searched for evidence.

The Chief of GOPOL sent a request to every other Chief Constable in the UK, asking them to take action on their suspects over the same period. Tom knew from experience it wouldn't be possible to arrest everybody. Some intelligence would be placed on file against a certain suspect, some would act as a tipping point for action, whilst others would be arrested without hesitation. The one thing he knew for sure was that offenders would be arrested for many years to come from intelligence received from the combined efforts of COCET and Cleveland Police.

It was two days from the beginning of the week of action and the appearance of Thompson in court, when Tom, who was about to call Niall in Thailand, received a phone call from John Bressman, of the RCMP.

"We will be arresting 'The Lord' after all, Tom."

"I can't believe it! How have you managed that? Tom replied incredulously.

"A sixteen year old girl walked into her local Police Station and made a complaint of domestic violence on Michael Stephens, aka 'The Lord'. It turns out she has been living and having sex with him since she was around 13 years old."

"Didn't anybody know she was there?"

"No. Sounds like she knew all about his sexual deviancy and was OK with that, but the beatings made her go to the Police. We have a statement. He will get arrested for the assaults on her, and we will search his place for child pornography at the same time."

Buoyed up by the great news he rang Niall, who was in Bangkok. After relaying the news, he got onto the main reason for the call.

"So. What are they saying today?"

"They came back empty handed, Tom. Bottom line is we are not going to resolve those two IP addresses. They want fresh intelligence."

"OK. I will get Dale to send an email now. Are you at the hotel?"

"No. Out for dinner with two of the Royal Thai Police who are working with us. Courtesy of Interpol." Tom read between the lines of what Niall was saying that he was greasing the wheels of justice.

"I will get Dale to send the email now. I won't bother you tonight unless I have something."

"OK. Good luck."

He should have been disappointed with the lack of progress. After all, Niall had been there a week now. But the news from Canada had replaced it with a tangible sense of achievement, and it had been against all the odds. He went in search of Dale and found him, Jane and Anna in Covert Ops.

"Send that email, Dale!"

"Yes, Guv!"

As Dale sent a prewritten email to PTC, Tom broke the news on 'The Lord'. The news was infectious, with Anna shooting off to inform the rest of COCET, and to send a message to Cleveland Police. Tom went to inform Supt. Burrows, and later joined the whole of the Intel Cell for a meeting about the Canadian list of missing persons, which had arrived from Interpol that morning. Jane chaired the meeting, with Tom there as an observer. They were discussing proposals on how to deal with the data, and had been in the conference room only a few minutes, when Dale interrupted them.

"Got a reply!"

The news brought the meeting to a standstill and the room went silent in anticipation. Anna Farley, surprisingly, was the one to break the silence. "Have you captured comms data?

"Yes," Dale said with a smile, the short exchange breaking the silence.

"What did he say?" Jane asked urgently.

"Just that he was killing time. What you really need to know, Guv," Dale said, now looking at Tom, "is that the IP has a country code of Thailand."

The news caused everybody to get up, and although the meeting was reconvened 15 minutes later, none of the officers had their minds fully focused on what was being discussed.

Niall got the news just as he was going to bed. He set his alarm early, and got to the Royal Thai Police Headquarters by 8am the next day, armed with the new information. He could tell by the Thai officers' faces that they weren't expecting him and the new information so early, if at all. One senior officer sent two lower ranking officers with the information to the internet provider, whilst Niall waited impatiently at Police HQ. Two hours later, the two officers, who had left with faces of worry and concern, arrived back with big smiles, claiming success.

Niall, from experience, knew he had to press home the advantage with the local Police before it got too close to lunchtime, otherwise there would be a long delay whilst lunch was taken. Again, courtesy of Interpol.

He used the air of excitement, and with two cars of officers from the Royal Thai Police they set off for the address. As soon as they got there the Police officers went straight to the apartment that the email had been sent from. The corridor that led to the apartment door was narrow and not air conditioned. Niall, who was suffering from the heat, was at the back of a long line of officers, the front ones being at the now open door.

After a few minutes of rapid discussion in Thai, none of which Niall could understand, two officers went inside whilst the others waited outside. One of those called Aroon who could speak English well, approached Niall.

"The address doesn't look good. They are checking it out now to be sure, but we have the wrong address. You must check your information, then we go back to the internet company and get them to check again."

Ten minutes later, the two officers who had entered the apartment reemerged to confirm it was not correct. The senior officer, who couldn't speak English, made a decision that the whole team would return to Police Headquarters. Once there, he requested that Niall check his information. Niall handed over a copy of the email containing the relevant IP address. The senior officer checked it against the one he had, and then dispatched the same two officers back to the internet company. Through Aroon, who was still present, the senior Thai Police Officer said, "This will take some time. Best we go for lunch."

Niall, recognising there was nothing to be done, went for an early lunch. Whilst they were at the restaurant the two officers who had gone to see the provider returned. There was a short discussion in Thai with the senior officer, who then spoke with Aroon, who then spoke to Niall.

"They say it is the same. You must do it again!"

Niall didn't believe for a second there was a problem at the UK end. But without a reasonable alternative he didn't have much option. He checked his watch to see what time it was in the UK. It was too early for another message from Dale in any case. Which meant the whole thing would go over for another day due to the time zones. He texted Tom, telling him the news. Tom, who was asleep, got it moments later.

Later that day, with one day to go until the lid came off Operation Resolve, Detective Sgt. Dale Walters sent another email to PTC, and got a short reply back a few hours later. The IP address was transmitted to Niall, who received it in seconds, but it was too late. Not only had the Police gone home, but the internet provider would not be open again until the morning. Tom rang Niall.

"This is cutting it fine. At least you are ahead of us. Everything that is being activated starts at a point within GMT, which gives us some leeway."

"It doesn't add up, Tom. Something else is going on here. Just for the life of me I can't think what it is!"

For Niall the following day was a repetition of the day before. The officers got another address; this time in another block of apartments in the same street. Again they went in, and again they came out saying it was the wrong address. The difference this time was that the senior officer from the day before had taken the day off, and he had been replaced by a younger officer. He had a long discussion with his fellow officers, which Niall could not understand; but at the end of it, Aroon said, "We are calling the company down here. It must be their end."

Forty minutes later, a telecom van turned up which contained two technicians. The senior Police officer spoke to them for about three minutes, with him doing all the talking and the two technicians saying nothing, but Aroon could hear the conversation.

"My Boss. He explaining the situation to them."

As the Police Officer stopped talking, one of the two technicians said just a few words in reply, then pointed up to the mass of wires strung along the street, and at the many more that entered the apartment blocks at hundreds of different points. Aroon again translated what was being said to Niall.

"He say that we have the wrong address because everybody in the street is cheating." Aroon stopped as the technician spoke some more.

"He say that the company knows everybody stealing, but they don't care as long as somebody pays. He say that everybody stealing off everybody else!"

There was another discussion in Thai before Aroon spoke again.

"My Boss. He ask if they can fix this one case for us."

The technician muttered something in reply which both Aroon and Niall didn't hear, but Aroon didn't need to hear it, and Niall didn't need it translated, as the nod of the head told them what they needed to know.

"How long will this take?" Niall said to Aroon.

The technician, who was returning to his van, and who had passed by Niall, heard what he had said.

"Fifteen minute. No problem," said the technician in almost perfect English.

Niall rang Tom Ross immediately, thinking that finally they were closing in on LB.

Tom and the whole team were present at COCET that day, except for Sarah Dorsey, who was with the Chief and the other heads of GOPOL at Thames Valley Police HQ. A mass of media representatives from all over the world were assembled in the conference room waiting for the briefing from GOPOL, the trigger being the sentencing of Philip Thompson. Tom assembled his team in the conference room and got Niall to ring back on the conference room speaker pod. Unbeknown to Tom, who was facing the speaker, Supt. Maggie Burrows had entered the crowded room and stood with her back to the wall. Within minutes Niall's voice came over the speaker pod.

"They have worked out which is the correct address. We are on our way there now. It is only two minutes away."

With an open phone, everybody in the room could hear the unmistakable cacophony of noises of a busy Asian street. They could also hear the sounds start to disappear as Niall entered the apartment building.

"It's up two levels, we are taking the stairs," Niall whispered.

As the room watched and listened to the sound of heavy breathing emanate from the speaker pod, Tom and Jane looked at one another. For them this was to be the end of a long road upon which they had both made many personal sacrifices, and which had changed them as individuals for ever. Tom was thinking that he needed this now, to help him move forward. Jane was thinking that her Michael had always been a lost boy, and maybe that was what LB stood for. Both knew for sure that the next few seconds would be with them for the rest of their lives. Niall watched as the Royal Thai Police knocked on the door. Then, as it opened, the officers entered the apartment quickly, shouting commands in Thai.

At COCET they heard the knocking and then someone shouting in a foreign language. Then Niall said, "They're in. They're in."

EPILOGUE

A mariner, when working out whether a particular location is a safe place to anchor, has to take many factors into consideration. The main one being 'Will there will be sufficient water under the hull as the tide drops to its lowest point?' What might seem to be a safe haven, with plenty of water beneath, can quickly turn to disaster and ruin, from a lack of information or a wrong calculation.

At that moment, the man known to COCET as LB was boarding a flight to Phnom Penh, Cambodia. He had a new passport, a new identity, a new face and a new future. One where nobody knew who he truly was.

CPSIA information can be obtained at www.ICGtesting.com
Printed in the USA
LVOW07s0530030816
498779LV00001B/38/P